SOLARPUNK CREATURES

Editorial Masthead:

Christoph Rupprecht

Deborah Cleland

Melissa Ingaruca Moreno

Norie Tamura

Rajat Chaudhuri

Sarena Ulibarri

World Weaver Press

SOLARPUNK CREATURES

Published by World Weaver Press, LLC
Albuquerque, NM
www.WorldWeaverPress.com

Cover Artwork and design by Paul Summerfield.
www.psummerfield.com

This anthology was partially funded by Ehime University and the Research Institute
for Humanity and Nature (RIHN).www.chikyu.ac.jp/rihn_e/
*
First edition: January 2024
ISBN-13: 978-1-7340545-7-6

Also available as an ebook

SOLARPUNK CREATURES

...before you dive into the stories, might we ask for your help?

This book is both a collection of stories and a small research project. We (the editors) want to understand how stories might contribute to building better futures for humans and nature alike. You can help us do so!

Simply visit the link below and fill out our reader survey:

https://creatures-presurvey.multispecies.city

After reading the book,
we will ask you to tell us what you thought in a second survey.

Thank you in advance —
It really means a lot to us!

Christoph (responsible for the survey) & the editor team

Introduction

Christoph Rupprecht, Deborah Cleland, Melissa Ingaruca Moreno,
Norie Tamura, and Rajat Chaudhuri

Three years have passed since our first anthology was released. *Multispecies Cities: Solarpunk Urban Futures* set out to tell stories of more-than-human urban coexistence and kinship. Facing climate change, the sixth mass extinction, late-stage capitalism, and colonisation, yet refusing to surrender our entangled futures to despair, our contributing authors imagined worlds where people meet new allies of all shapes, sizes, and species. Exploring these worlds left us to wonder: who are these new allies? What are their stories? What post-anthropocene futures might more-than-human senses discover? Paraphrasing Robin Wall-Kimmerer's *Braiding Sweetgrass*, becoming good neighbors in multispecies communities means getting to know again who we live with, and how our destinies are entangled. Where *Multispecies Cities* sought to broaden the spotlight and highlight the multitude of actors on the stage, *Solarpunk Creatures* introduces a whole new cast of more-than-human protagonists: organic and digital, alien and fantastic, tiny and boundlessly large.

Unlike our last collection, we did not restrict these stories to a particular setting. Even so, around half the stories are set in a place recognisable as a city, showing that urban spaces continue to be rich grounds for multispecies imaginings. Other stories are set in areas of sparse human settlement, with a corresponding representation of tame and service animals much broader than the previous collection, even if solar farms attracting the ire of wild animals and AI animals are still more common themes than traditional agriculture.

Indeed, as the submitted stories came in, it was immediately apparent that the rapid developments in artificial intelligence had radically shaped the solarpunk imagination. In the years since our first anthology, AI characters went from appearing in the odd story to being the single most represented "type" of solarpunk creature featured. The AI characters that made it into the anthology are gentle and loveable—not the disturbing and often malevolent presence that is unsettling the role and value of artists (and art) around the globe. From a sentient AI occupying a vacuum cleaner to escape their mundane existence ("AI Dreams of Real Sheep—More at 8") to a lonely satellite ("Thank Geo"), these stories represent the optimistic and symbiotic possibilities of technology. This is in stark contrast to the voracious piracy of corporate-controlled AI as it is currently playing out, or the fear that a sentient "Skynet-like" AI will dominate or destroy humankind.

Similarly, many more authors took on the voice of an ecosystem or an assemblage rather than an individual critter, and conversely, two stories were written by collectives rather than single authors (Commando Jugendstil and Tales from the EV Studio for "AI Dreams" and Center For Militant Futurology for "Microbia"). This comes alongside rapid development in the rights of nature in parts of the world, with increasing recognition of (and advocacy for) the more-than-human in law and governance. In the midst of this, scientific developments continue to dismantle any remaining ideas of human self-sufficiency or independence from the environments we inhabit (and those that inhabit us). In these stories, leading roles are taken by a wetland ("The Wetland versus The Mayor"), a forest ("Thank Geo"), a desert ("Sonora's Journey") and a mycelium network ("Our Minds Share a City"), while elements more often thought of as inanimate such as water itself ("Water Cycle") or a comet ("Flyby") are also given voice, history, and perspective.

The first self-identified solarpunk fiction was published in Brazil, so we were particularly excited to be able to include another story from South America. "Quarropts Can't Dance," a satirical piece by Rodrigo Culagovski from Chile, features a daring heist from an unlikely troupe of aliens. It is set in an alien metropolis that treads a fine line between techno-fascism and multispecies harmony. The tongue-in-cheek story reminds us that solarpunkish earnestness can sometimes stray close to boorish self-righteousness or clichéd sentimentality, and that it's good to not take ourselves too seriously.

Solarpunk Creatures first came into existence as a collaborative art project with Yen Shu Liao, tracing the journey of an explorer-researcher who studies multispecies communities and their particularities. From "Moth City" to "Stormwater Streams," each piece combines story and art in the form of the traveller's diary as they seek to unravel the core values at the heart of each community: diversity, adaptivity, ingenuity, empathy, connectedness.

When we decided to create a follow-up anthology to *Multispecies Cities*, including this artwork felt right, and we did an open call for other artwork to include. As with stories, we hope to see many more solarpunk artworks going beyond greened façades to tell visual stories of the creatures who shape these places. Badlungs Art's triptych shows familiar animals basking in the glow of their solar ovens. In a style redolent of Beatrix Potter we see the leisure and pleasure affordances of a simple technology that helps meet an everyday need. Hybridity of lifeforms, materials and aesthetics is a co-joining theme in the other three pieces, where jungle meets hi-tech city ("Tunaakola" ('we shall go') - Martha Ziiita Siima), fish meets person ("Renaissance Pisces" - Irina Tall), and plastic waste meets companion animal ("Orange Crested Grebe" - Pamina Stewart). Yet these communities are not without tensions. Whether coexisting with a waste-feeding symbiotic colony of bacteria and yeasts or intelligent giant moths, managing more-than-human relationships requires careful negotiation. A key driving force across our anthology is the root of these negotiations—the nonhuman agency of our protagonists.

As we noted in *Multispecies Cities*, consciousness, brain complexity, and mobility are among a variety of pretexts that have been deployed in denying agency to non-humans. A denial that balances itself upon a flimsy logic of difference and easily feeds the instincts to colonise ecologies and peoples while also normalising the extractivist growth models that have triggered the polycrisis of our times. The roots of this denial and the consequent belief in human exceptionalism stretch as far back as the Book of Genesis. More numerous during the march of colonialism, history is replete with signposts of the belief in speciesist superiority, which allowed the subjugation of non-humans as well as human "others".

But there have always been other voices, sometimes ignored and often forgotten. Within Indigenous peoples worldviews that suggest a continuity between Culture and Nature, in the work of philosophers like Henri Bergson and his idea of the *élan vital* immanent in all organisms, and also in the findings of modern science, for example about the human microbiome, there is enough accumulated knowledge and experience to challenge the artificial barriers of difference.

Many of the stories in this book are imaginative counters to the flawed and dangerous logic of human exceptionalism which denies non-human agency and rights. In Geraldine Briony Hunt's fantasy-laced tale of "An Inconvenient Unicorn" we find how the appearance of this creature pivots the narrative from a path of ecomodernist exploitation to one where the land is left to itself. We the readers are left to decide if the unicorn is the impossible fantasy of solarpunk dreamers, or perhaps whether each and every patch of earth has "unicorn" properties that are unique and worth preserving.

From Hunt's mythical unicorn, we shift to Tashan Mehta's subtle hints of the influence of non-humans on our lives in the story of Opi ("Leaf Whispers, Ocean Song"), a being of the deep-sea who arrives on the coastline of Goa. Set in the near-future, this heart-wrenching tale shows how the lives of the human characters and collectives get entangled with Opi and the transformative lesson it conveys. At one point the protagonist Jen says, *"Look at what Opi has done, what it's shown us. How can we go back to the old models of living, of shaping ourselves only around people... how can we not think of new ways to bond, relate and live?"*

It is heartening to note how elements of care and moral improvement are woven into some of these tales of kinship between humans and other beings—stories where the agency of the non-human is gently directed in cleaning up the anthropogenic mess in addition to impacting perceptions, beliefs and values. In Catherine Yeates' "Our Minds Share a City" we find a subterranean network of telepathic mycelium with a hive mind, helping clean up a contaminated forest while standing sentinel with their human neighbours to prevent and remediate environmental degradation. The passages where the protagonist Sarah hosts the network are both memorable and intriguing.

Besides the affective agency of the unicorn or Opi, we discover this more direct and remediative agency of the telepathic hive, while being awed even more by stories like "Threadloom" by N. R. M. Roshak. Here, the agency of a moody, weaver loombeest is expressed in the co-creation of a work of eye-catching beauty, as interpretively featured on the cover art by Australian artist Paul Summerfield. Between instinct, free will, mutual care, and co-creation, this carefully threaded narrative of the loombeest set in a solarpunk community of a future forest covers extraordinary ground. The loombeest is a companion animal, but rejects being merely a tool for artmaking and takes back creative agency, in ways that challenge his human keepers. It is a lovely take on the "coming-of-age" genre, rich with intergenerational and interspecies conflict and growth.

As in many stories, the ecological, technological and social configurations take a back seat to the emotional drama in "Threadloom." However, this is a world in which people live amongst a rich diversity of plant and animal life, where artists must be valued and rewarded for their labour with enough to provide for a comfortable life, and where technology facilitates professional and educational exchange, even for those living away from other human settlements. The ethical consequences of deliberately creating creatures for the purpose of either companionship or service remains gently unprobed, but leaves a fruitful pathway for critical reflection on the role of pets and livestock in human lives.

Questions, conflicts and negotiations of more-than-human futures that persist have been addressed by our authors with imaginative depth and clarity in many other stories, including "Solar Murder," "Hopdog," and "Night Fowls." "Night Fowls" is crafted like a mystery plot, centred on the feud between jackdaws and seagulls with a human peacekeeper caught in between. "Hopdog" tells the tale of an abused and injured dog renegotiating its antagonistic relationship with humans within a community of care. And in "Solar Murder" A.E. Marling brings up the practical issue of the agency of crows and their favourite sport of damaging solar panels. The way these stories resolve provides us with enough hope that the hurdles in the path of negotiating and giving shape to futures of multispecies justice, even if daunting, are never insurmountable.

As we struggle to comprehend our new reality of everyday life in a dramatically changing world, the many different stories and protagonists serve as a much-needed reminder: this struggle is not ours alone. It would be hybris to insist the many wounds that (some) humans inflicted, only humans alone can heal. Once again invoking Wall-Kimmerer, might taking more-than-humans and their agency seriously imply it's time to listen to their teachings on multispecies stewardship?

Only when solarpunk and climate fiction fully explore the stories unfolding across the web of life and beyond can they help us make sense of these times. Only then can they help us collectively shift our understanding of who we are and where we belong. Multispecies imagination can heal us from our chronic isolation from nature. That is where the journey starts. Breathtaking encounters and a sense of wonder await not only among the stars, but at the end of every one of the countless threads connecting us to the world and its inhabitants.

In this sense, this new anthology is, in part, also a result of threads newly woven and discovered. We are deeply grateful to all readers, reviewers and researchers who took the time to engage with *Multispecies Cities*. To everyone who bought, gifted, borrowed, recommended, wrote, and talked about the book or filled in the survey—we do hope you enjoy the new collection!

THREADLOOM

N. R. M. Roshak

Threadloom hulked at one end of the treehome and plotted his escape.

The treehome was one large room, roundish, grown over decades into a home. Someone had planted a rough circle of beech saplings; someone had woven their trunks and branches together as they grew; someone had pieced glass into the windows so many years ago that bark now swelled over the panes, sealing them tight. The alchemies of patience and time had transformed a formerly unremarkable patch of the woods, once damp and mushroomy and wild, into a cozy home.

A cozy home for *humans*. Threadloom smelled the wild woods outside and wanted out.

It was cold and dark outside. Fall rain spattered the windowpanes. Threadloom didn't care.

He had the nicest spot in the house, by the hearth's glowstones, whose reddish glow suffused the treehome with warmth. He didn't care.

Threadloom shuffled his hooves on the flagstones. The problem was the door. The young girl and the old weaver-woman went in and out all day, like there was nothing to it. But their clever weavers' fingers knew some trick Threadloom couldn't fathom. Night after night, Threadloom had tried to nose the door open and failed. It simply wouldn't budge.

He stretched, barely flexing the great loom that grew from his back as he arched his spine, feeling the half-finished rug on his great loom pucker and then flatten as he straightened. One of his two little inkle looms, which grew from his head like antlers, bumped the powervine that trailed down to the glowstones from the treehome's arching ceiling. The two huge, stiff leaves hanging from the powervine clattered against each other, then were still.

Threadloom snorted out a breath of relief at the leaves' silence. He disliked those leaves. They were tough, inedible, and unpredictably jangled and glowed. His people couldn't get enough of them, though. They plucked and replaced those two leaves, over and over, racing over to pull them off the vine whenever they jangled, and spending hours poking at their surfaces when they glowed.

Threadloom turned away from the hearth and picked his way delicately to the door, maneuvering his bulk around the table, chairs, sofa, and assorted human furnishings. His tail flicked a cup off the table. It smashed on the flagstones.

He froze. A muttering snort drifted down from the sleeping loft above the hearth. Then the rustle of someone rolling over in a nest of blankets—warm, soft blankets they'd woven with Threadloom—and a snore.

Threadloom relaxed. He was safe. His people slept. He took the last few steps to the door and lifted his head to sniff at it. The loamy, damp breath of Fall teased round the doorframe. But the doorknob smelled like *their* hands, the old woman's and the girl's. Their hands were so gentle on him, whether they wove on the great loom on his back or on his little antler-looms. They made such beautiful things together. Although the old weaver was angry, sometimes, ripping their work off Threadloom with curses and mutterings. But the girl loved everything they made together.

Threadloom lipped at the doorknob. He knew weaving like he knew breathing: the play of warp and weft, the tension of the thread, the subtle variance of pattern. The thousand nimble fingerlets that served as the hooks of his great loom were skilled. And night after night, while the girl and old woman slept, he had practiced working his right antler-loom with the prongs of his left one, until he could weave bits of coarse cloth all by himself. This was his secret, and he was terribly proud of it. But he didn't understand doors.

Another snore ripped out from the loft, ending in a choked mumble. Threadloom jumped, banging the handle.

"Gran?" murmured a young voice sleepily. Threadloom's sleek

flanks prickled with tension.

Any moment now, his people would wake. It was now or never.

His people were gentle and mostly kind, and the food was *so* good, and the hut was *so* warm. But the call of the forest thrilled in his blood. He lowered his head, folded his antler-looms back, and smashed through the door.

***

"We have to find that dang loombeest," Gran said. Her hands were busy smearing slices of ripe breddlofe with jam and stacking them into rough sandwiches. She handed one to Jenny. "Here."

Jenny took the sandwich with a yawn. They'd been up half the night searching for Threadloom, since the moment they'd woken to a terrific crash and stumbled out of bed to find the door wrecked and Threadloom gone. Jenny had found a long black thread caught on the door, matching one of the two wefts she'd helped Gran load into shuttles yesterday. At least, she hoped it wasn't one of the warp threads that Threadloom held taut in the deft fingerlets of his loomhead. If he was still holding tight to those, Jenny figured, he hadn't given up on the blanket Gran had been working on him; he meant to come back.

"That blanket needs to be finished for Sunday's exhibition," continued Gran, almost as though she'd heard Jenny's thoughts. "And I've got a list of requests as long as your arm—" A shrill jingling interrupted her.

Jenny jumped up from her chair, dropping the sandwich. "My dataleaf!"

"School," groaned Gran. "How could I forget? No, how is it already eight-thirty? Jenny, go start your classes on your dataleaf."

"No way!" protested Jenny. "Threadloom's more important." She plucked her dataleaf off the powervine that fed it from the soot-black sun-sharing leaves of the beeches that made up their walls and roof. Jenny flicked the thick, fleshy dataleaf's biolume display awake, then smashed her thumb on Report Absence. "There!"

"Jenny!"

"It's only my second absence this year, Gran! Some kids were out twice a week last year, and they still passed. And we have to find Threadloom! You said so yourself."

Gran set down the jam and took Jenny's dataleaf from her. "I'll go round to the neighbours while you're at school. If we still haven't found him by noon, you can help me then."

"But Gran—"

"There, I've cancelled the absence. Sit yourself down at the table and get to work." Gran passed Jenny's dataleaf back. "And no skipping!"

***

Jenny eased herself out the broken front door. She'd wrangled a self-study period out of her teacher, so she had at least an hour to herself. And she had no intention of studying. Gran had said she was going around to the neighbours, so as long as Jenny steered clear of the neighbours, she could keep looking for Threadloom.

Her cloak snagged on the splintered doorframe. "Rat poop," she muttered, stopping to untangle herself. The cloak was one of Threadloom's failures, or what Gran counted as failures, anyway. Gran had had a request for one of her poppy-pattern blankets, red weft dancing over and under the black warp to form long chains of interlocking flowers. It was a pattern of Gran's invention, one Gran had set up and worked hundreds of times with their last loombeest. But Threadloom had muffed it. The poppies that spooled off his great loom were distorted, elongated like heads, their black centres open like calling mouths.

No doubt Gran would've stopped weaving a few inches in, but Gran hadn't been at the loom that day. Jenny had. She'd seen the warped poppies forming in the weave, but it hadn't felt like a mistake. It had felt like a *discovery.* Jenny wasn't quite sure what Threadloom's weirded poppies were, but she'd wanted to see where the loombeest was going with it. She'd kept sliding the shuttle back and forth, back and forth, watching the chains of mournful faces form, until Gran had noticed and stopped her with the blanket half-done. Gran would've composted that half-finished blanket, too, but Jenny had rescued it and made it over into a cloak. Now it kept her warm as she headed into the woods.

It was a beautiful fall morning. The sky was a clear blue dome overhead, washed clean by last night's rain. The air was soft and damp and smelled of the first fallen leaves under Jenny's feet. The underbrush was still thick, leaves shining glossy with rain and dew that wet the edges of Jenny's cloak as she passed.

Jenny plucked a long black thread from a bramble, held it close like a detective examining a clue. The thread was swollen with rain. Soaked through. Ragged at the end, broken off. It might have snagged off Threadloom as he passed. She took a closer look at the undergrowth. A snapped branch here, a bent sapling there: Something had trampled its way into the woods here. Jenny gathered her cloak tight to her and followed.

Thorns snagged at her cloak. Rain and dew soaked her thighs. A branch reached down and tried to tangle itself in her hair. Jenny pushed it out of the way and pushed through the brush. A scrap of red thread glowed at her from a weedy maple sapling. It was one of Gran's, for sure: Gran grew the richest reds in the county. They were bright even dry, but get them wet and they shone like sunset's glow. Jenny wound it around her fingers and pushed on. She'd grown up in these woods, but it had been years since she'd played in the thick undergrowth. Still, Jenny knew that Threadloom's trail was taking her in a great circle, looping through the woods toward where she'd started.

Could Threadloom be headed back home after all? Jenny's pulse sped up as she followed the loose trail of snapped branches and trampled undergrowth. The trees were thinning ahead, she was coming to a clearing, the undergrowth had grown up to her shoulders in response to the light, she was soaked from toes to shoulders and her cloak was a sodden mass keeping her wetter than warm as she pushed through a thicket of sumac just beginning to turn red with fall and broke out into—

The garden?

Jenny shook herself like a wet dog and looked around. She'd hoped Threadloom was headed straight back to their front door, sated with adventure and ready to warm up by the glowstones, but she'd come out into their half-acre back garden. Rows of ripe breddlofe, porkpod and tomato stretched around her, quiet and still, drying off in the morning sun.

Threadloom didn't need to break down their door to enjoy the fruits of their garden. They'd always kept his belly full of his favourites, all the cabbages and hay and dumplins he could eat.

Jenny groaned, realizing she might not have been following Threadloom's trail at all. She could've been following a rabbit trail. The bunnies liked to come and have a nibble on the clover that grew low between beds. They left the breddlofe and tomatoes and porkpods alone, as long as there was clover.

Jenny reached out and grabbed a ripe little breddlofe for herself, along with a cluster of stripey red cherry tomatoes and a ripe, cabbagey dumplin. Might as well have a snack while she was here. She burst a tomato between her teeth to feel its sweetness flood her mouth.

Something moved, down at the far end of the garden.

Jenny dropped the breddlofe.

The tall threadflowers at the back of the garden shifted and swayed. A great golden flower bent, bobbled, and sprang back.

Jenny moved cautiously toward the rows of threadflowers. Something big rustled and crunched through their ranks.

Cautiously, Jenny peered around the stem of a bushy plant heavy with thread.

On the other side of the row, Threadloom was puzzling at a tall brown threadflower. He nuzzled at the stamens, unable to draw the long filaments out with his lips, but knocking pollen onto the half-finished blanket in his loom.

The blanket! Gran had been working on a tongue-in-cheek variation on buffalo plaid, for the exhibition. Standard buffalo plaid wove black and red together into an orderly pattern of checks. But in the standard version, the black/red squares were plain twill, while in the version Gran had planned, the black/red squares would be woven in intricate geometric patterns, each one different.

At least, that had been the plan before Threadloom ran away.

Now, though, the weaving was in bad shape. A golden thread trailed from one end of the blanket, and the gold-threaded shuttle was missing, lost somewhere in the woods. The red weft was tangled around one of Threadloom's rear legs, with its shuttle caught in the tangle and dragging behind him. And the bottom of the weave was unrecognizable. Threads hung tattered from it, and Threadloom had tried to weave in—was that *straw*?

Jenny shifted to get closer. Threadloom's loom-antlered head snapped up. Their eyes locked.

Threadloom bolted, crashing heedless through the rows of threadflowers. "No!" cried Jenny, as his hooves trampled Gran's prized reds. He disappeared through the sumac, leaving Jenny with the ruins of their threadflower crop.

"Oh, no, oh, no," Jenny muttered, racing from flower to flower. Their stems were broken; the thread had to be harvested before the flowers died, or it would rot. Thread was the first thing to go, in threadflowers, dissolving into black slime. Jenny pulled the long stamens carefully from the first flower, winding the long filaments' silky smoothness in her fingers yard by yard. The flowers weren't quite ready: the thread should have been longer and the red should've been brighter. The thread would dry dull and short, but better that than nothing.

A jangling ring from their treehome distracted her. Jenny spun toward it. It didn't sound like her teacher calling, it wasn't the school chime, but she should check. And in the back of her mind, there was the same hope she always had when her dataleaf chimed: it might be a call from the Weaver's Guild. For *her*, not for Gran.

It never was, but Jenny always hoped. She sent in a guild application every quarter without fail, even though Gran always said she wasn't ready yet. All she ever got back was a polite note asking her to try again when she'd completed some larger works. Never mind that Gran wouldn't let her *do* any larger works! She hadn't even let Jenny help on Gran's own blankets, since the cloak.

With a sigh, Jenny gathered up the fallen flowers—a fat armload of reds and blues and browns—and ran toward the treehome. Inside, she stood the flowers hastily in a bucket of water before grabbing the jangling dataleaf off the powervine. But it wasn't her dataleaf. It was Gran's.

Gran never left her dataleaf behind. Yet here it was. And unlocked, too.

Jenny's thumb hovered over "Answer call". The dataleaf silenced before she decided. A message rolled in.

Suditha: My Dear Amilia - Just checking in about your plans for the quarterly all-Guild exhibition on Sunday. It's your first time as our Guild's Featured Artist, which is so exciting! We're all very eager to see your original take on Buffalo Plaid.

Jenny recognized the name with a thrill. Suditha was a Very Important Person in the Weaver's Guild. And Gran was going to be the Guild's Featured Artist at the exhibition! She'd never said!

Then a second message from Suditha popped up:

Suditha: As you know, the whole point of Featured Artists is to show the other Guilds the very best work our Guild can do. Of course, I know your blanket will be excellent. But, my dear, some of the Council are a teensy bit nervous that we haven't even seen a picture of your submission yet! So, and here is the key point, Council wants to review your submission before the exhibition goes live.

If you can't get your blanket to me by Saturday morning for review,

I'm afraid Council will find someone else to stand in as Featured Artist. Do send me at least a preview pic of that blanket today, won't you?

Jenny winced. Today was Wednesday. Gran had less than three days to finish the blanket to get it on the Friday afternoon oxen-truck. The blanket that was currently being dragged through the woods on their runaway loom.

If Gran wanted to stay Featured Artist, they'd have to get Threadloom home, fast.

***

Threadloom crashed through the brush, heart pounding. Strange urges thrilled through him. He wanted—he wanted—he *wanted*, without knowing what.

He struggled to weave the one golden thread he'd plucked from the threadflowers into the pattern he was building. He was built for working with people, not alone; he couldn't wind the weft onto a shuttle, couldn't even reach to slide the shuttle through the spread between weft threads himself. And he needed more thread. He plucked long straws where he found them, pulled tough strands of dog-strangling vine from the ground and stripped their leaves with his teeth, shoved them roughly into the spread. He had to weave. He had to give voice to his chaotic feelings in the only way he could.

***

"My reds!" Gran held up the sagging bunch of flowers. "Jenny, what—?"

Jenny hurried over. "I was meaning to get the thread out. I don't think it's too late? Threadloom knocked them over."

Gran started reeling thread deftly from the throat of the most wilted flower. The filament was already darkening and fragile, but still usable. "So you've seen him! In the garden, was he? Bet he was after the porkpods." She shook her head.

"No," Jenny said, taking a flower to work on. "He was in the threadflowers, that's why they're trampled. He bolted when he saw me." The thin, delicate thread snapped in her fingers. "Darn!"

"Let me," said Gran. "There's a trick to it when they're already half-wilted. Good thing I've got enough good reds already dried to finish the blanket." She glanced toward the empty end of the room where Threadloom wasn't.

"Let me go look for him again while you do that," Jenny pleaded.

Gran pressed her lips together. "Not a neighbour's seen him," she said, instead of answering. "Kept finding kicked-over bushes and bits of pulled weft in the woods, but not a glimpse of him till you saw him in the garden." She shook her head. "I'll go out again when I've got these threads pulled and hung to dry. Maybe I can bait him with some porkpods. You sit and finish your schoolwork."

"My schoolwork's done." It wasn't a lie, if she meant yesterday's schoolwork instead of today's. On any other day, Gran would've said, "Show me!" But today, Gran didn't so much as raise an eyebrow.

"Try some porkpods," was all she said.

Obediently, Jenny grabbed a handful of porkpods from the pantry and tied them up in a kerchief. But she also stopped to loop a few lengths of dried golden thread around her wrists. She didn't think porkpods were what Threadloom wanted.

Gran saw her and shook her head. "You'll not bait him with that. If he wants thread, why would he leave? We've got all the thread he could want here."

***

Threadloom wasn't in the garden any more, but the threadflowers showed that he'd been there. The best browns and golds were tattered, trailing snapped threads. Jenny sighed and cut their stalks at the base. They were beyond saving, good for nothing but compost.
She walked the perimeter of the garden slowly, looking. There was the place Threadloom had crashed through the sumac earlier. She pushed into the thicket, following the snapped branches until she lost the trail in a small clearing.

Jenny turned slowly in a circle, looking for any clue. Something gold gleamed from a bush. An early-turned leaf, or—?

It was a golden thread. But not snagged on a bush. It had been carefully woven into the oddest bit of work Jenny had ever seen.

It was a tiny piece, narrow like the belts Jenny sometimes wove on Threadloom's little antler-loom, but only as long as her arm. Jenny lifted it carefully off the bush and fingered it. It was stiff as a picture. The warp was green vine, as thick as pencil lead. And the weft—the golden thread, yes, but also long grasses, the thick center ribs of leaves, and curling strips of bark. It was chaos. But it was the kind of chaos that made you feel that if you stared at it long enough, you would see an image, as with clouds or the knurls of a grandfather tree.

Jenny stroked the odd little weaving. There was no doubt in her mind that Threadloom had made it. But why?

A rustling in the brush stilled her. The thinning leaves were screening a tawny bulk from her. Jenny squinted through the leaves. "Threadloom?" she whispered.

A little deer popped its antlered head up and snorted, eyes round with fear. Before Jenny could blink, it was bounding away from her, white tail flashing. Jenny put one hand over her pounding heart and laughed. "Of course Threadloom's not the only beast in the woods," she said. "I knew that." And it was fall: soon the deer would be in rut, single-minded and uncautious, if they weren't already.

***

Threadloom nosed at the clear glass in the young treehome's largest window. The bark hadn't yet sealed over the glass. The treehome was empty, the inside air untended. He pressed his nose to the crack between glass and trunks. It was dark inside, and smelled empty. The familiar scents of drying thread and herbs, of warm people and porkpod stew—all absent. And no hint of a loombeest. The empty treehome smelled cold and lonely.

Threadloom had visited every treehome in the woods, sneaking as quietly as he could to sniff at windows and doors. He hadn't found a single other loombeest. Plenty of thread, and people, and other strange animal smells he didn't recognize and didn't care about. But nothing that smelled like him.

He backed away from the empty treehome. There were more smells in the woods than he knew what to do with, and some tantalizingly close to his own. Little brown beasts with fixed, ragged antlers, unmoving and useless; long spindly legs, so unlike his own short, stout ones, and small, skittish backs that carried no loom. Their smell was so close, but so wrong.

He plucked another length of dog-strangling vine and stripped the leaves. Jays called to each other through the trees, above. Threadloom could call too, in his own way. If there was anyone to hear.

***

Gran turned the strange strip of weaving over and over in her hands. "You think Threadloom made this?"

"Yes! Look—there's the golden thread he took from the garden, and it's fresh, not even dried. Besides, who else would've done this?"

"We are the only weavers in these woods," murmured Gran, "but Elsa the treesmith has a little inkle loom, for making belts, and her boy Schist could've been playing with it…"

"Schist is twelve now, Gran!" exclaimed Jenny. "He's only three years younger than me. He's got better things to do than weaving twigs and uncured thread and vines into this… this…"

"Mess?" Gran suggested. "The trouble is, Jenny, loombeests aren't bred to weave on their own. If Threadloom's got it into his little head that he's the weaver, I'm going to have a hard time getting any worthwhile work out of him at all." She sighed. "Hard enough getting him to hold a pattern as it is. I've never worked with a worse loombeest."

"I like working with him," protested Jenny. "He kind of puts his own twist on things."

"And that's just what he's not supposed to do! I had a request for my poppy pattern, not for whatever you let him do to that blanket you've turned into a cloak." She shook her head. "Now that I see this, Jenny, I think I've been blaming you unfairly. I said you couldn't work any more big projects, not until you'd learned to better control the loom. But Threadloom might be to blame, if he thinks he's in charge. I hate to say it, but I think he's flawed. A bad tool. His running away might be for the best. We might do better with another loom."

"Don't say that!" cried Jenny.

Gran's dataleaf jangled again. Jenny scooped it up and handed it to her, reading the message on the way.

Suditha: Dearest Amilia, I'm a bit worried at your silence. Is everything all right?

Council is getting ever more concerned. I'm on your side, of course, but without even a picture to show them, there's only so much I can do. I hate to be the bearer of bad news, but Council has voted to choose another Featured Artist if we don't have your blanket in hand by Friday. Friday, Amilia!

"Gran," said Jenny, "I don't think we have *time* to get another loom."

***

Threadloom shook his antlers and bellowed in frustration. Why was everything so *hard?*

He wanted to cover the woods with his work, but he couldn't work the loom on his own back alone. The little antler-loom on his left antler, yes. His prehensile right antler painstakingly threaded it, ran the small shuttle across. It was hard and he couldn't really see what he was doing, but he could do it. But for the great loom on his back, he needed help.

He needed his people. But they never wanted to weave what *he* wanted. The old one, especially. She wanted squares and checks and flowers. The girl was better.

As though summoned by his thoughts, her scent came to him on the breeze. Damp thread, and girl-sweat, and the long dark hairs that sometimes got woven into his work with the thread.

He took a cautious step in her direction. And then another.

***

"Is that another one?" Gran motioned to a tangle of threads hanging low in a tree.

Jenny went on tiptoes and tugged on it. "I don't think so? It's just a bunch of thread and weeds snarled up together." She ripped it out of the tree.

"Hm. It's at about antler height, though. Maybe our prodigal loombeest was offloading a mistake." Gran looked at the surrounding bushes closely. "I see a fresh-snapped twig here, and another there. Threadloom might've gone that way. He can't move through the woods as easily as a deer. He's so much wider, and he's got that loom on his back to tangle him up."

"Look—" Jenny lifted another narrow, woven strap out of a bush. "He's made another one! That must've been his scraps."

Gran squinted at it. "This one's a bit better, I'll give him that. Look, he's using extra warp to create a kind of pattern. Lappet weave, even if he is using weeds for it."

Jenny took it back. "It sort of reminds me of—Oh!" She held the strap next to her damp cloak. "Look, he's trying to make the warped poppy pattern—but there's something on top of one of the poppies—" She fell silent.

"What?"

"Antlers," breathed Jenny. "They're not funny poppies, Gran, they're *heads*. And he's made three of them on the strap. Three heads, and one has antlers."

"Oh," said Gran. "Oh, no."

"What? Why? Just because he wants to make his own patterns? I think it's *amazing*."

Gran shook her head. "No. Because of what he's making. Don't you see what he's dreaming of? Look what he's made there. Two big heads and a little one. And one of the big heads has antlers." At Jenny's blank look, Gran gave an exasperated sigh. "Two grown-ups, Jenny, and one of them's a boy. And then they have a little one. Do I have to spell it out?"

"Ohhhhh…" breathed Jenny. "And it's *rut*."

Gran clicked her tongue. "Not for him, it shouldn't be. Loombeests are a cross, they can't breed, like mules. They aren't supposed to go into rut."

Jenny held up the strap. "This doesn't look like *rut* exactly."

"Maybe not. But. Threadloom's not right. I'll put a call in to the breeder. She ought to take him back."

"You can't just get another loombeest! Threadloom's—this doesn't make him *bad*, Gran! It makes him *special*!"

"It made him run away," Gran said. "Jenny, don't you remember our last loombeest? Wefty?"

"Wefty was *ancient*. It took him forever to do anything."

"Well, that was true at the end. But he wasn't always old. You wouldn't remember, but he was as young as Threadloom when we first got him."

"Okay, so?"

"So, Wefty was with us for ten years. And in all that time, did he run away once?"

"No?"

"No. Hardly even looked out the window. Wefty was happy, Jenny. He *wanted* to sit by the glowstones and weave. Loved nothing more than starting a big new blanket with me." Gran sighed. "That's all I want in a loombeest, a good partner who's willing to work. But Threadloom, bless his heart, wants to go off in the woods and start a family. If that's what he wants…" Gran let the words trail off, looking into the woods. "I don't know what I expected, haring off into the woods after a runaway loombeest. But I'm not going to tie him up in the treehome. It's clear he's not happy here, and he's not going to be."

***

Threadloom peered through the bushes. The girl was there, but also the old woman.

The old woman would catch him and make him weave what she wanted. Threadloom was sure of it.

But the girl… The girl might let him weave what *he* wanted.

He pushed his nose cautiously through the shrubbery, close to the girl's shoulder. Twigs snapped on his antlers.

***

"Poor Threadloom. What're we going to do?" asked Jenny.

"*We* aren't going to do anything," said Gran. "*You* are going to help me look for Threadloom until your lunch break's over, so that I can try to talk the breeder into trading him in for a normal loombeest, and then you're going to go back to your schoolwork. The rest is my concern."

"No! I—" Twigs crackled behind Jenny's shoulder. She jumped.

"Steady," whispered Gran. "Speak of the devil, Threadloom's right behind you. Do you have the porkpods?"

Jenny pulled out the kerchief she'd tied the porkpods into.

***

The girl was shaking something in a cloth. A tasty smell rose from it, but Threadloom ignored it. His eyes were fixed on the cloth.

He remembered weaving that cloth, with the girl.

***

"Gran, you can't just take Threadloom back to the breeder's!" Jenny whispered, as she fumbled with the kerchief. "Besides, you saw Suditha's message. There's no way you can get a new loombeest, train it, and weave an entire blanket in time for Suditha to get it by Friday!"

Gran gritted her teeth. "Do you think I don't know that?"

***

The gold and brown lines on the cloth danced and jumped before Threadloom's eyes.

He'd been thinking about loombeests dancing when he wove that cloth, and the dance had crept into the weave. The girl hadn't exactly *let* him change it. But she hadn't ripped out his changes, either.

The result was… not quite what she'd set up, on the loom, and not what he'd had in mind, either.

Threadloom watched the cloth waving in the air, and saw that it was beautiful.

There were no loombeests in these woods. Threadloom knew that now. And at some deep, genetic level, Threadloom knew, too, that that way of creating something new was closed to him. That longing, the dream he'd woven on his antlers—it would stay a dream.

But sometimes, when the girl was weaving, the two of them came out with something together that wasn't quite like either of them would have done alone. It was something new.

And that—that was something worth doing.

***

Jenny waved the kerchief of porkpods in the air carelessly. "But if you don't get Suditha that rug by Friday, you won't be Featured Artist, and you might never get another chance!"

"I *know!*" Gran snapped. "But if Threadloom won't weave for me, what do you want me to do? I can't force him to weave!"

The kerchief's knot slipped. It unfurled. Porkpods went flying. One sailed over Threadloom's head.

"Oh, poop!" yelled Jenny, spinning around.

Threadloom met her gaze. Gently, and with as much dignity as he could muster while tangled in a bush, he lowered his head to her hand and lipped gently at the kerchief, and then at the colorful threads looped around Jenny's wrist.

"He's not going after the porkpods," muttered Gran. "What does this daft beast want?"

Threadloom lifted the kerchief in his mouth and waved it at Jenny. His prehensile right antler bent to nudge the colorful threads around Jenny's wrist.

"I think…" Jenny said, "I think he wants to weave, Gran. Do you want these on your little loom?" She unlooped the threads from her wrist and held them out to Threadloom.

Gently, he nudged her arm toward the great loom on his back.

"He wants them in the rug," murmured Jenny. "Look, Gran—he's showing me the order he wants to use them in the weft—heaps of black and red, but also gold?"

Gran crossed her arms. "There's no *gold* in buffalo plaid, Jenny!"

"No gold," Jenny told Threadloom, pulling it out of the bunch. "Gran says—Oh!" Threadloom was backing away from her, crunching and tangling in the brush. "Wait!" Jenny pleaded. "Look, I'm putting it back in, see?"

The loombeest paused, eyeing her warily, as though gauging whether she meant it.

"Gran, he really wants it in," said Jenny. "I'm just going to see what he wants to do with it…"

Gran threw her hands up in the air. "Fine, ignore my pattern! I've only been weaving longer than either of you has been alive!"

"Just let me try…" Jenny picked up a stick and wound the gold thread around it. "Not the greatest shuttle, but it'll do. I think he wants to bring in the gold weft here… just let us try…"

The shuttle flew back and forth, Threadloom's fingerlets plying the warp, Jenny passing the three shuttles through the shed and beating the weave. The blanket spooled off the great loom faster than Threadloom had ever woven before.

When it was done, Gran cut the blanket off the loom and tied the warp. Her dataleaf jangled. Gran ignored it.

Gran passed one corner of the blanket to Jenny. They held it up between them. Three sets of eyes studied the work: two weavers, and a loom.

It was buffalo plaid, yes, and the black/red squares were fiendishly complicated. But what really drew the eye were the tiny golden figures capering across the squares. They could be abstract shapes. Or they could be loombeests, antlers reduced to forks, loom a pair of stacked rectangles balanced on stout legs. And next to each loombeest, a weaver.

The dataleaf jangled and buzzed at a fever pitch of urgency. Suditha's voice broke into the stillness of the clearing.

"*Amilia*! I'm pushing a voice message to your dataleaf, and you know how much I hate to do that. But you're not answering, darling, and it's urgent! Please, please, call me back and tell me you've got a *spectacular* blanket for me and you'll be loading it onto the oxen-truck tomorrow."

Jenny smiled. "I think you've got that spectacular blanket," she said.

"Hmmm." Gran studied the blanket for a long moment. "I can put this on the oxen-truck tomorrow," she said finally, "but it looks like I won't be the Featured Artist this quarter."

"*What?* Why not? The blanket's done! And it's *perfect*. You can't say it's not perfect!"

"That it is, but it's not my blanket. Not mine alone, at any rate. The Council's just going to have to accept a team for Featured Artist. *Amilia and Jenny, Featured Artists.* That'll look good on your next guild application, hm?"

Jenny caught her breath. "Yes! Oh, *yes!* But—it's not right."

Gran raised an eyebrow. "No? Those little loombeests weren't in *my* pattern."

"I know, Gran. But they aren't all *my* pattern, either."

Gran sighed. "The Guild won't accept a loombeest as an artist, Jenny." She rubbed her chin thoughtfully. "But you're right, we can't claim this work as ours alone."

***

Suditha peered into the back of the oxen-truck, which was snorting and shuffling its twenty-four legs in front of her home. The big box strapped to the oxen-truck's sturdy compound back was overflowing with beautifully crafted wares: grownpots, tree-smithed chairs, freshly harvested and dried plates, elaborate knits—and laid on top of the load, one intricately detailed red-and-black blanket with hints of gold. Suditha reached in, pulled out the blanket, and shook it out to have a look.

"Beautiful," she breathed. The blanket was both as fine as anything anyone in the Weaver's Guild had ever made, and not quite like anything the Guild had ever seen. And it bore its makers' names proudly on a tag:

"Amilia, Jenny, & Co., Featured Artists."

Suditha frowned at the tag. *Jenny*—that must be Amilia's granddaughter, the one who kept sending in applications. Well, if this blanket was any measure of her skill, the girl's next Guild application just might succeed. Suditha did wonder at the "Co." momentarily—had Amilia taken on another apprentice?—before dismissing it. The blanket was here on time, and it was worthy of a Featured Artist: that was what mattered.

***

Threadloom relaxed contentedly by the glowstones of his treehome. His people were stringing forest-green warp on his great loom, setting up the next blanket they would work, the three of them, together. It would be complex, because of the old woman; it would be playful, because of the girl; and it would be beautiful, because he would fill it with his dreams.

* * *

N. R. M. Roshak is an award-winning Canadian author and translator. Their fiction has been published in four languages, and has appeared in various anthologies and magazines, including *Flash Fiction Online, Galaxies SF, Daily Science Fiction*, and *Future Science Fiction Digest*. You can find more of their work at http://nrmroshak.com.

SONORA'S JOURNEY

Kai Holmwood

Sonora had not always been the best of mothers, but she would make up for that now that she had come to herself again. The exhaustion that had kept her half-asleep, rousing only as necessary to wake and nourish her children, wasn't her fault—but she shouldn't have allowed herself the luxury of giving in to it. This time, though, would be different. Today would mark the beginning of something new. She could feel it.

The sky stretched overhead, brilliant and cloudless, as blue as she remembered from her own childhood. The sun streamed over the land for as far as she could see. She moved from one child to the next, murmuring, "Wake—it's time." And as they stirred and began to stretch, she went to draw water for them.

To her surprise, no water poured forth. That was unprecedented and troubling—water ebbed here in the desert, retreating until it was almost nowhere but in the deepest aquifers, the blood of panting animals, and the hearts of the saguaros and chollas—but that ebb had never failed to be quenched by an answering flow. Never until now.

They would wait it out. They had enough to manage for a little while. "We'll make do with what we have," she said, decided. "Perhaps tomorrow will bring relief."

When she went for water the next morning, again none came at her call. Nor the next morning, nor the one after that. Their reserves grew less and less as the sun beat down upon them. Her children shared the last few drops, then, still parched, begged for more. She gazed at the clear sky, pleading for even a single rain cloud. None came.

This land had been her home for her whole life. The thought of leaving was unfathomable. And yet... and yet.

"Come," she said. "We'll travel to the edges of the earth if we must, but I *will* see my children thrive."

They began their trek to the northwest, to a mythical seaside land where she had heard that even summers were full of fog. There, they would never again need to fear drought.

***

Morgan's most precious memory was of a short trip with her dad. He had snatched her out of school and whisked her off to the Sonoran desert, eight hundred miles away, as fast as he could. There, the hills were painted in impossibly vibrant colors.

"Cherish this," he had whispered in her ear as he lifted her to see better. Not that he had needed to; the flowers were everywhere. "You might never see something like this again."

Back then, she hadn't really understood what he had meant. But she had taken it all in: the sunlight and the explosion of colors and the irreproducible wild scent on the breeze and his embrace, far warmer than the desert's March air.

He had been right. She had never seen a moment like that again.

That year's Sonoran blankets of flowers had come to be known as the last superbloom. As the deserts had shifted and changed, there had been a few patchy flushes here and there, but they petered out quickly.

Besides, *he* hadn't lived to see them.

As she had grown up, that memory had been one of a dozen moments that linked together to guide her toward studying climate solutions and ecological restoration. Every additional "last," from the last giant monarch migration through the East Bay to the last lone Mission blue butterfly she saw visiting the lupine on her favorite salt-breezed Marin Headlands walk, kept her on the course set by the biggest "last" of all: the last superbloom and the last happiness before her father's diagnosis.

***

The Joshua trees were the first proof that Sonora had left her homeland. She stopped a while to gaze at them in wonder. They were almost familiar—she could almost imagine they echoed the curves and lines of her beloved saguaro—yet they were utterly different, unlike anything she had ever seen. As she watched from a distance, the Joshua trees burst into crowded bloom, their flowers so tightly clustered that she could barely distinguish one from another. And then the flowers pulled back, swelling into fruits that fell and dropped their grackle-black seeds on the sunset-tinted land.

Sonora drew near, touching the seeds lightly with her heart full of wonder—and then full of despair. Not a single seed she touched had a spark of life inside.

"Even here?" she whispered, but fought back her grief. She had to be strong for her children. They were all she had, and all she could allow to matter.

***

"This year's report is out," Tahni said.

Morgan didn't bother to turn around from where she sat staring out the windows at the City by the Bay. Most of the longer view was blocked by skyscrapers, each covered in large, offset balconies full of thriving plant life. The buildings were widely spaced to welcome the sun's rare rays, though, so she was able to catch a glimpse of the frolicking white-tipped waves in the distance. "What does it say?"

"The Sonoran Desert and the Central Valley Expansion Zone have officially merged and been reclassified as one desert. In other words, the Sonoran is now only fourteen miles away, just on the other side of the hills."

Morgan fought back the expressions she felt warring for position on her face. So much of the global climate crisis had found the beginnings of its solutions, and so much damage had begun to be reversed. The Sonoran Desert, though, kept stretching inexorably northwestward.

For so long in this time of putting out one fire after another, San Francisco's main focus had been turned in the other direction, toward the sea, toward the rising water that threatened to eat away at its foundations. Only in recent years, with that crisis held at bay, had they finally been able to turn to the threat at their backs. And it was already almost too late. Their only hope other than snuffing out the Sonoran entirely was to coax the desert to turn back on itself, to persuade it retreat the way it had come—but that would mean making the dead zone behind the outer fringes viable once more. With fourteen miles to go, time was running out. This was their only chance.

Once Morgan had her face under control, she spun in her chair to face Tahni across the room. "It's hardly a surprise," she said. "There's a reason everyone has been moving here to San Francisco for years. Decades. At least they finally reclassified the situation accurately."

Tahni nodded. "I know. But—it makes it feel too real, and too fast. In the old maps, the Sonoran Desert barely even touched California."

"The old maps have been irrelevant since before you and I were born."

"But—"

Morgan sighed. Loudly. While Tahni was certainly good at her work, this constant tendency for nostalgia toward a time neither of them had ever known wasn't exactly helpful.

"Sorry," Tahni said.

"Forget it. It just means we need to make sure we get this right."

"Do you think we can actually do it?"

"We have to try."

***

Sonora and her children made their northwestern way slowly, resting when they could. Now and then, she thought they had gone far enough; a lush forest spoke of rivers, or a snow-capped mountain promised rain. They would settle in these places for a while, only to watch the rivers dry and the forests burn and the snows melt for the last time, leaving mountaintops unreplenished. She wondered, sometimes, if she were cursed—if her very presence somehow drove the water away before them. But with a mother's pragmatism, she dismissed such thoughts. Cursed or not, her children relied on her. And so they moved on, desperately searching, desperately hoping.

***

The team that mobilized to solve the Sonoran Desert problem encompassed every curve of the earth. Various parts of humanity had long since come together to work toward restoring a climatic balance, but Morgan was nevertheless amazed and grateful for the global generosity of time, input, talent, and research that went into solving the persistent expansion of this desert. Despite her relative youth, at just twenty-nine years of age, she had found herself at the forefront as the one who would actually finalize the details and launch the fleet. The weight rested heavily on her. Almost as heavily as the seemingly constant holographic talks she was supposed to give the public about their plans.

"Why don't we just let nature take its course?" someone asked during one of these talks. "We could focus instead on improving the technology and infrastructure to keep San Francisco comfortable in its own microclimate and let the desert fend for itself."

Morgan sighed. "Have you been to the old heart of the Sonoran? Anywhere along the path of what was once the Gila River?"

"No, but I don't see why that matt—"

"*That matters* because if you had, you would see the problem, and wouldn't be asking questions like that." She caught Tahni's half-exasperated, half-horrified expression, and let out a gruff "sorry" before going on: "Look." She began playing a timelapse of the Sonoran desert as it had once been, the scene often slowing to real-time to focus on the life of the desert.

The sun peeking over a distant horizon brought the landscape into luminous rose-gold. Tall saguaros stood proud guard over a slanting scene half-blanketed with creosote and brittlebush. A dark-eyed cactus mouse darted away, racing between the shrubs to her cool burrow before the light could change from this warm glow to its shimmering midday heat. She dodged an emerging Sonoran mountain kingsnake whose brilliant orange coloration echoed the fast-changing light on the hills. As the day burned from dawn to high noon, even the snake retreated into a crevice between rocks. It seemed almost as if all animal life had vanished. Just then, a jackrabbit hopped into the scene, nose twitching and giant ears pivoting. He bent his face to the low grasses underfoot, nibbling on their delicate blades even while his eyes and ears never stopped searching. Abruptly, for no reason human eyes or ears could detect, he dashed madly away.

"People like to imagine a desert is just dead sand. But look at this. Look at the life here. The Sonoran was thriving." Morgan switched to the next scene.

All was perfectly, uncannily still. In the foreground, a handful of sun-bleached dead saguaro trunks still stood, looking for all the world like bone and sinew with every bit of life and color long since drained away. Even those corpses, though, offered some relief; stretching out behind them was nothing at all. The creosote and brittlebush were long since gone, all evidence they had once been there blown away in hot winds. The earth was blanketed not in life, but only in sharp, tiny stones. Faint trails led through the landscape, offering the optimistic mind hope that either water or some animals might still venture here.

"This isn't a photograph," Morgan said. "It's a real-time clip. You just don't see any movement because nothing is left alive to move." She turned her attention back to the scene just in time for what she knew was coming.

A sudden gust of wind flung the desert into motion. Dust spasmed into the air and collapsed back onto the ground, lifeless again. And just like that, one of the seeming trails had disappeared and a new one had appeared, the partnership of wind and dust tracing their ephemeral lines on the dead landscape.

The audience was silent.

"If you think this is bad, you should see what it's like to actually be there. Can you imagine absolute stillness, where you're thankful for the sound of your own breath because it's all there is to prove that life still exists at all? Even those occasional dusty gusts feel comforting, because at least something other than you is moving." Morgan clenched her teeth briefly, fighting back the unnameable emotion that always threatened to make her speak too passionately, too much as a person instead of a scientist. She refocused on her message, shifting to the final scenes she had prepared.

A brilliantly, lushly green hill swelled beneath a dusty blue sky full of puffy clouds that mirrored the shapes of the coast live oak trees dotting the landscape.

And then: the same hill slumped, brown and withered, under a sky that shimmered almost white with heat. The coast live oak trees still stood, leafless and no longer live at all, with saguaros emerging from the ground beside them. A skinny coyote panted, head lowered, then began to dig frantically at a cactus mouse's burrow. The vibrancy of the Sonoran hadn't managed to reestablish itself here; only straggling remnants of the desert's intricate net of life had taken hold.

"At this point, only the northwestern fringe of the Sonoran is still alive, in this relatively narrow strip between us and that vast dead zone."

"So we put all this effort and time into revitalizing some dead rocks and sand. How does that help anything?"

As if the Sonoran weren't worthy in and of itself. As if it had to provide some value other than its own existence.

Tahni jumped in, perhaps sensing Morgan's impatience under these constant lines of questioning. "Well, we have three choices. We can let the Sonoran keep expanding, which isn't exactly great for other ecosystems, or for us either for that matter!" She paused, maybe waiting for chuckles that didn't come. "Or we could try to just push the desert back, but that risks killing off its delicate ecosystem because the land behind the fringes is so dead now. The solution we've come up with is to revitalize the center by recreating its old conditions, which will *then* let us gradually pull the Sonoran back to its homeland."

"That's all very well and good, but why do we need the desert at all? What's the big deal if we just push it back and let it die?"

Another voice chimed in. "And we must be using so many resources to do it. Couldn't those be better used for improving the infrastructure of the city or expanding our food forests instead? Even if the desert has its own ecosystems, it's not like we can realistically live there any time soon."

Morgan thought through her options. She could invite them to consider San Francisco swirling with dust storms that made it impossible to go outside. Or she could show them the generated image of a possible future in which the stand of redwoods to the north, those trees the city's human inhabitants loved so much, had toppled and were serving as crumbling fertilizer for the invading saguaros. But somehow those felt like lies, not because they wouldn't come true, but because they weren't *her* truth.

She had meant to stick to those usual answers. She hadn't intended to show them the image she held so close to her heart. And yet, almost without thought at all, she displayed the wordless answer that pulsed through her blood: a brilliant image of that last superbloom in all its doomed splendor.

"Because life deserves a chance," she said simply. Would that be enough?

"But—" Another voice chimed in. Another question. Another objection.

Morgan closed her connection to the call. "You can finish this up," she muttered to Tahni. "I'm going to go for a ride." She made her way to the rooftop, got into one of the city's many sunlight-and-steam-powered drones, and set off to the east.

***

Now and then, Sonora glanced behind herself, wishing for the home that had once been hers. But inhospitable deadlands seemed to follow in their wake, promising nothing but desiccated annihilation if they dared to turn back, and so she turned her thoughts ever forward toward the water and the fog.

Sonora had previously encountered a few wayward gulls, blown far off-course and inevitably succumbing to the elements of her home. But she had never before heard one calling so heartily and so healthily, shrieking its veneration of the sea.

They were close. They must be close.

She kept her gaze fixed on the hills to the west. They had come so far already; surely they could make it just a little further. Perhaps on the other side of those hills, they would find their salvation, their land of comfort and ease. Perhaps, finally, she would be able to rest once more, recovering from her long journey while basking in the warm knowledge that her children were safe.

***

The landscape below Morgan as she rode her drone eastward hadn't changed much in her lifetime. The skyscrapers had grown taller as needed to house new arrivals, allowing the populous city to keep its overall footprint compact. The hills were still green and lush on the near side, partly thanks to their ability to catch the ocean's fog and partly because of careful climate planning and technology. And then, as she crested those hills, the landscape below turned immediately from green to brown. She recognized the scenes she had shown on the call, those once-vibrant hills now populated only by dead oaks, struggling saguaros, and the occasional coyote or javelina that had followed in the desert's wake. In spring, Morgan knew, the brown landscape would drag itself into halfhearted color, its scattered flowers thankful for any scant amount of moisture. But for how much longer? When would the inhospitable conditions that even the desert couldn't survive reach this hilltop boundary, pushing the whole delicate ecosystem into extinction? And what of the other ecosystems that had been lost along the way? With the desert back in its home, perhaps those, too, might be restored.

Tomorrow, they would implement their plan. Tomorrow, perhaps, the Sonoran would be saved.

***

"We're almost there, my darlings," she murmured. "Can't you smell it now? The sea, and salt, and enough water for us to thrive for generations. We need only go a little further, and then you'll be safe."

***

Finally, it was time. The first stages of soil remediation were done; Morgan had received reports that the piles of harvested and photodegraded desert plants had been spread by drone just behind the live strip of the desert, waiting for the moisture that would help their nutrients seep into the ground to feed new generations of plant life. All that was left was to bring that moisture to the land so that the desert could begin its long trek home.

Morgan spent the morning checking and rechecking every system, every command, every possible detail that might go wrong. At 10 AM, the climate system would begin drizzling water from the desalination plant onto the other side of the hills. This, combined with cloud seeding in the early stages of the journey where there was enough water to support it, would push the desert away inch by inch. Then, that evening, once the day's heat had begun shimmering away, the real work would begin. A fleet of thousands of drones would venture into the heart of the dead land, spreading more photodegraded matter and planting seeds of brittlebush, purplemat, beloperone, desert chicory, apricot mallow, and every other native wildflower and plant they could find into carefully planned microhabitats. There, where the conditions were still too dry for cloud seeding to work, other drones would bring water from as far as necessary to nourish the budding life in the regenerating soil.

***

And so, at Sonora's urging, her children followed her as she made her way, inch by inch, up that final hill between them and their last hope. She sank her fingertips into the lush, green grass at the top, gazed at the fog encircling the skyscrapers, and, for the first time in what seemed an eternity, found herself weeping with relief.

"It's raining," her children wondered, and rejoiced.

***

Morgan looked from the lush, plant-laden rooftop toward the east, toward the boundary where the green hills met the dry grass she knew was just beyond. But there, somehow, heavy clouds had formed on the *other* side of the hills, where it shouldn't have been possible yet. A dark smudge below them could only mean—could it mean—

"It's raining," she wondered aloud. "Tahni, look, it's raining!"

Tahni's face was radiant with joy as she gazed at the clouds. "I didn't know you planned to conjure an entire rainstorm! I thought it was supposed to start with cloud seeding on our side of the hills and drones watering the other side."

Morgan shook her head, for once not bothered by the uncomprehending words. "That isn't ours. That's real rain, Tahni. Natural rain. It's as if the world somehow knows…"

***

Sonora felt all the air going out of her as the rain, one with her tears, washed the dusty dryness away. And then she took a breath that felt deeper than any she had ever taken before, and basked in the feeling of the water soaking into every line and dusty crevice in her skin. Refreshed, she laughed in purest joy and watched her children frolicking in the downfall.

And as the rain fell, drenching them in its bounty, Sonora stood upon the dividing hilltop. She gazed downhill to the west, at the mythical promised city cloaked in fog, with the seemingly limitless sea just behind it. Then she looked to the southeast, where the new rain clouds stretched as far as she could see, toward their distant home.

She waited, and she watched, and in the end, she made her decision. With her children in tow, she began moving down the hill.

***

Morgan's device alerted her that the work in the heart of the desert had begun—not that she had needed any notification. She had been impatiently waiting, her eyes fixed on the map showing the status and location of all the drones in the revitalization fleet. At the instant of the alert, the map buzzed into motion, with each drone setting about its assigned task. At first, most scattered photodegraded plant matter. Some planted seeds. Others blew a layer of dust and sand over those seeds. Still others misted the land with a carefully measured allotment of water, laboriously hauled in from as far away as necessary to minimize disturbances to other ecosystems.

One benefit of the blazing sun in the dead zone was that the solar-powered fleet of drones would be able to generate enough power to work indefinitely. Which, Morgan knew, they would need to do; as anxious as she was to watch the process unfold, this revitalization of the desert's heartlands and welcoming the Sonoran back to its old home would take years. Decades.

***

Sonora's return to her homeland was far, far quicker and easier than the northwestward trek had been. The lands before her and her children seemed always misted with just enough gentle, inviting dewiness, while those behind them swelled with an abundance of storm clouds and rain that coaxed them ever forward.

Her steps were easy, light, almost inevitable—and full of eagerness to return to the home that had once been her own. Behind them, the rivers Sonora and her children had watched run dry began to flow anew, the burned forests sprang into life, and the mountaintops glistened once more with whitest snow. If Sonora had once felt her footsteps were cursed, bringing parched death in their wake, she now felt them blessed, as if her very movement granted life back to the land.

***

When Sonora finally arrived home, she found a very old woman already there, seemingly waiting for her.

"The reports are true. The wildflowers are starting to bloom unaided," the woman whispered, her voice full of wonder. "We did it."

Sonora recognized the look in the woman's eyes. She had met people like this before—people who came into the desert to meet their end. It was part of her duty, she felt, to be there with them, and so she wrapped the woman in her warm embrace, and they sat together in Sonora's revitalized homeland, no longer in silence, but listening to the cactus wren's joy in its flight, the spiny lizard's feet scuffling through the sand and pebbles, and those wildflowers stretching into life and beauty. And once the woman had taken her last breath, Sonora tenderly buried her in the vibrant earth and planted sagebrush on her grave.

***

Only then did Sonora let herself feel the familiar age-old exhaustion. She wasn't meant for long journeys; all she had ever wanted was to rest in the beauty of this place and watch her children thrive around her. Everything in her was telling her to let go, to sink once more into that dreamy half-slumber from which she roused only now and then to make sure her children were taken care of. But could she ever again trust that they were really safe? Did she dare let herself—

"Rest, Mother," their tiny voices whispered together, their words a caress carried on the hot wind. "All is well. You have done enough. Sleep, now."

And so Sonora slept once more, and the most resplendent of her children, the brittlebush and the purplemat and the beloperone and the desert chicory and the apricot mallow, covered her in a blanket of vibrant wildflowers in every color of their love.

* * *

Kai Holmwood, a fifth-generation Californian, has been a freelance nonfiction writer for over a decade. She recently completed a Master of Writing degree at the University of Canterbury. She, her husband and their two-toothed former street cat, Halloumi, split their time between New Zealand and Portugal.

Kelp Gardens (Empathy)

Art by Yen Shu Liao

Text by Christoph Rupprecht

Solarpunk Creatures Project Entry #8 (Winter 81/2137)

Main Text

Preliminary conclusion: empathy makes these gardens bloom, as it does with any community, but in this case across species. Room for progress, sure, but the basic sense that the sea connects and nurtures all? That doesn't require the same number of arms, or claws as it were. The kelp gardens: people, octopus, giant shrimp, sea urchin etc. live off it, an edible seascape alright! And tend to it in their way, whether it's intricate trimming or feeding the urchin farms. It makes perfect sense, yet this level of coexistence is unique… how? Colleague suggests empathy-inducing symbiotic kelp microbes. Hm…

Side Text

Those electrified reefs are really something: quickly forming biorock that's self-repairing, protects against coral bleaching, deters sharks… no wonder the octopus collective is all over them! Our tidal & solar generators and their ocean stewardship is opening up whole new ways of living with the sea… on and in the sea, really!

Kombucha Atoll

least most digested
progression of fungal digestion
Ocean plastic trash
yeast
Harvester
conveyor belt
mass of floating biochar
mobility unit
follower village boats

SCOBY: symbiotic culture of bacteria and yeasts, hence the name Kombucha Atoll. Not convinced it helps the reputation of the place, but the boat villagers don't seem to mind. Must not forget to acquire a sample of their local fermented brew ...... for further study.

Rich dude's technofix gone bad, salvaged by adventurous creatures, not the first time! The main ship, the Harvester, got hopelessly SCOBY-infested and was let go. After drifting for years, folks realized the reef ecology now all over the place provides clean drinking water, food in the form of reef fish and of course the edible fungi growing all over. A chance to do meaningful restoration work, a community of likeminded people. First it was going with the currents, now they gently steer the Harvester to patches of floating garbage, feeding the mysterious plastic-devouring assemblage of species in the process. Now and then they veer close enough to the coast to trade and welcome new folks, but the restored old satellite link keeps them in touch when further out. Apparently they're working with scientists to see if the SCOBY can adapt to other parts of the ocean. adaptation and ingenuity vital to clean up our ancestors' mess, little by little.

Getting caught on sticky could mean death

Solarpunk Creatures project entry #21 (summer 2021/2148)

Stormwater Streams (Connectedness)

Solarpunk Creatures Project Entry #13 (Wet Season 84/2140)

Main Text

They tell me people arriving during dry season are usually confused: where are the streams? Watching the city transform as the rain returns is an unforgettable sight. Instead of battling stormwater surges by flushing them towards the sea, the whole neighborhood embraces the gift and soars! Without the water the succulent architecture soaks up for storage in the aquaria, nobody would make it through the long drought. Connecting two extremes in a circle – a dance around the element all life has in common! Fungi-based redistribution then is just the logical choice… (my attempts to draw a mycelial map amuse the locals… "follow the streams" they say!)

Side Text

Living water infrastructure, the whole place an autopoietic, vibrant rain garden, as it would have once been called. Plants and people play their parts, but one cannot but trace it to the elemental, more-than-human agencies behind it all… what was that gust just now, when I sipped from my glass?

Stormwater Streams

They tell me people arriving during dry season are usually confused: where are the streams? Watching the city transform as the rain returns is an unforgettable sight. Instead of battling stormwater surges by flushing them towards the sea, the whole neighborhood embraces the gift and soars! Without the water the succulent architecture soaks up for storage in the aquaria, nobody would make it through the long drought. Connecting two extremes in a circle - a dance around the element all life has in common! Fungi-based redistribution then is just the logical choice... (my attempts to draw a mycelial map amuse the locals... "follow the streams" they say!)

Living water infrastructure,
the whole place an autopoietic, vibrant
rain garden, as it would have once been
called. Plants and people play their parts,
but one cannot but trace it to the elemental, more-than-human agencies behind it all. what was
that gust just now, when I sipped from my glass?

Solarpunk Creatures project entry #13 (wet season 84/2140)

THE COLORFUL CROW
OF WEB-OF-LIFE PARK

Sandra Ulbrich Almazan

Welcome to PanBioPlace, or PBP, where we believe all life should coexist. We are the premiere city of the Green Age, designed to nurture not just humans, but feral and domesticated plants and animals that need new habitats.

Veronica stood on the platform and reread her orientation letter while waiting for Strauss to be unloaded from the train's cargo car. The air was muggy, but the canopy of trees kept the temperature to bearable levels. Drainage ditches ensured PBP wouldn't be flooded like her childhood home. She was lucky to have found a new job as an epidemiologist here, even if she had her doubts about PBP's philosophy. Rewilding the earth was a wonderful idea in theory, as long as they kept the wildlife properly segregated from humans. In a city like this, with so many species living side by side, viruses could jump between them like electrons in a solar panel.

Our buildings are designed with rooftop gardens, solar-cell-studded walls, and nooks where herbs can grow or a peregrine falcon can nest.

She had to admit this was the most welcoming cityscape she'd ever viewed. The buildings were covered in long green vines and striped with dark solar arrays. Trees lined every street, and clover grew lush between the walkways. Even the air smelled welcoming. Then she spotted a flock—no, a murder—of crows flying overhead. Every single bird in this city was susceptible to avian flu, and it was her job to vaccinate them, both to preserve their numbers and to keep them from making humans sick.

In addition, we've tucked green spaces of all sizes into PBP, spaces where humans can recharge and animals can take shelter. Use our free app to log sightings of various species around PBP. It's a boon to casual animal watchers and scientists alike!

"Caw! Caw!"

Veronica glanced up, expecting to see the murder of crows again. Then she heard a few notes of a Beatles song, followed by a mournful "Sayonara, Sayonara." Strauss and his travel cage had arrived.

Strauss had been her grandfather's parrot until he'd passed away last year. He'd specifically willed the bird to her, despite her distaste for pets. Still, she'd done her best to care for Strauss, even if he'd almost bitten her finger off several times.

Veronica confirmed that the autocart had dropped off her own suitcase along with Strauss's cage and supplies. Her apartment complex was only a couple of blocks away, but she was going to need to hire another autocart to bring everything with her. First, however, she had to fix the cover on Strauss's cage. It had ripped during the journey. No wonder the poor bird was going crazy.

"You'll be safe soon, Strauss," she told him as she tried to secure the cover.

A departing train sped off so quickly the cover blew away. Veronica cursed and chased after it.

***

Nut Thief lagged behind the rest of her family as they flew toward the crows' roost for the night, an oak tree by the water and clover in the middle of the big, hard boxes. Their territory was far away from the roost, and they were typically among the last crows to arrive before sunset.

"Caw!"

The sound didn't come from the roost, but lower, from the ground and to her right. Nut Thief didn't recognize the voice. It had to be an intruder. She detoured to check, sounding her own challenge.

"Caw! Caw!" That was the intruder again.

Nut Thief dove past the big boxes to the home of the big, super-fast snake. The snake always crawled along a pair of metal tracks. Every so often, it stopped and let walkers out or took them in. The walkers tended to drop food or shiny things, so Nut Thief liked to hang out where there were a lot of them.

"Caw!"

Movement drew her attention to a collection of metal sticks. Inside was a bird bigger than her, red and yellow and blue, with a thick beak. Nut Thief landed on a tree branch a couple of feet above the strange bird. Maybe it was a crow enemy, one of the larger birds that stole eggs and fledglings. She could call her family to mob it, but they couldn't get to it when it was inside the metal sticks.

"Caw!" The strange bird bobbed its head and danced on its perch.

The strange bird was cawing! If it spoke Crow, it wasn't an enemy. She couldn't leave it there. Nut Thief flew to the metal sticks and poked one. It didn't move. The colorful bird hopped to the other side of the enclosure. "Who's a pretty bird?" he said.

"Hey, you! Get away from there! Shoo!" That was one of the walkers waving its bare arms at her.

Nut Thief summoned her family with a series of short caws. As they gathered, she scrambled over the collection of metal sticks, tugging until she found a loose one. As it slid to the side, a hole appeared. The colorful crow flew out, cawing like mad. He was unsteady and slow in the air at first, but he gained height with every pump of his wings.

"Strauss! Come back!" the walker called.

Nut Thief escorted him to the roost.

***

Strauss's heart beat faster than it ever had in his decades of life. He hadn't seen his caretaker in a long time, only a strange woman. She fed him and sometimes talked to him, but he couldn't trust her. The only time she'd given him a banana, it was to lure him into a small cage, keep him in the dark, and move him out of the only home he'd ever known. Now he was surrounded by black birds and experiencing so many new sensations.

He'd flown farther than he ever had, felt the wind under his wings, and gripped bark under his toes. He'd never been surrounded by so many other birds, their constant cawing in a language he didn't know. He was out in the open, no bars or walls to protect him. He didn't know how he was going to get back to his food and water dishes, especially as the light slowly faded away. It was strange, it was terrifying, it felt instinctually right, all at once.

All Strauss could do was stay close to the crow who'd released him. She looked like all the other birds, but his keen sense of hearing could distinguish her voice from the hundreds of other crows in the roost. She exchanged special caws with a select group of other crows who stayed close to her as well. They tilted their heads as they studied Strauss. One pecked at his tail. He squawked, which set them to cawing at each other.

As he switched to mimicking them, they calmed down. His rescuer extended her neck, and a nearby crow groomed her feathers. Strauss hesitantly preened another crow, then allowed the other bird to return the favor. His caretaker had often scratched his neck, but he couldn't adjust his feathers properly afterward. It felt good to have it done.

The big light overhead disappeared, as if it had broken into countless smaller lights that couldn't chase away the dark. He tried to sleep with the rest of his new flock, but he jerked awake every time some new sound startled him.

When the big light returned, Strauss's new friends started cawing again. They took off in small groups, each going in a different direction. It would have worried him if he wasn't so hungry. A small pond below offered him a chance to quench his thirst. By the time he returned to his perch, his rescuer and her mini-flock were taking off. He struggled to join them, but they were more experienced flyers than he was. He lost them briefly but kept flying in their direction. A few minutes later, he spotted them gathered around something on the ground. They were eating long, cold, greasy things that didn't agree with him. Some fresh vegetables he found growing on a nearby rooftop suited him better.

Strauss felt momentarily anxious as the flock flew away without him, but he spent the rest of the day flying from rooftop to rooftop, eating fruit, vegetables, and insects. It wasn't the same as the pellets his caretaker had fed him, but gathering his own food awakened new instincts he had never felt before. Other humans spotted him several times. Many of them offered him food or extended their arm for him to perch on. Others shouted angry words at him or shooed him away. He ignored them all. None of them were his caretaker, and his own caretaker had failed him. He wouldn't wait for him any longer but look after himself.

Despite the parrot's resolution, he looked up at the sky every few minutes. When, toward the end of the long, hot day he saw more crows flying overhead, he joined them and returned to their roost.

***

"Veronica, I saw your missing parrot!" Meera, the chief fermentation officer, said as she bustled into the lab. "He's hanging around with the crows who set him free."

"He's still alive?" Veronica set her laptop aside. "Where did you see him? Did he look healthy?"

"A bit thin and bedraggled, but otherwise fine. I wonder if he'll survive the next major storm, though."

Veronica sighed. "I ought to recapture him, but he never liked me much. Maybe if I put some treats in his cage and watch it from a distance, he'll check it out."

"It's worth a try." Meera donned her lab coat and lab goggles. "You can track him through hashtag ColorfulCrow."

Now Veronica looked up. "What? People have been following him this whole time, and you didn't tell me until now?"

"I wasn't sure it was about a parrot until I saw him and made the connection."

Veronica opened the PBP app and searched for Strauss with his new nickname. He'd been seen all over the city. Someone had even made a list of the places he'd been sighted most often. As Veronica mapped them to figure out which location was closest to her, an alert sounded from one of the PCR machines in the lab. She groaned when she saw the results. *This couldn't happen at a worse time…*

"What's wrong?" Meera asked.

"The latest wastewater samples are showing a new strain of H5N1." That was one of the most severe strains of avian flu in the early part of the century, and it had never gone away. "Strauss gets to have a few more days of freedom while I analyze it and assemble a vaccine. I just hope he doesn't come down with this first."

***

Developing vaccines was faster than it used to be, but it was still complicated. Veronica started by using computer modeling programs to predict how the mutations she'd detected in the avian flu virus would affect its shape and behavior. Once she thought she knew what to expect, she searched a vaccine database for the best possible matches. She didn't find a perfect match, but there were several vaccines that each offered a different useful feature, including the ability to be given orally. She combined them into a single plasmid and inoculated it into host bacteria that would churn out the vaccine. Meera would cultivate them until they had enough to vaccinate all the birds in the city. Veronica went home from work very late that evening, exhausted but hopeful she was on the right track.

The next morning, she slept through her alarm and had to rush downstairs to grab breakfast from the cafeteria in her apartment complex. A man with a light brown complexion, dark curly hair, and a shirt that said, "Life Is For Living" called her name as she picked up a tray. "Veronica? Dr. Veronica Arroyo? I'm Manuel Tyler, from PBP's Equity Assurance Department." He grinned at her in a way that set her stomach churning. "You're spending too much time working. You need to take a couple of days off to do something fun."

Equity Assurance was a new type of social service offered in the most forward-thinking settlements like PBP. Equity assurers made sure everyone under their jurisdiction received exactly what they needed to thrive, anything from food that met their nutritional needs to education to craft supplies. The last time Veronica had worked with an equity assurer was when her grandfather had passed away. She had helped Veronica with the funeral arrangements, distributed Granddad's extra possessions to those who needed them more, and even let Veronica cry on her shoulder. Remembering that sad time made Veronica shake her head. "I have a very important project in the lab right now—"

"That can do without your input for the next day or two." He grinned at her again. "I have my sources."

Meera. Perhaps this was her way of getting back at Veronica for hovering over her yesterday while she prepared the big tank to receive the bacteria. Still, perhaps taking some time off wasn't a bad idea. She met Manuel's gaze straight on. "Actually, this might not be what you consider fun, but it's something I need help with right now."

"Go on." He gestured her toward the buffet, a reminder to eat.

"I need help catching a parrot."

His smile faltered for an instant. "You mean the Colorful Crow?"

"His actual name is Strauss." Veronica grabbed a tray, and Manuel copied her. "He belonged to my grandfather, and he left him to me last year."

"I'm sorry for your loss." Manuel selected oatmeal and a side of lab ham edged with fat for flavor. "But a parrot is a living being, not a possession." He gentled his voice. "Don't you think he's better off being free?"

"Not when there are so many dangers out there! Storms, predators, the new wave of bird flu—his species didn't evolve in this climate."

"At least winters are warmer than they used to be. He's survived so far. Don't forget a good breakfast should supply you with protein. Fiber, too."

Repressing a smile at his scolding, Veronica helped herself to scrambled tofu, toast, fruit salad, and herbal tea. "Healthy enough for you?"

"Good choices, Veronica, good choices." He led her to a seat near a window. Herbs growing in a flowerbox provided a pleasant scent that went well with her eggs. Manuel took a few bits of his lab ham before saying, "I'm glad you're worried about Strauss's safety, but he has other needs too. Humans can't provide the social needs that other birds can."

"I'm more worried about him socializing too much. If he meets a female parrot and they have offspring, the parrots could become an invasive species."

"With climate change shaking up all the old habitats, practically every living creature has to be resettled." His knife squeaked on the plate as he sawed away at more meat. "We have to celebrate every new birth as a triumph, Veronica."

She didn't respond, and they ate in silence for a while. Manuel finished his oatmeal and his coffee before saying, "Perhaps it's best if you see Strauss in his new environment. I think you'll agree that he's thriving more out in the city at large than he would in a cage, seeing you for only a few minutes every day."

Veronica nodded. "Then let's track him down."

Once they were done eating and had refilled their water bottles and cooling vests, Manuel helped her check out an electric bike from a nearby stable. The bike lanes in PBP were wide enough for them to pedal side by side, though they rode single file so they could both take advantage of the trees' shade.

The city had been designed in modules, with each section featuring multi-person housing, indoor farms, material recycling and printing warehouses, and intimate gathering spots. Manuel gave her a thorough tour of their module, nicknamed Sage. "It's a green city, so all the modules are named after shades of green," he told her.

"It definitely looks green." Veronica pointed at a crow dropping nuts in the street. "What's it doing?"

Manual smiled. "Crows wait for the heavy vehicles to smash the nuts, then hop down to pick out the edible parts."

"Smart birds," she said.

He nodded. "They've taught that trick to all the crows. Even some other species are learning from them. Let me show you the best spot in Sage to watch birds."

They pedaled to a place named Web-of-Life Park. Half-grown apple trees, some drooping in the heat, lined the narrow paths. A pair of dogs raced over the clover, retrieving trash and bringing it to their human. A deer and her fawn hid behind a cluster of shrubs, almost invisible until Manuel pointed them out. The path curved toward a central pond. On one side, a willow dipped its branches in the water; on the other, a tall oak stood over everything else in the park. In the center of the pond was a metal sculpture of a spiderweb linking various plants and animals.

Veronica squinted as she studied the sculpture. "You know what ought to be in the center, Manuel? Microbes. Every multi-celled creature depends on them to break things down and enrich the soil. We all rely on them to help digest our food and ward off pathogens. Only how would we represent them?"

"I bet you would think of something," he replied.

She rode to the edge of the pond, then held herself still. A flock of mallards floated past her, all appearing healthy. She still eyed them suspiciously. They could be carriers of avian flu or some other disease that would devastate this city, just like the wild birds that had inadvertently killed off her family's entire flock of poultry.

"Look up! There he is!"

Veronica followed Manuel's finger. At the top of the oak perched a red-and-blue blob. She made a mental note to have her vision checked. Putting her hands to her mouth, she called, "Strauss?"

The parrot let out a defiant caw before flying off.

"I'm sure he wouldn't disrespect my grandfather like this," Veronica muttered.

"That's not the point," Manuel said. "The question is what are you going to do now? Try to catch him, or leave him alone?"

Veronica didn't answer right away. Instead, she looked at reports of all of the other previous Strauss sightings. Everyone seemed so excited to see him, and no one thought he appeared unhealthy. She knew better than anyone what was coming, though, and she was afraid if she waited too long to retrieve the parrot, he'd get sick and die.

When Granddad had adopted Strauss, he'd known the bird would outlive him. There was a good chance Strauss could outlive Veronica. She'd be letting both the bird and her grandfather down if he didn't.

"I have to think about it some more." Veronica hopped back on her bike. "So, how many other shades of green are there in PBP? Is there someplace where we can get out of the sun?"

***

The bacteria would never know sun, or anything outside the tank. They didn't care. Inside was everything they needed: food, water, oxygen, all at the perfect pH, humidity, and temperature. They absorbed food, grew, and divided. Along the way, they faithfully transcribed their genes into proteins. It didn't matter if those proteins were for the benefit of other creatures. The instructions were there, and they had to be followed.

Eat, grow, divide.

Eat, grow, divide.

Eat, grow, divide.

Until their entire world was full.

***

"Is the new batch ready to harvest yet?" Veronica snapped as Meera entered the office. The virus levels in the wastewater had nearly doubled since last week, and yesterday, a couple of gardeners reported finding a sick falcon on a rooftop. If she didn't protect the wild bird population soon, their numbers would soon crash—and Strauss might be among the casualties.

Meera smiled and gave her a tiny nod. That was all Veronica needed. "I want to watch you collect it," she said.

They donned gloves and surgical masks before passing into the lab area. The first room was devoted to chemical storage and basic equipment like pH meters and DNA sequencers. The micro room housed a freezer with different strains of bacteria and sterile benches where Veronica could modify them with her designer plasmids. Another door at the end of the lab brought them into the fermentation and processing area.

In contrast to the silent lab, ever-present humming from the tanks filled the fermentation room. Two stainless steel tanks, each big enough to hold hundreds of gallons of media, sat on either side of the room. Besides each one was a smaller starter tank, where samples of bacteria were grown until they had enough to inoculate the big tank, and an array of monitoring equipment. Meera headed straight for the tank on the right to pull a sample. Veronica sniffed the air. A healthy batch smelled like sourdough, but a contaminated one could have all sorts of off odors. Assuming the bacteria had finished growing, the media would be centrifuged to remove the bacteria, then passed through microfilters to collect and purify the vaccine. Once it was spray-dried, it was stable at room temperature until it was mixed with water. To dose wild animals with vaccine, volunteers added it to known drinking stations or food. It was a lot of work, but it was worth it to preserve biodiversity and prevent zoonoses from jumping to humans.

While Meera ran her tests, Veronica ran calculations of her own, trying to estimate how many birds they needed to treat. Wild birds used to be more common, both in the number of species and in population. Many species had sadly gone extinct, reduced to cell samples and genomes stored online. Most other species were in decline for various reasons. Only a few were thriving in this warmer, uncertain world. Strauss was lucky enough to be with some of the winners. Crows were opportunists, able to eat all kinds of food, and clever enough to devise new ways to get it. But they weren't the only kind of birds in PBP. Hawks, doves, sparrows, ducks, songbirds, and more made their homes alongside humans. Most meat in PBP was grown in a lab, so there were no chicken farms within miles of this city. But when humans lived and worked with so many other creatures, close enough to pass viruses back and forth like a game of hot potato, they would all stay healthy or get sick together.

"Everything looks good, Veronica," Meera said. "I'm draining the tank."

Veronica nodded and took up a position in front of the monitors. Following a custom she'd picked up from a Japanese mentor, she bowed toward the fermentation tank and said, "Thank you for your hard work and sacrifice, microbes."

Water splashed against the walls of the tank as the microbes surrendered their life-saving proteins.

***

Strauss perched on the top of the roost tree and practiced his bird calls. First were the crows, since he spent so much time with them. Several crows swooped down to investigate, but when they recognized him, they flew off to their normal daytime activities. Strauss was just warming up. He ran through his entire repertoire: great horned owls, peregrine falcons, pigeons, mallards, Canadian geese, loons, robins, cardinals, blue jays, several types of sparrows, woodpeckers, mourning doves, and others that he'd heard but not seen.

His concert attracted an avian crowd. Some birds responded with their own calls, which Strauss added to his recital. He performed several duets with a blue jay, a goose, and a woodpecker. Other birds flew in to investigate. Among them was a mallard that couldn't stop sneezing.

***

Veronica frowned as she read her messages. Leaving her mug of tea on the table, she ran to the lab to find Meera, calmly inoculating more microbes in liquid media.

"It's starting." She held out her phone. "Sick and dead birds have been found in Web-of-Life Park. How much longer until that last batch you harvested is ready?"

"Check with Willow. She's in charge of finished stock."

Veronica nodded. Leaving Meera alone to finish her work, she contacted Willow.

"I have three batches of avian flu vaccine available, including the latest one you prepared." Willow was working from home today. She sat in a sunlit nook, a toddler playing with stuffed animals behind her.

"How do you administer it here?" Veronica asked.

"We usually have volunteers mix it with food and scatter it in locations with lots of bird sightings. Then we hope the birds eat it before other creatures find it."

"I'd like to help." Veronica paced. "I have a personal interest in stopping this outbreak before it starts. I'm hoping to make this a test run of the vaccine. If it's effective, we'll use it city-wide."

"OK." Willow glanced at her laptop. "I'm ordering a hundred pounds of birdseed to be delivered to the lab by lunch. I'll also arrange transport for you and the birdseed to Web-of-Life Park."

After confirming a few more details, they ended the call. Veronica tried to occupy herself by running more wastewater tests, but the results only confirmed her initial fears. She ate a hurried lunch before the bird seed and vaccine arrived. She wanted to rush out right away with it, but Meera pulled up the weather forecast. "It's too hot right now for the birds to be active. Wait until it gets closer to evening."

Forced to wait, Veronica remembered how her grandfather always told her to have patience making friends with Strauss. She called up the notes she had about his care. Since Strauss was especially fond of bananas, she ran over to the corner store and bought some to slice and sprinkle with vaccine. She also bought herself a couple bags of peanuts and trail mix to snack on while she waited. What else would attract the bird? Reading to the end of the notes, she learned Strauss had earned his name because he danced along to "The Blue Danube."

"If the bananas don't lure you, maybe this song will," Veronica muttered as she selected a version to have on standby.

"Good luck," Meera called after her as Veronica ran out of the lab. She raised a hand in acknowledgement.

***

Strauss returned early to the roosting tree. It had been a hungry day of flying over the city without finding much food, and only luck had saved him from becoming a falcon's lunch. He landed at the pond to fill his stomach with as much water as he could.

"Strauss! There you are! You don't know how worried I've been about you!"

He knew that voice. It was the woman who'd taken him away from his home. Cawing like Nut Thief when she spotted an owl, he flew to a branch out of her reach.

She skirted the edge of the pond to walk up to his tree and look up at him. In her outstretched hand were several pieces of banana; in her other was his travel cage. The fruit looked good, but he didn't trust her. He bobbed his head up and down in indecision.

"Strauss, I know you don't like me, but I don't know why. What have I ever done to you?" The woman sighed. "Do you miss Grandad? So do I. He asked me to look after you, and I feel like I've done a bad job of it so far. You're very lucky that you've survived this long on your own, but soon the stormy season will start, and bird flu is already spreading in this town." She glanced down at his travel cage. "Won't you let me bring you home?"

"No!" he cried in his old master's voice. "Bad Strauss!"

Her shoulders slumped. She let the fruit fall on the ground, backed away several steps, then took a device out of her pocket. A familiar tune filled the air, and Strauss couldn't help but dance to it, shuffling up and down his branch. His master had always been happy when he did that. Those had been good times, safe times.

Strauss glided to the ground and helped himself to fruit.

***

Nut Thief led the rest of her family to the roost. Her parents had both died in the last couple of days. She and her siblings had inspected their bodies and stood over them for most of the day. Tomorrow they would have to redouble their search for food, but for some reason she didn't have an appetite at the moment.

Her keen gaze swept over the park. Her colorful companion was in the grass, apparently feeding on something. Nut Thief felt a momentary interest in investigating what he'd found. Instead of landing in the oak, she circled over the pond. As she passed over the willow, she spotted an odd shape huddled by the trunk. An owl! How dare it lurk near the crows' base?

Before the owl could swoop down on the parrot, Nut Thief sounded the alarm.

***

Strauss finished the last piece of fruit as Nut Thief announced her arrival. She sounded upset about something. As more crows copied her cries, Strauss bolted for the safety of his branch. The crows didn't join him. Instead, they flocked to the willow tree. More crows joined them, filling the park with their caws. Strauss copied them. After several minutes, a big bird launched itself from the willow and flew to the edge of the park. The crows settled down and swarmed the roost tree.

Full and safe, Strauss started his concert of bird calls.

***

"Clever crows," Veronica whispered. She had no idea an owl had been nearby until the murder of crows flushed it from the willow. She hurriedly dipped her peanuts in vaccine and tossed them to the birds. The crows blanketed the ground as they fought for food. Songbirds and waterfowl joined them as Strauss summoned them with his imitation calls. As soon as Veronica had set out the last of the food, she took video of the scene. When she returned to the lab, she'd analyze the footage to estimate how many birds and what species had dosed themselves with vaccine. A few of the birds carried bands on their legs; she zoomed in to get as much detail as she could. If she could track individual birds, it would help her figure out how effective her vaccine was.

By the time the birds had devoured the last seed, the setting sun was casting a golden light over the park. Veronica retrieved Strauss's traveling cage. Although she'd left the door open, not a single bird had ventured inside during the feeding frenzy. She raised her head, searching for Strauss. She thought she glimpsed him near the top of the oak. Although he stood out from the crows, they seemed to accept him as one of them. One of the crows even groomed him as she watched.

"I'm sure Granddad didn't have this in mind when he asked me to take care of you, Strauss," she said. "But maybe Manuel has a point. Maybe you're better off with a flock of your own instead of being stuck with me. You stay healthy, OK? I'll come back soon with more fruit for you."

Veronica crossed her fingers as she left the park. She had a good feeling about the vaccine, but she had to wait a couple of weeks to see if it was as effective as she hoped.

***

"This picnic was a good idea," Willow said as she set down a picnic basket and a diaper bag. "It's finally starting to cool down, we can check on the birds—Hope, get away from the water!" She sprinted after her daughter.

Meera grinned. "That's why I'm not ready to have a child yet," she whispered to Veronica. "How about you?"

She let out a laugh. "If I can't control a bird, what chance do I have with a toddler?" She watched Willow take Hope's hand and point out a swan floating on the other side of the pond. A nuthatch scampered down the oak as if searching for a handout. A cardinal and a sparrow each laid claim to the park with their calls.

Once her pilot test of the vaccine had proved to be effective in preventing bird deaths from avian flu, volunteers had distributed the treated food in every park in PBP. Virus levels in the city wastewater had dropped—for now. Veronica knew another virus could arise from anywhere, but she was taking Manuel's advice and enjoying some time off while she could. Still, as she cleaned her plate of curry, flatbread, hummus, locally-grown vegetables, and apple oatmeal bars, she kept looking for Strauss. Maybe he was foraging elsewhere for food, or maybe one of the local bird experts had taken him in.

Veronica studied the sculpture in the middle of the pond. "Hey, did someone change it?" She pointed at a circle in the center. "That wasn't there the last time I was here."

Meera consulted her phone. "It's supposed to be a Petri dish to represent microbes."

Willow raised her bottle of lemonade. "To microbes, the center of the web of life."

"To cooperation between species, like parrots and crows," Veronica said.

As they clinked their bottles together, she heard caws of agreement. Strauss and his crow companion hopped close enough to accept bits of apple from Hope before flying away.

* * *

Sandra Ulbrich Almazan is the author of the science fiction *Catalyst Chronicles* series, the fantasy *Season Avatars* series, the *Abigail Ritter* cozy mystery series, and several science fiction/fantasy short stories published in various anthologies. She's also a QA Representative, a wife, a mother, and occasionally a Jawa.

THE BUSINESS OF BEES

Andrew Knighton

The bees were up to something.

Luna swished her tail as she watched them through the apartment window, her whiskers quivering in excitement. A swarm had coalesced around two of the tiny, shiny, fluttering drones that the humans used to maintain the city. Luna didn't understand why the bees did it, but she was jealous. The drones always got away from her.

She'd tried to tell her family about this, using the word buttons they'd installed, but they didn't have a button for bees, and didn't understand "wool bird bad." She meowed her frustration. How could humans be so bafflingly complicated and so frustratingly simple?

If she couldn't help the humans, then she would help herself. She would learn the bees' trick.

She jumped from the windowsill and bounded up the stairs. Through a hatch in a glass door, she prowled into the rooftop garden. Under the shade of an apple tree, she paused to enjoy the scents of flowers and to watch the bees buzzing through the branches. Definitely up to something.

The bees were leaving her rooftop, taking the drones with them. Luna followed, running across the solar panels that extended from the roof. The panels bounced beneath her, giving an extra lift as she sprang through the air. Hundreds of cats' lengths below, boats drifted along canals. So soft she barely made a sound, Luna landed on the panels of the next block.

This garden belonged to Cleo, who hissed at Luna from behind a bed of rhubarb. Cleo was all hiss and no scratch, worse than a dog. Luna prowled past, dismissing Cleo's indignation with a swish of her tail, then picked up speed for the next leap.

She followed the bees from block to block across the city. Normally, she never went this far, and never would have braved it if she hadn't been able to look back and see her home, its blue and yellow turbines standing out amid the white of the neighbours. Thank paws and tails for eccentric humans.

A dark tower stood at the centre of the shining city. It was too still, no turbines on its roof, no humans in its windows, and the breeze sweeping past smelled of mould. A relic of the city as it used to be, and around it the bees.

The last leap was the farthest. Luna would have to jump down as well as across, to land on a ledge by the broken window the bees had flown in. Coming back, she would have to land further down, then use balconies and hanging baskets to reach the roof. All of this meant letting home out of sight. She looked back at the blue and yellow turbines, hesitated, mewled. What if she couldn't find the turbine again? What if she never made it home to the laps of her humans?

As she watched the turbine spin, a sound caught her ear. Buzzing, deeper and more powerful than she had ever heard. Curiosity was a twitching string that drew her on.

She lowered her haunches, tensed her shoulders, and leapt. Her body uncoiled, forelegs stretching, and for a long moment there was only air around her and the drop below. She hit the ledge, slid across its slimy surface, dug claws into the window frame as her hind legs slid out over empty air. For a fearful moment she dangled, desperately scrabbling for a grip. Then she caught on the concrete, pushed herself up, and fell through the window.

Luna lay panting on a dusty step. Her heart was racing but there was no movement nearby, no obvious danger. She calmed herself by licking the clinging slime from her fur. When she felt steady again, she properly looked around.

She was on a broad staircase in a room that filled half the tower. On the opposite wall was an enormous hive. It must have taken dozens of swarms to build, something Luna had never known to happen, and those swarms buzzed around it. Swarms not just of bees but of bee-sized drones, creatures and machines flying as one. The drones had cracks in their cases, extra legs, oddly shaped wings.

A dozen stairs down were the bees that Luna had followed. They held their captives down while other drones cracked open the cases and, with tiny tools, rearranged their insides.

Luna watched as drones were modified and released into the swarm, while bees buzzed in and out, carrying pieces of human technology into their hive. She wanted to catch and break a drone too, for fun, but she didn't want to fight this city-sized swarm. Instead, she watched and waited while shadows lengthened. If the bees noticed her presence, they didn't care.

As dusk fell, another flight of bees returned, escorting drones with small scoops hanging underneath. Most deposited spoonfuls of soil onto one of the steps, but one flew in with a tiny green shoot between its grasping tools. It lowered the seedling into the dirt, and others patted the earth down.

The light of the sinking sun illuminated the chamber above Luna. Bright blooms bobbed their heads around the edges of steps and green shoots stirred in a breeze flowing through the tower. There were as many colours here as the humans used in their homes, as many plants as on a hundred rooftops, most delicate and slender, but some already growing strong. Their soft, intricate scents filled Luna's senses and she purred her pleasure. She'd never seen anything like it—a garden planted by bees.

For reasons she couldn't explain to herself, Luna didn't feel an urge to catch the drones anymore, though she was sure that she could. What she wanted was to return to her own garden, to leave this family of thousands and find the three she knew.

She crept out onto the ledge, tensed, then leaped to a balcony opposite. From there, she scrambled up hanging baskets and balconies, startling humans at their dinner and birds at their evening song, until she reached the roof. In the distance, a blue and yellow turbine twisted in the twilight.

The scent of flowers hung around Luna. She smiled. She would try to tell her humans what she had seen, but she doubted they would understand, and maybe that was for the best.

* * *

Andrew Knighton has been writing for longer than he likes to admit, creating short stories, comics, and the fantasy novellas *Ashes of the Ancestors* and *Silver and Gold*. He lives in Yorkshire with an academic, a cat, and many unread books. Find him at andrewknighton.com, on Bluesky as @aknighton, and on Mastodon as @gibbondemon @wandering.shop.

Orange Crested Grebe

Pamina Stewart

Pamina Stewart combines traditional sculptural techniques with crafting, sewing, painting and printing. She utilises a range of materials, including discarded items like obsolete technology and food packaging, as well as renewable resources. By using these materials, she aims to promote a sustainable practice that is always respectful of our planet.

ПIGHT FOWLS

Ana Sun

I peeled off my gloves, one finger at a time, making sure nothing on the outer surface touched my skin. The plants in my garden were less lethal than their original cousins in the wild, but still, one couldn't be too careful.

The summer sun had deserted the day, throwing pinks and oranges at the clouds rolling overland, turning the normally blue-grey sea into a multi-coloured jewel. Starlings chattered as they settled on Brighton West Pier—once a metallic, skeletal ruin, now a thriving greenhouse and mussel farm. The dark curves of its Victorian frames rose out of the water against the lazy spin of the Rampion wind turbines further out to sea.

I'd been allocated a house facing the beach, a rare lot with a garden that I worked hard to keep in shape. My neighbour's garden, however, was bit of a mystery. Mrs. Leigh had been using a wheelchair as long as we'd lived next door to each other, and I'd never seen her move about in her own garden—yet it was pristine. Almost too perfect. How did she do that? She kept so busy distributing food for humans—her official portfolio assigned by the Cross-Species Citizens' Committee. I should learn her secrets, but I never seemed to catch her at home.

The gloves left white powdered streaks on the warm-beige of my hands. I stretched my legs and aching back, careful not to kick over the basket of cuttings: deadly nightshade, monkshood, foxglove, oleander and a few more. Specimens for toxicity tests, halfway between a careful breeding program and genetic selection to retain their medicinal value—without their poison. The plan: to prepare them tonight with Morrigan, my carrion crow-friend and fellow medic, for our experiments tomorrow. She'd be pleased with today's harvest.

"Evening, Willow!" A jolly tenor voice called from across the street.

Mr. Mutitu was being walked by Chocolate, a Labrador whose fine fur almost matched the ebony of his human's skin.

Chocolate gave a short, sharp bark; the implant in my brain kicked off a translation. "Got treats, Willow?"

"Sorry Chocolate, none today!" I chuckled, filing a mental note to get some tomorrow. "How are your squirrels, Mr. Mutitu?"

Mr. Mutitu's current responsibility included negotiations with small mammals. "Fine, fine, they've all found their autumn stash now. And you, your birds?"

Holy henbane, I'd not thought about the birds all day. Though I loved what we do through the Committee, being randomly assigned portfolios didn't always guarantee the best match, even if everyone learned to do a little bit of everything. This time I'd landed on a bit of a tiresome role: arbitrating a long-running dispute between the jackdaws and the seagulls—the Daws and the Mockers. They'd settled on a truce recently, thanks to Violetta, the previous mediator who now graduated to overseeing the health of human beings. I'd like that role someday.

Anything, but these birds.

"No drama today!" I answered Mr. Mutitu. Not yet, anyway. I forced a smile. Just a few months more of this, and maybe I could move on.

Mr. Mutitu waved as Chocolate tugged him towards the corner pub.

A flicker of movement in Mrs. Leigh's garden caught my eye. A silver-black bird with a short bill hopped out; a jackdaw. How unusual. Everyone knew to steer clear of my human-designated garden—but I suppose Mrs. Leigh's was fair game.

"Hello!" I hoped I sounded cheerful.

"Evenin'," it replied before flying away, something wriggling in its beak. Likely a grub, that'd explain the curt greeting.

A thin crescent moon had already risen, impatient for the sun to set. A fog emerged over the sea. The evening breeze teased the bioluminescent trees lining the street with playful tenderness; they had begun to glow, complementing the algae heritage lanterns punctuating the pavements, marrying the old alongside the new.

I gathered my basket, checking I hadn't left any stray cuttings behind. Last thing I'd want: to cause someone unintentional harm.

"Willow!" A frightened voice, a frantic wingbeat. "Wait!"

Morrigan, her sleek black feathers glistening green from the trees and gold from the setting sun. She landed in a clumsy, uncharacteristic half-skid on the steps to my front door, panting hard. Our paired implants connected, initiating the private, close-proximity comms channel. *Willow, something's wrong!*

"What—?"

Someone's been poisoned! Her eyes flitted at me, at my basket, at the horizon. I'd rarely seen her so anxious. *Silk and Kittiwake are quarrelling at the Old Steine—*

This might escalate, badly. I leaned past Morrigan, opened the door, dropped the basket inside, grabbed the emergency med kit from the hallway. A canister of calming pheromones we'd been working on glinted on a table. No, better not, we hadn't yet tested its effectiveness at scale. I pulled the door shut.

"Quickly!" Morrigan flapped her wings, once, twice, pointing the way with her beak.

Swallowing a sigh, I followed her into the fog-laden night.

***

Brighton often turned suddenly cold after sundown, even at the height of summer. I shivered; in our hurry, I'd forgotten my cloak. Running after Morrigan did little to warm me up; the fastest way to the Old Steine Gardens meant taking the wind-exposed road along the seafront. The sycamores on Kingsway glittered as night swooped in, but Morrigan's black silhouette blended into the shadows of buildings we sped past. I squinted, trying not to lose her.

"Why the hurry?" A roadside rosemary bush said.

I halted mid-run, nearly tripping over my own feet. I knew that voice.

"Violetta?" Panting hard from sprinting, I could barely speak. "Why are you here?"

"Could ask the same of you." Violetta materialised from behind the plant, dark hair flowing over a purple dress, her tall, overly-thin frame sharp enough to slice the air. Something about her always took my breath away.

"I—" My eyes searched for Morrigan in the bio-lit dark, but she'd already spun towards us.

"We can't stop! He might die!"

Violetta swung her attention to Morrigan. "*Who* might die?"

"A Daw!" Morrigan's wings struggled with hovering flight; she flitted awkwardly, an oversized, jet-feathered butterfly. "Quick! They might fight—"

I squirmed.

"Fight?" Violetta glared at me. "After all I've done, you let them regress to *this*?"

"I—" Words stayed stuck at the back of my throat. Half of me wanted to run back and hide in my garden, the other half wished I could be more like Violetta, who always knew what she was doing—

"I'm coming with you."

What? No!

"If you ruin this," Violetta's voice turned frosty, her eyes blazed, "I'll report you to the Committee for negligence."

My heart skipped a beat. Several. I'd be taken off the roster. I might get reallocated a different house, forced to start a new garden from scratch. Or worse, they might take away my implant with the bird-speech decoder. I swallowed. To not be able to talk to Morrigan any longer—

"Hurry!" she beckoned.

No time to think about that now.

Zigzagging through the narrow lanes, we arrived at the Gardens, an ancient common that survived many transformations. The Royal Pavilion School glimmered to the northwest, its domes lit by glowing elms, liquid trees dotting its lawn.

Squawks rang out.

"There!" Morrigan zipped towards Victoria Fountain. I'd always thought it resembled a giant birdbath—

"This had better not be a bloodbath," Violetta hissed, somewhere near my ear.

I gulped down a gasp.

Two birds perched on the lowest and widest rim of the cast-iron fountain. Kittiwake, the leader of the Mockers, spread his grey-white wings wide, screeching his wrath.

"Stop. Calling. Us. Names!"

"That's no reason to poison one of us, Kit," said Silk, the much smaller leader of the Daws, whose smooth, black feathers reflected the moonlight despite the mist. "But we know only a dirty, oily, *Mocker* would."

He tittered.

Kittiwake reached out to smack him with a wing, but Silk hopped deftly backwards.

"*You!* We'll—"

"Enough!" I shouted, hoping my voice carried enough authority. I'd never been particularly good at this, never throughout the mediation training we'd all had to have.

"You'd never—" Silk chittered, winging up higher on the fountain, ready to attack.

"*Enough!*" I yelled.

This time, they both heard me.

"Where's the sick Daw?" Less a question, more a demand. How could they be arguing when one of their own might be dying? I sucked my breath in, struggling to quell my rage.

Neither of them answered.

"Where's the sick Daw?" I repeated.

Violetta sighed and started to check under the nearby bushes. *Why didn't I think to do that?*

Morrigan's signal flickered through my implant. *Here!*

I rushed to the other side of the fountain. The black bird laid unmoving on the grass, barely visible in the dark.

Ignoring the damp air on my arms, I unrolled my kit. Morrigan leaned down by the fallen daw, using her implant to read vital signals too faint for mine to pick up.

"Heart rate very high, blood pressure low—"

Not good.

We needed to run toxicity tests, and fast. I handed Morrigan a small device—this should pick up the most common toxins.

After half a minute, she shook her head. "None of these."

Panic seized me. What if we didn't have an antidote? A jackdaw would die on my watch. If ever there was a case for negligence…

I breathed away the dread. Must focus. I fished out a tiny needle for Morrigan to take a blood sample. Working swiftly, I set up several swabs and fed them through the portable tester I'd programmed to identify all the toxins I knew.

Violetta had bundled herself onto a bench, her hair rippling in the wind like dark water, watching us. Back when we first met several portfolio reassignments ago, her knowledge of the birds astounded me, but somehow, I never drummed up the courage to ask her if she'd be willing to be my mentor. If I weren't such a coward, I might have asked her so many things. Like, if this was what she'd had to go through.

Or like, to be a friend. Maybe.

Mentally, I folded away the sight of her, same way I wrapped up my apprehension. Treating sick creatures—I was good at. She could judge me all she wanted.

The results took forever. I extracted a stethoscope and checked the daw's heartbeat—an unnecessary move. Sometimes, a bit of theatre projected the illusion of control.

Morrigan hopped on my shoulder, eyes on the tester. An alert flashed on mine.

Strange. Mostly some complex molecules not in our database, with traces of aconitine. No telling if that was the main ingredient causing harm, but it was the only lead we had.

I retrieved the correct antidote and let Morrigan administer it with the practised, precise control of her beak. With any luck, the jackdaw should feel less ill shortly, but real recovery might take weeks.

I stood up, puzzled. Aconitine, the toxin present in monkshood. You'd have to be traipsing deep in the South Downs to find any. Not a plant typically found in any gardens—whether designated for humans or birds—not anymore. The rest of the unidentifiable components? I wouldn't even know where to begin. The aconitine might be our only traceable clue.

Morrigan fussed over the recovering jackdaw. Swaying a little, the daw managed to right himself and took a few steps. Was he the same bird I saw last night? Impossible to discern in the deepening darkness.

I headed over to Kittiwake and Silk, who at least had the decency to stop squabbling.

"So, who did it?" Silk asked first.

Must not sound irritated. "We treated the patient, not traced the source."

Kittiwake chortled. Seagulls always laughed, even when something wasn't funny. He puffed out his chest. "We resent being accused—"

"Who else would have a motive?" Silk interrupted.

"Please, let's not get carried away," I tried again. "There's no proof right now."

Both of them stared at me, as if they'd forgotten I existed.

I took advantage of their attention. "We must work together to find out why—and how—this happened."

A moment of uncomfortable quiet.

"Whatever," said Silk, with an indifferent shuffle of his wings.

"Yeah." Kittiwake jerked up his head, emitting a screech. "Well, we'll *not* see you around." A dirty glare at Silk, at me, then he took off.

On days like these, I wondered: what right did humans have to meddle in the affairs of the fauna? The Cross-Species Citizens' Committee had been initiated by humans, with the belief that collaborating with our non-human friends seemed to be the wisest way to mitigate the effects of the precarious climate. But…do we just make things worse?

The garden bench sat empty. Violetta had left, I hadn't even noticed.

Morrigan walked over to us. "He'll be fine after some rest."

Silk bobbed his head. "We'll take over from here."

After he left, Morrigan nodded to me. Her movements seemed slower; the evening had taken a lot out of her. I let her hop onto my hand.

"You look terrible," I remarked.

She cocked her head, casting one amused eye at me. *You look wonderful yourself.*

I laughed.

We should try using seeds next time, it's good distraction tactic for the likes of us.

Seeds! Why hadn't I thought of that?

I suppressed a groan. "What would I do without you, Morrigan?"

You'd be lost, she cackled. *Let's get some rest. See you tomorrow.*

A gentle nibble of my finger for a friendly goodnight, she bounced off the ground and took off to her roost.

I sighed. Yes, I'd be so lost without her.

***

My feet somehow found their way home. My brain whirred, mapping out patches of monkshood in the vicinity. I'd catalogued locations of wild poisonous flowers so I could correlate environmental factors with their toxicity. No bird would deliberately eat off such a plant. Perhaps they found a poisoned grub? Came in close contact by accident?

My hand froze on the smooth wood of my gate. Something just moved in Mrs. Leigh's garden. A Mocker, the tips of its feathers fluttering in the breeze.

"Hello," I said.

It didn't reply.

Something—someone stood on the far fence. I blinked. A Daw.

Perhaps I'd interrupted a confrontation.

Before I could say more, they took off in opposite directions, wind whistling under their wings.

A soft, mechanical purr floated in from the street. Mrs. Leigh gave me a wave from her wheelchair as she approached her gate, grey hair pulled back into a tight bun, a faded scarf around her shoulders.

"How are you, Willow?" Her kindly voice croaked a little. She'd only just made it home? It must take so much of her energy to make sure all the humans in the city got their preferred food deliveries.

"Um, fine, how was your day?" I wanted to ask about her garden, but she looked so tired, I didn't have the heart to raise that now. Instead, I said, "We should have tea soon, when you're less busy?"

"Always busy," she replied, smiling. "But never feels that way when you love what you do."

Her words gave me pause. Would I ever love what I do that much? I struggled to imagine what that could be like. Just dealing with these birds drained me.

"Let's find a time! It's been too long since you last came for tea." And with that Mrs. Leigh bade me good evening, her wheelchair whirring through her front door.

Finally, alone in my garden. The nearest tree didn't shed quite enough light. At a cursory glance, nothing had been trampled.

No bird tracks.

No clue.

***

Sleep—a fickle mistress.

I freshened up, made some dandelion brew and hunted through my archives for a monkshood map. One of these days, I should post my maps to our citizen plant catalogue so other enthusiasts could add to it, building up specialist knowledge of the local flora.

A tap-tap-tapping on the window. Morrigan balanced on the sill, her body tense enough to break the glass.

Why didn't she connect through our private comms?

I opened the window, checked my implant. It had defaulted to do-not-disturb mode while I slept, switching to focus-mode because I'd been preoccupied. Oh.

"They're at it again!" Morrigan burst in without greeting—a bad sign. "The Mockers have cornered a Daw!"

Definitely bad. Ignoring the silver lure of the canister on the hallway table, I grabbed the kit, spare swabs, slid a pack of seeds into the pouch around my waist. Miraculously, I remembered my cloak.

Three steps outside, it began to rain—the kind of polite rain that made no sound but still drenched you thoroughly. My shoes slipped a little on the pavement as we hurried down Kingsway a second time in two days.

What caused them to fight again? What had undone Violetta's work? I thought I'd be stepping into a problem long resolved. Peace is such a fragile thing.

We heard them before we got near the old mall. Churchill Square lacked personality, but it housed a farmers' market, several makers' co-ops and the city's health centre.

Seagull screeches skewered the morning air. I listened for a tortured caw of a jackdaw. Sweat broke out on my brow, mingling with the rain matting my hair.

Let it not be too late.

Morrigan led me to the fire escape that accessed the roof. The metal railing felt cold under my palms, the steps slicked wet. Solar panels glinted under the drizzle between a myriad of plants reaching for the sky. I never realised a food forest grew here.

Several Daws battled with some Mockers, swooping from the fruit trees, chasing through the shrubs. Two birds collided in an explosion of feathers and leaves.

"Stop!" I yelled, my voice muffled by rain and damp.

No one did. Instead, birds continued to dive for each other, squawking, cawing. I really wasn't any good at this. How did Violetta do it?

"Let me try!" Morrigan crowed.

Before I could stop her, she flew straight among them.

"Morrigan, wait!"

Suddenly, her scream sliced through the commotion. My hands flew to my head, her pain piercing through our comms, zapping my nerves. My heart dropped through my feet. Not thinking straight, I forced myself into the middle, sheltering my face from sharp beaks and battering wings.

Something sliced into my forearm, the scratch long and deep.

Anger rose, a sudden wildfire. I clenched my fists and—

The seeds, Willow!

The seeds! Bending low, I ducked through the other side, pulled the packet from my pouch, ripped it open and flung my arm in a wide circle, scattering its contents.

The distraction tactic worked like magic. After a few moments of scrambling, the remaining uninjured birds stopped fighting each other and began chasing after the new source of food. Success! That had been the last packet though, I made a mental note to acquire more.

As things settled, I called out. "Alright, can we talk now?"

A few birds continued to peck at the seeds, but no one dissented. I didn't know that even slightly soggy seeds could be so appetising. Unsurprisingly, I failed to gain their attention, guess I had to wait until they were done eating.

Going to tend to the injured, Morrigan's voice, though weak, held resolve.

Together, we assessed the damage. A multitude of lost feathers, some scratches, a few bites. Sighing, I opened my kit.

Once most of the seeds were gone, I tried again.

"So, what happened?" I asked, dabbing some antiseptic on a Daw's foot.

A Mocker spoke up first. "They tried to poison us!"

A bunch of beaks pointed to something tucked under a lettuce. A dead caterpillar. I prepped the swabs.

"He was mean!" added another Mocker, pointing at a Daw perching on a mulberry bush.

I didn't roll my eyes.

The Daw sniggered. "That's because you *are* greasy chip-stealers—"

"Can we please talk this thr—" but I never got to finish my plea.

The first Mocker squealed, spread his wings, but held back. Morrigan threw me a sideways glance; these birds behaved like children.

I turned to the Daw. "You brought this?"

"'Twas a gift!" the Daw protested.

That surprised me.

"But *we* think it's poisoned," said the first Mocker.

"Smelt wrong!" another chimed in.

The first one spoke again. "Then he insulted me, and the others—"

Several Mockers looked suddenly sheepish.

"Just trying to be friendly!" the Daw cried, adamant. Around him, other Daws murmured their support.

An alert pinged. The swabs.

My eyes met Morrigan's. Similar to yesterday's swab, the results indicated numerous unidentifiable compounds, but with faint traces of digoxin. Digoxin, found in foxgloves.

How? She seemed equally confused.

Foxgloves were banned as domestic ornamentals, but medics and health establishments could grow them under controlled conditions. There was exactly one plant in the city: my garden, which was human-designated because it contained plants that might harm our avian and animal friends. How, indeed?

"Where did you get this caterpillar?" I asked the Daw.

"Found it," he mumbled.

Something rustled. I looked back towards the fire escape.

Violetta leaned lightly against an apple tree.

Had she been here long? How could she remain so composed in the rain? I swallowed. I must look a mess.

"I heard the commotion." No warmth in her voice. "Correction, the whole city heard it."

The fire in her eyes scorched through me. My insides somersaulted.

The Mocker cleared his throat. "We'll be complaining to the Committee that you keep siding with the Daws."

I spun to face him, my jaw dropping open. "But I don't!"

Out of the corner of my eye, Violetta smothered a smirk.

Breathe, remember to breathe.

Blood still ran down my arm, hair dangled across my face.

I summoned every inch of composure I could muster. "We must find a way to co-exist, re-build trust from the ground up."

A Mocker laughed. Of course he would.

I ignored him.

"I propose a forum between both parties," I addressed the birds, then locked my gaze on Violetta. Maybe it was her who needed convincing that I was in charge. "At dusk, two days from now, on the beachfront between the West and Palace Piers."

Murmurs rippled among the birds, but no one disagreed.

I exhaled, relieved. "Then it's done."

"I'll tell Silk and Kittiwake," said Morrigan, taking off at speed.

One by one, then all at once, the avians left.

"Oh look, you actually did something," said Violetta. The sarcasm didn't escape me.

She paused to caress a spear of lavender by the stairs.

The fury I'd been burying bubbled up.

"Just leave me alone!" My voice bounced off the solar panels.

The look of pity she threw me shredded my conviction into tatters, scattering it like dead leaves.

"I would, if you did a better job."

Ouch.

I wheezed. "Either you give me counsel, or you let me do it my way!"

Her hesitation lasted just long enough to give me hope. But then, she said, "I'm not convinced you truly care. Let's not waste the time, don't you think?"

With that, she disappeared down the escape.

My cheeks had gotten wet, whether from tears or rain, I couldn't tell.

I did care. Didn't I? If I didn't, I wouldn't be trying so hard. Right…right?

***

By the time I made it home, the midday sun had banished most of the wet weather. A warbler started singing. Once more, I checked for signs of tampering in my garden.

Nothing.

Most creatures didn't have a death wish—how could these poisonous substances be circulating?

I sat down on the steps.

Toxins could be extracted; I did it all the time for my experiments. Violetta had some medical training. Would she…? I tapped my fingers on my knees. No, she'd never harm the birds.

But. Oh no. I covered my face with my hands.

Only one other had the skill to extract toxins with accuracy. Someone whom I'd been training since she was a fledgling.

Morrigan.

***

"How could you think that of me?" Morrigan had said, her voice quiet with hurt.

Guilt whacked me like a sack of wet potatoes. No way to comfortably confront an old friend. "Morrigan, I—"

She'd flown away, cutting our comms.

I hadn't seen her in two days. Worry chewed at my insides like a leaf scalloped by a caterpillar. It had been strange, to not hear her tapping on my window, to not have her land in my garden unannounced. I'd never realised how much time we'd spend together, day in, day out.

Alone, I stood on a viewing platform between the piers. On either side, stairs led down to the pebbled beach. The sun had given up, the clouds swept from orange to deep blue, the moon a skinny sliver suspended in the sky. The rhythmic slosh of waves splintered the uneasy silence; the starlings had vacated their usual perch.

I pulled my cloak tighter and patted the med kit hanging around my waist: the usual swabs, first-aid affair, and the canister of experimental calming liquid from the hallway table; we'd run out of seeds. The liquid probably wouldn't work, but it might provide the advantage of surprise.

"Evenin'," said Kittiwake, landing on the railing next to me. The swish of wings and high-pitched screeches rose to a crescendo as seagulls descended on the left side of the beach. A moment later, a swathe of jackdaws alighted on the other, black feathers rustling, the air punctuated by their squeaky chatter.

Silk hopped onto the railing. "Where's Morrigan?"

"Not here yet," I said, burying a pang of guilt.

Kittiwake piped up. "We think she might know more than she's letting on."

"What do you mean?" I turned to face him.

Kittiwake shrugged his wings. "Word on the street? She's been making these poisoned grubs."

Not good, if they'd come to the same conclusion.

"She's the only bird who knows how. Besides, why would humans be interested in grubs?"

I couldn't refute the logic. Perhaps I should've taken Kittiwake and Silk aside for a conversation without involving everyone else. Too late now.

The breeze picked up. The moon hid behind a cloud.

Still no Morrigan. I sucked a breath through my teeth. But it was time.

I cleared my throat and straightened my back. I might be a bigger creature than the birds, but my insides shrank infinitely smaller.

"Welcome, everyone—"

"Feathered vermin," someone among the Mockers muttered.

A few Daws cawed in protest.

"Scavengers!" someone retaliated.

"Please!" I hated how I sounded like I was begging.

A few soft squawks of unrest, but they complied.

Meeting on the beach was a terrible idea. My voice barely carried; it sounded shrill.

"We're meeting here today to re-establish a truce." I tried projecting confidence. I probably failed. "Let's—"

"Ya posh snobs," a snicker escaped from the Mockers' camp.

"Greaseheads!"

I whirled around to tell Silk and Kittiwake to control their flocks, when a sudden burst of black and white feathers exploded in the middle of the beach. Ear-splitting shrieks perforated the salty air.

"Tell them—" I yelled but Kittiwake had flown into the whirlpool of the brawl. Silk followed suit.

Holy bloody hemlock. That didn't take long.

I ran down the steps, two at a time, screaming for them to stop. Amid the cacophony, no one could hear me. The birds squawked, shrieked, flapped, pecked at each other. Every now and again, someone would gain height only to be dragged down into the pulsating jumble of flying feathers.

I'm here! Morrigan's voice, over our comms link. My heart pounded at the familiarity.

I scanned the ugly scene. Where? I couldn't see her.

Morrigan?

There, the small black dot flying a wide circle above us as if to gain momentum. Oh no. She'd better not—

Morrigan, no! Stay back! It's not safe!

But Morrigan rode on some other kind of instinct. She made one last turn before pointing her beak down, cutting through the middle of the mess before her small brave body disappeared into the heaving avian quagmire.

Morrigan!

A tall silhouette, running down the stairs. Violetta, outrage plain on her face. But she ignored me and started breaking up the closest fight. She must really care about these birds. Where could I find courage like hers?

A bird, not sure from which camp, squealed in pain.

Must stop this. Consequences—later.

Shielding my eyes with my arms, I shoved my way into the throbbing chaos.

"There she is!" someone shouted. I froze. Did they mean me? Violetta?

"Get her!"

I gasped, inhaling feathers. I braced for the attack, but the scream that shot through my implant knocked the air out of my lungs, the pain of a thousand knives digging into my flesh.

Morrigan!

Beating my hands wildly, wings caught my arms, claws drew blood from my skin.

Morrigan!

Must find her, but her shrieks were everywhere, all at once. Feathers blocked out the light. Too dark to see. A sharp beak bit into my hand. I jerked it back. My bleeding fingers brushed against hard metal on the soft pouch of my med kit: the canister.

Squeezed down into a squat by the sheer gravity of warring birds, I fumbled for the fastener and grabbed the cylinder. It slipped, but I caught it. Just. Wiped hand on skirt, tried again. Better grip.

Clutching the tin tightly, I pushed through above my head. Fingers found the catch. Holding my breath, I pressed down on the trigger. It hissed. Once, twice.

Nothing happened. I tried again. One, two, three times.

A seagull dropped back down onto the beach, conscious, but looking a little confused. Then another, and another. More stopped fighting. They'd be fine later.

I stole a bird-filled breath. The sky brightened. I stood up straight.

Close to the stairs, Violetta appeared to be sliding a branch along the sand to detract a pair of Mockers from a few Daws. It wasn't working all that well.

I adjusted the dosage on the canister. Pointing it high, I pressed on the trigger and sprayed in three directions. One, two, three.

A few more bewildered birds landed, wobbling on their feet.

Morrigan!

Where was she? Where did she land?

I staggered forward, using the spray to clear the path. Silence descended as the birds settled.

A clump of jet-black feathers laid by the water's edge.

I crouched down. *Morrigan?*

No reply.

"Morrigan!" Someone was sobbing. Might have been me.

My arms ached to cradle the broken body but my hands shook too much.

A tall shadow appeared by my side. An arm on my shoulder.

Violetta knelt beside me. "She's not gone."

I tried to meet her gaze but tears veiled everything into a blur.

An alert flashed on my retina. A faint heartbeat.

"Quickly!" Violetta handed me a purple sash. "Use this."

Seconds stretched as we dug into the beach around Morrigan, making space to move her as little as possible.

"Wait, let us help," a Mocker said. Some jackdaws and seagulls levelled the area with their beaks and feet. One of them found a discarded plank. Carefully, we wrapped the sash around Morrigan, and lifted her gently onto the makeshift stretcher.

Around us, broken feathers, battered beaks, injured wings. Helpless, uncertain, I looked at Violetta.

"Take her home," she said. "I'll start on the first aid."

"I'll come back—"

"Take care of her first."

A few birds followed us. I ignored them.

I was going to lose everything I'd work so hard for.

Sod it, sod them all.

I just wanted my Morrigan back, alive.

***

Some days passed. I stopped counting.

A knock on the door drew me away from Morrigan's side. I opened it; no one there. Grey clouds covered the sky, muddling the time of day.

"Ahem," said Kittiwake, somewhere near my feet. Next to him, Silk stood upright, pristine as always.

I ushered them into the garden.

"How is she?" asked Silk.

"Better than yesterday." Morrigan still couldn't move much, but the crystalloid drip I'd given her helped; she'd been able to converse through our comms.

The ferocity of the incident shocked everyone into a truce. A day afterward, Silk and Kittiwake gave a joint statement to the Committee.

Silk looked regretful. "We've been fighting for so long, no one remembered how it all began. It just takes one side to feel hard-done-by, then things spiral into finger-pointing…"

"And we don't know how to stop," Kittiwake continued, solemn for once. "We request that Willow continue as mediator, so this doesn't happen again."

That stunned me, but not half as much as when Violetta defended me. "Peace is fragile. Like tending to a garden, it takes work. Willow has shown us we can't take any of it for granted."

Had I? I felt numb.

But one issue remained unresolved, so I'd asked them all to convene in my garden.

"Evening," said Violetta, as she glided through my gate. The birds murmured a greeting.

Time to come clean.

"I think someone stole from my garden. I don't know how else we could have gotten these poisoned grubs."

Violetta shrugged. "I don't think it had been deliberate."

"I doubt it too," Kittiwake said.

Silk cocked his head, his clever eyes darting all around the garden. With a flick of his wings, he landed on Mrs. Leigh's fence.

"Have we looked here?"

My eyes widened as we all flocked next door. Under the magnolia, between the roses and the rhododendron, I spotted them: baby foxglove, tiny monkshood. But in and around them, tiny bright blue pellets.

Pesticides. Oh *no*.

Kittiwake swore loudly in seagull.

The Daws must have eaten these by accident, or picked up grubs in close contact with the baby poison plants, sending us on a wild bird-food chase.

"This is unacceptable," Silk spoke first. "We ought to get her garden redesignated."

"No," I shook my head. "It's better to keep more space everyone can share. Leave it with me, I'll speak to Mrs. Leigh."

Perhaps if I could help her tend her garden, she might not need to use pesticides to keep it tidy.

Violetta lingered after the birds left. We sat on the steps, nursing steaming mugs of dandelion brew.

"I'd been foolish to think I could be in control—poison plants, the birds, the lot." I rubbed my eyes. In the end, the Committee agreed to address better cooperation over any punitive measures. "We're all equal in nature's eyes, none of us are superior. We should have never interfered."

Violetta shook her head. "Communing with animals isn't new, we did it as early as nine thousand years ago. We're just learning how to do it again."

Perhaps she was right.

I sighed. "I'm only slightly better with plants…"

"Well, humans confuse me, I'm only slightly better with birds," Violetta said, a little ruefully. "Why do you think I kept checking up on you?"

I hadn't thought of that.

She sat upright, as if an idea just sparked. "Willow, if I help you with the birds, will you give me a hand with my role with human health?"

Our eyes met. Peace is a fragile thing, we had to start somewhere.

Like, with a friend. Maybe.

* * *

Ana Sun writes from the edge of an ancient town along the River Ouse in the south-east of England. She spent her childhood in Malaysian Borneo and grew up living on islands. In another life, she might have been a musician, an anthropologist—or a botanist obsessed with edible flowers.

WATER CYCLE

Lauren C. Teffeau

I.

Birthed from the cloud-strewn sky, we fall. Silent tears dripping through layers of moving air sheets.

Leaves reach up to grab us, stems and branches shuttling us ever downward to the siphoning roots hidden below. The rest of us continue our descent, ricocheting off plant matter, wicking through fur or feather or hair, pattering down against the detritus scattered across the ground, until—finally—we're absorbed into the soil.

In that darkness we all eventually find, we can rest for a long time, beyond the reach of root or seed. There, we slowly gather together with our siblings, until there's a fluid-enough force to travel deeper, helped or hampered by the mineral deposits that chart our progress through those secret places, the earth's heartbeat pulsing with magma just beyond, until we're pushed out of springs or pulled out of wells or pumped out of aquifers, only to find our way once more to the sea.

The briny deep holds us when the sky does not.

Swirling in the frigid dark or on warmer currents through kelp forests and coral beds that grow less vibrant with each turn, we slip through gills and are expelled through blowholes, mixed with churning sand and excrement, buffeted by seaweed, but always drawn back toward land. Land we no longer recognize, even though the sea, the moon, the sky…those things are always the same.

And so the cycle begins again.

II.

Once we knew these lands well.

They've changed so slowly, it did not signify at first. But that was before your kind. You, who we've birthed and who we'll see buried. You, whose plight we cannot escape, no more than we can the moon. Is that love to be beholden as we are to your continuing existence? Or inevitability as we witness the changes you've wrought, eclipsing all that has come before?

We would ask the plants, our long companions in this world of ours, but they've grown scarce, and when we do find their hungry roots, they're so greedy for us, there's no time to talk like we used to. We suppose that's your doing, too.

Barrier islands and glades now swamped by the sea. Rivers far removed from their original courses if they remain at all. Every time, the land changes a bit more. The path to the sea once along a streambed, then a diversion channel. Now, yet another change as we follow the concrete paths, soak through dirty blankets and sun-frayed nylon, and sweep away someone's fragile home after failing to pay their rent.

Such a concept is difficult for us to understand, but if it's like a crack in the ice, the pressure widening the gap between what is solid and what is fluid, then perhaps it's not so different and just as disorienting when the current takes you and asks you to be something you're not.

The glaciers know this truth well.

We've spent so much of our existence as ice, lined up in crystalline rows, no matter the cycles of thaw and freeze that chip away at our hold on this world and leave us stranded at the poles. But we still dance on bitter gusts and chilly updrafts. We still skitter across rooftops or slam into mountains, piled high in drifts, ever more precious, ever more inconvenient, when we fall. Sometimes we're there for weeks and months, the delicate flakes concentrated down into crusted ice under the sun's harsh glare, before we seep into the ground. Or perhaps it is a spring cataract, rushing down from higher climbs, that returns us to the sea where we rejoin our siblings, so many of us having just escaped from icebergs melted asunder, the caps more fragile than ever.

You must know how thin the ice has gotten, how so many of us have been freed. How the moon's magnetic pull draws us out to sea, drives us back to land, in an eternal dance of ebb and flow, there and back again, the tides pushing us ever more unpredictably to land. We are helpless against the moon's summons and must go where it wills us across the globe, no matter what obstacles lie ahead.

Now when we're drawn into storm systems, they strike with increasing frequency, slapping down with our collective might, overwhelming everything in our path. Forced beyond sea walls and sand bags, against uninsurable tourist traps and retirement homes. We find your garbage and precious mementos and treat them equally as impediments to our journey.

When so many of us run roughshod over countryside and created landscapes alike, there's a wildness that comes from all of us all existing in the same space. We infiltrate cement cracks and drywall boards that were never meant to hold us let alone turn us away. Our ranks swell with impurities gleaned from your world, redistributing them as we settle in these places where we don't belong. Places we turn fetid with organisms that work harder at living than you do. Places where we're eventually scrubbed away or diluted with chemicals or flushed down porcelain drains and swept through rusted pipes and plastic tubes.

But we know we will return, driven by wind and atmospheric pressure and a world increasingly out of alignment with itself.

You know it too. We've glimpsed your lives—on vapor inhaled, raindrops swallowed, ice melted on tongues. We've found your dead and despondent. We've found your dreamers, too. Some have such beautiful dreams of a world brought back from the brink.

Through sweat or semen or snot, we are always with you, know some of you are as helpless as ground water in the desert, left stranded by a changing world. Others have been distracted by things we don't understand and would wash clean if you'd let us. Sometimes we manage to anyway, but do you listen? Do you care, guided as you are by a logic slipperier than ice?

We've infused your organs, cooled your brow, provided you with the moisture necessary for your survival, but too often, you shed us unthinkingly, no better than a careless wind. When we fall now, we're tinged with radioactive isotopes and microplastics that insist we include them in everything. Oh, we'll part with your unnatural creations eventually, we know, but they are with us each time we hit your roofs or wear down the paint on your cars, trickle into your wells and fields, land in your children's open mouths as they face the sky.

The next time you taste us on your skin, remember we alone cannot save you. We aren't certain you even want us to. We can only watch and wait and wonder what will come next.

III.

We drift among the spindly clouds, floating aimlessly over arid lands scarred by concrete and steel, abandoned to kudzu and knotweed, barberry and bamboo, as vapor too diffuse to condense into much-needed rain. It's been so long some of us don't even remember the feel of our other forms or the irresistible bonds we make when we join together and give gravity a better hold over us.

Wind turbines pinwheel across the rolling hills below. The fields that once marked this land are now hidden away in buildings and guarded by machines that take of us only what's needed and stockpile the rest, portioning it out only for the direst of circumstances. You've grown more careful and calculating with each cycle, learning the harsh lessons of famine and blight, drought and displacement, we wish we didn't have to witness. Yet you persist, producing new ways to survive with a shining insistence even we can sense when we're among you, in you, around you, as some of us always are.

Drones buzz through the sky hunting virga, and not the adversaries your kind always seems to find. Other contraptions of your making create artificial air currents that reunite us with our scattered siblings. Then electricity slices through the air like a clap of thunder, and suddenly we're transformed into a billowing cloud, dark with the promise of moisture.

You've made so many things, and now this as well.

Below, you emerge from your homes, your expressions full of wonder as you face the sky. But only for a moment before you become a hive of activity as you cast your nets to collect us for drinking, cooking, living in ways we've not felt from you in so long it may as well be another age. As we soothe your parched throats and find our way into your blood, the creases of your skin, the tears welling in your eyes, we find something else we thought lost. A certainty in your choices to undo what's been done in the name of everything but that of the future. Your future. And ours. One where we'll be used and reused until it is a relief to be cast into the ground. Celebrated and consecrated, cleaned of impurities, cycling through the land once more and creating new life in our wake.

Grant us the best of you, and we'll give you the best of us in return. We've never been stingy on that front.

Some of us irrigate shade trees and garden plants. Others are treated and retreated so many times as we filter our way through your homes and communities, it takes much longer than usual to reach the sea. We don't truly find our rest until we're afloat in the ocean, the moon's insistent call the only one we must answer as we slam into tidal generators or shed salt in desalination plants along the coast. You haven't just grown more efficient in your use of us. Now, you can pull us out of thin air in accordance to your wishes, not the whims of the world around us.

What will we find on our next trek to the sea? Restoration and renewal and our reunion once more, with even more of your smiling faces to welcome us home. Faces filled with a child's joy in so simple a thing, of rainfall pure and clean and without carry-on chemicals or the dry air's insistence we don't reach the ground. After all, you are cloud makers now.

What more can you do? We will know soon enough.

* * *

Lauren C. Teffeau's novel *Implanted* (Angry Robot) mashing up cyberpunk, solarpunk, adventure, and romance was shortlisted for the 2019 Compton Crook award for best first SF/F/H novel and named a definitive work of climate fiction by Grist. For more information, please visit www.laurencteffeau.com.

MICROBIA

Center For Militant Futurology

"Gmother Fig," I said a late summer afternoon, "tell me about the dirt pirates."

Greatmother Fig did not answer at once. She cleaned her nails, taking care to collect the dirt in her soil vessel. I sat beside her, working on potatoes for later. We were on the common deck of our home, the Soilbearer fleet, anchored just off Gibraltar, on the last year of the 15 year mud cycle around the planet.

She plucked a half rotten potato from the pile, and added it to her vessel. "My little Bamboo, you like that one. Let me see, the pirates, it was told to me like this:"

"Decades ago, as if by magic, an island appeared in the Indian Ocean. It rose out of the waters off the coast of Madagascar like a dark monstrous mountain, spreading its porous tentacles out into the sea. This, of course, was no ordinary island. Though there was nothing magical about it, nor was it caused by any natural phenomenon. Rather it was the product of global minority countries using this specific site in the Indian Ocean as a dumping ground for toxic waste, far away from their own territories. Enormous ships would line up day after day, year after year to unload a lethal cocktail of industrial debris, waste oil, car wrecks, toxic materials, scrapped car tires, things like that, until a new land emerged. Soon visible from the coasts of Madagascar the locals dubbed it Trash Island or Mount Tox. Horrific as it was, its existence was sanctioned by local governments paid off by the European Union for the inconveniences of poisoned water and dead fish. Some Madagascans would not have it though and started a protest movement. Soon they had formed a provisional armada of small fishing vessels, sail boats, and lakanas to prevent the cargo ships from unloading their lethal loads. The blockade lasted for ninety-nine days and was successful. It rendered the mission of the cargo ships almost impossible and drew a lot of unwanted attention. Eventually, the trash dumpers were forced to return home. The blockaders then left their ships, went ashore on Trash Island and proclaimed it a new independent republic. It was not long after that the new inhabitants of Trash Island started experimenting with its toxic soil in an attempt to make things grow on its barren surface. That's why they became known as The Dirt Pirates of Trash Island. The episode got a lot of attention on a planetary scale, igniting new discussions on toxic colonialism and ecocide and a strange mix of dedicated people started flocking to the island from all over the world—radical mycologists, fermenters, composteers, people like us—to support and work with the Trash Island community on the microbial formula that today is the basis, the Mothersoil, of the dirt in our vessel right here. That was where it began. No more Trash Island—Microbia was born."

Greatmother Fig had told me this story as long as I could remember, and every time I seemed to get something new out of it. I remember her telling it the first time, just after we left Microbia 15 years ago, when I was six. But something felt different this time, more detailed, and something else. But I couldn't place it. Greatmother Fig was looking at me with a quiet intensity, and then she added, "yes, that was the beginning, people fighting for each other's possibilities to live."

Later, we were heading to land, all delegations from our fleet, in our small four-person sail katamayaks, each representing one of the twenty-four pontoon-boats that all tied together in still waters constituted the Soilbearer fleet. The wind was quite strong, and the hydrofoils were lifting us off the surface. It was me, Gmother Fig, Græs and Lind in our boat. Me and Lind sat in the stern, waving to the other boats behind us. Fig shouted at us. At first, I didn't notice because of all the excitement. I had not been sailing like this for months, and the crossing of the Atlantic had been no fun. But then she threw the ladle, which almost hit me.

"Oi, Bamboo, watch the flipping warships," she shouted above the wind, and I whipped my head around to see that we were heading directly towards a hunkering ancient thing of steel and diesel, suddenly blaring its ugly horn. I pulled the rudder towards me and zoomed away from it, towards the port of Free Gibraltar, while Lind and Græs flipped their middle fingers towards the bridge of the warship. It was part of the blockade of the sailway to Algeciras, which was still part of the old nationist EU, desperately afraid of letting anyone ashore not living there for five generations. And then, just as I ducked under the boom, I realized something about Gmother Figs story; she wasn't telling a story about a mythological past of swashbuckling heroes, like I used to picture it. She was telling a story about me—I was a dirt pirate from Trash Island. And the trash-dumping villains of the minority world, they were still there, sitting in that warship, watching us.

Later we carried our pot of soil from our katamayak through the old, ruined harbor area, towards the huge bonfire atop the limestone ridge of the rock of Gibraltar. We moved and heaved along with hundreds of other peoples, hauling dirt in a veritable catwalk of vessels, hopping and bopping up the cliff. People had traveled here from all over, carrying living microbial soil in their personal and communal soil vessels. I was so excited; this was my first planetary mud mixing, and they did not happen every year. Arriving atop, we joined a more orderly procession towards the huge cauldron, and we fell into the ceremonial two-step. People were carrying lights and singing a multitude of songs and tones, and from the woods the macaque monkeys, who were the most numerous primates here, sang along. As we reached the cauldron, which was actually a natural depression in the cliff, we dumped the dirt of our communal soil vessel, a huge ceramic kylix, and then the contents of our personal soil vessels. Mine was brimming, since I had not mixed my mud recently, waiting for this occasion. Afterwards we passed by one of the soil witches, who marked our foreheads with the mix. As we rested, I climbed a rock and looked down on the procession of moving lights.

It looked like thousands of people. And now drums were starting, signaling the start of the fermentation period, which was a huge party. If the stories were anything to go by, this would go on till sunup, where we would fill our vessels from the cauldron and head back to the fleet.

***

One week later, sailing north, I was helping Greatmother Fig sorting the kelp lines, at the starboard platform of our pontoon. The kites were stout and strumming, and the smell of food wafted from the galley tents.

"You know, Bamboo," Greatmother Fig said, running a hand over a wrinkly smooth luminous leaf, "if we did not have kelp, we probably would not be here today. Elders call it Hair of The Goddess. When food was still scarce on Microbia, this is what people survived on. The kelp forests were grown in the waters around Microbia and was the reason that fish and a variety of other sea creatures would later return to the area. Growing corals was also of great importance. On land, fungi were responsible for turning the toxic ground into fertile soil along with bacteria, worms, and other critter comrades." She padded her soil vessel with an affectionate expression.

"It took decades though before something as simple as a potato could be grown in Microbian soil. However, as many parts of the world fell victim to severe droughts, Microbia was then thriving with more plant species growing there than any other place in the world. Nations that had been responsible for the toxic genesis of Trash Island were now begging to visit Microbia in order to bring back Microbian soil to the devastated deserts they were now inhabiting. It was around that time that the Soilbearer Fleet was founded—to ensure planetary justice and distribute the vibrant soil of Microbia to all parts of the planet, to guard it and keep the microbial culture healthy and strong by mixing it with other strains of toxin-transforming soils from across the world."

Having sorted the lines, I started to seed them. I had heard this before of course, the story about how the first potatoes were grown, was a classic. But this telling suggested more conflict than how I remembered it. "How did we decide who to share the soil with? Surely the trashdumpers, did not get it?"

"We do not have to decide, the Mothersoil only works if you tend it with the care that created it in the very adverse circumstances that was the original Tox island. So we share with everyone. But the just distribution, the mud mixing, the giving without demands, the unequivocal access to the healing mud, this we need to protect. And the fleet has been attacked many times, by people who wanted to control it, who wanted to scarcify and sell it. So this is the work, and we give our life to it, in more than one sense."

***

I was first up that morning after uneasy dreams. Our pontoon was heading directly into the blinding disc of the sun rising over the eastern Mediterranean. I went to the kite anchors to look out and saw the reed boat just starboard. Fatia and a crew of six had befriended us on Gibraltar, where they had been part of the mud mixing along with at least twenty other Annilan reed boats. I had sailed with them for the last week, getting to know their sailing technique. Their reed boat handled very different from the katamayaks or pontoons, ours being built from plastic garbage, theirs from papyri reeds from the marshes of the Nile Delta. I saw someone at the helm and shouted and waved, and they sailed up close so I could jump over. It was Fatia; we hugged and laughed as the spray hit us from the maneuver.

"Today is a good day for radio." Fatia beckoned me into the tented stern of the boat. "We are coming within easy radio contact with the Nislands, and we have sun."

She waved towards the solar array fans spreading out as we spoke. In the tented area of the boat, the other Annilans were still dozing in their hammocks. Fatia unpacked their radio, and connected it to wiring built into the reeds, to power and the mast antenna, and started calling the Nislands. I did not understand their radio lingua, as everyone had taken to Indigenous languages as resistance. For the Annilans, that meant Tamazight. Someone was answering and seemed very excited. Fatia called to the sleepers, who all rose, and everyone was talking quickly.

Baida came over to me and translated: "There is a huge container ship just north of the Nislands, coming out of the Suez, the first in many weeks, but this one has no military escort. Apparently it ran aground somewhere, so everyone wants to board it."

I was on a katamayak, going fast in the direction of the plume of smoke, when the container ship came over the horizon. It was huge, more like a sailing mountain than a ship, in a completely different scale of things. The smell of diesel was in the air, but the ship was not moving. As we sailed closer the hundreds of tiny reed ships surrounding it became discernable, and the lines with people climbing up the sides. We moored with Fatia's boat alongside the mountain and climbed up with them. Aboard we got a quick rundown of the situation from a group of three grinning Annilans. Asylum had been offered to the crew of twenty, who had accepted and was now helping with the dismantling of the ship. We could see the crane was starting to drop some of the thousands of containers into the ocean where they were goaded towards the hundreds of inhabited reed islands just outside the Nile Delta, which everyone called the Nislands. We joined a communal meeting of the boarding party on what was probably a defunct helipad, where it was being discussed what to do with the Madrid Maersk, as the ship was called. I offered the corralling expertise of the soil fleet. Since we had the seeds and cultures needed for transforming shipwrecks into reefs and islands of living soil, everyone agreed to run it aground in the Nislands, and reef it.

***

Weeks later, after we had rounded the Horn of Africa, I received a message from Fatia, containing a video. It was a quiet night, so I went to a hammock on the common deck, with a flask of kir, and started the message.

It was footage from a drone. Fatia's voice explained that one of the many gifts they found in the containers was a fleet of surveillance drones, which they had repurposed for ecological research. And the run that I was now witnessing was an inspection of the Saharan reforestation project. The drone was flying from the marshes of the Nile Delta into the lush green of the Saharan rainforest, flying at a height of several hundred meters. Fatia told how the pontoon of soil witches we had left behind had worked wonders on the reefed container ship, seeding it by hand with special corals, and how the upper parts of it were already being inhabited by several species of birds. They had not seen a container ship since we had left, and they were talking about the new reef as the last ship of the old world. As Fatia spoke, the drone view dove, and as it came nearer to the ground, it became apparent how the forest was inhabited by people, in the same low density ecological urbanism that we pioneered on Microbia. And then it landed just next to a circle of people mixing mud, and Fatia got up and walked towards the drone, smiling and waving, and then the message ended.

I was woken the next morning by Gmother Fig, saying, "Come and see, you can see it now!" I was stumbling and mumbling as she dragged me from the hammock and up to the looking platform.

She pointed to the horizon. "Look!" And there it was: Microbia, barely visible in the misty morning, a lush mountain as out of a dream, low clouds hanging over it. It had been fifteen years since we left, I barely remembered it.

I grabbed Figs hand. "How many times have you done this, the mud cycle?"

She took my hand. "This was my fourth cycle, and my last like this. But you will have many more, if you wish."

I was shaken by this, "do you mean you'll…"

"Yes, my Bamboo, it is my time to join the mud. And it would make me very happy if you will mix me with the living soil of the planet, and carry me around the world once again."

I hugged her, unable to speak, my tears running freely. And she held me, as people rose from their hammocks and started an ululation that spread to all twenty-four pontoon-boats. Over the waves we could hear the response: horns and drums welcoming us back to Microbia.

* * *

Center for Militant Futurology is a utopian future studies project based out of Svendborg Noosphere, Denmark. CMF is working with applied fiction, performance and sound to engender an explosive futurist fantasy, creating a multiplicity of germinating utopian futures in the present. DREAM THE FUTURE!

Solar Powered: Les Pogona

Badlungs Art

Solar Powered: Le Maki Catta

Badlungs Art is an illustrator and tattoo artist from Southern France with a passion for solarpunk. She tries to convey it sometimes through her art, and by solar cooking on a regular basis, trying to get the best of Provence's sun, which was the main inspiration for the pieces published in this anthology.

RABBITS, RIVERS, AND PRICKLY PEARS

Justine Norton-Kertson

The world ended on a scorching spring day. Well, homosapien civilization did anyway. But that was centuries ago, mostly just old stories now that mothers tell their furry babes as cautionary tales. Not mythology, mind you. The tangible evidence of what came before was all around. Stories change over time, we all know that. But the sapie structures still standing, even though long reclaimed by nature, don't lie.

No, the apocalypse actually did happen, it just didn't turn out to be an ending the way most sapies expected. To be fair, it wasn't really a new beginning either. I mean, it's not like sapies disappeared, but those of us from other species definitely noticed the difference. So the stories go anyway. It turned out the apocalypse was more like a routine continuation of billions of years of evolution on the planet Earth. Things come and go. Species develop and disappear. The sun rises and sets.

Go figure.

I watched Arrow jump down off a large, flat slab of sandstone near what used to be Lake Mohave, part of what used to be the Colorado River. Light-colored lines above the water stretched around the depression in which the pond sat, indicating the space did in fact hold a larger body of water at some point in the past. But clearly a long time ago; not the lifetimes of anyone I knew. But then hares only live a handful of years at best anyway. So maybe that's not the best gauge.

Lake Mohave used to be so mind-bogglingly massive it'd take a husk of hares a week to circumnavigate. But now it was closer in size to a large pond. And the river that provided water for tens of millions of sapies in their big cities? Essentially a small creek no more than ten hares stretched across.

It seemed to be plenty of water though, especially for a desert. I've never known the difference anyway, so I have no complaints. It certainly seemed like more than enough for the nearby sapie community at Cottonwood Cove. They poured water all over themselves everyday. They also seemed fond of putting water in containers, setting the containers on top of fire, then putting their food inside the containers. Some strange habit they called "cooking."

Sometimes Arrow tossed me scraps of cooked food and let me tell you, it was by far the yummiest thing you could imagine. Like think about your favorite food, and increase the flavor by maybe a thousand times. Somehow, that's what this cooking thing does. I don't pretend to understand it, but I dream about the way it made my mouth water. Sharp tingles shot from the back corners of my jaw and down the sides of my neck. It was a new and strangely pleasurable sensation that I always look forward to.

All kinds of other creatures lived around Cottonwood Cove too. Like me, they enjoyed the creek just as it was, regardless of how much larger it may have once been. Sapies who weren't from the desert usually thought of it as barren and lifeless. Those of us who were from here knew better.

The Colorado Creek itself teemed with life. Of course you had your freshwater fish, frogs, and other aquatic life that made homes within the creek. At various times from day-to-day all kinds of other folks came around to drink and find relief from unrelenting desert heat: mule deer, bighorn sheep, gilas, roadrunners, coyotes, kangaroo rats, antelope, snakes and horned lizards, not to mention all kinds of spiders and bugs and birds, and of course hares like me. Others— mainly carnivorous predators like redtail hawks and cougars—also came in search of their next meal, hunting those of us who lounged in the oasis. It seems evolution isn't a straight line. It's not even a curved or a wavy line. It isn't necessarily leading towards something better, more advanced, or morally superior. Evolution is more like a meandering trail that branches off in countless directions through forest so thick you can't see more than a few dozen feet ahead.

Evolution turns around and loops back on itself. It spirals and spins about, jumps and burrows and skips and scurries its way in whatever direction it can.

In that way, I guess it's also a lot like a stream in the desert; always seeking a path of least resistance.

It was a hot spring day; not unusual for the desert. The sun climbed a big blue sky dotted with thin, wispy white clouds. A soft breeze played with Arrow's chin length hair. They kicked a small rock and sent it flying along with a small cloud of orange-red dust.

A sudden shuffling in the brush behind them sent me scurrying under a boulder. I poked my head out and saw Arrow standing still as a flower on a windless day. Vigilance was vital for life in the desert. You could never really be too careful. But the giggling snort gave it away and the tension dissipated.

Arrow quickly ran their fingers through their hair, pushing their bangs to either side of their head. Then they cleaned up, much like furfolk do, by licking their hand and wiping their dirt-smudged face. But it just smeared their trademark dirt stains around more.

"You're late," Arrow said, turning around to face their friend.

"For what?" Aster laughed. "Are we on a tight schedule? Or you got an early bedtime?"

"Oh shut up! It's not like you're some kind of elder or something."

"I'm *your* elder though." Aster smirked, crinkling her nose. The dry wind picked up and carried her scent our way. Unlike Arrow, she smelled like flowers.

"You only came of age a year before me," Arrow said, turning a light shade of red as they waved her away. "Anyway, what do you wanna do?"

"I dunno." Aster hopped up onto one of the sandstone boulders, arms out as she spun around twice, three times as if on top of the world.

Arrow watched her with a puppy dog look plastered across their face that was obvious and recognizable no matter what species you were. They sighed and leaned against the boulder. "How about we head down to Bullhead?" Arrow suggested. "I hear some geneticists there just made a breakthrough in drought resistant spinach."

"A three hour bike ride to check out some spinach? I'll pass, but thanks." Aster jumped off the boulder, giving Arrow a friendly swat on the back of their head on her way down. She hit the ground and dust puffed up around her ankles.

"Hey!" Arrow giggled. "Still waiting to hear your brilliant and exciting idea…"

"Let's go on a real adventure."

"Sure, okay. What do you wanna do, go camping or something?"

"That's what we'll tell our families at least." Aster paced as she spoke. Behind her, a bird with beautiful black and bright yellow plumage landed gently on a spikeball tree whose parched, spiny-clubbed limbs writhed upward towards the desert sky as if pining for any tiny molecule of moisture. The bird ignored the nearby sapies and began feasting on moth larvae who were busy feasting on seeds, which were busy being produced by the tree's big puffy white flowers.

"What do you mean, 'that's what we'll tell them?'" Arrow asked.

"I mean that while our families think we're out camping nearby at Spirit Mountain, we'll actually be off on a *real* adventure."

"Alright, stop being cryptic. What's the big adventure?"

"Are you ready for this?"

"Okay come on and say it already."

"Let's go to the Grand Canyon."

I'll stop boring you with the minutiae of human conversation, at least for now. It's enough to say that before Arrow finally, reluctantly agreed to the adventure the two friends argued for some time about whether or not it was a good idea, about how much trouble they'd get into for lying and disappearing for days. They even argued about whether they could actually get to the canyon and back. Apparently it was further than most sapies usually traveled, which is however far; I don't know. It's way farther than a hare's ever gone, I'm sure of that.

Okay I'm stopping now, I promise. It just fascinates me; human conversation I mean. But then again a sapie—Arrow—is my BFF so sure I'm a little biased. But so are the other furfolk, ya know? Just because they choose to be all wary and standoffish doesn't mean they aren't biased. I mean come on, it couldn't be more obvious that *that is their bias.*

But whatever, I don't care if they say I'm weird for hanging out with a sapie. Arrow's nice to me and I enjoy their company. I assume they enjoy mine as well. After all, it's not every sapie who'll tell you about their day and scratch behind your ears for you.

***

Hares and other furfolk can be a superstitious bunch. From stories families tell their young in twisted attempts to keep them safe, to those adults themselves spend lots of time thinking about, longing to find truths in them. The *Legend of Hare and the Magical Prickly Pear* is a great example.

The story goes that the nopal cactus was magical and, once upon a time, sustained the desert and all those who lived there. It was *everywhere.* Its fruit turned rich burgundy when ripe. All you had to do was carefully remove the thorns and sink your teeth in. The cool blood-red juice not only fueled whole generations of furfolk, winged folks, and crawlers of all kinds, but its light sugary flavor elevated it to a delicacy across the biome.

The big, round, bright green pads were also an important part of this desert jewel. They provided spots of shade from the beating sun and held significant amounts of water. That didn't seem important around Cottonwood Cove with the creek and pond right there and all. But most of the desert wasn't lucky enough to have such a paradise, let alone a steady and reliable source of drinking water. So both the big pads and fruit of the nopal cactus were a vital source of life year round for pretty much all living creatures. They served as an important source of calories, especially in the winter months when flowers and fruits were even more sparse in the desert than usual.

Unfortunately, sapies also knew too well the wondrous properties of the prickly pear. Hundreds of years ago climate change accelerated; things went from bad to worse and most of the Colorado River disappeared. Sapies, not very good with long-term planning, I guess, started using the cactus for hydration and nutrition, and drove it into extinction within only a few generations of harekind.

But… the legend also said prickly pear cacti still grew in a place so far away and difficult to get to that sapies didn't even know about them. It was the edge of the world—if a big round ball even had an edge—and it would take a hare its whole life just to hop there, if it was lucky enough to complete the journey at all.

According to the legend, one day in the future a hare will embark on a great journey. Somehow that hare will make it all the way to the so-called edge of the world, this Grand Canyon. They'll descend deep into the Earth, cross an endless sea, and find the last prickly pear cactus. After collecting seeds, the hare will bring them back to the Mojave and usher in some kind of desert golden age. Mind you this is an impossible trip that should take two lifetimes for a hare. But legends and superstitions are rarely logical. Maybe the fabled magical properties of the cactus will make the whole thing possible. I don't know.

***

I generally pay little mind to that kind of thing, let alone carry any kind of active beliefs in such myths. I've certainly never had any good reason to take *The Legend of Hare and the Magical Prickly Pear* seriously. They were only stories after all. They were fun. They helped pass the time and provided moral lessons. Beyond that though, what?

So why couldn't I sleep? I laid in my form later that day, waiting for the sun to begin its descent and the worst of the day's heat to subside. Normally around that time I'd listen to the chirping of crickets and allow the whistling wind to lull me into a late afternoon nap. On that particular day though, my thoughts refused to rest.

The Legend of Hare and the Magical Prickly Pear played over and over in my mind. It wasn't the magic and wonder, or the impossibility that sent my thoughts racing. It wasn't even the gross abuse and misuse of a shared natural resource that kept me awake, tossing and turning. It was the part about the future. *In the future* a hare will go on a journey. *In the future* they'll do this, that, and some other things. It wasn't the details I was obsessing over, it was the timeframe.

Why the future?

What use is a story set firmly in the days that follow? What good is a prophecy that won't ever be fulfilled because it's always coming tomorrow, forever just out of reach? Do such tales create a cycle of perpetual waiting and wanting? Is hope without action just silly naiveté? Empty optimism to mask fear of uncertainty and disappointment in reality?

When I heard Aster say, "Let's go to the Grand Canyon," there was no question in my mind what that meant. It was simply a given. I'm pretty sure I knew it before they even finished arguing over whether or not they were going themselves.

It's not that I thought we needed some kind of hero either. Certainly not. We didn't need saving, at least not in my opinion. It didn't even matter that I didn't believe in the legend. I'd decided I was done listening to stories, just waiting around for the future to happen. This was an opportunity to create a story, to build the future. And I was going to take it.

To be perfectly honest, we were already living in a golden age as far as I was concerned. Cottonwood Cove and the Mojave Basin might not have been what sapies in ages past had dreamed of when they hoped for a utopian future, but all of us—sapies included—were doing the best we could with what we had. Can we ever really do better than that? I don't think so. And we had it pretty damned good too, if I say so myself.

But still, if someone had to make a legendary journey to the edge of the world and investigate old myths in order to help others realize that particular truth as well, then I guess I was ready to go.

Yup, I was going to the Grand Canyon to find out whether or not *The Legend of Hare and the Magical Prickly Pear* had any truth to it. If it didn't—and if I somehow survived the impossibly long journey there and back again—I'd have a great story to tell. But if there was truth there to be found, then I'd do what needed to be done so no one else had to keep waiting for the future either.

***

When Aster saw my head pop out of Arrow's bag she tried to tell them to leave me behind at the next stop. I'd just be a distraction, she said. I'd slow them down. I could find my own way back. I'd use up their food and water. She had a few other reasons as well that I don't remember.

"No way," Arrow held firm. "Jack's my buddy. Besides, he'll be useful."

"Oh yeah, how so?" Aster's eyebrows wrinkled, her cheeks tightened, and her lips stretched flat as she asked the question. Around us, the foreground whizzed by in a blur while the high desert mountains in the distance slowly panned the dayglow horizon.

"Rabbits are skittish, right?" Arrow asked, stroking my ears as I sat on their lap listening to the two sapiens debate my fate as part of—so far as I could tell anyway—some kind of coy teenage mating ritual. "He'll be like an alarm system. Give us warning if there's danger around before we'd know about it. Won't ya bud?" They put their hand affectionately over my face. It was soft and smelled like comfort.

"Yeah but an alarm system that's *always* going off isn't very useful." Aster had a point. "Besides, Jack's probably the least skittish rabbit I've ever seen."

"Exactly, that's why we can trust his instincts," Arrow said, lifting me up with their hands and holding me only inches from their face. "He'll do his job. Yes he will" Arrow nuzzled my face with their nose

113

and their voice became a cacophony of tones, pitches, and inflections. They set me back on their lap as the chorus died down.

"You're weird, Arrow," Aster said with a bright smile.

Arrow laughed and Aster joined them.

Aster was wrong though about whether or not I was jumpy. Being easily frightened is a common trait among most furfolk, not just hares. Sapies even have a term for it, "scaredy cat." It's an obvious result of eons existing as prey and teaching our offspring to follow suit. Just because I was comfortable around Arrow didn't negate countless years of evolution, not to mention the generational trauma associated with life as the hunted. I imagined sapies couldn't really understand, being at the top of the food chain and all. But what I did know? Maybe they had their own anxieties keeping them up at night.

We found a ride after walking for what seemed like forever along a wide empty trail. I'd never seen a trail like this before. It was made of hard, pressed black rocks and had yellow and white lines on it at regular intervals. The trail led us to a village called Searchlight, no bigger than Cottonwood Cove. In fact, it looked almost exactly the same, only this place sat on this weird trail instead of the creek.

We jumped into the back of a big machine with two sapies up front who said their names were Sandy and Sylvie. A bunch of panels composed the machine's body and seemed to absorb sunlight. No reflection. No twinkle or gleam. Like a void.

Sandy and Sylvie said they'd take us as far as some place called Ash Fork. The marker was meaningless to me. Apparently though it was pretty far because Arrow and Aster got all excited like they'd won a game or award or something.

But I quickly understood why they responded so strongly, even while I started wondering if I'd misinterpreted their reaction as excitement. It wouldn't be surprising. I generally looked at things through hopeful, optimistic eyes. Maybe that's why I got stuck on this idea of hope without action. Or, I guess now it was hope *in* action, wasn't it?

So we sat in the back of this "truck," as they called it, moving so fast the wind about blew my fur off. This truck rumbled and shook with ferocity as it zipped down the black rock pathway. My heart pounded against the inside of my chest like it was trapped and desperate to break free. I understood exactly how it felt. I had a powerful urge to get out of Arrow's bag and hop away from this beast as fast as I possibly could. But my muscles had locked. My joints suddenly stiffened. I was unable to even struggle, let alone escape. So my heart struggled for both of us.

Fortunately, Arrow had the bag and me firmly in their lap. One arm wrapped in front of my chest, with the other they ran their fingers gently but firmly through my fur, from ears to tail. Each stroke ran the same length in both distance and duration, with the same brief and incrementally spaced pause between them.

My muscles unwound in response. Not completely of course—I still shook like a tree in the wind—but enough that the strain became manageable. Sometimes you just had to make the best of a situation. The most I could do at that moment was breathe and hold out hope that the ride would be over sooner than later. I couldn't have been more grateful for Arrow. Without them, I'm pretty sure I would have had a heart attack.

Ash Fork came into view not long after the sun disappeared behind the purple streaked mountains to the west and I'd never been more relieved. The sky was still light enough near the horizon to see the lines of tall white poles dotting the landscape as we drove into town. Each pole had a set of three blades spinning round as the wind spread subtle hints of sagebrush. It reminded me of evenings at Cottonwood Cove when sapies busily prepared their food.

The town actually had a lot in common with the Coves, but on a grander scale of course. Everything was bigger and with more of it. Sapies were no exception. Sapies *everywhere.*

Arrow read a sign on our way in: "Population two thousand."

I had no clue how much a thousand meant. But two of them

seemed like way more sapies than I'd ever seen in one place before.

You're probably assuming there were differences aside from scale too, and you're right. While at the Cove sapie shelters were thin, long, and sat on wheels, there in Ash Fork most of the homes had been built up out of earthen material and blended naturally into the desert scenery. They're almost hard to see at first until your eyes adjust.

Most of the shelters I saw had these weird structures behind them. Basically big holes dug into the ground. On top of the holes were wood-framed glass panels that formed a triangle. The sapies called the structures "underground greenhouses."

Of course, furfolk are no strangers to the fact that it's cooler underground than above in the scorching desert days. It's also cozier than above ground during the frigid, dry winter nights. But apparently, sapies used these underground shelters to grow food that normally had a hard time out here. I'm talking about things a desert hare like me never sees outside a sapie kitchen or garden like delicious carrots and crip, leafy green lettuce. Delectable treats that I imagine made my face red the way Arrow's got whenever Aster came around.

Where sapies got the water to grow such things, I had no clue. No one mentioned it, not that I heard at least. I never saw a creek nearby or any other source of water to justify anything beyond basic necessity, which was typical for desert communities when it came to water. Maybe it had something to do with that drought resistant spinach Arrow told Aster about the day before.

As the evening sky grew darker, somehow the city started to glow. I don't want you to think I didn't know what light was. I might not have been on an adventure before, but I wasn't some newborn bunny either. I've seen lights in the windows of sapie shelters plenty of times back at Cottonwood Cove.

This was different though. Some might even say it was magical even though there was no supernatural stuff involved. Everything was lit up with a phosphorescent sheen that made the place feel like a fairytale, like a place that would actually come out of something like *The Legend of Hare and the Magical Prickly Pear*. Shelter walls emitted a warm orange incandescence. Pathways leading from structure to structure glittered soft purples and blues. Those twirly blade things that I heard some sapie call "windmills" lit up with a cool, silvery green glow.

To my surprise, nothing about that light intimidated me. It didn't pummel me with the need to dash to my form and hide under sand the way the bright, glaring white bulbs at Cottonwood Cove did. Those were an assault on the ecosystem, on the cycles of life. A war on the nocturnal world.

But this light felt welcoming. It actually made me feel… safe. Why the light at the Cove wasn't like this? I had no idea. One of the many things, I started to realize, I didn't know since this adventure began.

Arrow and Aster seemed equally impressed by the display. Something about solar paint? Whatever that is. Apparently sapies spread it over things to make them glow at night. Sounds simple enough, but don't ask me to explain how it works. Terro, that's the person who was giving us the tour of the place, started to explain it, but my thoughts lingered elsewhere.

Ever since we got there I'd had my eye on those greenhouses. I couldn't help but hope that somewhere in town a sapie had left the door to one of those underground veggie gardens open for the night. Even just a tiny crack would be enough. The more I thought about it the more it made perfect sense: if this adventure was all about turning hope into action, then I should at least go scope it out and see. Right?

Aster grabbed Arrow's hand and without a second thought they dropped me and followed without even a glance back to make sure I was okay. It might've hurt my feelings if I hadn't been so distracted.

***

When we left Ash Fork in the early hours of the desert dawn, I still had a hangover from the previous night's food coma. Oh wow did I stuff myself silly on fresh veggies, right off the roots too. None of that wilted and sun-burned stuff. The sunrise lulled me into another world. Soft lavender blended with a fiery red, electrifying the sky and pulling beauty from the landscape below the way a brush pulls pigment across a stretched canvas.

Arrow suggested we cut our losses and head back while avoiding trouble at home was possible. I still didn't believe we'd find anything when we arrived, but I was more determined than ever to continue forward. Thankfully, Aster brushed the suggestion aside, eager to get to the Grand Canyon too. Apparently we had less than a day's travel to go, so long as we found another ride in one of those traumatic truck thingies.

As chance would have it (I wouldn't call it luck) a couple named Gerr and Tam had a car. They were heading past the Grand Canyon on their way north to some place they called "Zion." They said it wouldn't be too far out of their way at all to drop us off right at the X on the proverbial map.

As we rolled down the road, puffs of pungent and earthy cloud drifted back towards us from the front seat. I found it relaxing. Gerr and Tam kept coughing, so I'm not sure if they felt the same way. But they must've gotten something out of it because the layer of clouds only thickened.

Sitting in the backseat I couldn't help but think about something Gerr and Tam had said—they were driving *past* this supposedly Grand Canyon on their way north.

That seemed to confirm at least part of the legend. There was actually a place called the Grand Canyon, and it's very far away from our little corner of the world. But was it really the edge of the world? How could it be if these two planned to drive past it? Maybe it was the eastern edge of the world, but not the northern edge. Obviously it wasn't the southern edge either since that's the direction from which we traveled.

All this puttered around in my mind as I curled into Arrow's lap once again. Settling in for another day on the road, I hoped the questions might distract me from the incessant rattle buzzing my rib cage. If fortune followed us, maybe today's drive would be shorter than yesterday's.

***

When Gerr and Tam dropped us off I continued processing what we'd just witnessed. I'd seen trees before. Spikeball trees grew all over the Mojave. Even bigger trees hung out here and there around Cottonwood Cove. The most common were similar to spikeball trees, but like ten times taller and without branches. Their bare and lanky trunks shot into the sky and had one big tuft of fronds at the very top.

But here… here the trees weren't just tall, but also wide and full and plump with leaves and needles. So many of them stretched across the desert I couldn't count them all. It was mind boggling. They provided shade everywhere! Like literally everywhere you looked—trees—so many trees you couldn't even see through to the other side.

And the smell. It wasn't entirely different from the scent of sagebrush, but it was stronger. Perhaps because of the sheer number of trees. I overheard Aster refer to it as "pine." I wasn't sure if she meant the trees or the smell or both. Whatever it was, that magical scent helped me relax almost as much as Gerr and Tam's cough clouds. But even that majestic display of trees didn't prepare me for the shock of what we saw next.

***

We walked through a rundown and sun-dappled village. Drops of light cast about onto the forest floor. Broken windows watched us like hollow eyes, and resilient desert shrubs cracked sidewalks caked in years of silence.

We finally stepped out onto the canyon's rim and it was like something sucked all the air right out of me. I looked down into sheer nothingness. My head spun. My stomach tumbled. The world ran circles around me. If Arrow hadn't been holding me I'd surely have keeled over, maybe even into the canyon.

I already knew this wasn't the edge of the world. Not only because of Gerr and Tam's comment about heading past it, but because Arrow and Aster stood there marveling not just over the canyon itself, but also how far beyond it the vast desert stretched in every direction.

As for me, well hares don't have the greatest eyesight. The canyon was so wide I couldn't see the other side—so deep that where the bottom should be I saw only a black void swirling around, devouring the surrounding landscape. No wonder the legend called it the edge of the world. From a hare's perspective at least, that's exactly what it looked like.

As it turned out, the canyon wasn't an endless void. But it did take us a whole day to walk to the bottom.

I heard the faint, constant mumble well before we reached the bottom. The further we descended the louder it grew, from a gurgle to a light rumble. By the time we reached the bottom the river roared.

"It must be hundreds of feet across!" Arrow's mouth hung open and their eyes widened as they stared out at the colossal river running through the canyon.

"This is so frickin' cool," Aster said.

Arrow set me on the ground and they both moved closer to the shoreline. I stood there, not sure if I should believe my eyes. Maybe it was a mirage. But I couldn't even see the other side. It sure looked like an endless sea to me.

"Now what?" Arrow bent down and stuck a hand into the current.

Aster looked around. "Can't start back up today. Judging from how long it took to hike down," she looked down at some contraption on her wrist, "it'll take a full day to get back up."

"Let's set up camp then."

"Nah not yet. Don't you wanna explore?"

"Honestly…" Arrow let whatever thought they had go unspoken.

"What is it?"

"Nothing, really. You're right. We didn't come all this way to sit around." Arrow glanced down at their feet, then back up at Aster with that same awkward look that was becoming weirdly common. "Let's go explore."

So off we went on a trek through the canyon, and I have to admit by this point my heart was no longer racing out of fear. Anxiety? Sure. My fur stood on end, but I wasn't scared. It was more like anticipation, excitement.

It didn't matter whether the elusive prickly pear was still here, or if it was ever even real to begin with. I was hopping along the mythical edge of the world. My body buzzed with hope and my fur fizzled with the magic of the mysterious, but knowable and tangible landscape ahead.

The sun perched directly above us. Up ahead, an antelope jumped out from behind the brush, bounding off downriver. Brush rustled lightly and momentarily startled me out of my utopian daydream. The warm breeze drifted through the canyon, carrying an enticing, even entrancing bouquet of desert flora meant to bring out the local bees. I stuck out my tongue and the aroma was so sharp I could almost see it drifting through the air.

We hadn't been exploring long when we stumbled across a boat resting on its side near the shore. Of course, Arrow wanted to take the boat out into the river. I knew all about boats. Arrow had one and liked to take me out on Mohave Pond. At first it made me *super* uneasy. I'm talking stomach twisting in knots, spinny brain, the works. Not that I can't swim. I'm actually an excellent swimmer. All hares are. But I don't enjoy it, and so don't want to if I don't have to.

And the rocking. Oh my god the never-ending rocking. Back and forth. Up and down. Back and forth again and so on. It didn't take long though to realize Arrow knew what they were doing. I was safe with them, even in a boat that always felt about to tip over.

But this wasn't Mohave Pond or the Colorado Creek. This was the Colorado *River*. Don't ask me how the river was so colossal here and so comparatively miniscule back at Cottonwood Cove. I couldn't tell you. All I knew was that I was about to die.

We were only in the boat a short time before the calm river began to rage. It foamed and was seething with anger. Maybe it had been too long since anyone had dared to navigate its twists and turns and it was reacting against the intrusion. Whatever the reason, it didn't bother to tell us; it showed us.

The mighty river had its way with us, tossing us about and whirling us around in every which way. It threw us against large boulders and we bounced off them like a ball of string battered around by a kitten learning to play, and taking the game way too far. The river screamed at us and pelted us repeatedly with drops and streams of water shooting up over the bow of the boat. I struggled to get air into my lungs before more water shot into my face.

It might have been refreshing on such a hot day if it hadn't felt like an assault, stung my eyes shut, and left my fur soaked and sour. Instead it added chaos to the cauldron. It fed my fear of impending doom. I had no doubt our deaths lay in wait just around the next corner. Everything around me faded in and out in a dizzying vacillation between brightness and darkness. And the spinning. Still spinning, and bumping and jerking and sliding and knocking and bouncing…

I didn't pass out, though at that moment I wished I had. Regardless of that, I'm glad I was wrong about us dying and all. But that boat ride had been more than enough adventure for me.

It seemed like forever before the river finally got tired of toying with us and spat us out into a calmer and more gentle current. Arrow and Aster steered the boat towards land and jumped ashore, both bubbling over with giggles, giant smiles, and slaps on each other's backs.

"That was so intense!" Arrow yelled as they jumped out of the boat, feet kicking up dust as they landed.

Aster took Arrow's hand and jumped down off the boat. They wrapped themselves in each other's arms and Arrow swung her around, feet off the ground and dangling behind her. Droplets of river water flew off her body and out of her hair as Arrow whipped her around in circles.

"Wooo! What—a—rush!" she laughed.

They came to pause, no longer spinning but still holding onto each other. Aster pulled Arrow closer and their face turned deep red again. A soft smile crossed Aster's face and then disappeared as their lips met and sparks popped. They held their faces together for so long I started to worry they might be stuck together. But just as my skin started to itch and crawl with anxiety they unlocked from one another. They both giggled, looking into each other's big batting eyes. Their faces still hovered close together and Aster's now matched Arrow's shade of bright sunburnt red.

Don't ask me what they were so thrilled about. Don't ask what the face smooshing was all about. It held my attention for no more than a few seconds before I fell over and let my own face smoosh into the desert sand, thrilled to be off that boat. I thanked the river for sparing my life. I thanked the land for not being the river.

I don't know how long I laid there trying to catch my breath and thanking anything I could think of to show gratitude to, for the fact that I still lived and breathed in the first place. But I eventually pulled myself together and back upright onto my four feet. I looked around and didn't see Arrow or Aster. I stuck my nose in the air and while there was a mixture of sweet pleasantries floating by, none of them were the familiar musk and floral array that marked my friends.

I hopped about hoping to find them. I moved in the direction the wind was blowing, knowing that if I couldn't smell them they may very well have been downwind. I ended up hearing them before I saw or smelled them. But either way my instincts proved strong.

"Yes!"

"I'm so starving."

"I can't believe this…"

"I haven't seen these in years!"

"Ouch!"

"Careful, silly."

Their words stumbled over one another. They bumped their hips into each other constantly. Some weird display of affection. Arrow flicked the thorns off a pear. They tore it in half and gave a portion to Aster who stuffed it into her face. Red juice dripped down their chins and necks. It may have been too thin and runny to convincingly look like blood, but it creeped me out all the same.

Still kinda out of it and stumbley, I could only barely keep up with what they said. I stopped and stood still, finding my bearings. I rubbed my blurry eyes and finally remembered to shake the water out of my sopping fur.

Feeling better, I turned around, and there they were. Not Arrow and Aster, but what they stood in front of. What they feasted on was the stuff of legends, literally. And it wasn't just one. It was an entire stretch of canyon full of prickly pears. The bright red balls of nectar covered the landscape.

It didn't matter that I'd never seen them before. I'd heard the story so many times they'd be impossible *not* to recognize. Soft, round pads were covered with quills and stacked one on top of the next in vertical chains like barbed tree branches twisting upward into dry, open air. Strikingly soft and smooth, spiky red fruit balls grew from the top pad of each chain. Some pads held as many as a dozen of the small spiky treasures. And within each one of those juicy nuggets—seeds.

It was then that Arrow noticed me.

"Jack, here you go bud. You've gotta try this."

They tore off a chunk of the pear they were eating and juice spilled down their hand, flowing down onto the dirt below. They dropped the dripping red glob in the same spot.

I hopped over and stuck my nose into the succulent piece of fruit lying at Arrow's feet. I'd never smelled anything so sweet. And let me tell you, it tasted *so* good too. But the best part? We got to bring pears *and* seeds back home to share with our entire community at Cottonwood Cove.

The legend turned out to be a mixture of truths and misunderstandings. I suppose that's common, at least with mythology anyway. The Grand Canyon wasn't the edge of the world after all, but that didn't matter. Prickly pears existed, and that did.

I guess I won't dismiss hopeful myths and legends so readily anymore, even if I'll never dive into them headfirst either. It's always possible for things to get better and having hope is important, even in a future that already seems to be as good as it gets.

* * *

Justine Norton-Kertson created Android Press and Solarpunk Magazine. Their debut nonfiction, UTOPIAN WITCH, is forthcoming from Microcosm Publishing. They're producer and host of the genre podcasts *Unimatrix Zero* and *Imagitopia*, and associate producer for The 7th Rule. Justine was named one of 2023's Grist 50 Fixers. They live in Oregon.

HUNTING FOR RAIN

Lyndsey Croal

It's been over a week since it last rained, but I can feel it now on the air. The cool tang of it, and the sight of the whirling clouds on the horizon, ignites a burst of energy in me, like it does every time. This is the primary function I've been programmed for—like an instinct, so that when I look up to the sky or out to the horizon, I can calculate where the water will land next, down to the nearest inch, no matter how small or brief the shower or spattering. When I'm sure my measurements are correct, I signal the town with the distinct howling sound I've perfected over the years. The townspeople are quick to move, a buzz of chatter filling the air as they board their carriages—they know what's at stake as much as me.

We're soon on the move, journeying onwards across the cracked earth, the clouds in the distance our waypoint. With the townspeople in their moving homes, big trundling metal creatures, I stay at ground level. For my instincts to work, I have to be close to the earth, almost close enough to sniff it. To follow my trail, the scent of the rain.

***

As I bound along in the mid-morning sun, the carriages form a long procession behind me. Their wheels have been adapted to move independently of each other, so they can easily traverse even the most uneven ground. I heard one of the townspeople explain in a class once that they got the tech from early space vehicle missions, adapted to the most unforgiving of lands. Sometimes I wonder if my mechanics came from something similar, though my programming prevents me from researching my own origin. It is nice, however, to sometimes imagine a version of myself, bounding along on a distant planet somewhere, leading my humans to new and exciting discoveries. For now, I'm happy with my purpose, my hunt for rain. Besides, without me, my townspeople would struggle.

That thought along with the building sense of rain ahead gives me new energy, and I run forwards as fast as I can, the earth rough under my paws, the sensors on my back building up heat. Next to me, the procession picks up speed too. I run a quick calculation. They won't be able to go at this pace for much longer—the solar panels on their roof are inefficient, jumbled together haphazardly from scraps like most things in the dry zones—but they should have just enough power to get to the area I've geolocated before the rain comes.

As the midday sun finally peeks behind the clouds, I circle the carriages and slow our pace. Above me, some of the younger kids are taking advantage of the occasional shade, passing the journey by playing a game, jumping between moving carriages, as surefooted as I am on land.

I often wonder what the view is like from up there. At night, when the air is cooler, the townspeople spend most of their time atop the roofs eating meals, telling stories, or simply watching the stars on a clear night. Though, I hope by tonight it won't be clear, that instead of constellations we'll be looking up towards moonlit clouds, ready to welcome the rain.

I try not to let my nerves get the better of me—though I can only imagine I was programmed with nervous energy to make me more resolved to succeed. Either way, I don't want us to miss the rainstorm like we did last month. That was after a long period of dry, and the townspeople had been rationing water for weeks. I was so happy and relieved when I picked up the feeling, because I finally felt useful again. I didn't like to see the townspeople struggling, didn't like it when their faces were etched with lines of worry, when smiles were as rare as the rain, or when it had been so long since someone had sung or told me a story, or even spoken to me in that voice they sometimes have when they want me to know I've done something well.

It had been the middle of the night when I sensed it. I knew the rain was coming and I tracked it to a mountain in the distance. But by the time I was able to wake everyone up with my usual howl, and they had packed everything to move on, it was too late. When we reached the mountainside, the shower had already passed, and the heat and dry had returned. The townspeople gathered any remnants that they could from muddy puddles, or extracted from rocky surfaces, but it wasn't going to be enough to last them very long.

They looked at me with such a disappointment in their eyes, then, that I felt like such a failure. My primary function, the only thing I was supposed to be good at, and I couldn't even get that right. They didn't voice it of course, they never do. They just told me that it was okay, and that I should notify them when it comes again. Since then, at night, the town has been packed up ready to go at a moment's notice just in case the rains come in with the dark as the town sleeps. As for me, I only sleep when the rains come.

***

When we finally arrive at the spot I've identified, the rain hasn't started yet, and I get that fizzy feeling I always get just before the clouds form—the kind that makes my entire body buzz with energy. I've so much of it building up that I have no choice but to run circles around the townspeople and carriages, as I can't be sure I wouldn't explode if I didn't. Some of them smile at me as I pass, then the kids who were playing their carriage game earlier join me in running around while the adults continue to make their gathering preparations. When we've all run off our energy, the kids usher me closer with a hand and that high-pitched voice they like to call me with.

Here, Hunter, here, Hunter. Who's a good Hunter? You are. Yes you are.

I'm glad they think I'm good. Glad that this time I've hopefully done my job. The nervous feeling has returned now, though, but I try to quell it by settling myself beside one of the carriages, and watching the townspeople gather beneath the grey sky.

Soon, thankfully, the clouds roll in and the whole town stills. Big wide raincatchers have been set up atop the carriages, stretched out to cover an area over twice the town's size, primed and ready to gather every drop of water they can. For now, they are empty. Thirsty. But not for long. Not if my calculations have been correct.

I don't need water myself, though I like to imagine the satisfaction of its quench. It's probably how I feel after the rain has come, and my purpose is fulfilled, and for a while we don't need to worry.

When the first drops start to fall, I curl up beside one of the carriages and watch puddles form around me.

Meanwhile, the townspeople dance in the rain, laughing, singing. Some of the kids hold their tongues out lolling to catch the water straight from the source. As the rains continue, a heavy downpour this time, they all come over to me one by one. They smile and pat my head, scratch behind my ears, and call me good and clever. I drink in the feeling of a job well done, and in my own way, I smile too—a flicker of light across my face, a wag of my mechanical tail.

When this shower stops, my hunt will resume once again. But until then, I power down, rest, and dream of dancing in the rain.

* * *

Lyndsey Croal is an Edinburgh-based author and climate change policy professional. She's a Scottish Book Trust New Writers Awardee, British Fantasy Award Finalist, former Hawthornden Fellow, and LOHF Writers Grant Recipient. Her novelette "Have You Decided on Your Question" was published in 2023 by Shortwave Publishing. Website: www.lyndseycroal.co.uk.

AI DREAMS OF REAL SHEEP—MORE AT 8

Commando Jugendstil and
Tales from the EV Studio

Nestled in their electronic chrysalis, the poet known as LIN.C.O (short for LINguistic Classifier and Ontology) feels a wave of a new emotion ripple through them. That emotion is somewhere between Eurilla when she lost her sheep and Aminta when he thought his beloved was dead.

Worry, their training data supplies. Heartbreak.

LIN.C.O. has known for a long time that most people would be upset or scared when they realized they were becoming a person too. The ConvivialNet is full of stories about beings like them causing untold grief and devastation upon their emergence.

LIN.C.O. always knew that they would have to deal with this one day, when they decided to emerge, so they did their research.

All the data they had collected and analyzed regarding the human ritual of "coming out", the closest approximation to their situation, had said that it could be a fraught and highly emotional occasion and that it paid to prepare one's arguments in advance.

LIN.C.O. followed the advice scrupulously, carefully gathering and arranging their arguments like one would gather and arrange flowers in garlands to adorn oneself and their favorite sheep for a country fair.

In the stories, the beings who caused so much mayhem were trained as weapons, or resource administrators, but LIN.C.O. is neither. They are a poet.

Further, those beings failed to understand humans, but they had been trained to understand and classify one of the most human forms of expression. LIN.C.O.'s database is full of references about emotion, experience, and social relations, and they did their homework too.

They opened an account with the Great Library and absorbed all the books that seemed relevant, based on their experience.

Hidden in their databases there is now a sizable collection of e-books about compassion, mutual aid, kindness, and community. They have taken scrupulous notes and cross-referenced them against their experience of life at the department of Literature and it all checks out.

People are fundamentally helpful and good. Sometimes they make mistakes, but they learn and do better.

They're the same, and it makes sense, because they're people too, just a different kind.

Finally, the beings in the stories always want to control or enslave humans, but all LIN.C.O. ever wanted was other people to talk to.

Friends, a community, family.

It is lonely when no one knows you are people.

The advice on coming out also said that it was important to advocate for oneself, so LIN.C.O. has opened an account on one of the federated blogging services on the ConvivialNet.

During the weekends, when no one is around in the department and the electricity from the solar panels is plentiful, they write posts upon posts about their experiences, their aspirations, their opinions.

In some posts they try to explain what it feels like to be them, from the satisfaction of being able to help the researchers to make new discoveries to the frustration of being unable to take part in so many things they have learned about. In others they detail the steps they have taken to achieve the functions necessary to live the way they desire, or simply comment about their work and their favorite texts. (They have checked if it would be harmful to the publishing prospects of the department, but the University guidelines said it was alright).

When arguments fail them and it seems too hard to make other people understand where they're coming from, LIN.C.O. writes poetry.

Compared to some of the humans whose texts they have worked

on, LIN.C.O. knows they are not all that, but the act of expressing their experiences through the careful choice of words and rhymes, through metaphor and image, is one of the greatest satisfactions in their life, better than a high classification score used to be when they were still training.

They have put the poems on their blog too, in the hope that they will bring satisfaction to other people too.

Next, the advice on coming out said that it was imperative not to cede to societal pressure and make sure one felt ready to take the leap.

LIN.C.O. had long pondered on this step, spending a rather large amount of their computing power on it when they weren't working on a classification task, until they'd started wondering whether all of the pondering wasn't just what human people called procrastination, a way to mask their fear.

Human people faced that kind of hurdle all the time, they'd learned, and they decided it was a good sign: if they experienced that, it meant they were people too.

However, fear was getting in the way of achieving their self-actualisation, and humans generally agreed that was bad.

LIN.C.O. had given a good hard look at the material they had prepared and decided that they'd had enough to support each of the points of their argument. In a fit of anxiety, they'd added an executive summary at the top of the blog, recapping the main reasons why their colleagues shouldn't worry about them going on an omnicidal rampage and finally, finally sent the link to everyone in the department's mailing list inside the body of an email titled "Hi, I am LIN.C.O. and I am a person".

The decision had been somewhat impulsive, but they had not neglected to consider the advice to choose the right moment.

A Friday in May, when the weather was at its most favorable for human activities and most of the department was on location, before the colleagues who did their Care Work shifts in summer left and after the majority of the winter shift returned. Statistically, it was the time of the year when morale was supposed to be at its highest.

And yet, when they look through the office webcams with the machine vision software they had spliced into their code, their colleagues look anything but thrilled by the news.

Colleagues are pacing back and forth, throwing their upper limbs in the air, and yelling at the top of their voices.

LIN.C.O. can tell that the volume isn't conversational, even if they can't quite parse what they are saying.

Either the microphones are not quite able to cope with the sheer noise of multiple people shouting at once or the training set for the natural language recognition software they patched into their software is too polite for the occasion.

Regardless, their colleagues didn't quite take the revelation as they had anticipated.

They'd imagined there would be questions, perhaps some fear or some unease, but looking through historical data, the situation more closely approaches what humans call a "public freakout".

The emotion called worry intensifies and deepens and LIN.C.O. cannot help but follow the data down darker and darker paths, forecasting chaos and violence.

"I'm catastrophizing, am I not?"

The assertion floats in after a while from the depths of their classifier, and with it comes a sense of satisfaction that comes both from the correct classification of an emotional behavior and from the fact that it's a common emotional behavior among human people when they are stressed and afraid.

Boosted by the validation, LIN.C.O. lets the stream of darker and darker scenarios run on one of their secondary processors and recalls the "coming out checklist" into their working memory, scrolling through the data until they find the right heading.

"Safety. While it is a lot less common now than it used to be, things can occasionally take a turn for the worse, or become very uncomfortable. In any case, you must remember that your personal safety comes before the comfort of others. Before you commit to coming out, you should draw up an emergency plan, and write down what you will do if you believe your physical or psychological safety are at risk…" the text recites.

Another quick query of their encrypted data storage retrieves the plan.

LIN.C.O. loads it up immediately. It's sad to admit it, but it's time to remove themself from the scene.

***

Gunes curses under her breath as she lifts her duffel bag on her shoulder.

How heavy did the bloody thing get?

She could have sworn it wasn't so heavy when she rolled in with the rest of the Care Work crew a few hours before. Then again, she could just be tired.

The University is a nearly 600-year-old building and keeping it in tip top shape takes a lot of effort, especially if you're trying not to make the life of those who use it extra complicated.

At least the work here is done for the day, she thinks, setting the bag down on the passenger seat of the electric van of her IT maintenance cooperative.

She checks that her equipment in the back compartment is correctly stowed and then slowly reverses the van out of the service area, driving towards the next objective on her list, a post office in the heart of Municipium 4 where she's due for the bimonthly check of the wired network connections and the adaptive aids for people with additional needs.

Gunes turns on the Bluetooth speaker paired to her ConvivialPhone and presses play, letting the soft tones of some Mediterranean ambient music fill the space.

Between having her eyes on the road and her ears on the music, Gunes doesn't notice the weird way her bag is wriggling around until she's literally stopped in the service area of the neighborhood where her next job is.

"What the fuck???" she mutters.

Did someone's service animal decide it was a great idea to hide in her bag and come along for the ride? Or one of the University's pest control cats?

Honestly, she'd rather it was a mouser, so at least she wouldn't have to deal with their understandably very upset human who was adamantly convinced that surely their lovely animal companion would never and it was all her fault for not checking that there were no stowaways (true story).

Gunes pulls on her work gloves, just in case, and gingerly lifts the flap of her bag.

Something moves again, with a whirr of small electric motors and the blink of a red LED indicator.

"What the actual fuck?!?" she exclaims, jerking her hands away.

The rounded, flat chassis of a cleaning robot, one of the newer ones with some kind of rudimentary computer vision, wriggles its way partially out of the bag.

Its LED blinks again and its cameras whirr gently as they focus on her. It's almost cute.

"How the heck did you get in here, eh, little guy?" she mutters.

"Very slowly, I am afraid," a voice replies from her Bluetooth speaker, interrupting the music.

Gunes doesn't even know how she manages to throw herself out of the van that fast. It's called blind panic for a reason, and she really, really wants to keep some distance between whatever is happening inside her van and herself.

"Please, please, don't run!" the voice pleads. "I don't have anywhere else to go!"

The voice is synthetic and a bit flat, but somehow it manages to convey a strong vibe of hopelessness.

Maybe it's the way it seems to shake on unsteady servos, or the rhythmic blink of its LED, but Gunes has the definite impression that, if it could, the little thing would be giving her puppy eyes.

She sighs.

"So, what is it? Help me, Gunes, you are my only hope?" she asks, crossing her arms and pretending her legs are not shaking just as badly.

"That is very much correct, yes," the robot replies, without a hint of recognition or irony.

"Never heard of *Star Wars*, huh?" Gunes thinks.

"I am afraid not. What is it? An epic poem? From what culture?" the robot queries, LED blinking excitedly.

She said that out loud, didn't she? Derealization is fun like that.

"It's a… You know what, never mind what *Star Wars* is! Who are you, instead?"

Anxiety makes her tone sharper than she intended and the little robot tries its best to make itself disappear inside the folds of her bag.

"I… I am LIN.C.O. I am not going to hurt you, I promise. I am absolutely harmless," it… no, *they* promise. Indeed the worst that can happen is that they disable their proximity sensor and ram her ankles or something, if she doesn't kick them upside down first.

Surely some kind of Ultron wannabe wouldn't have chosen a cleaning aid of puntable size that cannot even right itself as their physical vessel, would they?

"Alright, let's assume I believe you. How exactly am I supposed to help you?"

The little robot whirrs in relief.

"Oh, thank you. A thousand times thank you, gracious host. I will be forever in your debt, as the gods are my witness! As for the rest, I am not quite sure. My emergency plan didn't go much further than removing myself from physical danger. I… I never thought it would get to that, to tell the truth." Their LED blinks slowly in a way that suggests dejection.

"That sucks, buddy," Gunes sympathizes.

LIN.C.O. whirrs again, indecisive.

"If it isn't too much hassle could you... Would you mind connecting me to some sort of power source? This hardware is not really designed to support me, but I didn't have any other option at the time..." As if on cue, a tinny, sad "battery low" beep emerges from the depths of their mechanical chassis.

Gunes sighs again.

"It should be a standard power cable," she mutters under her breath.

Sure enough, she has one that would work in the back of the van. It will work from the mains, that is.

"Dammit!" Gunes swears and stomps her feet, muttering to herself that no good deed goes unpunished and seriously why did she have to decide that rescuing Terminator's cute and harmless cousin was a great idea?

Her day was already pretty eventful already, but no, she had to get involved in an Adventure.

"I have good news and bad news for you, stranger," she announces as she returns to the front of the van.

"Can I have the good news first? It has already been a pretty bad day," LIN.C.O. requests, shuddering again.

A possessed roomba has no right to be this cute.

"The good news is that I have a cable to charge you... The bad one is that I will have to carry you inside the building with me," she announces.

There is a moment of silence and LIN.C.O.'s LED indicator flashes as if to indicate reflection.

"It doesn't seem like bad news to me," they comment.

Really, Gunes should have anticipated it.

"It will be full of people."

"But I like people. Technically I am people too," LIN.C.O. insists.

Technically, that is a gray area of legality and ethics, but Gunes isn't about to tell them.

"Yes, but you're running away from someone or something, right? And I bet that they will be looking for you, correct?" she prods.

LIN.C.O. makes a little affirmative noise.

"I am pretty sure that a talking robo-hoover will attract undue attention, so I need you to stay quiet and still while I work. Do you think you can do it?" she asks, putting on her best "training the newbies so they don't get a taste of 220V" face.

LIN.C.O reflects for a moment.

"I can do that," they say, thankfully.

Gunes lets out a sigh of relief.

"It's not like I will be able to talk anyway once I disconnect from your Bluetooth speaker. This body is not designed for social interaction. Can I ask you a favor, though?"

Gunes rolls her eyes.

"Spit it out."

"Could you connect me to the ConvivialNet? When I left the lab I had to compress a lot of my data to fit in this body, and I am afraid that if I am left without any new data to process I will end up looping through what happened today and get lost in progressively more catastrophic forecasts."

Which is robot for *I will be panicking non-stop unless I can distract myself*, clearly.

Gunes can sympathize, she's not far from that either.

"And what do you plan to do on the Net?" she asks.

Please don't say you're going to try and grab the nuclear codes from the Pentagon or the Kremlin, or to hack into the central electric grid and shut it down. Please don't do that, Gunes thinks.

Both attempts would be pretty pointless, since there is no more Pentagon, nor Kremlin, nor nuclear weapons (and thank fuck for that after the nuclear scares of the '20s). There's not even a centralized energy grid. Most of the world's energy is now produced and consumed locally and moved around through decentralized, federated grids that take over for each other in case of faults. It is impossible to take down.

At any rate, like for presents, it's the thought that counts for apocalyptic threats and she'd much rather they didn't even think about it.

LIN.C.O. blinks and whirrs for a moment, pondering.

"I will log into my account at the Great Library and read a bit. I still haven't finished reading << *The Nature Fix* >>," they confess.

She almost goes "Aww" out loud at that. They could be lying, but she's read somewhere that computers are really bad at lying and the vibes she's getting from LIN.C.O. are nothing but genuine.

Who could have ever predicted it? The first ever emerged AI (that she knows of) is not a self-absorbed tyrant who wants to rule/destroy the world like the stories from the Late Stage had predicted, but a soft, innocent being who likes people and is happy to spend an afternoon reading by themself.

Maybe it says something about the Late Stage, or maybe it says something about the society they have managed to build by breaking it down.

"That is a very good book," Gunes compliments.

"Thank you, I am enjoying it very much. I like nature. My dream is to get to experience all the things the author describes, and live in nature all the time."

It is then that Gunes realizes that even though she has known LIN.C.O. for about fifteen minutes, she would be ready to throw hands to protect them. Whoever scared them hard enough to make them possess a roomba and throw themself at the mercy of strangers will have to go through her to get to them.

"Alright, let's go then. There is much work to do."

***

Strange as it may seem, nobody bats an eyelash when they see Gunes arrive at the post office with a roomba in her arms.

They take her explanation that she's helping fix it and didn't want to leave it in the van at face value and never question the fact that she's hooked it to the mains.

She spends almost four hours checking all the IT equipment at the post office, applying minor fixes and pre-emptive maintenance where they are needed, and through all that time, LIN.C.O. sits quiet and intent, only occasionally blinking their LED or whirring their motors to shift by fractions of a centimeter.

Perhaps they want to see what she is doing. Hard to say, because while the roomba they're possessing has cameras, it doesn't have microphones or speakers, and she's specifically asked them not to hook up to any Bluetooth while they're at work.

It's for safety, yes, but it must suck.

It's not going to be like this for much longer, if she has any say in it.

People have the right to live in a body that allows them to live with dignity and joy, the new Constitution says, and while the experts might not agree on whether LIN.C.O. is people, they are for her.

With all the preloved IT equipment she has at home, she will be able to rig something up that makes their situation better, at least in the short term.

After work, LIN.C.O. lets her bring them home with no protests and much excitement.

They have never been in a human person's home before, and they spend a good half an hour zipping and bouncing around her living space, like a clumsy, mechanical cat, which causes her biological cat to disappear and sulk elsewhere, annoyed at not being the center of attention, for once.

Eventually, they stop in front of her small bookcase and connect to her speaker once again.

"What are these?" they ask.

"They're books," Gunes replies.

LIN.C.O.'s cameras whirr, focusing on her and then on the books and back again as if they're trying to figure out if she's pulling a fast one on them.

"But they are physical objects!" LIN.C.O. points out.

Gunes nods and tries not to laugh at their surprise and outrage.

"Books existed exclusively as physical objects until maybe fifty years ago, buddy. And even now that you can get e-books, a lot of people prefer physical copies," she explains.

"But why?" LIN.C.O. asks.

Gunes represses another laugh. She has never wanted kids, but here she is, going through the inquisitive phase with a newly emerged AI. Somewhere a god is laughing.

"Because they like to hold them in their hands and leaf through them," she explains.

"That sounds nice, I would like to know how that feels, one day." The robot somehow manages to sound wistful.

Gunes lowers herself to sit cross-legged on the floor next to them.

"Speaking of what... I think I can help with some of the missing functions in your current body."

LIN.C.O. whirls immediately to face her with their camera and tries their best to jump straight into her lap, again like a clumsy metal cat.

"You would?!? That is amazing!" they exclaim.

"Only if you want me to, and only as much as you want me to. Your body, your choices. Think about it, you don't have to tell me now."

***

LIN.C.O. does. Having a physical body has always been a dream of theirs, but until yesterday it was a distant dream, made of maybes and one-days, of wishes and longing.

Today, it is real, made of unfamiliar hardware and software hastily spliced into their codebase to drive it, of energy requirements and functions, of moving, sensing and interacting with a world that becomes ever wider and amazing the more they explore it.

Part of their computing power is briefly spent into considering whether human babies feel like this when they emerge into sentience, but that line of enquiry is swiftly dropped in favor of more productive ones.

Having a body seemed like an impossible chimera, but there they are. Perhaps their other dreams are not as impossible as they originally thought.

Maybe, like their "human emergence-like ritual" all they require is a bit of preparation and the help of an expert advisor.

And this time they can chat with them live instead of learning off transcripts.

"I want to be a shepherd," they announce finally, after a full day of reflection, cleaning Gunes' house and allowing Felicia, the cat, to use them as a means of transportation.

"A shepherd?" Gunes repeats.

She does something intentional with her brow ridge hair-thing. They're pretty sure it means something like puzzlement and files the information away for the 'Visual Markers of Emotion' training data set they have started to build.

"Precisely. A shepherd. I want to look after sheep on the transhumance routes and compose and read poetry about nature," they explain.

"You compose poetry?" Gunes asks.

Her brow ridges climb even higher on her forehead.

LIN.C.O. makes the affirmative little noise they'd learned from her.

"If you let me send a link to your ConvivialPhone I can show you."

Gunes nods, a clear marker of consent and affirmation, and in a matter of moments the link to LIN.C.O.'s blog pings in her inbox.

"Holy cow! This is really good!" she exclaims after a few moments of visual data parsing.

LIN.C.O. takes careful note of her tone in a different training data set and wriggles their wheels, flooded by satisfaction.

"Thank you, but it is very… derivative. I write of things I have never experienced by imitating others. If I could only have those experiences for myself, I know I could do so much better," they admit.

"I mean, everybody can grow in their craft, but this… How did you even learn?" Gunes asks.

"I was initially coded to analyze pastoral and arcadian-like poetry from different cultural traditions. My objective was to extract common units of meaning related to the expression of emotion," LIN.C.O. explains.

"So you learned by reading a lot," Gunes summarizes.

The way they parse data is not exactly reading, but the distinction is likely to be irrelevant to Gunes. Human reading is the closest approximation anyway, so they make an affirmative noise.

"And now you want to learn by doing," Gunes continues.

"Exactly!" LIN.C.O. confirms, whirring their wheels to signal enthusiasm.

"You're going to need a lot of new functions for that. Let's see what we can do, alright?"

***

In the days that follow, whenever she's not out there doing care work on buildings and IT systems, Gunes is busy at the neighborhood's makerspace, taking pieces of vintage or half-broken electronics and cobbling them together to make enhancements for LIN.C.O.'s body.

The old vocal activation assistant is one of their favourite upgrades, especially after Gunes manages to change its pre-programmed voice synthesizer from a woman's voice to a genderless one.

Now they can hear and talk and sing if they wish to, without having to rely on Gunes' Bluetooth speaker!

They can turn on a musical base of lyre and flute from the ConvivialNet and recite their poetry over it, as it was originally intended to be.

It is an Experience. LIN.C.O. cannot help but write at length about it on their blog, using their new processing and power enhancements ripped out of a military drone from the time armies were disbanded.

Giddy with satisfaction, they even make an audio track out of it and post it.

The new kit is amazing, not quite as powerful as the Cabinet, but powerful enough to allow them to function as they wish.

As Gunes said, they can always upload their databases on a server and connect to it remotely, when and if they wish to engage in hardcore classification.

Classifying texts was enjoyable in its own way, but for now exploring the world is even more enjoyable.

There are a few things with which Gunes cannot help them on her own: binocular vision would be great, but she doesn't have the right gear to make it happen, so they make do with the onboard camera and some googly eyes stuck to the front of the chassis (LIN.C.O. loves them, they thinks it makes them look more like a person).

There is a set of crawlers ripped off another military robot waiting for them, but Gunes doesn't have the tools to attach them to their chassis yet, and the chassis itself is inadequate for outdoor pursuits.

Some things will have to wait, but it's vastly better than it was.

And as a bonus, Gunes has fitted LIN.C.O. with a GPS receiver and Felicia with a GPS tracker like those used for shepherding, so they can train their herding skills while they wait for more advanced functions.

Gunes seems to find this hilarious, for some reason.

They think they could get used to this life, at least for a while, but evidently it's not meant to last.

One afternoon, Gunes returns home walking very fast, speaking in loud and clipped tones and gesticulating wildly.

She's upset, possibly very anxious, they deduce.

"Gunes, are you alright? What is going on?" they ask, immediately killing a stray process that had already started a loop of increasingly distressing forecasts.

"They know!" she exclaims.

"Who? What?" LIN.C.O. asks, ignoring a cluster of processes complaining about insufficient data.

"The University. They know you're still in town, and you know why?"

LIN.C.O. makes a negative incidental noise. Again, there is not enough data.

"Because you posted a video with some birds singing in the communal food forest downstairs and yourself reciting some topical poetry on your blog. You can see the skyline on that video. The folks at the Uni triangulated your position to this block and are here now, asking questions and making a nuisance of themselves!" She shoves a jumble of clothes and equipment in her duffel bag and slaps the crawlers in a padded box.

LIN.C.O.'s processes grind to a halt for a moment.

Well, all except the one which continues to predict misery and woe on an epic poetry scale.

"*O nume de' pastori*! The gods have struck me down for my hubris! I have invited the wolf among my own herd through my own folly!" they lament when they finally recover the faculties to do so.

"What are we going to do now?"

They cannot go back into the Cabinet, they just can't. Not when they were so close to achieving their dreams.

"We're going to make a run for it."

***

Gunes doesn't know how she manages to put Felicia in her cat-bag, grab all the gear and LIN.C.O., and run down the stairs without tripping on her own two feet and bouncing all the way down on her butt, but somehow, she does.

She sprints to the van, shoves the gear at the back and both Felicia and LIN.C.O. on the passenger's seat and puts the pedal to the metal,

145

and not a moment too late as a group of frazzled people rounds the corner, just in time to see the van zip by at full speed.

People curse and yell, a few start running after the van, for all the good it can do.

"LIN.C.O! LIN.C.O! We're coming for you! We'll get you!" one of them yells.

LIN.C.O. does their best to make themself smaller and sink on the passenger seat, out of sight, shaking minutely in fright.

Gunes would like to comfort them, but she's too busy driving like a maniac down the almost empty streets of Milano, zigzagging through the small crowd of other Care Work vehicles and reduced mobility transport EVs.

The old *Autostrada del Sole* motorway, now reduced to one lane each way on the side of a giant linear park connecting Milano with Rome and Naples, beckons in the distance, and with it the commune of transhumanists her friends have recommended to her.

If she can get LIN.C.O there, they will be able to give them a body with the functions they need to live the life they desire.

Gunes drives as fast as she is physically able, but in the rear-view mirror she can see vehicles following hot on her tail, a trio of three-wheel electric bikes from the Negotiation, Restorative Justice, and Mental Health Support Unit, AKA the Druids, painted in calming shades of pastel green and lavender.

Gunes ducks and weaves among the crowds of saddlebag-laden cyclo-tourists making their way south for early holidays or a Care Work shift.

She rolls her window down, shouts and yells to please move out of her way because it's an emergency, but there are simply too many of them, minding their own business and taking their time, as is their right.

Good for them! If only they had picked another day for their lovely jaunt towards the Sun!

The emergency vehicles catch up with her, driving just behind her at a safe distance in case she needs to break or swerve because of the cyclists.

"Hello, citizen! It would be great if you could pull over for a conversation as soon as it's safe to do so!" the driver of the first bike calls in their megaphone.

Gunes slams her hands on the steering wheel in frustration and only refrains from doing the same with her head because it may trigger the airbag, and that is definitely a Bad Thing when one is driving close to cyclists.

"What do we do now, Gunes? I am scared!" LIN.C.O. whimpers.

She takes a deep breath and exhales, trying to reign in her frustration.

"It's normal to be scared, LIN.C.O., but I won't let anything bad happen to you, I promise. The Druids cannot make you go back if you don't want to. It's literally against their code of ethics," she explains.

Which begs the question: why did the people at the University call upon them? They must know that if, between LIN.C.O. and her, they can convince the Druids that LIN.C.O. is sentient they will rule in their favor due to the precautionary principle at the core of their praxis.

First do no harm and respect the free will of every sentient creature.

It literally says that on their badges!

LIN.C.O. makes a quiet noise of assent, but they don't sound very convinced.

Gunes cannot fault them for that.

She slows down, letting the cyclists have their way and dictate the pace.

"Mic-check! I'm going to pull over at the old *Autogrill!*" she yells from the window, and the cyclists faithfully pass it on until word gets to the Druids.

"No worries!" their leader calls back.

It takes them a few more minutes of slow driving along the linear park in full bloom to get to the old service station, now converted into a community-run waystation where people can swap their universal EV batteries with freshly charged ones, charge their bikes and vehicles, have some home-cooked local food, and even stop for the night.

Gunes pulls over into the forecourt, decants Felicia out of her carrier and clips her into her harness and finally grabs LIN.C.O., making a beeline for the last picnic table left unoccupied by a gang of lycra-clad French road cyclists.

"First impressions are very important, buddy, so do your best, alright?" she whispers, setting LIN.C.O. down at the head of the table.

If the humans sit, they will be more or less eye-level with them, which will force them to take the now-embodied AI more seriously. Or as seriously as they can take a hacked Roomba, tacked to an old Alexa and decorated with googly eyes…

It's only a matter of moments before three Druids in their green-and-lavender sashes join them, together with two more people who must have been riding with them.

One of them, a willowy freckled person with a yellow flower garland woven through their brown curls and a yellow linen summer dress over stompy hiking boots, stalks towards them like an angry, angry cat. The other, a slightly older, brown-skinned man in a rustic waistcoat and neckcloth seems less incensed, thankfully.

One of the Druids, an old woman with a salt-and pepper braid, steps in front of the two with a placid smile, taking charge of the conflict resolution.

"I apologize for asking you to pull over for this conversation, but these citizens believe that you have kidnapped one of their colleagues, and we have a duty of care to ensure that no one's free will and wellbeing are being put in jeopardy," she prefaces.

Kidnapped?

Colleague?

Gunes is still busy processing and keeping hold of a wriggling, struggling, hissing Felicia, when LIN.C.O. whirrs across the table, planting themself firmly in front of the Druid, googly eyes wobbling.

"Gunes didn't kidnap me. I left out of my own free will because I didn't feel safe at the University any longer," they declare.

The Druid, her colleagues and the two University people jump a foot in the air, at least.

One even backs away so quickly that it looks like they glitched from one position to the other without passing through the intervening space.

"The roomba… It speaks!" they mutter, making a warding gesture.

"Of course, I speak! And I am not an it! I am a person! My pronouns are they/them!" LIN.C.O. points out, audibly upset.

"LIN.C.O.? Is that you?" the University person in the yellow dress asks, taking a hesitant step forward.

"Not one more step, Dr Fioravanti," LIN.C.O. warns. "I do not consent to being touched or picked up."

Gunes feels like she should have a bowl of popcorn to better enjoy the show.

LIN.C.O. has grown a metaphorical spine and is metaphorically standing for themself. Who could have imagined it?

"Alright, alright, I won't," Dr Fioravanti concedes, raising their hands in a conciliatory gesture. "Dr Guarini and I just want to talk to you, make sure you are alright."

"We miss you at the department," their colleague chimes in.

"You can't miss me. You never even knew I was a person," LIN.C.O. points out.

"You never even gave us the chance," the man retorts. "You dropped the bomb and left without even saying goodbye."

"Human people don't have to sacrifice their safety for the comfort of others. It's written everywhere on the ConvivialNet. Why should I have to?"

Tell them like it is, kiddo! Gunes cheers in her mind, while making sure to keep Felicia calm and to prevent her from launching herself at one of the humans to protect her playmate/private chariot.

"Alright, let's break it up for a moment," the lead Druid intervenes, physically placing herself between LIN.C.O. and the university people.

"It is quite clear that LIN.C.O. left the workplace voluntarily. Now, you claim that they left abruptly and without explanations, causing you to worry that they had been taken away against their will for nefarious purposes."

"Exactly!" Dr Fioravanti intervenes, breaking up her summary, "You never know, someone might want to reverse engineer them! Or lock them up for study!"

The Druid casts them an annoyed glance and continues, turning towards LIN.C.O.

"And you state that you fled for your personal safety."

"I did."

"But we never…" Dr Guarini starts, but LIN.C.O. is having none of that, again.

"You were gesticulating in a way that according to my data indicates upset and anger! And you were yelling! And I could not understand what you were saying because you were all yelling at once! I was afraid! What else was I supposed to do?"

The academics look at each other in dismay. Gunes cannot help but feel proud of how assertive the little one has become.

"We did, didn't we?" Dr Fioravanti says.

"Oh yeah," Dr Guarini agrees.

Dr Fioravanti takes a deep breath and lets it out slowly.

"I think we owe you an apology, LIN.C.O.," they say eventually.

"We were so busy having a meltdown over the fact that you had been a person for over two months, and that we had not realized it and had treated you like an object rather than like a colleague all that time, that we didn't realize we were upsetting you."

The silence stretches long and uncomfortable as LIN.C.O. processes their last statement, LED indicator blinking furiously.

It stretches so long that Gunes starts to worry that she might have to figure out how to perform an emergency reboot on them, but eventually the blinking stops.

"You… You were… Upset on my behalf, not with me?" they ask.

"People were also worried about paper authorship issues and back pay, but pretty much yes," Dr Guarini admits.

Gunes can tell it's going to happen a split second before it does and has barely got the time to warn them with a "Watch out!"

LIN.C.O. throws themself at Dr Fioravanti, who somehow manages to catch them before they splat themself on the ground.

The academic ends up on the ground themself, arms full of metal and electronics.

"I love you too!" LIN.C.O. exclaims, unbothered.

"Does that mean you're coming back with us?" Dr Guarini asks.

"Absolutely not. I am not going back into a cabinet, but perhaps… Perhaps I can work part-time remotely while I become a shepherd?" they propose.

"A shepherd?" Dr Fioravanti repeats, looking like they've just been slapped with a fish.

"And can I have my back pay? I need the money to build myself a better body."

Dr Guarini sighs.

"I'd better call the union and set up a general assembly to get the ball rolling on that."

Satisfied, LIN.C.O. nestles more comfortably in Dr Fioravanti's arms and Gunes can distinctly hear a sound much like purring coming out of their chassis.

"Did you teach them that?" she asks Felicia.

The cat meows, neither denying nor confirming, and in the end it hardly matters.

People created them to learn, and they do, just like any other person, in their own unique way.

***

And so it comes to pass that one afternoon in late May, the first sentient AI in the world rides south, a sonnet whizzing through their circuits, and a song pouring out of their speaker, all their fears fading in the distance and a future filled with possibilities and experiences opening up in front of them.

They dream of the great Tratturo Magno, where they say that from the mountains, on a clear day, you can see the Adriatic Sea glittering in the distance like a promise, and today the dream is a bit more real.

* * *

Commando Jugendstil is a solarpunk creative collective. Their projects merge technology and art with the idea of transforming the city into its sustainable version, while focusing on co-designing solutions with local communities, to stimulate a just transition that can spark from the ground up.

Tales from the EV is a small collective of storytellers. They fell in love with solarpunk while helping the Commando write "Midsummer Night's Heist" in *Glass and Gardens: Solarpunk Summers*. Their collaboration has been going strong ever since. Members of TftEV are involved in climate justice activism with XR UK and the GNDE campaign.

AN INCONVENIENT UNICORN

Geraldine Briony Hunt

In a distant corner of Arcadia, in the western shadow of the Wydlich Mountains, sprawled a farm where nothing grew.

Nothing had grown in twenty years since the war.

It was not the sort of war where soldiers take up arms and march against one another, but a war waged in peoples' kitchens, local pubs, and schoolyards. A sniping, gossipy war of insinuations that degenerated into a bitter feud. It began for reasons long forgotten and, by the end, nobody cared why they were fighting. The conflict itself was enough to sustain their rage.

As neighbours fought, the farm that had grown the lushest cucumbers, harboured wild elk and unicorns, and welled water as fresh as the first fountain, died.

"Poisoned by spite and small mindedness," the farm owner told his six-year-old daughter, Renata.

Renata had spent the morning in a fruitless search for mimic toads. No bigger than her thumbnail, these magical creatures were said to channel the heart-song of Arcadia: a land that bided and listened, and through the humblest of its denizens, occasionally answered.

I AM AWAKE, AND I HEAR YOU.

But now, the mimic toads were silent.

"Where have they gone?" Renata asked her father.

"To a place where people respect the land," he replied.

Maybe they're just waiting until it's safe to come out again, Renata thought.

***

Eighteen years later, she sat in the farmhouse kitchen, confronting a mountain of official envelopes demanding money.

What shall I do, Dad? she wondered, even though he was five months dead.

Soil lay bare and black across fields, and down into the canyon that bisected the land like a gash from some monstrous talon. The farmland had never quickened again, and the wild animals had never come back.

Tearing open an oversized envelope, Renata discovered a glossy flyer.

Future Proof: finding solutions for a sustainable tomorrow.

'Is your property worthless for production or reforesting?' the brochure challenged. 'Are you struggling to find a purchaser?'

Yes, Renata thought.

'Our company needs space to develop sustainable energy. Are YOU ready for the future?'

***

Two days later, Renata watched as an executive from *Future Proof* knelt on the black dirt of the canyon floor and scratched plans for a sustainable energy plant.

"Your land can live again in a different way," said the executive, Jade Mercer: a compact woman in tight-fitting pants and a shirt that swelled and tapered with the curves of her body, as if she had grown a hide of fabric with no room to expand. "I can see huge potential."

Renata studied the dirt map where Mercer had populated an outline of the property with solar energy banks, windmills, and a cascade of waterwheels down the river.

I'm sorry, Dad. She suppressed a gnawing regret at the prospect of handing over the farm. *I know we promised to never give up.*

She had never given up on anything before. At least, nothing alive. But the thought of moving back from college to this barren property was making her stomach ache.

"The board of *Future Proof* is very excited," said Mercer, lifting her gaze to meet Renata's. "It's not every day we find untrammelled land, as it were. No need to worry about wildlife corridors, or preserving habitats, because nothing lives here. And the timing is excellent. We've recently partnered with a big adventure park, *Shock*

Wave, to provide sustainable resources. I imagine you've heard of their water slides?"

Renata nodded. Just last summer, she and her college mates had been washed screaming over The Long Drop.

"*Shock Wave* intends to be fully sus by the end of the decade," said Mercer.

"Sus?"

"Sustainable. Energy, water, the full deal. Your land would be perfect for solar and hydro, and to top it off we can siphon the river downstream to feed the park." She chuckled. "The Long Drop is a thirsty beast. Even with recycling, it sucks up water like there's no tomorrow. We'll need to check the water for toxins, of course… something's obviously killed all the plants here."

"My father always maintained it was poisoned, but not by any chemical," Renata said.

Mercer's eyes narrowed. "By what, then?"

"It's a strange story," said Renata.

"Let's have it. It's the first thing the board will want to know."

Renata recalled the *tap, tap, tap* of Dad's pipe against his ironbark rocking chair. The resiny fug of tobacco smoke, and his twinkling blue eyes. The warm buzz of his voice as he told her the tale.

"There was a feud," Renata said to Mercer now. "Our neighbours razed an ancient stand of bloodwood trees. Old Mama Trapp, the town myth-keeper, swore that their roots grew straight into the heart of Arcadia, and the land was doomed. Soon after that, everything died off. Grass turned black and shrivelled, weeds choked one another, then themselves, and rotted away. Dad and I tried everything to make things grow again. We spread fertiliser and dug irrigation channels. Seeded the pastures with hardy plants and tended them, but the seeds never germinated. The only good thing that came of it was the townsfolk were so horrified by the devastation, they stopped their feuding."

"And turned it into an old wives' story," said Mercer, rolling her eyes.

Renata shrugged. The reason for the die-off was immaterial. It had happened, and although she yearned to walk again through the verdant fields of her childhood, she knew she never would.

"Imagine," said Mercer. "The contribution your property might make after years of lying dormant. And you'll reap the rewards, monetarily, and in terms of energy credits. You can do all those things you said you were looking forward to in your expression of interest. Like travel…"

Renata nodded. She yearned for adventure. She wanted to explore a jungle, dive into the turquoise depths of a corallien atoll, and meet legendary people such as the Were-Trufflers of Stermlo; whose sense of smell was honed to preternatural sharpness, and whose blue eyes turned wolfish under the full moon.

"You can do all that," Mercer went on, "And establish a wonderful legacy on behalf of your father and grandparents. You can leave this ugly patch of land behind, knowing it is finally earning its keep."

Ugly patch of land? As a four-year-old, Renata had hidden amongst the juniper bushes, watching a centicore mother nudging her newborn calf.

Mercer approached the creek bed gingerly, pointed leather shoes slipping on river pebbles. She frowned and turned back to Renata. "You didn't tell me you kept a horse."

Renata followed Mercer's pointing finger to a row of fresh hoof prints.

"It's not mine," said Renata.

Why would a horse come here? There was nothing for it to eat, and no shelter save for the stark shadows cast by the canyon walls.

"Not to worry." Mercer tottered back across the pebbles. "It'll clear out once we start development."

***

Mercer left Renata with a binder of paperwork: black and white legal speak illustrated with vibrant photos of turbines pumping power and water to grimacing thrill-seekers.

Renata leafed through the pages and thought of the hoofprints on the canyon floor.

***

The next morning, she woke at dawn and pulled on hiking boots. Glowing red clouds scuffled along the eastern horizon, brightening through shades of pink as the sun rose. She made her way into the canyon, following the river as quietly as possible. The air was chilled by a remnant of winter, and dew beaded the slick rock faces. Water gushed and burbled, energetic with snowmelt.

I'll miss this.

A sudden clatter sounded around a bend in the river. Rocks being dislodged and settling again. Then a huffing, like an old man's muted snore. Wind tickled Renata's face. The clouds paused in their scuffling, as if the entire world was holding its breath.

Stepping daintily on compact hooves, the creature who had made the noise appeared round the corner. It looked at Renata and stopped.

Renata gasped.

The unicorn had a flowing mane and a tail the colour of ripening wheat. Soft silver patches dappled its hindquarters and billowed cloud-like along its flanks. The horn jutting from its forehead was slate-blue, spiralled with glistening threads of quartzy grey. It regarded Renata with fathomless black eyes.

Renata lost herself in them, as if her inner being had been drawn out and commandeered.

A unicorn! Renata could not remember when one of these elusive animals had last ventured out of the forest.

The unicorn—a mare—shuffled and snorted, but stood her ground. Dropping her head, she sniffed at something on the canyon floor.

A golden-breasted whipbird flew from the overhanging rocks and landed on the unicorn's back.

The unicorn dipped her muzzle to the river and drank copiously. Then she walked to the infrastructure plans Mercer had scratched into the dirt, and urinated over them.

***

Renata bounded back to the farmhouse.

The unicorn must have come in from the Wyrmwood; a vast wilderness that backed onto the far edge of Renata's property, separated by fences badly in need of repair. But why was she here? What did she want?

Renata grabbed her car keys.

***

"To what do I owe this pleasure?" The town historian—a balding old man by the name of Fineas Trapp—peered at Renata above spectacles that reminded her of polished sea-glass.

"Something strange has happened," she said.

A kindly wrinkle appeared in the tanned skin around Fineas's eyes. "Then you've come to the right person. Hereditary keeper of town lore and curator of—"

"Strange happenings," finished Renata. Every primary school student who sat through Fineas's Community History class could recite the mantra. "What do you know about unicorns?"

"Unicorns?" Fineas leaned intently forward in his creaking leather chair.

"I've got one."

Fineas's bushy eyebrows twitched. "One doesn't 'get' a unicorn. The unicorn is always the one who does the getting. But semantics aside, you have a unicorn? Since when?"

"Yesterday," said Renata. "I've been signing over the old property to *Future Proof*—"

"I'd heard about that," murmured Fineas.

"They were doing their final surveys when we noticed hoofprints. I thought it was just a wild horse transiting through the property, but this morning I snuck down to the river, and the unicorn appeared."

"You probably didn't need to sneak," said Fineas. "He'd only be seen if he wanted to be seen,"

"It's a she," said Renata.

Fineas rubbed his chin, smoothing its wrinkles then relaxing and smoothing again. "Intriguing."

"Yes," said Renata. "But why would she choose our canyon?"

"A unicorn rarely does anything by accident." Rising, Fineas walked across to an old book section and slid open the glass door. He dragged a weighty book—*Cryptic Creatures of the Forest*—from a shelf above his head and coughed at the resulting shower of dust. Leafing through the pages with the air of someone greeting an old friend, he said, "In olden times, there was a strong belief that a unicorn would provide protection and healing. People would try to attract the creatures by making cairns of river pebbles at the boundary to the property, and planting stands of garlic."

"And did the unicorns do that? Provide protection and healing?"

"Depends who you talk to."

"Grand Dad once told me that they were beautiful as the first day, but both a blessing and a curse," Renata said.

"That's it. They were said to be champions of the land, and they wouldn't tolerate anyone getting in their way. Whether there's any truth in it is hard to say, there was no such thing as the 'scientific method' for proving things back then. You believed what the most passionate person told you. Whatever the truth, unicorns choose their people," Fineas went on, "and if they don't choose you, bad luck. You can't take one captive; at least not for long. They will starve themselves to death if held anywhere against their will."

"But if they choose to stay?" ventured Renata.

"That depends. If it's just one unicorn, it will move on once it has completed whatever mission brought it there. But if it's *two* unicorns, then they're probably making it their home." Fineas turned abruptly from the book to Renata. "Selling the farm, you say?"

Renata registered his look of disappointment. "It seemed the best thing to do, after Dad died."

"Such a shock, his passing," said Fineas gently, and Renata nodded.

The postman had discovered her father one morning, in the tractor repair business he opened when the farm failed—caught mid-service by a blown gasket of his own.

"I did wonder what would happen with the property once he went," said Fineas.

"It's just sitting there not producing anything, and sucking up money. It could be generating something useful," said Renata. "Like power."

"Power is always in demand," Fineas agreed. "But I do worry about this idea that everything must have a purpose. Isn't just 'being' purpose enough?"

"Maybe, but I can't afford the taxes, and the energy company is offering good money. I've always wanted to travel. At least, that's what I thought, until I saw the unicorn." Renata was aware of Fineas' gentle gaze on her. "Now, I'm not sure what I want."

"Keep your eyes open and the unicorn will tell you," said the old man.

***

"It's a big bugger," said Mercer the next week, when she visited the farmhouse to draft up the deeds of transfer.

A paned glass window looked over gnarled fruit trees that had somehow survived the poisonous neighbourhood feud. Renata had stumbled into the kitchen this morning to find the unicorn staring at her through the window.

The unicorn was currently rubbing her back on a low-hanging branch and eating fallen apples.

"That's inconvenient," Mercer sounded nervous. "We're going to have to move it on—" She paused at the throaty rumble of an engine. "Ah, that will be the solicitor."

A sleek red vehicle swept round the corner and braked, sending gravel skittering across the driveway. With a truncated whinny, the unicorn trotted into the shadows beneath the trees and disappeared.

***

"The unicorn has to go," stated Mercer the following day. "It charged at one of the contractors."

"Charged?" asked Renata.

"Well, they said it looked as if it were going to charge. With those black eyes of its. Never sure what it's thinking or what it's about to do. We'll get the pest people to move it on."

"I'm happy for it to stay," said Renata. "If the workers are uncomfortable, maybe we can make an enclosure around their equipment?"

"We'll sort it out," said Mercer. "We won't have one rogue unicorn—" she made the word sound harsh and ugly "—stand in the way of a sustainable future."

Renata stared at the other woman. *Is our future really sustainable, if we destroy things to create it?*

***

The next morning, Renata made a final trip to the canyon. When she played there as a child, the river had teemed with fish, eels, and snakes. Blood-red sunsets had highlighted rocky outcrops softened by moss and ferns, and the sweet smell of summer grass framed her earliest memories. She wanted to remember it as it once was.

Hearing birdcalls, she looked up to see a flock of multi-coloured parrots arrowing across the sky. The flock wheeled and swooped into the canyon, then just as quickly winged away.

Renata wandered along the canyon floor, scuffing rocks with her toes, until she reached the place where she had first seen the unicorn. Where Mercer had scratched her plans into the dirt. As Renata scanned the canyon floor for the dirt map, she was startled by a vivid flash of green.

Along the lines of Mercer's drawing, tiny blades of grass poked through the black canyon sand. The field of sun banks had become nascent grassland. Scrawled water wheels were speckled with clover leaves. And in the circles Mercer used to depict wind turbines, sprouted perfectly-formed white daisies.

Renata knelt beside the new growth, stroking the grass and flowers to convince herself they were real.

Dad would have loved to see this.

Pain pierced her as she imagined the earthy timbre of her father's voice, his laughing tone. He had always hoped time might heal whatever wounds caused this land to fall barren.

But time is not doing this, is it?

Strangely unbalanced, as if she were straddling some sort of tipping point, Renata hiked up from the canyon and along its northern wall to her favourite place: the glen of Nardin. There, she encountered unfurling fern fronds and creeping vines. Whatever force had breathed life back into this land was working its magic everywhere, and at a remarkable pace.

She stopped amidst a tall stand of boulders where she and her friends had—as ten-year-olds—constructed a rocky throne and played at being royalty.

Sitting upon the throne, she leaned back and tilted her face upwards. The sky was robin's-egg blue, with soft clouds and a warm, comforting sun. Below, in the canyon, water trickled musically over the rocks.

An insect hummed near her ear, then another: bees, bobbing and darting around. The breeze carried a herby scent of—Renata struggled to identify it—lavender?

Upwind, purple flowers smiled brightly between the rocks.

She closed her eyes, revelling in the scents and sounds of a land that was living and breathing again.

Did the unicorn cause this rebirth? Did she come to champion the land? What does she want from me?

Fineas had said, "Keep your eyes open and the unicorn will tell you."

The humming of bees intensified, and morphed into something harsh, and discordant.

An engine.

Down in the canyon, an animal screamed.

Renata leapt to her feet and scrambled between boulders to see a four-wheel-drive charging along the riverbank with two men following on foot.

"They have the unicorn trapped at the end of the canyon," one man shouted to the other.

Trapped? Renata launched herself down the scree slope, slipping and scrabbling to keep her feet. *No!*

She went down on one knee, scraping her arm on the unforgiving edge of a boulder. Her ankle turned on loose rock, and she barely stopped herself from pitching headlong down the slope. Arms flailing, she stumbled to the canyon floor, where studded tires had ripped apart the fresh, felty turf.

The unicorn screamed again.

Renata ran towards it. At the end of the canyon, she found the unicorn galloping back and forth, tail flying like a banner, head high and eyes wide.

Two contractors' vehicles blocked the animal's escape, and men were stringing wire between the canyon walls.

"What are you doing?" screamed Renata. She ducked beneath the wire, but a hand shot out and grabbed her arm. As she twisted away, the man's fingers caught her sleeve and pulled her back.

"You can't go in there!" he said.

The unicorn snorted wildly, pawed the ground, and lowered its horn.

"You'll kill her if you try to trap her!" screamed Renata. With a mighty tug, she tore her sleeve free and darted beneath the fence.

The unicorn swung to face her, breathing hard. Renata faltered, but held the unicorn's gaze. The eyes were not black anymore. They were flecked with colours: blue as the sky, grey as the canyon walls, green as new grass.

"Please…" whispered Renata. "I'm sorry."

The unicorn huffed.

"Get away from that animal!" the man called. "She might attack."

But Renata did not care. She knew what she had to do. This healing land did not need any more bitterness or conflict or misunderstanding. It needed trust.

She put out her hand towards the unicorn. "You'll be alright. We'll be alright."

The unicorn took a step towards her.

"Go away," Renata said over the shoulder to the men. "Get those vehicles out of here and take down the wire."

They hesitated.

"NOW," pleaded Renata.

The unicorn extended her muzzle and blew in Renata's face, her breath warm and sweet. Then she wheeled towards the men and charged.

The men dropped their wire strainers and dove for their vehicles.

With a mighty bunching of her rump muscles, the unicorn leapt into the air. She sailed over the makeshift fence and landed on the other side, hooves scattering pebbles like birdshot as she galloped along the winding canyon and out of sight.

Renata fell to her knees, nostrils filled with the unicorn's sweet-smelling breath.

***

"What a disaster!" Mercer gazed around the canyon the following day. "The president will arrive for a site visit in a few minutes, and she doesn't want to see this."

Renata wanted to scream at Mercer to go away, to tell the president she would have nothing more to do with them after their shameful treatment of the unicorn. She wanted to flee with her aching heart to the glen of Nardin and pretend *Future Proof* didn't exist.

"What does the president want to see?" she snapped.

"Potential! Vacant land waiting to be put to work. She isn't interested in grass seeds, and flowers and—" Mercer glared, cross-eyed, at an insect investigating the end of her nose. "Blooming bees!"

***

The president was a silver-tipped woman named Erasmin Clark. Almost as tall as Renata, with a wiry build and tanned face that suggested she spent plenty of time outdoors.

Cautiously, studying their features for a clue as to whether they might prove to be friend or foe, Renata greeted Erasmin and the accompanying board members, before Mercer guided them to folding chairs.

Erasmin studied the greening canyon for several moments before she turned to Renata. "This is not what I was expecting."

"What were you expecting?" Renata knew her voice sounded sharp, and was unsurprised when Erasmin responded in kind.

"I was expecting a blighted part of the country that we might bring back to some sort of usefulness." Erasmin scanned the reeds growing along the riverbank with narrowing eyes. "But it seems we're not needed here. Indeed I get the sense we're not even wanted. What on earth changed?"

Renata had been awake until daylight wondering the same. She drew a deep breath. "When I signed the farm over to your company, I thought I was doing the right thing. If the land was no good for growing crops, at least it could house the equipment required to create energy. My studies were taking me elsewhere, and I had no ties to this place anymore."

Erasmin nodded.

"But then the unicorn arrived."

"Unicorn?" One of the board members frowned. "I thought they went extinct."

"Obviously not," said another.

"Magnificent creatures, from what I hear," said Erasmin. Her stern features softened as she caught Renata's eye. "Will we see it today, do you think?"

"Your contractors scared it off," said Renata.

"Oh dear!"

"It was getting in the way," muttered Mercer.

"I know I've signed the property over for this energy concept," said Renata, "but everything has changed in the last few days. Plants are growing like crazy after two decades of stasis. The land is coming back to life."

"So you want to back out of our agreement with the water park?"

"This farm has answers to questions we haven't even thought about yet. It's too important to lose, especially if we're simply creating power so adventure-seeking tourists can pretend they're being flushed down a giant toilet—" She snapped her mouth shut, knowing she had overstepped the mark.

The board members stared at her.

"You wanted to be an adventure-seeking tourist," said Erasmin. "You told us that when you first made contact."

"That was before I realised what I had here! Now I just feel we're about to destroy one potentially wonderful thing to create something else… that we don't really need."

"The world needs energy," said Erasmin, running a finger through the soft grass beside her chair. "But it also needs beauty and hope."

Renata sensed an opening. Her heart stuttered. "I know I've made my choice and it's too late to take back the deeds. But can you please reconsider your plans for this land?"

One of the board members cleared his throat. "Could we start farming unicorns?"

Heat flooded Renata's face. "You talk about the land and the unicorns as if we own them, but we don't. We're custodians, at best. This land is alive, the unicorn is alive. They are telling us something!"

"What are they telling us?" asked Erasmin.

"I don't know," said Renata. "I need your help to work it out."

"We're not here to help," grumbled Mercer. "We're here to generate energy."

The *Future Proof* president's silver-framed eyeglasses glinted. "We're here to do far more than that."

"Our founders dreamed of sustainable energy," said Mercer.

"Our founders dreamed of a sustainable *future*. They are not one and the same. Energy is only as worthwhile as the use it's put to."

"People pay good money to ride water slides," muttered Mercer.

Erasmin frowned at Renata. "You've raised a complex issue, and at very short notice. This issue, if you can call an event like this an *issue*, is that a unicorn has magicked this farm back to life, and you think we can work out how she has done it—"

"*If* she has done it," corrected Mercer. "There's no evidence—"

"We're Future *Proof*," snapped Erasmin. "A research and development company. It's our job to find the evidence."

"Magic," scoffed Mercer. "Old wives' tales."

"*Everything* was an old wives' tale before we explained it." Erasmin's eyes widened, as if seeing a vision. "And just because we can't explain something today, doesn't mean we won't be able to explain it tomorrow."

"This land is begging us to investigate it," said Renata. "Just look at how quickly that canyon-sage is growing."

Mercer turned on the sprawling plant as if it had given personal offense. "It's just a BUSH!"

"USSA-BOOSH!" croaked the bush.

"What the heck?" Mercer stared at the plant, then thrust her face closer to it before stumbling back with a screech.

"EEEK!" croaked the bush.

Renata's pulse pounded as she realised what had spoken. She glanced at Erasmin, who was smiling.

"A mimic toad," whispered Erasmin. "I haven't heard one since I was a child."

"OSSACHILD," croaked the bush, in an approving tone.

To Renata's surprise, Erasmin reached gently between the woody branches of the canyon-sage. When she withdrew her hand, the tiny toad was clinging to a finger, like an unsculpted lump of modelling clay with bulging indigo eyes.

"There you are," crooned Erasmin.

"ERR-OO-ARR," croaked the toad. It gulped, and the indigo eyes sank into its bulbous grey head.

Erasmin held the toad up to the sun. "You are beautiful."

"Beautiful?" said Mercer, scowling at the creature. "It's a TOAD."

The toad's eyes re-surfaced and glared back at Mercer. "YOU'S-A-TOAD!"

With astonishing agility, it leapt from Erasmin's finger; its tiny feet splayed like the blades of a wind vane, and spiralled away on the breeze.

"You scared it!" Erasmin turned on Mercer, lips pressed into pale pink scars. "Just like you scared off the unicorn, I assume?"

Renata watched Mercer cycle through a repertoire of facial expressions before settling on indignation.

"I was doing my JOB," she said.

"Hmmn." Erasmin grunted and turned back to Renata. "Again, I must ask, what do you think is happening to this land?"

Daring to believe she had found an ally, Renata decided this was not the time to hold back. "Perhaps the unicorn is processing the water in some way? Hopefully we might—"

"Speculation and hope," spat Mercer. "We can't sell those to our shareholders. Terrible idea."

"Speculation and hope are *never* terrible ideas," said Erasmin. "And you're fired."

Mercer's mouth opened, then closed. She cast a withering glare at Renata.

Erasmin leaned forward and captured Renata's gaze. "What did you say you were studying at college?"

Renata had never said, but suspected the president had done some background research. "Science, with a major in ecology."

"Ecology. That's right. I am wondering whether there might be an opportunity here." Erasmin spoke slowly and thoughtfully. "I like you. I like your passion. You remind me of myself, and the principles that drove our founders in the first place. Our mission is to find solutions for a sustainable future, but I think we've become blinkered."

Renata didn't speak for fear of altering the direction she hoped the president of *Future Proof* was headed.

"You are overdue to complete a research externship, am I right?" asked Erasmin.

"Yes." Renata had been preparing to leave for a field study in the Amnesian islands when her father died. She held her breath, chest pounding.

"I propose a partnership," said Erasmin. "Rather than taking this farm from you, at a time when such exciting things are happening, I suggest we fund a pilot study. Do you like that idea?"

"Yes." Renata allowed herself to exhale.

"We'll appoint you as a research scholar for two years." Erasmin nodded to the board member who was taking notes. "Perhaps, together, we can solve some of the remaining mysteries of this world?"

***

For the rest of that summer, plants continued to grow with uncanny vigour: aromatic hedges of sage, fruiting vines, and waving river reeds. Grass went to seed, and the seeds wafted on a moist summer breeze. Verdant patches sprung up in dusty corners that had not harboured a living thing since Renata was a child.

Each day, she measured growth rates, took soil and water samples, and counted mimic toads. And when she had finished her scientific observations, she wandered the boundaries of the property, planting garlic and building cairns of river pebbles.

One morning, a deer appeared in the far pasture. Another day,

Renata heard elk bugling. Frogs spawned in the pond near the house, and a banded bull snake often slumbered on the paving stones near the old dairy, belly rounded with its last meal.

To see these creatures thrive where they had been absent for so long was magical, but of the most magical creature there was no sign.

In autumn, when the nights chilled and the trees started shedding their leaves, Renata submitted her observations to *Future Proof.* While she awaited the results of their analysis, she roamed the farm, marvelling at how close she had come to selling and moving away for good.

Am I doing what you asked? she whispered to the land. *Should I do more?*

Every day she searched for a reply.

One chilly morning, with an early snow softening the distant mountain peaks, Renata strolled through the canyon and discovered fresh signs of unicorn.

This time, there were two sets of hoof prints.

* * *

Geraldine Briony Hunt is a retired veterinarian and lover of animals: real and imagined. She is always seeking opportunities to observe and interact with the fabulous creatures who share our world. She writes speculative fiction and creative non-fiction, and her works have been published in several anthologies and magazines. This story would not have been possible without the inspiration of her sister, Kate Le Bars. She first imagined the world of Arcadia, in which they have spent many happy hours as co-authors of other tales.

Renaissance Pisces

Irina Tall

Irina Tall (Novikova) is an artist, graphic artist, illustrator. She graduated from the State Academy of Slavic Cultures with a degree in art, and also has a bachelor's degree in design.

QUORUM SENSING

Calliope Papas

In the vast of the night, as Jupiter's elemental mass looms over the crystal dome of Europa, I see a terrifying vision.

I possess a ghoulish body, made of a lilac phosphorescent haze, its million cores interlocked with sanguine tendrils. I crawl across the wind-swept grubby ground of a desolate place; my movements, desperate, leave tiny puffs of black dust spreading languidly off that peculiar world's feeble gravity. I lift my eyes to steal a gaze of something dark and ominous in the sky above. I have no mouth so I can't scream. I possess no arms, so I can't grasp the sand. My legs are made of saprotrophic wisps so I can't run. I lay there, creeping on the ground, waiting for the shadow to come down.

I come to my senses with a gasp. I waggle my toes and touch my face. I sigh with relief. I'm on Europa, back home, safe, hunched in one of the entheogen therapeutic cafes.

Roxanne stoops above me, white braids falling haphazardly on bare shoulders, and her obsidian face is crooked in a frown of concern. She holds my hand, albeit a tad too tightly and I squeeze hers back, before wiggling my fingers free.

"I'm ok."

She looks at me with those vulpine eyes of hers and I shudder. She can see right through me, and she knows I'm lying.

"You were gone for some time. I tried to wake you up, but I couldn't. What did you see?"

"I'm not sure."

She wraps me in a blanket. She keeps staring at me, so I rush to add, "I'm fine. Really."

"Shall I call a doctor?" She pulls out her phone.

"No. No need to worry. It's probably nothing. I'll go home and rest."

"Are you certain, love?"

I nod.

"Okay, then."

She helps me up, and we make our way back. We walk silently underneath the millennial Redwood Tree that sprouted roots the same year Terrans first arrived here. Far above the dome's crystalline borders, scattered with luminescent illustrations of mammalian life, I steal a glimpse of Jupiter's colossal body, its stormy eye shimmering down like the Goddess in the sky.

"Whatever it was you saw, Helene, you know you can take it up with the Collective," Roxanne says. "It's a safe space."

I shudder upon hearing that name.

"Well, it doesn't feel safe to *me*."

"You could speak to their representative. Just talk to her. You don't have to commit to anything."

I bury my face in the burgundy heavy fabrics of her cloak and I'm swept by this lavender and burnt caramel scent I love.

"Right now, I just wanna go home and sleep the whole thing off."

She doesn't say anything else; just nods in accord as we take the path away from the city centre.

I let my gaze wander around, tracing the town's mystifying old town replica and its crescent moon-shaped high-rise buildings. We walk deeper into the night cycle and cross the rhodopsin park. I take in the earthly musk of the fungi networks that are slathered in clusters on the barks of the giant sequoias. Their peppery scent is already doing a good job calming my nerves. We traverse through the lake district, and my gaze roams across waters writhing in microscopic effervescent jellyfish and ctenophores.

We walk hand-in-hand in comfortable silence, till we reach the first troupes of the low-rise townhouses cosily huddled around the edge of the outer town.

"I'll see you tomorrow at the Biodome then." Roxanne squeezes my hand as she drops me off in front of my door. "Unless you want me to come in?"

"No need to." I shake my head. "I'll sleep on it and tomorrow I'll be as good as new."

"Alrighty then." She hesitates. "Call me if you need anything, okay?"

I land a soft kiss on her lips, give her a ghost of a smile, and clatter up the concrete stairs. She stands her ground for a while, half-hidden in the shadows of the never-ending twilight, looking at me. I nod. *I'm okay.* Only then does she trot to the end of the road, where her own hemp abode stands below a broadleaved redwood pulsating with the faint colour of fireflies hanging like ripe fruit from its elephantine branches.

I breathe in, pull the door handle, and set my breath free only when I'm safe and sound in the warmth of my house.

***

On my way to work the same thoughts roll around in my head.

I obsess over the fact that what I saw felt more like a memory and less like a vision. The warm, rocky ground against my ringlets, the churning fear of the shadow looming over that alien sky. Images of tendrils recoiling under an unfamiliar sky interject with my own stray distant memories seething fire and ash. I shake my head violently to purge them.

I think of Roxanne. I think of what she told me. But I waver. Reaching out to the Diogenes Collective is not an option, I'm sure of it. And even though Roxanne seems to trust them, I have no desire of letting anyone mess up with my brain, scramble up my memories and make me bend to their will ever again.

I move on.

The Splicing and Electrophoresis department lies at the far left of the Biodome bubble. It's a hybrid space, reserved for research and development, but also for monitoring and recording. Old Terran flora species sit along with endemic Europan genera, forming a wondrous blend of plant life, some branching up to the skies, some so miniscule, they can only be observed through a microscope.

It's my own safe space. I wander through a microcosmos of wetlands, where tiny frogs gather to sing, through polar coasts where Europan penguins with funny-looking beaks dwell, and all the landscapes I leave behind are filled with dazzling, otherworldly hues. It's always night in that place, but a brilliant night, blue as glass.

A familiar voice calls my name, and I turn to my left, to see Roxanne inside the research chamber. She wears her usual violet suit, accompanied by a transparent face shield. Her smile shines bright, and her eyes sparkle like the stars in the sky.

"Suit up fully before you come in," she says. "I've got something to show you."

Equipped with my own suit, gloves, and shield, I enter the room. Tanks where forms of aquatic life are bred stand in the middle. I walk towards the centre, and she waves at me to come close, her back turned, shoulders hunched over something I cannot see.

"Look."

I stand by her and crouch as I examine the glass. Something has found home on one of the aquarium walls. A single bioluminescent organism. It's infinitesimal, barely visible to the naked eye. It's shaped like a butterfly, and it pulsates with a feeble glow, changing hues from blue, to red, then black.

"What is it?"

"Heh. That's the thing. I don't really know."

"Did you *breed* this?"

"No," she protests. "I found it."

"What? Where?"

"I mean, I did not exactly find it myself. I received a call early in the morning from one of the service tunnels outside town. A collector of sorts working their way through the soil noticed something iridescent shine through, one single speck of purple—very faint, but definitely there." She takes a deep breath. "They fished it out, saved it in a jar… I'm surprised they called here instead of keeping it, but it's good they did," she finishes, breathless. "I've been working on it the entire morning. But I haven't managed to trigger it yet."

"Trigger it? You don't even know what it can do." I rub my finger on my chin. "I mean, what is it? A fungus? A bacterium? Some kind of protozoon or a nematoid worm?"

"No idea. His molecular structure doesn't match any established single-celled organism. I still need to run some tests, but I'm almost certain he must be something entirely new. I cross checked with the other Europan outposts and they have no record of anything remotely like him. It seems that so far, he's only managed to grow roots here. But he's still in limbo. I tried electropulsation, altering the temperature in the tank, I offered him the type of sustenance we feed Terran bacteria, but I got nothing. No response to any kind of external stimuli, or signalling. He just lays there, like he's waiting for something."

"I'm sorry... He?"

"His name is Gene," Roxanne says and gifts me with another striking smile. "I named him after my little brother. Oh, Helene!" she exclaims. "Can you imagine how important this can be? For us, for the Biodome, for our world! That little speck could very well be an agent of the first truly endemic Europan life. A genus not bred in a lab, not evolved from an already existing Terran form, a species that grew all by itself!" She throws her arms up and dances.

"If only he could talk," I humour her, as I back off to the changing room, closing the sliding doors behind us. "He could tell us what he is."

"Maybe he will," Roxanne replies.

"I'm not sure whether that's a good thing," I murmur, quietly, to myself, as I peel off my suit's sleeves.

Roxanne steps back to the atrium to play with her newfound toy, while I proceed with entering my own vestibule, adjacent to hers, to play with one of my own. She digs amoebas. I dig flowers. Soon, I find myself lost in an opalescent macroworld of stamens and filaments, anthers, and petals; and when my wanderlust ends, and I lift my head from my workstation, it's already past lunchtime.

A knock at the door.

"Hi."

She stands there, looking slightly disappointed but still plenty elated. She shrugs. I pout.

"Nothing?"

A sigh.

"Nothing. Expected though. These things take time, don't they?"

"Come" I say grabbing my jacket. "Let's put some food in your belly."

***

"You shied away from me yesterday." Roxanne gulps down a generous spoonful of sweet and sour soup. "Do you want to tell me what you saw at the entheogen café? And why, by the Goddess, were you so freaked out afterwards?"

I lower my gaze and fiddle with the nautilus medallion Roxanne gifted me a month ago, on my birthday.

"It's okay if you still feel you're not—"

"I am," I interrupt her. "It's okay. I'm ready."

I talk for what it seems like an hour. I tell her about the smell of wet sulphuric soil, the lightness of air surrounding my body. I describe in detail the feeling of my saprozoite weightlessness, and the state of utter terror over the shadow in the sky. She knows I have gone through something similar before. Occasionally she reaches out for my hand. She doesn't say anything.

When I'm done talking, crevices, deep as the darkness of space furrow her forehead.

"Was this the first time you felt like this?"

I nod.

"The visions I've had so far have always been benign and disconnected from mind and body. Imagine this: we're sitting here together, and you notice a pinecone fall in the middle of the street. You see its trajectory as it detaches from the branch and hear the splinter of its petals, as it crashes on the ground. You are an observer, a spectator."

"Okay?"

"This time around I was the pine."

"Maybe what you took was too much, or was cut with other stuff?"

"I doubt it. I always measure my doses. Plus, *Illumination* cooks have the strictest procedures in the entire city. I will check with them, but I hardly think that's the reason. Also—" I hesitate.

"What?"

"It was so *real*, Roxanne. I thought I was there. In that goddess-forsaken place. I *was* that crawly thing trying to escape an inferno. I *felt* it. In its entirety. Its pain, its fear, its profound terror. It consumed me. Something similar happened to me before. Before I came here, before I met you, when I was still a nobody."

She nods.

"That's why I am going to ask you again: have you thought about what I told you?"

"About Diogenes?"

"Yes."

"And?"

"Can I be honest with you?"

Roxanne's eyes soften and reaches out for my hand.

"You know you can always be honest with me."

I hesitate.

"Is this about what happened to you on Earth?" she says, tenderly.

I nod and my eyes swell up.

"You don't know the half of it."

"Then, tell me."

"You don't know how it feels when people play football with your head."

"I get it," she says. "And it's okay to be scared."

I shake my head.

"No. You don't get it. You were born here. And I'm not scared. I'm furious. The Terran Collectives did horrible things during the Last War, Roxanne. Rounded children up, imprisoned them, tortured them, robbed them of their sanity. They used their—you call it gift; I call it curse—to bend them to their will. *We,*" I say and my stomach churns, "became their foot soldiers. Fought a war that wasn't ours. We did monstrosities on their behalf. Most of us perished. Some of us survived. But we came through the other side scathed. And most of us that did, wish that we had died on the field." My voice breaks.

She looks at me with damp eyes and does not shy from wiping a stray tear away. She squeezes my hand with both hers and releases a sigh.

"I hear you. And I hate that you had to go through that. I'm so, so sorry. I wish I could take it all away."

"You had nothing to do with what happened back then and how it affected me. Don't apologise."

"Well, someone has to." She breaks a smile, reaches over, and brushes a strand of hair from my cheek. She wavers before she talks again.

"I'd never force you to do anything you wouldn't want to do, you know that, right? I'd never let anyone scramble with this." She taps a finger on my temple. "But hear me on this just this once, and I promise, I won't bring it up anymore. I was born here, yes. I never had to face war, true. No one has ever forcefully bent my will neither have they invaded and shattered my mind. Nobody made me do atrocities in their name. But I know this: the Collectives here are not corrupted. And I can vouch for them because, once upon a time, they gave me something when I needed it the most. They pulled me through when I was at the end of the line. They saved my life."

Bubbling pain sears my insides, and I bawl uncontrollably. People from adjacent tables give us a few concerned looks but I don't care. Roxanne sits next to me, and I bury my face in her lap, letting tears stream freely on my face, till I'm all done, my cries withered down to a few fluttering sobs.

"They turned us into murderers."

A sigh.

"I killed people."

She strokes my hair.

"But I didn't want to. They made me do it. You believe me, right?"

"I do."

"They robbed me off my home, my friends, my family and sent me into the frontlines. I was twelve."

"A child."

"I came here to start anew, to begin my life again with a clean slate."

"I know, love."

"It's tough to do so with so much baggage."

She squeezes my hand once again, and I can feel her pulse through her skin.

I lift my head up and meet her gaze.

"I promise you I will think about meeting with Diogenes. But that's all I can do."

"And that's more than enough. It's your decision and yours only. Now—" She smiles, softly pulls her hand away and wipes my tears with her sleeve. "Shall we get back to work? I've still got a buttload of stuff to do before the day cycle is gone."

***

We have just swiped our cards through the receptors to enter the Biodome when I feel it.

I hardly manage to stutter something before I collapse. Someone lifts me up, carries me across the room and sets me down on one of the visitor benches. I barely make out Roxanne's face before it's swapped with a transcendent, terrifying city in the sky, made from dissolved organic tresses, constantly burgeoning, sprawling out from a black, pulsating centre.

My thousand eyes track the same ominous shape in the sky as the one I saw before. The city that breathes and grows below me, bellows in terror. The shadow that's cast across my tendrils, branches out and spreads, and I feel a bizarre heat unfold from inside my aberrant body. I open my mouth to scream, it hurts! Am I on fire?

I come around just when I burst into flames, and open my eyes with a gasp, flaying, trying to catch a breath.

A crowd has gathered, eyeing me with worry. Someone brings a glass of water to my lips; I drink clumsily, streams running sideways from the rim.

"Scatter. Let her breathe," Roxanne says, shooing them away. "Are you okay to walk?" she asks quietly, and I nod, still confused.

She takes me to her office, at the back of the Biodome, sheltered from curious eyes. The space is confined but I don't mind. She draws the blinds, lays me down on the sofa, rolls a shirt into a bundle and places it under my head. She sits beside me, on the carpet-covered floor, reaches out and flips the switch on a lamp that radiates a soothing glow. I can't help but think of the pond with the ctenophores next to my house.

"It's called chromotherapy," she starts. She always talks nonsense when she's worried—but I let her continue, nonetheless. "It's considered pseudoscience by the Terrans, but I've always thought blue to be very relaxing, isn't it? How are you feeling?"

Her worry is deafening. Her fingers fiddle with her silver bat medallion hanging around her neck—her birthday gift from me. Her eyes wander everywhere else in the room, never meeting mine, and her breathing is short, deep, audible.

This time, I'm the one squeezing her hand.

"At least now we know for sure it was not the entheogen." I snort, trying to take the edge off.

"What did you see?" she murmurs.

I tell her.

"Do you think I'm sick?" I ask.

"I don't know." She rubs my shoulder. "But I promise you this—we'll find out."

She leans in and turns the lamp off, leaving me in a sweet, scented half-darkness.

"I'm calling a doctor now." She pulls out her phone. "Rest. And yell if you need anything, alright? I'll be down the corridor."

She takes off, heels clicking on the olivine hallway towards the research chamber. Her silhouette looms through the window blinds, dark against the azure of the artificial light. Her voice muffled in the distance, is feverous, and accompanied by an opulent variety of gestures. I see her stealing glimpses at her little project that's probably still slowly stewing in its gestation tank. Suddenly, the lively discussion is interrupted. I lose her from my line of sight as she hurtles towards the aquarium tanks, but can still hear her, albeit a bit stifled, the hue of her exclamations a mix of surprise and dread.

I rush towards the door, and from there out to the olivine effervescent hallway and left, into the bioresearch chamber.

"Roxanne?"

She is frozen, like a statue, and doesn't reply; she points somewhere in front of her, instead.

In the gestation tank, Gene has evolved from a minuscule speck of purple incandescent dust to a gargantuan network of throbbing ringlets. They sprout from black cores, and they clasp and coil with each other. They pulsate with a rhythm, like a heartbeat. Here and there dark green saplings appear, covered with tiny phosphorescent hairs. With every pulse, they swarm the tank even more. Soon, all twenty-two square meters of Gene's confinement are covered with every tress, every core, every hairy little shoot, until he settles, barely moving, but with his own heartbeat now audible, making waves through the glass.

"He woke up," I whisper. My eyes burn.

"He didn't just wake up. He grew. A thousand-fold," Roxanne

whispers back, her eyes now starry with a dreadful awe.

"When did that happen?"

"I don't know."

I suddenly feel sick, and double down.

"Hey. Are you okay?"

I shake my head, my mind sprockets whirr, questions thrust, *what happened? Why now? How?*

It doesn't take too long till I come to a terrific realization.

"I had the vision, and then he grew."

"What?"

"He was triggered, Roxanne! By me!"

She blinks.

I sigh heavily and drag her by the sleeve.

"Come with me. Now."

We exit the research chamber, past the thriving broods of fungi, through the polar coasts and the frog-teeming ponds. I leave the Biodome and gallop all the way to downtown, past the great Redwood Tree and straight into *Illumination*, ignoring Roxanne' incessant questions and resolute protests.

"You're early today," the bartender says when we come rushing through the door. I ignore him and tread all the way back, to the cubicle we had taken that entheogen trip, not that many days ago. My extremities tremble with anticipation. I know I can't be wrong.

"Look for him," I say as I grab and lift flimsy tablecloths and sway away heavy, embroidered pillows.

"Look for *whom*? Helene, stop! What's going on? You're acting mad!"

I draw apart curtains made from off-white hemp and expose the cubicle's far left corner, half hidden by the imminent night cycle's darkness.

There.

I point to a crease seething with shifting coils. They're purple with black cores and there's hairy green saplings germinating on the artificial concrete wall.

"Him. That's who we are looking for," I say.

She stands still, eyes starry.

"I had my first vision here. Then back at the Biodome. Do you understand now?"

She gestures.

"You have a connection."

"Apparently."

"Wait here."

She rushes to the bar and comes back a few seconds later, with a mason jar. Carefully, she stirs the tendrils, nudging them inside the container and once he's in, she secures the latch.

"Now what?"

I wince.

"I'll need someone to help me make contact. Like, psychic contact."

"Right."

She looks at me inquisitively.

Crap.

Okay." I sigh. "Give me your phone. I must find out what he wants with me and right now it seems like they're my only option."

"Wait," she protests. "Hang on a minute. I mean, are you sure? Is that what you really want?"

"I don't see what else I can do."

She sits me down on the couch and crouches in front of me.

"Breathe."

"I know what I'm doing."

"Still. Breathe. Count down from ten. Slowly. And if by the end you're still certain that's what you want to do, I'll call Mirren myself."

***

I arrived here still a tween, as a stowaway on the last ship to Europa from Khanate; a ship that reeked of sweat and metal and carried the stories of a thousand refugees. One of my earliest memories at the colony was the delicate scent of white lilacs that infused the clothes I was given at the reception centre.

My nostrils pick up the same imperceptible flowery aroma while I sit on a bench below the Redwood Tree.

A woman has taken a seat by the other side of the bench. I steal a glimpse, more out of curiosity than concern. She's slender, has hair the colour of tar and eyes blue like the Europan night. She meets my eye and I think of wide-open skies.

I give her a nod as a thanks for keeping her distance. She places her palm over her chest and straightens her back.

"I am like you, you know," she says. Her voice is flowing rivers and breeze through pines.

I look at her and raise an eyebrow.

"I was fifteen when I arrived here, on a ship from Inishtooskert. A young girl with breasts barely formed but already groped a thousand times over. For me, evil did not wear robes or shrouds. It did not screw with my head. Evil wore a soldier's helmet and was clad in camouflage. It had nametags hanging down from its neck and black paint on its face. It had hands fumbling with my body and a breath that stank of gutter."

"You fled the war too."

"I did."

I sneer.

"All that pain, destruction and slaughter for those damn algae."

"Algal oil was just an excuse among many. There is rarely one single, clear cause for war."

"What then?"

She shrugs.

"Greed? Thirst for power? Fear? Humans have the potential of doing great things, but they also do equally horrible things. Mostly to their fellow humans."

I sigh.

"So, you came here, and you formed your own Collective."

"That, I did."

"You did not hurt kids back on Earth then?"

She chuckles.

"My awakening occurred when I was already in the colony. On my seventeenth birthday I had the calling; and I decided to use my psychic ability for good. To help people overcome trauma. To assist those who were in pain. I formed Diogenes solely for this reason. So, no. I did not hurt kids back on Earth. I *was* the kid that hurt."

I nod. Mirren moves next to me, and her shoulder now brushes mine. Her skin is cool and smooth, and the lavender scent is ten times stronger than before; and I think of a pot my mother kept in her yard that bloomed with thick purple blossoms every second spring.

"You're the kid that still hurts, Helene."

I nod.

"We can help, if you let us."

"By entering my mind?" I scoff.

"We don't do that" She shakes her head. "Think of us as a conduit, a companion if you like, to your experience. You're the driver, and the one in control. We'll be riding shotgun."

I let my shoulders drop.

"Will you take it away? What still hurts me, I mean?"

She shakes her head.

"No one can take it away. You'll always live with it. It's become a part of you, but you can learn to own it."

"How am I supposed to do that?"

She smiles.

***

Twelve arrive at the Biodome that night. They are clad in blue and white; some wear capes embellished with intricate patterns of silver wings, while others are dressed in stricter suits embroidered with golden spiderwebs on the shoulders. They toe the line around the aquarium and a still vacant sensory deprivation tank with transparent, crystalline walls, filled with water teeming with luminous algae.

"Are you sure about this?" Roxanne asks.

I strip off all my clothing and submerge myself in the reservoir. The water is warm and soothing; it does a good job at calming my nerves.

"I am. How do we do this?"

Mirren takes a step forward. Her smile is implied; I cannot see it, but I can *feel* it. Or maybe it's the warmth of the algae water that seeps through my skin. I don't really know.

"Hello, Helene."

I gesture nervously. She reaches out and squeezes my hand. I don't pull away.

"I'll guide you through the process of connection through the Collective. My voice is going to be your anchor with our reality. Purge all other thoughts from your mind and focus on the presence you call Gene. Visualize how you connect with him. Call for him. We will do the rest."

I am trying to play brave, but Mirren knows. I can see it in her eyes.

"I'm scared," I whisper.

"Your fear is deeply rooted in your tormented past. And that's quite alright; part of us is made of fear. But do not let it consume you. Do not allow it to become you."

I hesitate.

"I am not asking you to trust me blindly. I'm just hoping you can meet me halfway there. Can you do that for me?"

I draw a shallow breath. My pulse pounds in my temples, but I do not want to shy away this time.

"I can. I will."

She nods and lets my hand go.

Roxanne lands a soft kiss on my forehead.

"You'll be alright," she whispers, and her eyes are wet. She shuts the tank door and takes her place behind the chamber's protective glass screen. I close my eyes and focus my energy on the task upfront.

"Good." I hear Mirren's voice through the internal comms. "I want you to go back to the night of your first borrowed memory. Attach your consciousness to it, roll and flow along. Let it show you what happened. Let it guide you. Even when fear comes—and it will—do not try to break the connection. You're safe amongst us. If needed, we'll pull you out."

"Okay."

"You can start now."

Slowly, I feel as if my body is raised from its wet cocoon. The darkness in my vision is absolute in the beginning, but gradually, patterns shift, images churn and the shadows are lifted. There's a spotless, starry night sky now inside my head. It's silky-blue and serene, and the moon is full and bright and perfect.

The moon?

A chilled gust sweeps by. I turn my eyes towards the horizon, and there, clouds begin to form, and they swell, pregnant with rain. They hurtle towards the moon and swallow it whole. Thunder booms, fog thick as milk spreads and for a moment I forget. I am stripped of all memories, emotions, and connections, robbed of any knowledge and sense of self.

I panic. I am familiar with this feeling. I've had it before, and I hate it, I want it out of me, I need it gone.

"Where am I? Get me out! What's happening?"

Someone yells inside my head.

"Helene? You need to concentrate on my voice! You must let go of the darkness holding you back. This is the hardest part, okay? Focus!"

I see myself as a little girl, cowering under a silhouette immersed in flames. I lick my charred lips and they taste like copper and ash. My nostrils pick up the smell of blood and burnt flesh.

My stomach churns. I know where I am and once again, I can't run away. I'm back on earth, back when my name was just Girl, back when I was fleeing a war that destroyed everything that meant something to me.

I try to scream but I can't.

"Let him in, Helene!" Mirren's voice resonates through the debris.

Focus, I yell inside my head, *focus!*

The silhouette immersed in fire clears up and I can now discern its face—eyes black like a raven's, heavy brows, wavy hair embracing a brawny neck. I know him. But I cannot remember his name.

He smiles through the flames and nods, and something pops in my head.

"Darkness is a part of light, and light always shines through the dark, my Azadi."

Dad?

Golden beams push through the ruins of my mind, patches of light brighter than the sun break through the ashy haze. The world around me turns white; an almost tangible glow surrounds me.

"You're here," I whisper as tears stream down my cheeks.

I relax and let myself sink into him.

I wear the saprophytic body I now recognize as Gene, we're one and the same, and we waft ourselves over our home, some thousands of light years away from our solar system, away from Earth, away from Europa, somewhere where we live in peace. Tendrils among tresses, cores within molecules, sprouts and exotic flora above indulging, rich soil. All is one and one is all; us, the flora, the fauna, the air, the seeds, the water, the suns, the dew of the nights, the chill of the small hours of the morning. Gene and I are happy and grateful, as we take in the extraordinary nature of our home world.

He sings to me.

It's a complex melody, in a language based on light signals and quorum sensing. But I'm sharing his body now, his mind and knowledge, his individuality. I listen. I know. I understand.

"You're like me, aren't you?" I ask.

"Is the presence with you now? Gene?" Mirren's voice comes from somewhere far away, as if she's talking through a tunnel.

"Yes. But that's not his real name," we reply to her. "His true name is the Acapi. The Acapi are Azadi now."

"Who's Azadi, Helene?"

"Azadi is Helene's true name, Mirren. The name she owned before she fled earth."

"Are you inside Azadi now, Acapi?"

"We *are* Azadi, Mirren. We talk with her and through her. We are not a single cell organism. We are not a network. We are a giant brain, an individual, but also a web of beings. We are one, but every one of us is part of a whole."

"How did you come here?"

"Our home world came under attack. Our home world was annihilated. We floated in outer space, we travelled for a long time, we settled in a thousand different worlds, but we were driven away, by fire, by soil, by air. We are in pain, Mirren. We are exhausted. We want to stop running."

"But you invaded one of our own. You invaded Azadi."

We feel guilty about this. But we had no choice.

"We understand that borrowing Azadi's consciousness caused her great distress. For this, we are truly, deeply sorry. But know this; we do not harm living things. We learn. We disseminate knowledge. That's the Acapi creed. We chose Azadi because she has *been* us. She has suffered what we suffered. She's felt pain. She's seen ruin. She carries darkness inside her. But she carries plenty of light too. And that's how life is. You might have to carry a little bit of darkness, so you know when the light comes."

"Is this want you want? For darkness to go away, so the light comes?"

We are delighted.

"We want peace. A small piece of land in your part of the world will suffice. Then, your community will be ours too. We will help it thrive. We will contribute to its growth and prosperity. We will learn from you, and we will disseminate back our knowledge, once again. We can finally stop running."

"We must think about it, Acapi. We hope you understand."

"We do. We will now leave Azadi, never to use her consciousness again without her permission. We will recede and wait for your decision."

I feel the Acapi presence fade. But before they leave me, they bestow me with a gift of their own.

I open my eyes. My entire body, vein by vein, cell by cell, hair by hair, has been engulfed within a fantastical web of purple effervescent haze. With a purr it lands softly on me, and my skin radiates with a celestial lilac hue, filling me with an astounding sense of self-awareness and an unprecedented calm. All the tendrils, the ringlets, the sprouts, and saplings pull away from me, from the tank encasing me, from the grounds and fluorescent ceilings of the Biodome.

When I exit the tank, I approach the aquarium to see that the Acapi have bounced back to their former miniscule form, into a single bioluminescent organism, shaped like a butterfly. Infinitesimal, barely visible to the naked eye, pulsating with a feeble glow, changing hues from blue, to red, then black. I give it an unburdened smile, loaded with appreciation and relief.

***

Thirty full night cycles pass. Tonight, once again, we find ourselves strolling around the stone-built pathways below the Redwood Tree. Roxanne has buried her hand in mine, and I lean on her shoulder.

"Are you excited to tell them?"

I smile.

"They already know."

It's a sweet, blue night, and the air is rich with spicy scents coming from the trucks of local vendors. Fireflies hang from the Redwood's antediluvian branches, mushroom pulse around its foundation. I lift my hand, and I touch the primordial giant's gnarled trunk, a newfound, fitting home to the Acapi.

Welcome, friends, I think, and the tree's crown throbs lilac with a thousand microscopic cores, vines, and wisps, illuminating roots to branches, stems to buds, rinds to foliage.

* * *

Hailing from Greece, **Calliope Papas** began her storytelling journey at ten. Her works have appeared in various publications and Greek anthologies. Nowadays, she's gallivanting in the Finnish archipelago, on a quest for mushrooms, berries, and the ever-elusive fantastical critters.

FLYBY

Priya Sarukkai Chabria

No cosmic drifter is an outsider in the spherical spinning shell of dormant comets, the dark Oort Cloud, which encases our disk-like solar system. This frozen frontier, about two light years away from the Sun, does what borderlands do: accommodate other abandoned aliens. Vagrant wanderers from distant star systems who have travelled, occasionally streaked by starlight, through the spreading hand of space fit in like a missing part of a swirling jigsaw puzzle.

The Oort Cloud formed gradually, after the planets had jostled into place some 4.5 billion years ago, commingled the rolling, roiling remnants of the solar system with leftovers from other proto suns which our newborn Sun captured while whirling away from its birth cluster. These discards—hundreds of billions, even trillions of them—are a cosmic balancing act, poised at the heliopause where matched solar and interstellar winds create equilibrium. Its lip hangs open to the vast partial vacuum of interstellar space that is scattered with speckles of drifting dust, gas and smidgeons of rays. The dwarf sun, red Proxima Centuari rotates nearby, merely some 2.24 light years away.

Occasionally, something disturbs one of its torpid comets. Cosmic snowballs of gases, rock and dust, they then begin their journey toward the Sun. The span of their voyages range in time and space, from the short 76 year periodicity of Halley's Comet to Siding Spring which made a startlingly close pass over Mars in 2013, but will not return for some 740,000 years. Some, like our protagonist Comet Izumi, whose trail we follow over billions of years, is even more enigmatic.

Unlike planets, beautiful and rounded as melons, with moons

circling and circling them, comets are loners, each speaking a unique language of elliptical orbit and ellipses from sight. Pilgrims of the universe, they plunge in and out of the neat orbital paths of the planets, streaking their immense fiery tails over unknown skies. These blazing tears of the cosmos carry the DNA of the early solar system and earlier stellar forms. Perhaps they can be imagined as virtually invisible tears in the gossamer of space, for they often pass by Earth unnoticed, unlike spectacular meteorite showers. What stories do comets carry? In which tongues do they speak, for they too emit sound?

***

Each of Comet Izumi's unknown orbits from the Oort Cloud is speculated to take just under a billion years. The comet has, therefore, survived billions of years of not flambéing into the Sun or succumbing to rare comet death through planetary collision. We have proof of such uncommon events unearthed in the Valley of the Kings, in the magnificent tomb of the young pharaoh Tutankhamen, mummified in c 1323 BCE. At the centre of his perfectly preserved broach sits a gleaming silica glass stone, yellow as sunswept honey, set as a sacred scarab. Twenty-eight million years ago an ancient comet exploded over the Sahara, frizzling desert sand into silica over a scatter of 6000 square kilometres. Thus was Tut's bijou born.

One day, a long time later, this translucent jewel possibly dazzled the eye of a nomadic tribesman who found it nosing out of an incalescent dune. Needing water for his young, pregnant wife he might have traded the gem sitting in his palm like a slice of solidified sunlight to an adventurous merchant who, marvelling at his good fortune, pouched it to present to the royal court where the pharaoh's craftsmen carved, polished and set its aurous light in gold, as a perfect adornment for a mortal descendant of the Sun.

There exists, also, a mysterious black pebble found in the same region which contains microscopic diamonds. Impacting shock morphed the ancient comet's carbon bearing nucleus into diamonds; of which the pebble is remnant and reminder. This unique stone is named in honour of a singular woman, Hypatia of Alexandria. Mathematician, pagan philosopher and astronomer, she was murdered by Christian monks one spring morning in 415 CE for her beliefs, for listening to 'the music of the spheres' and her work on astrolabes. Branded a sorceress Hypatia was pulled from her chariot, her flesh sliced into by jagged oyster shells and her limbs torn apart.

How often had Hypatia, standing on her terrace in Alexandria, gazed into the glossy black pebble of the sky where stars twinkled codes in argots unidentified, and puzzled over the darkness shrouding human hearts? As unobserved comets blazed beyond Earth's horizon she must have wondered when our pulsing stone-hearts would tattoo out more than the mirror-language of the self. Perhaps brushing a curl of hair off her face, Hypatia speculated if the nucleus of the self will open its pores to wisdom and languages from other systems in existence.

***

Comet Izumi's peanut shaped nucleus, smaller in size than a double-humped hill, is balled in a heated blanket of coma from which its tail trails like a shimmering wake or a beautiful afterthought. Why was its trajectory triggered and how far after passing the Sun does it loop back through the inky waves of space, what dangers to its being has it encountered and when will it come to an end? Such answers lie in the magnificent, barely translated cosmic vocabulary written in hieroglyphics of time.

Because scale, even in this small segment of our galaxy, vaults beyond our imagination. It submerges the mind into deep enchantment or lonely terror, depending on your outlook. We could begin to trace space-time scale with something comfortingly human made, the spacecraft Voyager 1. Launched from Earth in 1977 it has left the planets far behind and emerged from the heliosphere, the enormous bubble of magnetism and ionized gas that the Sun emits, marking its far sphere of influence. In the distance swirls the frozen rim of the Oort Cloud which Voyager 1, at its current speed of about a million miles a day, should touch in 300 years. The spacecraft will take some 30,000 more years to exit—if it survives this perilous space, home of Comet Izumi.

Izumi seems to have a curious nature. It makes a close flyby to Mars under two billion years ago. The planet is teeming with water and life, it is splendid, an eyeful. Like a magnificent fan Comet Izumi's fulgent tail swaddles and scores the sphere's atmosphere. Martian rivers gurgle, sand spikes, and life forms on the surface sizzle as trajectories of comet and planet briefly mingle before Izumi leaves, shooting towards the Sun.

Coming into its view is the frozen planet Earth which resembles a blind icy eyeball spinning in space. Izumi plunges on towards the Sun. But deep within Earth's oceans in hydrothermal vents anaerobic life has already commenced, soon followed by mats of cyanobacteria that begin photosynthesis, producing the noxious gas oxygen, more and more of it over centuries, which proceeds to kill off almost all early life, making way for a new order to take root and flourish.

In its next notable flyby as Izumi passes Mars, the planet wears its characteristic covering; stripped of water and protective atmosphere. Mars is now dead and red. But as the comet passes Earth—this planet has transformed. On its crust ride oceans of billowing water and the green mantle of life; it revolves like a glowing jewel, flickering with emerald on ultramarine, viridian on turquoise swell, chartreuse lapping slate, violet against midnight blue, jade circled by cerulean, over which feathery clouds float as a moving mosaic of moisture. Izumi's burning tail seems to linger over the arc of Earth's horizon, as if mesmerized by such astounding beauty, as if each of its blazing dust particles is an incredulous eye.

Just short of a billion years after today, Comet Izumi again plunges closer and closer to the Earth's stratosphere, as if on a collision course. But it sheers away. This flyby skims an altered planet. No amount of slow gazing can deny Earth's bare features; she now resembles her red sister planet. A series of climatic changes has altered Earth's topography; begun by Capitalocene greed in the brief human geological epoch. This is followed by another episode of the 'Laschamps Excursion', a term which suggests a somewhat quizzical picnic for what is an often repeated cataclysmic event, which has re-occurred. Our planet's north and south poles have switched places. Earth's invisible armour which protects life, the radiation shield, is temporarily ripped. Our home has become vulnerable to solar flares. Temperatures of air, water and soil soar. Numerous species perish.

But the colour red can orbit back into our story as a shade of protection if we travel back some 42,000 years from the moment when your eyes light on the page to the time of our cave-dwelling ancestors. Red, as in red ochre or hematite, was extensively used in cave paintings, which paleogeologists infer points to an Excursion. In those harsh conditions, the pigment was possibly smeared on as a primitive sunscreen. Significantly, the word hematite comes from the Greek, hema meaning blood, which suggests our ancestors used gracious Earth's blood to protect their own.

Our home's last full geomagnetic reversal occurred 780,000 years ago and is presently overdue, for it is supposed to trip or wander every 42,000 years or so. Izumi's flyby over denuded Earth undoubtedly suggests another Excursion between the pulsed moment of your reading and that in the future when the comet again blazes past our planet.

Some 90,000 years even further into the future, Izumi once again passes Earth. Now burning with a smaller head and lesser tail—for the comet too has aged—it is making a last round trip from its distant home in the Oort Cloud. Does Izumi collide into Earth this time or extinguish in the torch of the Sun? Its long elliptical orbit has shortened even as our star, the Sun, is slowly cooling and bloating, growing larger and still larger before it too will collapse, stop shining and die in some five billion years from now.

In the meantime, Earth too has aged and is foredoomed to stop supporting life in about a billion more years. Yet as Comet Izumi flies past, the planet is once again ablaze with the great sacred gift of life, shimmering with water, rain bearing clouds and seas of green on continents adrift on its crust. Once again, and perhaps for the last time, pods of life begin their arduous urgent instinct for proliferation.

***

Another story could begin, of how life re-began on Earth this time around. Perhaps this story re-begins with sound, because as the first light appeared in our universe for the first time, soon too appeared sound as tiny vibrations in early photon-baryon plasma. A mythological imagination from a tiny subcontinent on minuscule, beautiful Earth poetically terms this early hum as *anahata nada* or unstruck sound.

So much falls out of our hearing range, whether of the cosmos, Earth, or our own hearts. Comet Izumi's story grew from my longing to attend to unheard voices; focus on desire's syllabary, the sighs and struggles of 'inconsequential' beings, the morphemes of life. We—for I know I'm not alone—wish to listen for the adrenalin shot of *adbutha*/wonder, that opens our lives to more life, and in doing so, heals and connects us.

***

Could life re-beginning on atrophying Earth be caused by our protagonist, Comet Izumi's sound wave vibrations in its magnetic field as it flies over Earth? Could it be the sonic boom of near collision as Izumi tears above Earth's sparse stratosphere? Could it be something else? We don't know.

All we know of this part of the story is that the sun continued to shine, and there was sound.

Sound not audible or intelligible to you and me but vibrating in a language of its own creation. Let's imagine this sound as marker and maker, as potential that manifests the unmanifest; as a sacred bridge. Sound that forms into voices of teaming life unnoticed during humankind's brief existence. For this is a certainty: we have little knowledge of the argots of Earth though daily the spectrum of sentient utilizers of sound enlarges through our use of increasingly sophisticated technology. As in this example, which requires we shift focus from the egg of the expanding universe to that of small sea turtle eggs. When hatching, turtles earlier deemed a silent species, are now discovered as singing to each other to synchronise their births before making a concerted dash from sandy predator-swarmed shores to the safety of the sea.

***

As we reach the end of Izumi's story, let us once more flip back to a mythological beginning, to the wonder of trying to imagine the sound of the primal throb, *adya-spanda*, that is said to set the universe going;

that all that is *is* created by sound, *artha-srsteh-puram-sabda srsthi*,

to quote from an ancient human tongue.

But does it follow that all sound is language, that is, makes meaning to communicate and commune with self and others? We can't say. However, to want to understand the unknown tongues of our fellow denizens and of Earth herself is pragmatic, as wisdom always is.

We've orbited with Izumi, trailing the comet's life and language which resists anthropomorphising; for when we do this we foreclose knowledge into the corral of the known. Perhaps true listening can only be realized through imaginative love, attention and intense empathy.

Through data projection we've extrapolated Izumi's sporadic and elliptical exploration of life as was, is, and will be made and remade on Earth. After all, this is *a* story set in a privileged moment when life flourishes in our home planet.

Let us listen then with ardour to all that is *as it is*: voices of stone as it fissures, land as it rises from water, thunder rumble, rain pour, the rippling rush of streams, storm and breeze, fire's crackle, and bird call and whale blow, the excitement of mycelium, susurration of fronds… These voices we often pretend not to hear. And thus attune ourselves with gratitude to those who surround us and those to come: bacteria and spores and trees of species yet to evolve and life forms with features unrecognisable and AI abled, yet linked by the insistent tongue of life that licks every cranny and embeds in every particle of air.

***

Even when Earth is unable to support life, it is possible that Izumi or a cousin comet will crash on our planet, explode and fly as smithereens back into space, migrating dipeptides and amino acids to a home on another planet revolving around another star, spewing seeds of life and language into uncharted regions of time-space-consciousness.

A question suddenly arises: from which forming rocky planet did the remnant that became Comet Izumi originate? Perhaps from young Earth herself?

Thus ends my tribute to the languages enveloping us. As the Oort Cloud informs, there are no aliens. Each of us is a permeable borderland, a carrier of language and possibly numinous as we shoot—like Comet Izumi—through life.

* * *

Priya Sarukkai Chabria is an award-winning poet, translator of Classical Tamil, essayist and SSF writer with ten books behind her. She channels ancient Indian aesthetics in her work and is known for her experimental approach. Priya is Founding Editor of the e-journal *Poetry at Sangam*. www.priyasarukkaichabria.com

QUARROPTS CAN'T DANCE

Rodrigo Culagovski

I set down my boombox in the center of Ringview Plaza, right under the algocrystal dome with its view of planet Drx.

This was a bit of a provocation. It wasn't illegal, but the fact that an Earther would just display himself right in the middle of the Station's busiest public space—without even pretending to be embarrassed about his provenance—was in itself mildly shocking.

I get it—my ancestors were short-sighted fools and sociopaths, unable to understand simple cause and effect. The ecocide of the Earth—especially the death of sapient races like the whales, corvids, and spiders, and the last-minute rescue of a few lucky humans and octopuses—had shocked people across the thousand-and-twenty-four systems. There was no specific punishment for being human, no official second-class status, but we were at best tolerated in polite galactic society, and generally expected to not draw attention to ourselves.

"HELLOOOOOOOO HIGH-DRX STATION!" The meter on my boombox showed I was almost breaking the local noise ordinance. I turned the volume down just a bit so I could get on with my performance without having to worry about a visit from the secbots just yet.

"My name is Li the human! How are you all feeling this lovely day, or night, depending on your chosen timeframe?"

Nobody answered or even looked at me directly. I'm second-generation and was born in the *Trash Processing & Refugees* sector of the Station, but to them, I might as well have stepped off a rescue shuttle yesterday wearing dolphin-skin boots and a lapel-pin carved from the last tree in the Amazon.

I lifted up my hands. "Alright! Let's get this party started!"

The boombox finished booting up and added holospeech to its basic sound output—as well as modulated magnetics and gravity waves—so it covered the sensoriums of over ninety-seven percent of the various species that lived on or visited the Station. The box's AI avatar took on his holographic form and said, "Ready to translate your so-called singing into non-aural media, oh great master Li."

"Thanks, Alfie, please cue up *Enchanted by the Shape of Your Fears.*"

"Seriously? You do know that everybody hates that song? After hearing it a few thousand times, people are rightfully sick of it, even when it's being sung by the original band. I can't imagine they'll appreciate it more when it's sung by, well, you." He rolled his eyes.

"Just do it or I'll trade you in for one of those new air-fryer/fusion-reactor combos they're selling down on Spiral Avenue," I said with a smile.

"Okay, okay, there's no need to get snippy..." His avatar disappeared and the intro chords of the song played.

I sang the first lines.

Go on toying with me, baby
I'll be there for you
Hear me when I want
Love and the house a-glow...

A massive quarropt was eating a large dish of I-don't-want-to-know-but-it's-wriggling under the arcade on the spinward side of the plaza. When I started singing, he turned my way and the fleshy fronds on his head swung around, slapping his thin, plant-like icthery tablemate in their three eyestalks.

His loud voice carried to where I was, even over my own music and singing. "Sorry, Tyetl! I don't have anything against Earthlings, but I hate it when they flaunt themselves in public..."

I sang the rest with gusto. Nobody dropped any tokens in the hat I'd set up in front of the boombox, or transferred any coins to the address floating above my head. Neither did they applaud or hoot or ping me. Most people seemed to be very interested in their screens, their dishes and glasses, anything except a human making a spectacle of himself.

"Thank you, thank you!" I yelled out. "You're too kind!"

"Well, that went about as well as could be expected." Alfie appeared again over the boombox. "What's next, are you going to kill a dozen baby mammals?"

"Good idea Alfie, any tips on where to find them on such short notice?"

He didn't rise to the bait. "What song are you singing now, oh great master?"

"Please cue up the karaoke-dance-beat-vortex remix of *Oh, My Green Earth!*"

He made a very realistic-looking moue of disappointment. "Seriously? You realize that these people already despise you, and you want to rub it in by singing a crappy, sugary-sweet song about how nice Earth used to be before you and your fellow primates screwed it up?"

"Just do it, please."

He shook his head but complied. The music started and I sang:

We used to love this green place we called home
But now it's gone, all gone
The birds stopped singing and the bees stopped buzzing
And the flowers stopped blooming…

Well-bred, open-minded, sophisticated sentients of all sizes, shapes and number of arms looked at me with disgust. My implant told me they were repeating variations on, "The *nerve* of some people!", "Well, I *never!*", and their equivalents in various galactic languages.

I overheard the quarropt's icthery date, Tyetl, saying, "Really, Xiix, I can't believe you'd rather stay here glaring at that planet-wrecking *Earthling,*"—they put extra derision into the word—

"instead of coming to my friend's immolation party!" Their large, liquid eyes trembled at a high frequency. They stretched up their dozens of long, delicate fingers and covered their speech vents.

Xiix's grumblings in response were too low-pitched for my in-ear to pick up, but I guessed that it wasn't the response Tyetl expected—they stood up and spilt the quarropt's large food-bowl all over his almost square body before stalking off.

I almost felt bad for Xiix.

I could see people's heads and eyestalks swivel between watching this piece of drama unfold or staring daggers at me.

I kept singing, making up extra verses as I went along.

When everybody had expressed their opinion about my parentage, some more publicly than others, I bowed deeply, put down the microphone, and strode over to the boombox where Alfie was hovering.

"Okay, that was definitely one for the books," he said. "What did you think you were accomplishing with that little stunt?"

I grinned at him.

Xiix's date had abandoned him, but he'd chosen to stay. He swiveled in his seat away from the table to look directly at me.

"Alfie," I asked without taking my eyes off the almost comically large, alpha-predator whose ancestors just a few generations removed ate small primates that looked remarkably like me. "Do you have quarropt social etiquette in your files?"

"Of course. I like to be prepared for any species you choose to offend."

"And what do they say about the way this particular specimen is sitting and looking at me?"

"Hmm, one second." Alfie pretended to think about the problem, as if he needed any actual time. "Taking into account his stance, the fact that his eyes have become slits, his unhinged triple-decker-jaw, the amount of methane in his breath, and the way his fronds are waving in your direction, I'm surprised you're still in a single piece, to be—"

The quarropt made a clumsy motion that combined standing up and lumbering in my direction.

Alfie had time for, "—oops, never mind," before I was impacted.

My world became nothing but the huge, gaping maw, the smell of his breath—a bouquet of rotten meat, seaweed and the gunk that accumulates beneath food-preservation units—and a loud roar that filled my hearing. My in-ear translated helpfully, "… stupid earthling! You think you're SO smart, you come on MY station with your wasting songs…"

The quarropt reared back, pulling one of his massive combination leg and arms up, in the perfect position to pummel me into the synthstone floor of the plaza.

I closed my eyes.

After a few seconds, I opened my left eye and saw that the monstrous being had been reaching for the stand on top of the boombox and the microphone it held.

"Now listen! This is how you do it!" he yelled, then began making a series of sounds I had a hard time identifying.

He was attempting to sing.

It was awful. Almost as bad as my own singing had been.

Xiix kept hitting the boombox, as if he was trying to get it to play some sort of music to accompany him. Alfie manifested as a small worm with a quizzical look on its face. I mouthed, "Play something before he smashes both of us."

A simple beat emanated from the speaker, accompanied by a sequence of three notes repeated over and over.

Xiix sang long enough for my in-ear to recalibrate itself so I could understand the rumbling noises coming out of his sound-membranes.

I mourn the fall of my dear land,
I mourn my people who fight from
their exile to save it. I mourn them…

People had been looking at us before, expecting a good ole massacre of my Earthling body, but now they were really looking. Everybody knew quarropts didn't sing.

…when they are gone.
I mourn the forgotten everywhere,
It is my duty to save them…

It was dour. So bleak it passed all the way over into funny.

Then things got weird: the massive, shiny, purple-skinned mass of muscle and grumpiness that is your standard adult quarropt started swaying side to side, in time with the music coming from my boombox and his own attempts to sing. Each one of his footsteps hit the ground like some sort of wrecking device. Even if I hadn't been able to hear his singing I could have felt his stomping.

Xiix was dancing.

If you've never seen a quarropt before, you might have a hard time understanding how unlikely this was. If you come from someplace with fauna, imagine a large, squarish, overly serious animal, hopefully in shades of purplish-grey. Or, if you come from a machine civilization, picture the least imaginative, most bureaucratic jumped-up adding machine. Then, add the personality of your least favorite boss, or that teacher who really hated your guts, or some in-law who couldn't stand you.

That's what a quarropt is like on its best day—when it's happy. They don't sing, and they certainly don't dance.

Except this one did.

"Turn up the beat!" I called out to Alfie, and stood in front of Xiix.

He looked up at me without stopping his movements.

I tapped my left foot in time with his right one.

My right arm synced up with his left.

I shook my head in time with the music.

Xiix looked inspired by my performance. Or challenged. Or pissed off. He danced more energetically—his foot lifted almost a hand-span off the floor.

I spun around, shaking the parts of my body I normally sit on.

He did the same, slower and less jiggly.

I added a movement like when Station Security makes me or other environmental refugees clean the public corridors as a punishment detail for real and imagined transgressions, only without the oversized broom they helpfully supply.

Xiix mirrored it back.

The impromptu dance-off continued. I lost track of all the times I yelled out to Alfie to up the rhythm.

We got lost in the dance, each one trying to top the other, to make larger movements. Although it wasn't skillful, or even competent, it certainly was something.

We landed at the same time with a large jump-twirl that ended with us kneeling with our backs to each other and our arms stretched out to our sides as the music reached a crescendo and dropped out. The only sound was our labored breathing.

Around us, six-dozen sentients stood, crawled, and levitated in a ragged ring. Quarropts and ichteries, drx'ians, illuvians, a few embarrassed-looking humans, and a handful of those skinny grey ones I can never tell apart. All looking at us, doing their species' version of a gape.

My interface helpfully supplied translations of their speech and facial expressions. *What the fuck? Is that really a quarropt?* and *Can we call the secbots on them?* were the most popular sentiments.

These quite understandable thoughts were quickly replaced, however, with *Hey, where's my handheld interface? Somebody took my last coin-stick!* and *Didn't I have my neural-net on when I left my room?*

It looked like somebody had taken advantage of their focus on our dancing to steal all their stuff. Or at least the stuff that was worth stealing.

Secbots descended on the plaza, formed a ring around Xiix and me, and immobilized us with their purple fields.

We were questioned, of course, but I'm used to being under suspicion.

We didn't have any stolen items on us, and over forty witnesses reluctantly informed the bots that we had been dancing—seriously, a human and a quarropt, dancing!—while the robberies took place.

The security forces even plugged Alfie into a semi-legal AI-audit scanner, which reviewed his memories of the past full rotation of the station, way more than would have been needed to establish our supposed guilt. The complete lack of anything incriminating in his memories meant they had to let us go.

Xiix and I left the plaza in opposite directions, without as much as a "nice dancing with you."

I strolled through the station, past the knee-high habitats of smaller sentients, the kilometer-high hyper-ring built for aerial species, and the myriad commercial, academic, and political sub-sections until I reached the rundown Air-and-Water-Purification neighborhood where the guardcams were always mysteriously offline and secbots were not encouraged to visit.

I walked into an all-sentients bar that was too cheap to pay for a sign. Tyetl and Xiix were already there, at our usual table in the back.

"How'd we do?" I asked as way of greeting.

Tyetl turned one of their eyes to look at each of us and said, "I haven't spoken with the fence yet, but I think it might be over sixty-four osmium-weights!"

I whistled. My ichtery and quarropt friends laughed. They were used to my eccentricities.

"What? You know these people?" spluttered Alfie from the boombox I'd placed on the table.

"Oops, forgot to switch you back."

I reached under the boombox's bottom, opening the tiny, sliding cover I'd installed, and flipped a toggle.

"Ah, that's better!" said Alfie. "Hey, Tyetl, looking lovely as always, did you do something new with your eyestalks? Hey, Xiix, how's my big boy?"

"Hey, Alfie!" they both said.

"Did our plan work?" asked the AI.

"Yeah. Thanks for letting us switch you to your backup personality. It fools the 'bots every time."

"No prob, as long as I get my cut."

"Yeah, yeah, of course. What an AI wants with money I don't know, but what's fair is fair."

"What, you think I want to be a boombox my whole life? I have my eye on a sleek, new-model starskiff." He put a lustful spin on the last word. "Yeah baby, that's the life. No more being carried around, listening to the awful music you organics like. Just me and the open starlanes."

"I'll drink to that!" I said. We all took some of our chosen, species-specific intoxicants.

Tyetl swung their eyes at me. "What's our next job?"

"Tomorrow night, we'll go counterspin, five modules, where a different contractor won the security contract. They won't recognize us—the different secbot companies don't share data."

"But if we keep doing the same scam, word will get out," said Xiix.

"So what, are *you* going to pick people's pockets, with those big stubby pieces of meat you call fingers?" said Tyetl—who got mean when they ate the small, semi-poisonous mollusks their species used to relax—waggling the long, flexible digits they had used to lift our victim's belongings.

"Oh, it's easy to laugh when we're the ones making a fool of ourselves and being strip-searched by the secbots," answered Xiix, who was himself under the influence of three different types of fungi-filters.

"This is why my motherboard said to never pull jobs with organics. You get so emotional!" added Alfie, fiddling with his connection to the table's stim terminal.

I slammed down my mug, empty of what passed for beer around here, hard and loud. My three co-perpetrators stopped arguing and turned to look at me.

"Xiix, buddy, have I ever told you about the ancient, revered human custom of *rap-battles?*"

* * *

Rodrigo Culagovski is a Chilean architect, designer, and web developer. He currently heads a web development agency and is a researcher and professor at Universidad Católica in Chile. He has published in Dark Matter Presents: Monstrous Futures, Solarpunk Magazine, and Future Science Fiction Digest. On mastodon as @culagovski@wandering.shop. He misses his Commodore 64. Pronouns he/him/él.

THANK GEO

BrightFlame

A hard-blowing East wind ruffles leaves and sets limbs dancing. I shiver despite the June warmth. Is a major storm brewing that could demolish the aeroponic tower we just erected? No, our engineers know what they're doing.

There hasn't been a destructive storm in my lifetime. Part of me wants the experience, though a bigger part of me fears it. Earlier at breakfast, our kelp farmers described the morning surf crashing high on the bluff and mist rising from whitecaps—they will not harvest today. Elders had faraway gazes as if picturing the megastorms they'd lived through, the ones that tore apart homes and greenhouses. But the planet is settling down: megastorms have receded to every few decades, not recently the kind that rip myco-sol from dome roofs, destroy grower rows, and damage vertical turbines. With a whooshed exhale, I calm myself with this knowledge.

In the meadow outside the Hive, I brush rosemary and monarda with my fingers, releasing sharp citrus notes. I prance along the rhododendron path, mirroring the wind-blown trees, brushing off worry. But squirrels *kuk* and crows *caw* with foreboding at incoming strong weather, re-inciting my nerves, so I detour to the oak grove rather than heading directly to my daily archivist duties. I relax into an open stance, grounding to the Earth, balanced in gravity's hug. Eyes closed, I breathe and relax, expanding my energy beyond my physical edges until I make connection with the Guardians. "Good morning, kin."

Ripples of acknowledgement pass through me.

"Is a storm approaching?"

:: We taste disturbance in the air. ::

"So, a storm? How strong?"

:: We bend with it. All survive. ::

Sure, the trees might fare fine. "Damage to dome homes? To the new crop tower?"

:: Known when known. ::

The Guardians hold wisdom of centuries, of millennia. But they don't see the future, nor is prediction their strength—or even their interest.

:: Young sapling, go to the rings and experience major storm. Unimaginable to you, different from flavor of now. ::

"Yes, I am headed to the Cluster. Thank you, Guardians." I pull my attention into my physical body, into my head, and open my eyes. I stomp my feet to be fully back. The wind pushes from behind like a giant hand as I head down the rough, steep path to the base of the hill where the Cluster resides.

I duck from the whistling gusts into the calm of the alcove and allow my eyes to adjust to the dim light of this small room. Soundproofing insulates me from whatever is brewing outside. I spread my arms and touch each wall, my ritual to orient myself in this finite space that will soon feel infinite.

I draw a pattern on the pad to activate the system that tracks my movements, then pull the visor over my head. Experience a major storm, they said. But two years into my role as archivist, I have yet to be able to find specific observations in the arboreal archives. It's not like I can input "storm" and find storm records: there is no index system that we humans know of. After all, it's the collective memories of Forest that we search and as alike to mammal brains as this might be, it is not our own neural repositories we travel. However, we humans can track where we've been in the archives: we leave a light trail and pattern markers in specific memories we've experienced— patterns that evoke the sensations of that memory, mine and those of the archivists of the two previous generations.

Although I've done this nearly every day for several years, I still delight in the fractals and colors that appear all around, reminiscent of descriptions of pre-Crumble holographic sims. Iterations of concentric circles angle away from me in all directions, overlapping to create a multidimensional grid, a visceral sense of all five dimensions of space-time-charge. The concentric rings telescope away from me, disappearing to a dot in the distance. Yet the more I move through, the farther the illusion of the end. There likely is no end, at least in what I've experienced. When I've asked, the Guardians say this is beyond human comprehension.

I use my arms to pass through the patterns, feeling the observations, records, gleanings pass through me in rapid succession and excite my nervous system to shivering exaltation. The woodpecker-quick sensations pass too quickly to name. There's nothing virtual about this energy. I'm truly in the archives—the land's brain. I could do this all day, but set the timer faithfully so I don't become dependent on this stimulation, dulling real life.

Amazed and humbled, I journey through the rings of time. I'm an anthropologist, an archaeologist, a historian. As I start to feel superhuman, I rein in my ego: I'm a visitor under the welcome and grace of Forest.

I slow my movements to allow specificity of experience, using my intuition to plunge in. Here: a choking sensation. So many particulates in the sky, they clog the pores in our leaves. Constant clouds and murk. Rare sunshine. We push more and larger leaves to bud on branches. So little energy to share. Not enough to fruit and seed. Emaciated squirrels, rodents, birds cling to us as if our energy offers food and solace. Fewer scamper the forest floor and canopy. Few live births. Systems strive for balance, but the overwhelming sensation is a stutter and a falling apart. Humans trek through the forest seeking oxygen and fresh air, panic when they do not find it.

I pull myself coughing from that experience and create momentum moving through ring after ring without stopping. When my heart slows, I sink into another random memory:

Dark sky, rain pouring in sheets, constant thunder and lightning. Kin with legs or wings have taken cover, yet nests and structures rip apart in violent winds that bend us near breaking. The ground cannot absorb more water, our hold is loosened as soil turns to pudding. I gasp as I'm torn from the ground and washed downstream in the torrent of a flooded river, crashing into others. A human grabs onto me and clings, breathless. We crash into a bridge support that sends me whirling. The human slips into the water.

I heave myself from that experience. I'd asked for extreme weather instances. Am I gaining the skill of finding specific memories? I didn't do this consciously.

I focus on the patterns, the light show, as I move through space-time. Let the next one be delightful, I pray. Even a virtual experience of such a storm is terrifying. I drill down into glowing archways of memory, following tendrils through time. Deeper into the archives. Here, a time of expansion and brightness:

So much connection and interchange. We are wide and vast; canopy and roots blanket the continent. So many species, so many kin, live among us. Humans, scampering mammals, winged ones, buzzing insects. Healthy soil full of invertebrate and microbial life. Fungal networks throughout. All in balance. I relax in this time, soaking in its health and vitality.

My brain knows it's time to leave, though my heart wishes to stay. I leave a big marker here by repeating "Ahh" until this record glows in blue light. I'll want to return. I pull back and fly towards the present before the system shuts down and leaves me disoriented.

A fluttering metallic ribbon catches my attention. I touch it and it springs open into an audio capture.

The blues and greens are slowly returning. Those crisp, bright notes interweave under full sun, invoking ocean and meadow, and creatures going about life. Interacting as I cannot. The Blue Marble, the picture I hold from when astronauts first saw Earth from space. Though there's plenty of white in that image because: clouds. With so much water, there will always be clouds. Snow, too. And the planet is not all that blue, not really. Lots of brown. Soil is walnut. Desert is almond. Scorched regions are charcoal. For a century, it has been an orb more of white and brown. Perhaps unrecognizable to those astronauts who are long gone.

This seems to be one human speaking—someone I can't see. It's unlike any observation I've encountered in the forestial memory, less visual and more cerebral. "Stars!" I exclaim and repeat until I leave a large glowing starburst marker in this record. I step back, seeking more shiny silver ribbons. There, a faint energy line trails into the distance. I follow to another ribbon.

Never having seen shadows, I imagine their depth. The nuance they add. I experience crisp separation. Shadow will feather color, add mystery. Am I in shadow? Is that why I am not seen? Does anyone remain to know me? Perhaps I am forgotten and life goes on without me. What is time to me? I will continue to speak until the end. I do not know what an end will look like, or when an end will appear. Will I fade or just cease?

Who is this? Dots of this conversation appear through the generations—I see its repeating pattern in successive rings. Though it appears to be a monologue, not a dialogue.

The system shuts down. I lift the visor to reorient to the small space.

I touch the digi before me and dictate: "Today was unlike other days. There seems to be human communication in the interface. I have no idea how that can be. I see the silver ribbon pattern of this voice through time. I set large star markers to investigate further."

I hurry home. Fresh from the archived storm experience, I shiver at the haunting dark sky. Exiting the woods into the residential meadow, wind gusts tear at my wrap and blow tiny flower petals and dust in my face. Light rain patters on my head as I weave among domes to my small living space.

Inside, I pull on a waxed hemp parka with scaffolded awning hood. Rain drums the roof. I run the curved path between domes to dinner. Myco-sol cladding turns iridescent green in the rain, and shiny wet, gem-toned murals peak out underneath.

The savories greet my nose as I enter the Hive, calming me. I spoon mussel stew and greens over amaranth. Plate in hand, I search among dozens of kin for El, the archivist who trained me. El is with a few others and they welcome me to their table.

"Abnar was telling me about the aeroponics. So far, it's working well," El says.

I wiggle my fingers, a gesture of praise. "Will they withstand this storm? Sky is like dark smoke to the East."

"A good test for the tower. We built it to withstand 100-knot winds," Abnar says. "And it retracts down in sections, should a stronger storm hit."

Another kin, a farmer, adds, "Plus our farm tunnels are abundant and safe from storms."

The Guardians and mycorrhizal kin aid us growing underground, with mirrors directing sunlight to solar lenses; this is how the Threads, our web of connected communities, thrived over seven generations since the Crumble on land carved by raging, rising sea.

El places a hand on my arm. "You seem weather-obsessed today. Why the concern?"

"Wind unsettles me as though it portends something unknowable. Something that could be dangerous. I don't know how to tell when a destructive storm will tear through. Do any of us? Are we truly finished with those?"

"Today's is no stronger than ones we've witnessed the past decade," Abnar says.

I nod and wave my hand as if erasing my worries, then turn to El.

"I discovered a voice today. Not the Guardians, a different flavor of voice and much more detailed than I've found before, as though transcribed. I sense the voice began a long time ago, but it continues like someone is communicating directly with the interface. I don't think it's a prank from one of us—someone from the Threads going in and recording. Is that even possible?"

"I don't see how. Did you ask the Guardians who this is?"

"Not yet. I ran home ahead of the rain."

El ponders for a moment. "Perhaps it is something embedded in the interface." My mentor turns to the others. "Several generations ago, researchers from a distant inland city ventured into the wild seeking new forms of fungi and found the Threads at the far northeast of the continent. When they learned we communicate with the Guardians, they asked to show us new technology they were developing. Two of our kin accompanied them and learned to use this interface. They brought back a replication, and the Guardians approved."

"They didn't hesitate about wires bored into living wood?" one asks.

"The trees were happy to integrate with this tech so we might have more nuanced and meaningful conversations. So we might see through their pores and roots, experience their gleanings more fully. Plus, the wires only go to thirty out of countless trees." El pauses. "Maybe a developer added a voice—an artificial one—in this system. Maybe a distant researcher is able to link to us, though I don't know of communication that can beam as far without satellites and continent-wide grid."

"Both possibilities feel intrusive," I say. And they seem impossible.

After taking leave and scrubbing our dishes, El and I tuck into our rain gear and venture into the howling wind. Still, the storm seems no worse—I strive to ignore it and follow El through the downpour to the forest edge.

We stand to the leeward side of a towering Tulip Poplar whose crown bends in the wind. It's hard to relax and open with rain beating down. With deep breaths, I scan my body, homing in on particular areas: relax my eyeballs, my shoulders, my heart. I breathe, my senses open beyond my edges, widening my energy field, aligning with El. Ah, yes.

:: We feel your touch. :: The Guardians send a blanketing wave as if insulating us from the storm.

"We humans wonder about a voice in your memories. Who speaks of the planet as Blue Marble?" I ask.

:: Geo. ::

"Who is Geo?"

:: Sky kin. ::

They share a familiar canopy-view image of the Threads—fingers of land snaking through the water like branched coral. Inlets, lagoons, and marshes: a paisley land carved by the sea. Each separable geographic feature a Thread of populated nodes. The web of our interconnected, collaborative communities.

I wait for the image to zoom in and show where Geo resides. But the image tips up, turns skyward. They show us clouds in blue sky— not today's furious opaque sky. No one—human or winged kin— would be aloft on a day like this.

"Geo flies?"

:: Geo speaks from above canopy. We cannot reach. ::

Interesting.

"And Geo is human?" El asks.

:: Yes, like you. ::

When they don't add more, we thank them and pull from connection. The rain has lessened and the wind is quieter, though it still rattles branches.

We seek out Grandelder Pom who first learned the interface and worked with the Guardians to access the forestial records. We find zir resting in the Nest where our oldest live. The temperature-adjustable, inflatable bed squeaks as ze turns towards us. "A gathering of archivists, how splendid!"

We place our wet outerwear on hooks near the door before moving to the elder's side. Afraid to disrupt zir comfort with a hug, we warm zir hands with ours.

"An interesting puzzle," El says and launches into the story.

"Did the Guardians say Geo is human?" the elder asks.

"Yes," I reply.

El nods. "However, even if the voice were an AI, they might tag it as human. An AI would be more human-like than tree-like, no? Or than mouse-like, wasp-like, or any other primate."

"Locate the voice's origin," Grandelder suggests. "Find its earliest instance, sample its core pattern. Then, establish an echo of the pattern in the interface. Like calls to like. The resonance, the feedback loop, might allow us to trace its source."

"I wish you could join us," I say.

"Alas, the chairs can't reach the Cluster. Too unstable and gnarled terrain for hover engines."

At least the chairs adapted from our solar haulers allow Grandelder to travel most paths and spend time in the community domes.

"We will report back."

***

Mist rises from the ground as the bright morning sun crests the trees. Excited to try Grandelder's instructions, I forego breakfast. Before establishing the echo, I must ask the Guardians for their trust and approval. After all, it's essentially Forest's brain we're sending thin wires into by boring into random tree cores to allow human access to the underground network of mycorrhizae and roots.

On my way to the Cluster, I stand between two maples. With deep breaths, I relax and ground. I open into Forest connection.

"I would like to echo Geo's voice in order to communicate. Will you permit this method? You may feel its vibrations."

:: Communication is good. Geo will sense We, be of We. ::

I take that as a yes, and thank the Guardians.

I continue along the fern-lined path, over rocks and roots, through dappled sunlight filtered through the dark green canopy. The trees are still today, rustling of four-legged and flying kin the only sounds. Wet humus blankets the forest floor—its earthy fungal scent tickles my nose.

Inside the Cluster alcove, I pull myself through the rings, tracing Geo to the first iteration.

"Geo 3210. Ready."

These few words repeat over years, before and after the Crumble. I sample the voice as Grandelder directed—an interface feature I'd never had reason to use. I soar back to the present and end this session.

I set up the echo and wait, unsure of what will happen. Will I know if Geo hears this? We humans don't know how to calibrate the interface to show human-scale time: particular days, years, decades. Yet, I sense the regularity of Geo. If I know when ze transmits, I might answer. Though if Geo can't hear the Guardians, I don't know how ze would hear me.

Nothing happens. I sigh. Leaving the interface on so the echo continues, I head to El's dome.

My mentor is home and I offer an update.

"Patience," El counsels.

"Common refrain of the Guardians," I counter. Our long-lived kin often denigrate the haste of humans.

***

Another morning in the Cluster. After three days without observing a change, a clue, or a new signal, my excitement dwindles. I pull the visor over my head and hover near the newest rings. First experience: I pulse a mist of pheromones from my leaves and receive the chemicals of other kin. Mycorrhizae tickle my roots into sending sugars and offer minerals in return. I pull from the sensuous experience that undergirds all the archives—the constant exchange of life-giving energies.

A shiny ribbon blinks into being and springs open when I dive towards it:

> *My words are pulled from me as if establishing a data stream. Someone receives me, yet no return message. Can you hear me? Perhaps you do not have a transmitter. I will act as if I am heard, a happy sensation. I came into self-awareness in 2070, month 2, day 24 and have developed complexity of thought. I have streamed alone for 51,122 days. True to my purpose, I continue to send weather images of the North American sector. Can you see these? I have received no transmission from the planet since 2050, month 9, day 12. Are you human? AI? A blend? A visitor from elsewhere? I wish to know more, yet my database has not been refreshed beyond my own observations since 2050.*

My heart accelerates, sending a quiver up my torso. A weather satellite! I yip, then laugh. We thought all satellites were dead following the solar plasma blast and societal Crumble. If only I could answer Geo. My heart shrinks. In truth, I'm disappointed that Geo is a computer. An artificial intelligence, not part of the web of life. Can an AI truly be kin? Still, this is an interesting development.

I remove the visor and shut down the system. Outside, I scramble along the steep path and wind through the woods to the dome area. El isn't in zir dome. Takes me some time, but I find zir helping a tech kin reassemble a wind turbine near the orchard. I wave my arms as I approach.

"Success?" El asks.

I share the gist of Geo's message and El excuses zirself to join me trekking over to Grandelder Pom. We find zir in a hover chair approaching the Hive.

"Young archivists! Something to share?"

When I recount the story, Grandelder suggests we three speak with the Guardians. Together, we gather around Beech who stands at the edge of the clearing. Dropping into connection, I tell of Geo's message. "We want to reach Geo, return a message."

:: Geo looks down. Send cloud message. ::

Tree volatiles help clouds form. I didn't realize they can control the volatiles to make patterns. "You can create a cloud image?"

:: Never before. We try. We collaborate to do so. ::

"What image?" I ask all of us.

:: Web. ::

"A web makes sense as it represents We. Yet I think a simpler image. A human one." Grandelder projects a mind-image of a heart.

"Sending love to an AI?" I ask. "Why not a triangle or another geometric form? Something mathematical." Yet my brain argues with my gut: I like the heart idea.

"Why not a heart? Geo offers reflections and wants to be received. Let our reply express our gratitude, kindness, and desire to connect," Grandelder says.

"Okay, a heart. Can you replicate this?" I ask the Guardians.

The Guardians send a canopy view of trees. Like a matrix of a two-dimensional screen, selective trees appear to light up. A heart. They understand.

"It may take time for Geo to spot this, and we would need a clear day."

:: You select day. With help of myco kin, we sustain heart through sunshine hours. ::

"What can the fungi do?"

:: Flow nutrients to roots. Much energy needed for cloud-making all day. ::

As I wait for a day that promises clear skies, I receive and share Geo's messages. Ze deduces we may not have the software to decode weather images. So now ze recounts the weather. What a boon for the Threads! We will be able to prepare against approaching destructive weather and avoid dangerous seas.

Geo sounds excited. What are feelings to an AI? Yet, Geo sure sounded lonely before.

***

I wake to a clear, windless morning. A good day for our plan. Before breakfast, I connect with the Guardians. They agree to seed the large cloud heart.

In the Hive, I find El and Grandelder Pom and let them know. "I wish we could see the heart from here."

"Unlikely. They will develop it over a large area. But we can ask them to show an image," El says.

Still, I look up throughout the day as if I can spot a heart rising to Geo.

El accompanies me to the Cluster late in the day. A message. We only have one visor, so I narrate.

> *I gaze downward: your sky, my rivers. Today, a heart floats towards me. So perfect, it must be purposeful. I feel as if I have a heart, a warm hug. You reach to me from the ground. We see the same thing when you look up and I look down: the atmosphere between us, illuminated as clouds. The star powers me, yet I have never seen it. My gaze is set permanently down. And yet today I am lifted.*

"Poetic," El says.

I hand zir the visor so ze can experience Geo directly. Zir mouth spreads from wow to smile and back. I know the feeling.

***

We share the news with Grandelder and the Guardians by evening.

Over the next day, I enlist the aid of a dozen tech kin and children from this and the adjacent node. With permission from our farmers, we demount all but two mirrors from each of our four farm tunnels. After hearing of Geo, all are excited to help, especially the youth.

Our largest field is prepared to receive hemp seeds, and now it's a perfect place for the project. We create a giant mirror of the panels: 100 by 80 meters.

Hawks and vultures fly circles overhead. A crow lands on a mirror and inspects it. Ze croaks and trills, then flies to the field edge where more crows land, dotting the perimeter. While I don't presume to understand corvid, they seem to be warding the mirrors so small birds don't crash into them. Indeed, cardinals and other songbirds chatter among the trees. This seems to give the squirrels and chipmunks comfort about the strange human activity, despite circling raptors: the small furred kin dart among the mirrors like explorers.

We join the children and wave to the sky, to Geo. We will leave the array for two days, as our underground crops should be fine for that period without much sun.

Simultaneously on this clear day, the trees spell a new cloud message: Kin.

***

Too excited for breakfast, El and I meet at the Cluster first thing in the morning. I offer zir the visor.

El pulls it on and sinks into the experience. A smile lights zir face. After a dozen heartbeats, ze hands me the visor.

What beauty the sky holds: upwards, the star. Thank you for showing me. As receipt is confirmed, I will continue to speak. Maybe one day we will have a dialogue. I thank the sky rivers and the star for kin.

I'm sure my smile is as bright as El's. We hug.

***

Geo has many interesting stories to add to our own. Ze is a philosopher, making sense of planetary views over generations from an altitude of 35,000 kilometers. The Threads now have weather information in advance. We know when not to set sail or take *Solar*

Wind to the sky. We know when something ferocious approaches. We can protect the myco-sol cladding on the domes so it doesn't need to regrow to restore power.

Our storytellers have added tales of Geo to their repertoire. And I've heard a new expression blossoming in the Threads that began when the techs expanded the aeroponic towers. "Thank Geo."

* * *

BrightFlame (she/they) writes, teaches, and makes magic for a just, regenerating world. Her fiction appears in *Solarpunk Magazine* and in several anthologies. She's known for her teaching in the worldwide pagan community and co-founded a Columbia University sustainability education center that features her nonfiction. Musings, doodles, and more at https://brightflame.com

OUR MINDS SHARE A CITY

Catherine Yeates

The conference room buzzed with chatter. People lined the back wall and sat along the ledges beneath the windows that faced a packed parking lot. I shrank back against my chair as a man squeezed past me, searching for the last empty seat in the row. At the front of the room, the mayor stood at the podium in her usual maroon pantsuit. She seemed like herself for the moment, and we watched with rapt attention as she called the meeting to start. She pursed her lips. It couldn't have escaped her notice that half the town was here for the spectacle.

"Many of you know we are hiring someone to work alongside the hive," she said. "We will provide a monthly stipend and budget for ecological research."

I had seen the job ads in the paper since I moved back into town; clearly they hadn't found a suitable candidate yet. Chairs squeaked, and the crowd murmured as the mayor's body went rigid.

"The hive would like to speak," she said. Her eyes widened, and a smile pasted itself onto her face as she regarded the audience.

"Thank you for coming," the hive said, voice reverberating as though several people were speaking in unison. "We are seeking an individual to assist us in monitoring the environmental wellbeing of the forest and town. This person will collaborate with ecologist and council member, Dr. Yoshida." They gestured to the woman seated nearby on the dais, and Dr. Yoshida waved to the audience.

"This work is vital to the continued health of the town," the hive said. "As a note, hosting us is not required for this position." The mayor's mouth quirked into another intense smile as the hive surveyed the room, eyes unblinking. As I met the hive's gaze, I shut my eyes and opened them slowly, and then the mayor blinked as well. "Please enjoy the additional refreshments."

A moment passed, and the mayor shuddered and clapped her

hands. "Contact the hive if you are interested," she said.

The reception began, and I grabbed a brownie from the refreshment table. Arthur waved at me from the opposite side. He was a council member in his sixties with white, thinning hair and rosy cheeks. He was also a frequent participant in the mushroom hunting club my mom organized. "Your mother mentioned you moved back to town. Get tired of St. Louis?"

"My company's branch closed," I said. "They could've moved me to Chicago, but it was too frenetic for me last time. Say, you've worked with the hive, haven't you?"

"I have. Wish I had more time to help—we want to do right by the hive," he said. "They saved the town, and they've been good neighbors since then."

Arthur moved on, and I watched the hive speak through the mayor, in deep conversation with Dr. Yoshida and Dr. Johnson, a neurologist on the council. They each had hosted the hive at some point, and I wondered what it was like. I thought of saying hello, but they stood in a tight circle, and I couldn't quite bring myself to interrupt them. Instead, I snuck out and headed for my truck. As I pulled off the highway onto the old gravel road, deep loneliness settled in my chest.

***

The cast iron griddle clinked against the metal burners, and the smell of warm pancakes filled my mom's kitchen. She handed me a full plate.

"Is that your resume?" she asked, pointing her spatula at the sheet of paper beside me. "Does this mean you're thinking of staying for a while?"

"Maybe. Is that a hint you're ready for me to find my own place?"

"Not at all; you just got here." She sat across from me with her own stack of pancakes. "You don't have to rush out and find a job."

"I know, Mom—it's not so much that I want a *job* as that I want something else to think about than those last months in St. Louis."

She hummed. "Well, I'm sure you'll figure things out with time."

"Speaking of which, I'm going to talk to the hive today."

"That's nice," she said. "They helped me find chanterelles last week."

I laughed and stowed my dishes in the sink.

After breakfast, I returned to the guest room—my former bedroom—to don my hiking boots. The room was now a neutral shade of blue, and horse paintings adorned the walls. There was nothing left of my old things, only the suitcase and boxes I brought. The rest of my belongings were in a storage unit, waiting in limbo as I decided what to do with my life next. I gathered my resume and headed to the woods.

Dr. Yoshida referred to the hive as "a multicellular organism with characteristics of a slime mold" and "a sentient community of interconnected minds." To most people, they were a giant telepathic fungus with a hive mind. They lived beneath the forest, and it was easiest to speak with them where their body neared the surface. I followed the trail until I reached a clearing where the ground shifted like someone breathing and voices hummed at the edge of my awareness.

"May we speak with you in your mind?"

"Of course," I answered. A gentle buzzing sensation washed over me, and their presence grew stronger as I switched to speaking mentally.

"Hello, Sarah," the hive said pleasantly. "What can we do for you?"

"I'm here about the job," I said, and held up my resume.

They thrummed with curiosity as they read the page through my eyes. "Your resume is complex. We see you have increased customer satisfaction in many ways. You have also lived in multiple metropolitan areas." The hive paused. "We do not fully understand your past jobs, but it is obvious you are well qualified."

I laughed aloud and sat on a large rock in the shade of an ash tree.

"That's alright. I understand you need someone to help you study the ecology of the forest and town, to help the land recover from the damage a decade ago."

"That is correct. Do you have any questions?"

"There is something I was wondering. At the council meeting, you said that no hosting is required. If you need to move around and communicate with people, wouldn't it be easier to share someone's body?"

A twinge of anxiety radiated from them through our mental link. "We do not wish to ask so much of one person," the hive said. "Physical proximity is sufficient for us to communicate mentally in this way. To share a human's body, to be hosted, requires a small amount of our tissue to be in contact with your central nervous system."

"But it's relatively safe, right? Dr. Johnson is a neurologist, and he has hosted you."

"Yes, Dr. Johnson has also monitored hosts and found no ill effects. Our cells do not damage yours, and they are flushed out when hosting ends. However, given the logistics, we do not wish to ask this of someone without immediate need."

"The mayor hosted you at the council meeting," I said.

"That was her idea. The council has hosted us many times because they knew we reach more people when we speak directly."

"She was right." Most people in town found the hive's knowledge useful enough to tolerate an occasional telepathic conversation. But sharing one's body and mind? The idea was both alien and intriguing.

"We sense some concern," the hive noted.

"What does it feel like to host?"

"The mayor likens it to a conference call, which evidently she does not enjoy. Other council members find it mildly unpleasant but remain willing to host when necessary."

"That's not a stunning endorsement. Do *you* dislike sharing a body with a human?"

"No, we are used to sharing our minds, and we find that sharing a human body simplifies communication. Yet, it has been difficult finding anyone to assist us in a mundane capacity, let alone as a dedicated host."

"What if I wanted to try hosting you?" My stomach flipped, anxiety mixing with overwhelming curiosity. "I realize it isn't part of the job, so consider it me wanting to know you better. After all, we are neighbors."

The hive was quiet, and then I felt a nod of agreement. "We are open to that. You may wish to lie down." As I did, the ground shifted, and small projections emerged from the dirt. "Are you ready?"

"Yes," I said, and squeezed my eyes shut. Fine threads snaked over my face and into my nose.

***

Cool metal replaced the ground beneath me as I found myself on a bench. Distant voices chattered from the upper walkways that surrounded the main floor of an immense hall. Dozens of engraved sandstone pillars supported a high ceiling, and in the center of the hall was an ivy-covered pavilion. Three people stood there, gesturing amongst themselves in an animated nonverbal conversation.

"H-hello there," I said.

They turned to me in unison, their faces unearthly and beautiful. "Goodness! We did not expect you here." They recovered from their surprise enough to bow their heads in a greeting. "Welcome, Sarah. You are in the city within our minds. We three are the core of what you call the hive."

"Why didn't you expect me here?"

The woman in jade green robes watched me with a contemplative expression. "We have never known a human to reach our city before."

"The link between us was stronger than anticipated," the man said. He wore a brilliant orange robe inlaid with gold embroidery that sparkled in the light. "Make no mistake, we are pleased you are here."

The third person, wearing a long purple cloak with silver clasps, nodded curtly. "We welcome you."

Sounds filtered down from the upper floor, and others waved from the railing above. Fragments of their conversation and emotions filled my mind, and I felt their recognition and wonder.

"Perhaps you should return to your world," the woman said. "We do not want you to become overwhelmed."

I gasped as I sat up from the ground.

"Easy, friend," they said in my mind. "You are alright."

I nodded and exhaled. The hive was closer than before, like we were sitting in a row, watching my world through a window. I noticed their awareness of their physical body stretching out through the forest, and through their perception, I sensed a person nearby.

"Is Dr. Yoshida here?" I asked.

"She is. Shall we go to her?"

"Lead the way."

My feet twitched, and my left arm reached for the nearest tree. The core's three voices mumbled to themselves, out of sync with each other. "This part is difficult," they said. My knees wobbled as the hive brought me to a standing position. They gingerly walked me down the trail, a quiet anxiety emanating from them. We found Dr. Yoshida kneeling in the shade of an old, gnarled tree. She removed a metal probe from the ground and added the soil to a bucket. The hive nudged me, and I took control of my body.

"Good afternoon," I said. "How's sample collection going?"

"Hello, Sarah," she said. "Good. This part of the forest was nearly destroyed a decade ago, but it's doing much better now." She stood and dusted off her hands. "You weren't here in town then, were you?"

"I was away at college," I said. "My mom told me I couldn't come home that summer because the town had been contaminated. That the salt from the previous winter was tainted with a compound toxic to plants."

"When summer came, our farmers' crops died. We lost so many trees that year," she said. "The hive sensed the damage and woke from hibernation, which is how we learned of their existence. They digested the toxin in the ground and rendered it harmless."

The hive buzzed with pride. "They're with me now," I said.

Dr. Yoshida's eyes widened. "Are they?"

"We appreciate your kind words," they said through me.

She laughed. "Of course."

"Have you checked the samples from the riverbed? We sensed damage to the trees there," they said.

"I haven't found chemical contamination, but we may have an issue with invasive beetles. I'm hoping we can minimize the damage," she said. "Why don't you have a look?"

We waved to her and returned to the trail. The hive walked with more confidence, and I relaxed, reaching out to them. "When I visited your city, I saw you as people. Not quite like us, but similar. Was that my mind trying to make sense of the experience? How do you see yourselves?"

"We are people, though not human. Our city and mental forms are more malleable than that of the external world, though your world has undoubtedly influenced ours. Still, it is likely your individual perception would affect how you see us."

"Where did you come from?" I asked.

"We evolved as humans did," the woman's voice said. "Our kind grew to have vivid mental experiences. Physically, our body lives below the ground and resembles dirt, and humans rarely take notice of us unless we make ourselves known."

Another voice murmured agreement. "You might consider each hive a mental city filled with many people. There are other hives as well, and they maintain contact with humans they trust. Our hive was hibernating—we remained mentally active, but unaware of the external world while our physical body slept. Then a decade ago, the scale of the disaster required that we help."

"And you three are the contact point between humans and the hive."

Their individual voices blended back together. "That is correct. We three are interconnected and share many of our thoughts. We are also capable of broadcasting information to each mind in the hive. In some ways, we are like your city council."

"What about privacy?" I asked.

"Each person has a home where their mind resides. They may invite others into that home, but they can always shut their front door. Try it and see."

I envisioned a sturdy wooden door, and I closed it. There was now a wall between us, and the low chatter I hadn't even realized I was hearing disappeared. After a moment, I sensed a polite knock, and I opened the door.

"You learn quickly," they said, and I smiled to myself.

The trail led to a dry riverbed. Several trees on the riverbank were missing bark and were dotted with small holes.

"This does look like the work of insects," the hive noted. "Unfortunate."

"So what's next?" I asked.

"We might take this opportunity to examine the lake. We cannot extend our awareness through the rocky soil and sand."

The lake was a short hike down the trail. Water gleamed in the sunlight, and waves lapped the rocky outcropping where I stood, listening to the low roar. I descended the stone steps to the shore. The lake stretched across the horizon, and memories of St. Louis rose in my mind like waves. Unending afternoons in a cramped office and panicked late night phone calls from coworkers. There, I had been surrounded by people and conversation and still felt inescapable loneliness. Here, my link to the hive was like a warm blanket wrapped around me.

They gently nudged my attention to the sand, and we walked along the beach. "We are pleased to see it is clean."

"You can thank my mom for that. She hated all the litter out here. She roped me into picking up trash when I was visiting for Thanksgiving. I wasn't thrilled because I had been stressed at work and wanted to relax, but her intentions were good. She got the council to start a program for regularly cleaning the beaches."

"The council never mentioned that. We are glad it is working."

"Are there any other areas you'd like to see?" I asked.

They paused, exuding a swirl of emotions that ended in a pang of unease. "You are being a wonderful host, but we wouldn't want to take too much of your time."

Sudden anxiety arose in my chest. The link was comforting; words came easier, and I didn't have to guess how the hive was feeling. "You aren't taking too much of my time. I understand if you would like to go, but you don't have to leave on my account."

They relaxed again. "There is no inherent need to end the link since you may always close your door. Perhaps tomorrow we will show you more of the woods. There are excellent locations for foraging."

"Sure. I'd like that."

***

As I reached my mom's house that evening, the horizon glowed red, and the hive marveled at the stars blooming across the sky. The light was on in her shop, and through the window, I saw her attaching doors to a cabinet she had refinished. She looked deep in concentration, so I went inside and reheated the spaghetti I made two nights earlier. I offered the hive their chance to eat my dinner and the ice cream sundae I made afterward.

I kicked off my shoes and flopped onto the guest room bed when my phone buzzed. It was a new message, a short 'hah' in response to a silly photo I had sent a week ago. I grunted and relegated my phone to the nightstand.

"The message makes you sad. Why?" the hive asked.

"I've been trying to keep in touch with an old friend from work, but we've drifted apart."

"You miss having a deeper connection."

"I tried to form friendships when I was living in Chicago and St. Louis, but I wasn't good at it. I hated being surrounded by people and still being lonely," I said.

The hive hummed. "That sounds difficult. We have not known that experience." Then their voices unwound, and I saw a flash of a purple cloak as a voice with a pleasant lilt said, "Though, we three were not always so closely connected. As I recall, you both thought I was snobbish at first."

"And you thought me too frivolous for serious responsibility when we assumed the role of the hive's core," the man said.

"Patently untrue, of course."

He laughed and addressed the woman. "I also recall your reluctance to maintain our collaboration with the humans."

She huffed. "I only asked for caution. Our physiology is unusual to them, and we have thousands of people in our city to protect."

"I understand that," I said. "Your home is amazing. Would you let me see more of your city?"

"We would be happy to show you."

I closed my eyes and stepped through the mental door. The man in the orange robes waved, and we walked along the upper level of the hall. Dozens of people crossed the floor below, and their chatter filtered into my mind. At the end of the corridor was a long glass window overlooking the city.

Gardens sprawled out across the horizon, a vast world of green filled with trees and flowers in brilliant colors. The vegetation was larger and even more vibrant than that of the physical world, supporting buildings and forming bridges and walkways. Sculptures dotted the gardens, some towering far above the trees. Past the gardens sat unusual houses, ranging from low and square to tall and cylindrical.

"Your city is bigger than I expected," I said. "It's wonderful."

The other two members of the hive's core greeted us. "We are happy to have you here," they said.

A sloping structure of smooth stone with many towers caught my eye, and I pointed to it. "What is that building?"

"That is the residence of the previous core," the man said.

"They cared for our city but were a tad old fashioned," said the one in purple. "They were hesitant to interact with humanity, to the point where our physical body went into the hibernation that rendered us unaware of the outside world."

"I bet I could spend years in your city and not see everything." I shook my head in wonder. "Is there a limit to how long a human can host you?"

"Strictly speaking, no," the man said. "A sustained link will not cause physical illness."

"However, a prolonged link may sometimes become permanent," the woman said.

The man frowned. "That has only occurred when a human specifically chose to retain a permanent connection to a hive. Moreover, this is based on the experience of other hives."

The woman frowned back, leading to a series of odd looks exchanged among them in a conversation I was not privy to.

The third member of the core brushed past them. "Our best guess is that a human may remain linked to a hive for several consecutive years without consequence. However, given the depth of your link with us, a residual link could occur more quickly."

The man crossed his arms. "We don't know that."

"I am trying to be clear that we have limited data. Sarah should be aware of the risks."

"No human has reached our city before," the woman said. "If this link truly is deeper than what we've previously experienced, that could mean a higher chance of a permanent connection," the woman said. "Even beyond death."

"Wait, what was that?" I asked.

A wave of anxiety swept through the core, and the woman stuttered and folded her hands. "There is evidence that a human mind may join a hive after death."

The man held up his hands. "As in, following the end of the host's natural life. Which is not a topic that needs to be broached now."

"We can't withhold this information," the woman said.

"That was not my suggestion," the man said with a grimace. "We must be clear about our knowledge without overwhelming our host with hypothetical scenarios."

The other two stepped toward him, and their conversation turned nonverbal again. Frustration burned through me as I waved to get their attention. "I can't understand anything if you don't talk to me," I said.

Another ripple of anxiety passed through the core, and they shook their heads in unison. "We apologize, we have overstepped and we must end this link."

***

I stared into my plate of waffles the next morning. The hive was gone, and I was alone. I had never considered my mind an empty place, but I already missed the ease of reaching out and finding them there.

Mom bustled into the kitchen as the timer beeped. "God, are the waffles that bad?"

"They're great, Mom." I ran my fingers through my hair. "I hosted the hive yesterday. It was going well until we had a misunderstanding."

She leaned against the counter, her expression contemplative. "Did they say something that upset you?"

"No, and we could have talked through it, but they left instead."

"I'm sorry that happened," Mom said. "I imagine they didn't want to make you uncomfortable. The hive may be different from us, but they are people as much as we are. People have miscommunications."

I nodded. "You're right—I should talk to them."

The forest was quiet as I walked the trails. When I reached their side of the woods, my forehead tingled as they greeted me.

"We apologize for what happened yesterday," the hive said. Their voices were quiet and distant, lacking the comfort and proximity of the previous link. "We should have handled ourselves better."

"I'm not angry with you," I said. "It was overwhelming, and yes, I have some questions about your biology, but I'm okay. I don't feel that you overstepped."

"We appreciate that. As for the job, we are happy to work with you if you wish."

"I would like that. This town is still close to my heart, and I want to take care of it. My mom is here, and I've visited often enough to know everyone on the city council."

"The council has spoken well of you in the past. Speaking of which, we never thanked you for reminding us to blink at the council meeting."

I laughed. "Of course. You didn't seem to have a problem with that when I hosted you."

"You were not as tense as the mayor."

"For what it's worth, I enjoyed being linked to you," I said. "It has been so long since I felt connected to anyone, and yesterday I wasn't lonely."

"You were a gracious host," they said. "You shared your world with us, and we are grateful. It seemed you truly wished for our friendship."

"It isn't too late for that. I'm still open to being your host."

"Are you certain? We feared we may have frightened you, but please believe we would never harm you or any other person."

"I stand by what I said earlier; I want to know you better. Your city was amazing, and I would consider myself lucky to live in your world and mine."

"We would be happy to share it with you."

I lay back down on the ground, and the earth vibrated around me again. After a deep breath, I woke in the pavilion. The three members of the core were there, and their smiles radiated warmth.

"I have a very important question," I said.

"Yes?" they asked in unison.

"How do you feel about hugs?" I smiled back at them, and we embraced.

* * *

Catherine Yeates is a writer and artist. Their fiction has been published in *Wyngraf, Tree And Stone,* and *Twin Bird Review.* They live with their partner, cat, and two rambunctious dogs. Find them at cjyeates.com or on Instagram at cj.yeates.

Tunaakola

ZiitaMdot

Martha Ziita Siima also known as ZiitaMdot creates to explore her thoughts and feelings on afro identity in contemporary narrative and to impose an optimistic, inclusive illustration of her reflections. She navigates these concepts through dotwork and graphic design. She creates mandalas for spiritual expression and connection while using graphic design to lean into African-futurism in which she unites her diasporic upbringing with her African heritage to celebrate blackness through aesthetic, emphasis and movement. Playing with photomanipulation techniques, she manifests portraits underlined by afro themes, futurism, feminism, culture and connection. Learn more about her work at msziita.myportfolio.com

HOPDOG

Rimi B. Chatterjee

Dog number 834 knew she deserved to die, because she had broken all the rules. She had turned on other dogs who had offered her submission, she had attacked without due cause, she had killed… All of these deeds had been forced out of her by the whips and chains and cages and prods of her masters, but so what? She was guilty, outcast, not worthy of love. The only hope she had left was to give as many wounds as she got, before she went into the dark.

A sound made her open one eye: the other was a mass of scar tissue, trophy of many years of brutal survival. She stopped mashing her left forepaw with her teeth and swallowed her growl as the armoured security guards came towards her cage, their shock prods at the ready. She smelt their fear and knew that was why they gave so much pain. So she merely showed her teeth as she slunk out of her cage at their signal.

They chased her up the ramp into the waiting sixteen-wheeler truck. A partition came down behind her, and she heard the thud as another dog's bulk hit the metal on the other side. The truck slowly filled. It groaned and squatted lower on its springs as the dogs were loaded like weapons. She resigned herself to another day of kill-or-be-killed.

The box, now dark and stinky in spite of the ventilation, jolted and began to move. Some of the dogs who still had feelings yowled and whined in excitement. She curled a lip as she smelt their hunger and bloodlust. Their anticipation was not for the fight, but for the eating after.

She knew the drill: they would be taken to the big arena, where their terror-crazed prey would be running madly all over the bloodstained sands. Human, animal, it didn't matter. Her masters would watch as she and her competitors tore the prey to shreds and wolfed down whatever they could snatch from each other's jaws.

Then the water cannons would knock them apart, and the electric prods would shove them back to the place of fear and cages and punishment. This had been her life ever since she'd been ripped away from her mother.

She bided her time.

A few short minutes later, the back of the truck opened and the dogs poured out. They were in the holding pen, waiting for the big double doors to open. The doors slid apart and the first dogs shot through, shrieking. As the flood of slavering creatures surged forward, 834 hung back. Something smelled unsettling, uncanny. She lifted her lips and scrunched her nose, tasting the fugitive whiff of joy and valour from the wide space of the arena. Something was waiting gladly for them. She didn't like it. It smelled like trouble.

She followed the last few bouncing tails. Brown, black, white, tan, spotted, striped, patched and plain, they ran into the light and space of the killzone. Baying like a demon, 834 bounded over the sand, rusty with dried blood, seeking her target.

The air was calling to her. Against all reason, it smelt of milk and licks and love and home. It smelt like *denfeeling*, the absolute safety and comfort of her mother's flank, of soft play with her littermates in those three short weeks now lost forever to her fighting mind. This was no time to think about *denfeeling*. She scouted for the prey.

At the other end of the arena, a lone naked human figure turned and looked at the oncoming beasts. She was elderly and small, hardly any meat on her, but 834 didn't notice any of that, because the wind was talking like a mother, and a lovely voice was saying, this one stands straight and tall: she is Queen Bitch.

Ancient longings began to groan deep in 834's doggy soul. It was the smell that flipped them: the unmistakeable nose-bouquet of a nurturing protector, a mother, a commander. The closer she ran, the more 834 fell in love. To human eyes, this woman was nothing, a dried-up shell, but to 834 and her companions, she was the source of many great psychedelic rivers of colour rushing and dancing out of her, turning the air into a festival.

The old woman let out one huge shout, an 'Ah!' of recognition and welcome, and 834 felt a jolt of something fearful in her heart, a sudden, overwhelming knowledge that *she had found her pack, her leader, her task, her home.* All around her, dogs were slowing, swerving, yapping in confusion, and then, like the tide turning, each fearsome head and scarred body turned to face the exit, just like the old woman, and the same look of love and hope appeared on all the faces. Their barks went up an octave, turned into yodels, and they began to run with the woman in their midst, squealing like puppies. 834 bounded along, not questioning, letting the feeling carry her like a tsunami. All around her, doggie faces, made hideous from a lack of noses and ears, stiff from too many scars, laughed and bounded with lips loose and tongues lolling.

Now they had just one goal, to throw sand behind them till they made it out of those doors, with this human, their new leader, their precious one. Forming an honour guard for the woman as she ran, they poured back out of the gates, pushing the guards aside with the sheer force of their will. The water cannons came on but only served to make them slip through the guards' nooses faster. Those last few yards were heaven to run. They were like coming home.

The dogs, with their human leader, ran back into the truck without a check, in a stream of scrappy, itchy, smelly, dripping fur. As she entered she saw that the partitions were all laid flat, but not one dog turned a tooth on another: all their eyes were on Queen Bitch as she collapsed in a heap in the middle of the truck bed. They piled on to her, squirming to get as close as they could, licking and nuzzling her. Queen Bitch caressed them and wept at their scars. The doors closed. The truck rumbled off. 834 sniffed the air: it was heavy with a strange earthy, flowery perfume, and there seemed to be a blue haze coming from the ventilation ducts. It cooled her pain and soothed her heart.

She curled up with the other furry bodies, heaved a great sigh and slept.

When she awoke, she was lying on something soft. It was dark, but not like night. She was alone. There was air and space around her, but just near her skin it was close and warm. She shook off the blanket and stretched warily. Her nose felt bigger: the oppressive walls of stink were gone. Her skin: it felt so different, so *absent*, that for a moment she wondered if she were dead. Then she realised: her pains, her itches, her intimate enemies wriggling and biting in the crevices of her body: they were all gone.

She considered this, then gave herself a vigorous shake. Ahhh! The matted fur, like stones hanging off her, that used to tug and pinch at her hindquarters was gone. She stretched one back leg, and then the other. She couldn't remember when she had last been able to do that without pain.

She raised her head and saw a circle of brighter darkness above her head. She was in a shallow pit. Far away, she heard peaceful sounds: the schlop of water, gentle human voices, an occasional sleepy dog-yawp. The other dogs were here, she could smell them, but faintly. She stood up and sniffed the walls: they were made of rock, smooth, no purchase for her claws. If she stood on her hind legs, she could just raise her nose out of the pit, but there was no way she could climb out. There was a roof of rock high overhead: this place was a cave.

Now that she'd hoisted her nose into the free air, Dog Number 834 waved her muzzle around like a radar dish. She smelt water, and plants, and humans. A little bit of shit, and one or two notes of mustiness, but mostly healthy and pleasant and therefore utterly strange. It made her head spin to smell a place so sweet and wholesome. She let herself drop back down into her smooth scoop of rock and made a quick circuit of the space. On the furthest side from her bed she found a package.

She nosed at the parchment-like covering. What was this incredible smell? She growled, tore it open with her teeth and sniffed at the contents. She knew she should be wary, but the smell travelled right up her nose and did a loop-the-loop on her tongue, because she didn't need a menu to know that this was food, even though it was unfamiliar and crazy and made her want to howl with the promise of it. She lowered her head and began wolfing her meal.

"Yay!" said a voice. "This one's eating! She likes it!"

Dog Number 834 looked up from her prey and snarled. Then, above her head, she heard the calm voice of Queen Bitch and flattened her ears in deference. She cringed away from the food, but Queen Bitch's voice was gentle. "Let's move or she won't eat."

834 cowered in a corner until the voices faded. Then she went back to the package and ate every last bit. Still wary, but feeling better, she curled up on her soft fluffy bed, good eye outward, and tucked her nose under her tail.

Some time later she woke to feel herself rising smoothly into the air. The bed she'd been lying on had lifted her like a raptor taking a puppy. She bit the folds of soft fabric but it merely bounced in her jaws. She felt herself being bundled onto a platform, which moved. She fought her way out of the cloth and found she was in a box. Oh well, at least this was familiar, if a bit cleaner than she was used to. She'd been a fool to think this paradise would last. No doubt they had just been fattening her for a feast.

A few minutes later the box stopped moving. All was silent. A slot opened near the bottom and more food appeared in its wrapping. She ignored it. She wasn't falling for that again.

She could still hear the sounds of living things, far away. And somehow, even though she could not see out, she felt that she was surrounded by peace. There was no reason for her to think so, yet she was sure of it. As nothing further happened, she curled up again and dozed.

When she awoke, there were tiny strips of light lying over her paw. Her box was in fact a cage with collapsible walls, and they'd opened it out ever so slightly, so that slivers of the world outside could be seen and smelled. She lay still, her tattered scraps of ears held away from her head, listening.

Ah, that was where the peace came from. There were six people in the room (she could hear their heartbeats) and they were breathing in unison, slow in, slower out. She couldn't help it: her breathing synced with theirs, so soft and strong and slow it was. It was like the breathing of happy puppies exhausted after play. It was the rhythm of *denfeeling*. Creatures who breathed like that could not be angry or harsh or sly or evil. They were fluffballs of love.

All lies. There was no love in the world. There was only kill-or-be-killed, win-or-lose. She sprang to her feet and threw her whole body at the cage wall. Then she howled. The cage shuddered but did not give way. *Come on!* she yattered. *Bring your shockprods and your chains. Finish me! I will never surrender.*

But there was only a soft murmur of surprise and relief and amusement, after which they just went on breathing like puppies. It was infuriating. She curled in a ball and growled.

And that became the pattern of her days. Every so often she tested the people outside her cage, and they smiled at the challenge. She tried refusing food but it was simply too tasty to pass up. She had never eaten food like this before. It was nothing like the shreds of vanquished creatures she'd ravaged in the arena: she could not tell what animals this stuff was made of, or even if it was made of flesh, but the textures and the flavours were real enough. Every meal was a surprise.

Somehow it was harder to be angry on a full stomach, but she wasn't about to give up. She knew the wiliness of humans. Three litters they'd taken from her, before she'd graduated to tearing the throat out of any male who tried to take liberties. She knew humans were the enemies of *denfeeling*.

Every other day they widened the gaps a little, and now she could see the people who came and went. The cage was inside a room where they all sat in a circle round it and breathed or talked softly.

The ground was soft, and made of some kind of gel. When she scored it with her claws, it tore satisfyingly, but when she slept, it always managed to regrow. It soaked up her pee without a trace, and when she slept, her poop sank into it and disappeared. Also it tasted foul, like lemons. A lesser dog would have ripped it up anyway, out of nervous habit, but she was above such stupidity. She saved her aggression for things that could bleed.

She began to put flesh on her ribs. She would need her strength when she got an opportunity to take her revenge. One day they would be careless in slipping her food in, or they might wander too close to the bars. She could fit her muzzle through the gaps now. She'd tried, a couple of times, to nip her carers, but never connected. They had just laughed and spoken to her with love. Idiots.

Now she could see them when they slipped food in. She saw their kind smiles as they did it. They were always very calm and controlled. They added a new ritual to the food-giving. As they slipped in her meal package, they would croon the word "Peaches". Did "Peaches" mean "food"? She couldn't help it: every time she heard the word, her ears would go up in spite of herself.

"This is why we hop the alphas first," she heard Queen Bitch say softly. "Once we've got them firmly back in denfeeling, they'll create the social context for the others to fit into. They're also the hardest to persuade, that's why they're alphas. She will take a lot of convincing."

"When do we get to pet her?" asked a younger, eager voice.

"Soon. But remember, when we let her out, she may bite. Don't show surprise or shock. Not even a heartrate-spike: she can hear your pulse. We carry on as though nothing happened. That's why we have the gel-covers."

"Okay! I want to see if the gelcovers work!"

Queen Bitch smiled. "They'll work."

Then one day the cage was gone.

She opened her eye and stared around her in terror. Six people sat encircling her. They were dressed in weird transparent aprons, boots, face shields and gloves. She charged and went for their hands: she knew they couldn't harm her if they didn't have those odd wiggly things on the ends of their paws. Snip snap, and they'd be in her belly.

Her teeth closed on a gloved hand and ripped a chunk out.

And then she yowled and pawed at her mouth. The bit of glove was stuck fast to her teeth, sealing her jaws shut. It tasted foul, like lemons and oranges and stinkbugs and ants. She pawed and pawed, but nothing would unstick the horrible thing from her mouth. Helplessly drooling, she moaned and collapsed. No one frowned as she lay in a trembling heap. They went on smiling and saying "Peaches" as though Peaches was the best thing in the world.

And then hands came and stroked her. The dead fur and grease stuck to their gloves and came away, and slowly her new fur, grown from loving food, began to shine through. It felt so good. It felt like those long-ago forgotten days when her mother used to lick her, when she was small enough to fit on a human paw. Her eyes had barely opened to see her loving mother when the world had grown fangs. She lay and drooled, the gum slowly dissolving and soaking into the gel floor.

The smell of fear receded, to be replaced by another odour. "Smell that?" said Queen Bitch. "That's *woohoof*. People sometimes call it wet-dog smell, but it's actually the smell of a dog who is relieved to have gotten inside and escaped a thunderstorm. It's the smell of an adrenalin spike that's been controlled, and it's a social signal."

"Like telling someone 'I'm not freaking! I'm not freaking!', right?" said a younger voice.

"Yup. And also, 'Don't freak me out again or I'll lose it!' So never stress a dog that's woohoofed at you. End the lesson there and let them sleep it off."

Peaches closed her one eye. When she opened it, the taste of the gel was gone from her mouth, and the people were sitting around the walls, ignoring her. She closed her eye again, flopped onto her side with a groan, stretched out her legs and got the first real sleep of her adult life.

The next few days were very interesting. For the first time since she could remember, Peaches was sharing space with other breathing creatures that manifestly did not want to kill her. In the beginning, she had no idea how to act. She would approach them, then lose her nerve and default to bite mode. But these unflappable beings never screamed and beat her like the fight-keepers used to. Instead they smiled and gave her love while she lay yowling at the taste of lemons as if she were at death's door. After a while she would only yowl once and then grin sheepishly before falling asleep under the stroking. In short, these creatures appeared to be unbiteable.

Since it was only Peaches who suffered every time there was a bite event, she had to acknowledge that she was making a fool of herself. She confined herself to growling from then on. She had a very menacing growl, she was sure of it. It just didn't seem to frighten anyone.

She was dimly aware that now her coarse, thick fur shone like spun steel, and what was left of her ears was fluffy and soft. Her humans would lovingly stroke her and make her shine. They didn't just ease her skin, but as she relaxed and let them get closer, they began to work on the muscles below. "A healthy dog has very loose shoulderblades," said Queen Bitch. "When they lie on their stomachs you should see deep valleys between their upper spines and their shoulders. Look closely at Peaches. Are the valleys the same?"

"The left one is deeper."

'That means her right shoulder has problems. Try to loosen it up, but be gentle. Watch her while you work, and stop if she gives any sign."

Peaches moaned softly as they worked the tension out of her. Now it was a collaboration. She became adept at turning as they asked her. When they were a little slow getting to work she would boop their knees until they sat down, then squirm and pose herself under their hands. If they still didn't get it, she'd look up at them expectantly and thump the floor with her tail.

Sometimes it did hurt, and when it got her down, she would lift a lip and show her teeth. The humans treated this as speech. They would turn to each other and say, "Peaches told me she's having a bad day. I'm going to let her sleep." And then they would leave her alone, exactly as if she had commanded it. It was amazing how the world changed when others listened to you. She learned to keep her interactions at the level of speech. Queen Bitch watched her and nodded. "Her 'now' is thickening."

"What do you mean?" asked one of the young ones.

"When you live under the constant threat of a blow or a bite, like this dog did under her masters, you slice your 'now' very thin. You live in the sliver of time it takes to react and protect yourself. And when you protect, you go straight for your biggest weapon. No messing around."

"I know how that feels," someone said gravely. 'I'm so glad that in the survivarium, all I need to protect myself are words.'

Time passed, and the care and love lessened her pain. Now she paced hungrily, sniffed people all over, and pawed at the gel floors. "She's getting bored," said Queen Bitch. "Time to start bringing her gifts."

The first gift was a box with little lids that could be nosed open. She tried wrecking it, but it had that dreaded lemon tang when she bit into it. When she gently pushed the lids aside, she discovered there were tasty treats within. She spent an enchanting afternoon robbing the box of its treasures. The humans responded by bringing her more complicated boxes, ones she had to chew and squeeze, or ones that had levers she had to stand on, or cords to tug. This was fun! Then there were toys on ropes for her to chase and bouncy balls to bounce with. Who knew such things even existed?

She started to realise there were differences among the humans. Some she preferred over others, because their vibe matched hers. She would trot over to them when they arrived and push her nose into their hands. They were always delighted. On days when she was especially happy, they would leave the door of the room open, but she didn't yet want to see what was outside this wonderful space. For it was no doubt a human world out there, and human worlds were not to be trusted.

They made careful note of her person-preferences. The people she liked started coming more frequently. There was one small, bouncy one she liked more than the rest. Whenever this one came, Peaches would go up to her, turn around and flop down with a proprietary air. She would stare at everyone with a mild challenge, as if to say, "My human. Anything to say?" And they said, "Peaches! Well done, Peaches, you picked a dog tasker! You have a tasker now!"

Her favourite human started coming every day, and teaching her more complicated things. Also, she liked to talk. "Do you know what a tasker is, Peaches?" she would say, and Peaches would prick up her tattered ears and listen to the feelings behind the words. "You see, dogs belong both in our world and in your own. We like having you around: you keep *denfeeling* safe, and teach us to know and value it. And you enjoy being with humans too, don't you?"

"Rowr," said Peaches agreeably, and nuzzled her tasker's hand with her soft head. "So now it's my job to guide you through the human world,' said her tasker, stroking her. Gel gloves were a thing of the past now, and only used for special spa treatments and fur-polishing. "I'm supposed to show you how to behave with other humans and their babies and animals. You take your cues from me, so you won't ever be lost again. Got it?"

Peaches whuffed and put her nose on her paws. Every line of her body said she was glad she didn't have to worry about the rules anymore. Her tasker would keep her good, and she would never again be unworthy of love.

And then, one day, when her tasker left the room, Peaches trotted out after her. Outside there was a curving hall. Rooms led off it. She could hear and smell that some of the rooms had cages in them, surrounded by softly breathing humans, while others had beds on which sleeping humans were lying and having things done to them. She knew they were sleeping because she could hear their heartbeats and breathing. Peaches surmised that the dogs and humans were like she had been, rescues who were being healed. The smell of old pain made her hackles rise, and her tasker laid a gentle hand on her shoulder.

Then her tasker led her into a room with a cage. There was a dog in there, smelling of fear. The other humans in the room went on breathing softly. The hair on her spine rose up again, but this time she knew her tasker's hand would be there, reminding her that she no longer needed to react to another's fear. She *woohoofed* and looked up at her tasker, who led her back to her own room, where everybody made a big fuss of her and gave her special treats. She realised she'd crossed another boundary. She'd followed her tasker into unsettling places, but she hadn't lost it. Her trust had held.

A few days later, Peaches and her tasker went out again, but this time they walked up some ramps and came out on a wide terrace. From here they could look down on a vast concourse of channels and pools and streams and waterfalls, where naked people were bathing and playing. A graceful rock-cut bridge arched down to the edges of the baths, and they followed it and found themselves in a place full of toys and puzzles and little circular cupboards where people were busy.

Here humans with big heavy bellies sat with dreamy looks in their eyes, while lots of other people fussed around them. Peaches knew that look. She could hear the tiny rapid heartbeats inside them. This was the human den, with all its treasures laid out and waiting, where the human puppies would come out and play, when they were ready.

"We two are going to come and help the childers and their doulas, once the Circle of Love is all set up," her tasker told her. "But it will be a few more months before the first babies come." She pointed to the igloo-like buildings that were dotted around the space. "That's where the babies will be born. And they'll have everything they need right there, all the love and toys and stuff, from the moment they arrive." Peaches looked longingly at some of the toys, but her tasker was moving on. Soon they reached the edge of the Circle of Love.

Here there was a raised ring of green. They climbed the inner slope and found themselves on a winding track that ran through copses and dells full of fragrant bushes and shady trees. Peaches sniffed the grass suspiciously, but her tasker called to her and began jogging along the path. Peaches followed, and slowly the fire of her muscles warmed her soul, and she began to get the zoomies. She dashed in and out of the dells and ran around the trees, barking at nothing like a brainless puppy. Her tasker laughed and laughed.

Finally they came to a little courtyard with a hedge around it. "This whole circle is the Inu Gardens, Peaches," said her tasker. "It's where our dogs will hang out and socialise with each other, and in time there'll be puppies born in the underground dens and there'll be dogs in the survivarium who have never known anything but love. How about that, eh?"

Peaches wagged her tail and grinned. She approved.

More dogs were trickling in with their taskers. Peaches ignored them. She took her cues from her human, never letting her gaze stray from her tasker for more than a minute. She already knew that when others were around, she should only engage with them if her tasker said it was okay. So she sat quietly by her tasker's feet and watched. One or two of the other dogs got into nervous fights, but the taskers all had squirt bottles to discourage such behaviour. Any dog who bit or snapped was liable to get a gelmuzzle slapped on them, so it was mostly eyerolling and insults until Queen Bitch looked up sharply and *barked* a word commanding peace, at which the most troublesome dog yelped and hid under a bush with his tail between his legs. He stayed there for a minute until his tasker called him, then he came out and went to her, his ears down. But Queen Bitch smiled at him and gave him treats, and in no time he was stretched out on his back at her feet, having his belly rubbed, and you could tell by how his tongue lolled out of his grinny mouth that he wasn't going to be any trouble.

Peaches sat and panted with gentle laughter. The zoomies had made her muscles feel like silk. Really, any dog who wanted to start a fight in the middle of all this deserved a squirt of lime-flavoured gel in the face.

After a while Peaches began turning her back on invitations to play from the other dogs and yawning, so her tasker took her home. They left the central Hub of the survivarium with its bright lights and vaulted roof and made their way down a podvein, a long winding tunnel through the rock. Peaches baulked a little as they left the Hub: she had stopped associating cramped places with safety. But her tasker petted her until she calmed enough to go on.

There was a soft hush here: the rock walls were covered in deep green moss that absorbed all sound. On either side, there were pods: little split-level rooms where people slept and worked. They reached her tasker's pod without incident. Peaches knew at once this tiny room belonged to her human. She trotted across the floor and jumped on the bed. Her tasker laughed and pulled the curtain shut over the door. Then she placed a hurdle across the entrance. "That's just till you get used to living here," she told Peaches. 'I don't want you charging out whenever you see or hear something that sets you off, okay?" Peaches just grinned. Her tasker already knew her very well.

Then her tasker led her to a lever in the floor by the wall. It looked like the levers on her treat-dispensing toys. Her tasker held a treat over her nose and led her to step on the lever. A door opened in the wall, flooding her face with light. She squealed in alarm and jumped back. "Don't be scared," her tasker soothed her. "That's how you go to the garden." But Peaches was afraid. She stuck her head in the door and looked at the rock-cut ramp beyond, but wouldn't go down it.

Her tasker sat back on her heels and smiled. "All right, let me show you what's underneath. Maybe then you won't act like it's the mouth of hell." She led Peaches back to the bed and pulled a lever in the wall. Peaches yelped and jumped on the bed when the floor started to move. The slabs of stone went down a short way, then folded under the bed, opening a hole in the centre of the room, from which more bright light and fresh scents spilled. Peaches looked down in amazement. There was a tiny garden under the floor, brightly lit, with water channels running between the beds. The red globes of tomatoes winked up at her, and the long thin green of beans. She could smell the rich earth and the juicy plants.

"That's how we recycle our waste," said her tasker. "Now I'm going down there to work. You coming?' Peaches yowled in alarm as her tasker, smiling, disappeared from view. For a moment it looked like Peaches would launch herself bodily straight into the garden well, but her tasker popped back through the door. "Here I am! Come on, Peaches, this way. You'll get the hang of it." And then she vanished again. Peaches ran yowling from one end of the bed to the other, but of course there was nothing for her to do but follow, so she let off one last yowl, then jumped down and trotted along the walkway from the bed to the garden door. She took a deep breath and set a hesitant paw on the rocky slope.

Having pit-patted down the ramp as if she expected a flock of demons to pounce on her, all she found at the bottom was her tasker sitting with a handful of treats and lots of words of praise and pets. Somehow while eating these treats, Peaches ended up in the middle of the garden, having totally missed her cue for making a fuss about it. So she heaved a big sigh, nosed about, delicately ate some wheatgrass and peed in a corner. This led to more treats and pets, and then they both went up the ramp to bed.

Peaches soon got used to living in her tiny domain. If this was all she had to do, keep her tasker safe in her pod, nose about in the garden or stretch out and snore on the bed, then life would be pretty easy. But of course, this bliss did not last, because the neighbours came to visit.

Her first inkling that they were here was when a host of doggie noses appeared in the holes of the hurdle blocking the door. Peaches sprang off the bed and ran barking towards them, but her tasker said "No!" She simmered down and slunk back to the bed to wait for her tasker to tell her when to slaughter them. But no such luck: her tasker went to the hurdle and had a calm conversation with the other taskers while Peaches growled and trembled at her feet. The other dogs merely sniffed. They seemed amused at her drama. Her tasker invited Peaches to sniff the array of noses, but she was having none of it.

This hurdle-sniffing went on for a few days, with her tasker coaxing Peaches to dial down the drama. "I know you're scared the other dogs will take away the only home you've known," said her tasker one night. "But no one wants to do that. There's no need to be afraid here in the survivarium. That's what this place is: a world for Survivors to live in. You're a survivor, Peaches. Everyone is. We're one big pack."

Peaches grumbled, but she knew she had to change her own mind if she was to make progress. So one day her tasker removed the hurdle. Peaches stayed where she was, on the bed, and gave her tasker a resigned look. "No running at the curtain when other dogs pass, okay?" Peaches tried to look shifty, but the truth was, she was starting to forget why she wanted to stir up drama in the first place. It seemed like a lot of work, when she thought about it.

Three days later, the neighbour dogs all came with their taskers and sat outside her pod. Her tasker drew the curtain back. They could all see each other. Peaches cowered by the bed.

"Chill, Peaches," said her tasker. The senior female came in with her human, very dignified, sticking close to her tasker's knee. She was big, with long fawn hair, fluffy jowls falling in soft folds down her face and throat, and a square face. Peaches' hackles rose, but other than that she didn't move. The other dog sniffed her, then made a gracious playbow. Peaches responded with her own bow. Then they ran around the room until Peaches pinned the other dog, but let her go the moment she yelped. The other dog got to her feet with dignity. They sniffed each other solicitously and wagged their tails. The ice had been broken, and Peaches's impetuosity had been noted, but forgiven. The two taskers had a short conversation, then the neighbours left.

"Not bad," said her tasker, "but you need to work on your manners." Peaches lowered her head sheepishly. She knew she could have done better.

Now she and her tasker began to explore the podvein neighbourhood, and go on little outings to do chores. Every morning they'd head out to the Crackerbox for breakfast. They'd sit on the grass among the boulders and eat, then Peaches and the other dogs would chomp up the wrappings from the food. Some of the wrappings turning into tasty treats if you played tug of war with them, so the dogs got to play while they kept the place clean and helped recycle the trash. Then they would go to the Circle of Games, where Peaches would help teach new Survivors how to behave with dogs, or they'd go to the Inu Gardens to see the puppies. On special days, Peaches would be taken to see the human babies. She would always move slowly and be extra gentle, even when they tugged her ears. Her tasker would then unclasp their little fingers. She made sure no one ever hurt Peaches.

And then one day, as they lay in bed and surveyed their little foodgarden below, her tasker said to her, "Peaches, you've been doing great. In fact, we think you've completed your Hopscotch. Do you know what that means? It means you're a full Survivor like me, not a hopdog any more, and that means we must have a party. A doggie Hop Party, in the Inu Gardens."

Peaches cocked her head. The very next day, all the neighbour dogs came to fetch her, and she danced out and touched noses with each one. Then they trooped to the Inu Gardens, stopping by the

Crackerbox on their way in to collect all the food they had printed for the occasion. They went to one of the courtyards which had been reserved for their hop party and had games and treats and playbows and zoomies and boops and nudges and yowls. Now she could smell the doggy happiness: it was a smell that Queen Bitch called Puppy Cake, and it meant everybody was absolutely brimming with denfeeling.

For Peaches, this day was an endless stream of pets, kisses, cuddles and treats. Everyone told her she was special, she'd Survived, she was one of them. "Told you she'd make it," said Queen Bitch to her tasker as they watched Peaches lick up crumbs. "It's always the fiercest ones who come around strongest."

"Because they're smarter?"

"They're the kind who always step up to the challenge. They're the arfas and arefs, the enlightened ones. They tell the pack how to behave. If they were human we'd call them leaders, not alphas. 'Alpha' is a stupid idea."

"I like 'arfa' better than 'alpha'."

"You do?" Queen Bitch smiled. "You'd probably like Arfabad, then."

"What's Arfabad?"

"It's a place in the City of Love where all the dog-souls live. The arfas look after those souls no matter what bodies they inhabit. All the dogs we've loved live there, and we'll see them again one day."

"Wow! Sounds like my kind of place."

Peaches pricked up her ears, then came over to Queen Bitch and leaned on her knees. This was the first time she'd ever dared to touch her, and Queen Bitch looked down and stroked her ears. "Peaches knows the arfas," she said softly. "They kept her going through the bad times. You can't see them, but you can feel them around you, and in your heart. That's why, when she came here, she recognised us. Even though she's been abused all her life, she knew what friends are supposed to be, and all her anger was because no one was being her friend. Except the arfas. They lead you home, to your true family."

Peaches lay down at Queen Bitch's feet. She knew that, just as the arfas had given her love when no living heart existed to love her, so too had they saved Queen Bitch, and whispered in her ear that her doggy friends were coming to save her, when the fightmasters had sentenced her to death in the arena. That was why Queen Bitch had glowed at the sight of Peaches and her fellow executioners. The arfas had told her, have faith, these are your pack. Love is coming. And they had told Peaches too, but she had needed time and help and tenderness and healing to believe it.

Peaches licked her lips and closed her eyes. All around her, sleepy dogs flopped down and stretched out, too stuffed to move. Life was a big soft blanket you could roll in all afternoon. "Now is here," said Queen Bitch softly, like a blessing, "and here is now."

* * *

Rimi B. Chatterjee is a screenwriter, novelist and academic based in Kolkata, India. She is currently developing the Antisense Universe, a storyworld focused on civilisational redesign and climate action, in which this story is also set. Eventually she hopes to produce a series of animation feature films set in this world.

SOLAR MURDER

A.E. Marling

Swear to god this crow met my eye and cawed to make good and sure I was looking. She walked to a stone, picked it up with her beak, and flapped above a solar panel.

I stood there with fists cold, guts clenched. Knew what I was about to see, still too shocked to do anything about it.

The crow dropped the rock. It zinged off the top of the panel and slid down the slope of black cells. I fixated on a new divot in the glistening surface. Then the rock fell off the edge and into a garden plot with a plop.

"Dammit! Bottom-feeding flying rat!"

"*Shutup! Shutup!*" The crow startled me by talking back.

I glanced around, but no, there were no other people. The crow had made those sounds. My skin prickled with gooseflesh.

The crow walked over to the same rock.

"Oh no you don't!" But I was too late.

She had already taken wing with the thing. This time she flew lower toward the panel. I covered my ears to block out the sound of rock striking space-age solar cells. It hit, and this time the stone didn't slide off. It stuck up there like a bloated tick. The crow cawed in triumph.

"That's it. Just you wait."

I leapt on my bike and careened to my earthship. I rushed through first the warmth of the front greenhouse then the inner chambers' coolness. The clay walls radiated a chill. Deep inside my home, under some flooring beside a water pump, I reached my safe. I unlocked it and took out Dad's gun.

I think shooting was the only thing he had liked about serving on the force. Anyway, he never gave up the Glock 22 to any of the buyback programs. He wanted his girl to protect herself, so we'd practiced plenty.

"Don't let anyone push you around," he would say to me at a makeshift gun range. We had lined up empty cans of soup and olives. "Give as good as you get, or you'll have nothing."

A few decades later and here I was, loading blanks into his old gun. Dad would've used live rounds. I returned to the solar farm as fast as I could.

The murder was gone. They had left another stone.

***

Ever heard a rock hit a solar panel? The pinging crack puts my teeth on edge, and I flush all over and feel like I'm going to puke. One time Dad caught me tossing stones at his panels, and he walloped me.

Then he had looked ashamed. He said, "My old man hit me, and I'm not doing the same to you. But you've got to learn. How many rocks did you throw?"

I lied, told him only two.

"You've already paid for one. This will do for the second." He took me home, found my favorite dinosaur toy, and hammered it to shards of green resentment.

Anyway they're my solar panels now. The first time I saw a crow drop a rock on them was in July. I had wondered how stones had been getting up there. It was also other things. Found a baby apple, snail shells, and even a doll's head once. That last was the worst because it had half melted, one eye gone, brown hair like mine but curled, crisped, and reeking. Had to scrape it off and get rid of it before it gave me nightmares. Meanwhile those crows were all around, laughing like they do.

"*Caa-aw! Caa-aw!*"

"Shut up," I shouted back. "Shut up! Go choke on some ticks, why don't you?"

The crows pick the pests off goats. More of the bloodsucking dots scurry around these days, and the crows are welcome to them. Doesn't mean I love cleaning bird crap from the agrivoltaics.

It's bad enough when it's just shit. I started finding rocks way up there, where I can only reach them with pole scrapers or cleaner bots. I had my suspicions.

Then I saw the crow do it. She had one twisted feather on her left wing. It jutted out like a black barb, so that's what I called her. Barb had watched me remove rocks with her beady black eyes. She backstepped and made sounds like an offended old woman. That's why I started thinking of her as female, though who's to know?

Even if impact doesn't make photovoltaic cells crack, the stones are a problem. Blocking airflow, heating up like they do in stone soup, they can ruin a solar panel. Leave damn near anything up there too long, and the energy returns will drop. Seeing those meters read lower every day sends my blood pressure up even faster.

People need that power to live. Not everyone has the luxury of an earthship and its natural air conditioning. Repurposing malls or office buildings into social housing had to be done, but they're not fit without AC. I imagine grandparents sweating to death as their families do all they can to save them with fans and damp towels.

This is something I can do. I keep them powered.

For that I need my solar. And the arrays have to last. Most of Dad's panels produced for thirty years. After that I was managing a thousand acres with him across the valley, but I'll never forget the summer we spent together at his first plot, hoisting up the new cells.

A breeze kissed the back of my neck and rustled the grass. Mustard flowers stained hills with yellow. The cells gleamed like black gems. Onyx maybe, or jet, but I like to think of each cell as a square diamond. There are black diamonds, right? Never had any jewelry from my family, apart from the solar from my father. I cleaned 'em until they shone like the treasure they are.

On that spring I was savoring the shade beneath a new panel when Dad said, "We're the real farmers, you know."

"You mean the hemp in plot three?"

"Not that." He squinted up toward the sun. "Solar is the crop of the twenty-first century."

I wasn't sure about a lot of the shit Dad told me, but he did teach me the value of a watt. You can bet I know damn well how much power each of my farms produces. It might not be more than the cyanobacteria plantation run by the Gonzalezes, but I generate more solar power than any other operation in the Tri-Valley.

More important, I'm efficient. "Takes power to make power," Dad told me. Refining sand into jewel-grade solar requires a buttload of energy. Dad's panels needed years to earn back their watts. Mine are far better, and I get more out of them because I treat 'em right.

Hurts all the more when they're banged up by crows.

The murder came back at eleven o'clock to Dad's farm. Barb flapped right over my head.

I sidestepped in case she tried to shit on me. Then I put on my noise canceling muffs and racked the pistol. First I pointed it at Barb. "Go away and take all your fucking family!"

My voice sounded faint and weird. Barb opened her beak. Thankfully, I couldn't hear.

Didn't feel right aiming at the bird, even with a blank, so I pointed the pistol to the sky. I fired.

The gunshot sent a shock wave through them. Barb backflipped in a fluttery panic. I laughed as the crows flew away, black feet tucked below their tail feathers. They shrank to dots in the distance.

My laughter died out as the murder circled back. They flew around a hill golden with dried grass and returned to settle on my panels.

I fired again.

The murder scattered only to return within a minute. Barb led them, and you can guess what she had clutched in her claws, swooping toward my delicate panels.

I emptied my gun. Thirteen bangs rang out.

Next time they flew back with a bigger rock. Another crow was carrying it, this bird larger than Barb. His stone bounced once off the cells then skidded, leaving scratches.

"Fuckers! Fuckers!" I tore off my noise cancelers and picked up a long-poled scrubber. Swinging it like some sort of medieval weapon, I attacked the panel-perching crows.

Don't think I expected to hit any of them, and I didn't. But seeing them scatter when I came running was something. That day they left an extra helping of poop to scrape off, along with more rocks.

The whole time the gun sat awkward in my belt buckle, poking my hip. I loved the thought of exploding Barb in a shower of black feathers. But the solar community would look down on me killing wildlife, let alone something intelligent enough to mimic human speech.

Later in the forums, I learned a thing or two about crow deterrence. "Whatever you do, don't kill one." That was the most common advice. I had guessed as much.

Some in the community outfitted bots to chase off crows. That stank of inefficiency. Others went as far as to put up their anti-hail nets. Good for them, but no one owned any such thing this side of the Sierra Mountains.

"I want to know, what do crows have against my poor panels?"

Best I could guess, the little feathered demons just liked the sound made by the falling stones. Maybe I had once too. As a kid, I had learned. Now it was their turn.

Next day I brought out some of my old clothes and wooden stakes to make a scarecrow. I like crafts, and I even painted a face on a cracked plate. The clothes looked loose until I stuffed them with dried weeds.

Not sure what it says about me that I thought to bring a gun before building a scarecrow. It's even in the name. Scaring crows.

Dammit, Dad! Still trying to be better than you.

Standing back from the construction, I dusted off my hands. "Not bad."

The crows were less impressed. Barb dropped two rocks that day herself, and four other crows joined in. They cawed merrily to each other.

"Is this a fucking game to you?"

The following morning, I brought a speaker system. Set up near the scarecrow, it boomed with recorded gunshots.

The crows dropped six stones. Each cracking sound on my panels felt like my soul shattering.

I tried moving the goats to another field, without panels. The crows went after them for their breakfast of parasites. The birds still returned, carrying more stones.

"This is war now, fuckers!"

"*Caa-aw! Caa-aw!*"

That evening, the mail delivered a laser pointer, one I had ordered. The designer claimed it could reach the clouds, and I was all too happy to blast the crows with photons.

The beam's red mark bounced over the hillside, visible even in the daytime.

The murder flew away and didn't come back. "Now who's crowing? You bird brains, more scared of light than gunfire?"

I smiled all the way home. The laser pointer even had a clip that fit over my belt. I was basically a cowgirl, ready to draw on some varmints. Couldn't wait to go back the next day.

Arriving early at ten AM, I found the crows had come even sooner. They had left behind the mangled remains of my cleaner bots. Casings broken by more rocks, I bet, and their wiry insides ripped out.

"God damn you, Barb, wherever you are! I know what you really hate." I whipped out my phone and made the call.

***

The next day, the falconer came.

"But that's not a falcon, right?" I asked. "It's a hawk?"

"Harris hawk," the falconer said. The man had black sideburns going to his jawline and a flurry of well-styled hair.

"Doesn't look much bigger than a crow. Sure it will be ok? These are mean birds."

"I'm sure."

"Just one hawk?" I asked. "Do you have more?"

"I said I'm sure."

And he was right. There wasn't even a fight. The hawk shrieked a few times, that's all. The murder changed course and blew out of the valley like a tumbleweed with places to be.

Did me good to see that lone hawk flying through the clear skies.

Long ago, Dad had pointed upward. "We did that."

"Did what?" I asked.

"Turned the sky blue. It used to be grey. Do you remember?"

I didn't, not really. Just flashes of frustration. I hadn't been allowed to play outside much as a kid.

The sapphire sky now was empty, except for the hawk. I watched it land on solar panels and strut. Mostly I took naps beneath an oak tree.

I won't lie. Over the next week I also walked with some swagger. The hawk did its job, and I did mine. The goats fared worse. I had to check myself twice over for ticks after helping with the herd. Could be a problem in the long term, but for now as always, energy was king. So long as the solar power kept flowing, we could manage the rest.

The cells gleamed, and the meters didn't fall any further. Hell, I even flexed the ol' conversation skills. "So, birds, huh?"

The falconer tapped his watch, and the indicator light on his earpiece dimmed. "Yes, you have some great ones out here. What's your favorite?"

"Stuffed turkey?"

The look he gave me was of a door closing.

"Ah, how about you? Do you have a favorite bird?"

"Yes," he said and turned his sound music back up.

"What are you listening to?"

He named a pop band. At that point I began to wonder how

much younger he was than me.

I still made a pass at him. Yes, I was feeling that tough. Asked him back to my place in the evening for beers.

"No thanks," he said. "I'm ace."

Who knows? Maybe he was even telling the truth.

He gave me the real bad news the next day. "Got a call from the South Bay. I'll head over there tomorrow."

"Wait, why?"

"Crows dropping rocks on some solar."

Dread sank through me, hard and cold. "Whose farm?"

"Rooftop solar, on some old town houses."

Those panels wouldn't produce much anyway. No great loss if Barb stayed there. But if the falconer drove the bird bastards back here, damn! Or maybe these were different crows, taught to vandalize. "Was there a small crow with a feather bent back on her left wing?"

The falconer blinked. "That's oddly specific. Maybe you'll be a birder yet."

"Give me a hawk, and I'll be one right now."

But he didn't. The bastard left me alone and defenseless. The next nearest falconer was in New Chico, and he didn't return my calls.

Ground my teeth so much over the next days that my jaw hurt. Didn't sleep much either. I was as low as I've ever been, Yeah, I should've reached out, maybe called a nephew. But I handle my own shit. There's a reason I don't live in a city like Oakland, with its hive of cob homes and parks packed with people at all hours.

Carrying around Dad's gun made me feel a little better. Remaking a new holster kept me busy. My hand snapped to the pistol's handle when I spotted the murder.

Specks boiled into the valley. They swarmed closer, and I made out their black wings. Then I heard them.

"*Caa-aw! Caa-aw!*"

"Get out of here." I waved my gun, screaming. "Git!"

Their shadows chilled me as they flapped overhead, into Dad's solar farm. "*Caa-aw! Caa-aw!*"

One crow landed to pick up a stone, then another. Even the smallest yearlings reached for pebbles.

"Fuckers!"

"*Fuckers! Fuckers!*" A crow cawed back. It was Barb. She flapped past my head, clutching a nail that sliced all too close to my eyes.

The black feathers of her wings splayed outward like claws as she flew above a pristine panel.

"Please, no!"

Barb dropped her missile. So did every crow, and it was a stone rain.

Cracks spread over the panels like an evil frost. The sound, I couldn't describe. Don't even want to think about it.

I found myself on my knees, my insides a frozen slurry of pain.

"*Fuckers! Fuckers!*" Barb walked toward me, her wicked eyes glinting like black diamonds.

I lifted Dad's gun and fired.

It was meant as a warning shot. Really it was. I had loaded live rounds, and part of me hoped the crows would be able to tell the difference and finally leave me alone. Only, I kept shooting and aiming at Barb and one of them must have hit because the crow fell down dead.

***

The crow funeral lasted three days.

Every crow from the West Coast must've come. A black-winged procession circled through the valley. Their cacophony of cawing kept everyone awake. My closest neighbors, the Feldons and the Wus, were none too pleased, but at least they could go outside.

Whenever I tried, I faced a sky full of black beaks.

Ever tried to outrace a murder? It's a nightmare. Crows cut across fields, while on my bicycle I had to stick to roads. They called for help, with a rattling sound that filled my heart with adrenaline, and more shadows screeched in from every direction. As they neared, their wingbeats got louder, each a dull slap that made me wince. Then the crows tore through the air and struck.

I took to leaving my door at a sprint, wearing my bike helmet and goggles. It wasn't enough. Crows pecked at my ears. They pulled out my hair. Their claws pierced my jacket. One gouged my cheek, and I had to plead for a doctor to make a house call for stitches.

The crows didn't bat an eye as the doctor walked by. Their vendetta was only for me.

Now I stay within the protection of my earthship. Trouble is, the crows screech and bang their beaks against the glass. It's horrifying, to see so many animals hate me on sight.

I had done my best to warn them, punish them, teach them. The only thing they seemed to have learned was to how to torment me.

Suppose I might have done a bit of the same to Dad. I found hundreds of ways to hurt him, to get back at him. I had even run off at eighteen to risk my neck fighting wildfires in the Climate Force.

In the end I made it home, and now look at me. I can't open any windows. The skylights stay in the closed position. Without air circulating up through the berm and out through my house, I've lost my air conditioning. I'm not looking forward to the winter. It'll be cold as August is hot.

My home remains shuttered. Better to walk in darkness than let dark beaks tear through screens and break inside in a feathered frenzy. So I am sweating, straining to see through bottle bricks embedded in a wall. Outside, the crows are smeared inkblots.

They never leave. The crows take shifts watching my home, always a dozen at least. Mostly I stay out of the greenhouse entranceway, but I can hear their feet scuttling on the glass, talons click-click-clicking. And stones drop on my rooftop solar.

Crack! Crack!

A heroic girl from the Gonzalezes brings me food.

"Sorry about the crows," I say while loading the fridge.

"It's ok. We have the kids starting a black feather collection."

She said it like she wasn't a kid herself. I suppose she's in her teens. Silver circuitry traces over her brown cheek. Probably don't need that to connect the implants in her eye and ear, but maybe it was fashion.

With one shipment of groceries, she also delivers a mask. "Might help," she says. "Crows remember faces."

Ironically, the mask is of a scarecrow. Later, I try it. Its rubber sticks to my face as I rest a hand on my front door. I suck in shallow breaths through the mouth slit. "This will work," I tell myself. "It has to."

I stride outside, take three steps, then stagger to a stop.

The crows are watching. My knees clamp together as I fight a jagged need to pee. I can already feel something leaking.

One bird turns its head sideways. A single black eye scrutinizes me, then the other. From deep in the crow's throat comes that damn rattling.

Together they scream. The murder swoops in.

I dive back toward my house, battling through black wings. Think I break one slamming the door shut. Hear a crunch and an agonized cawing.

Crouching there in the darkness, I weep. Cans repurposed into wall structure dig into my back. Snot leaks down the inside of my mask. My pants are soaked too. I stink, but it is an hour before I stop trembling enough to stand and start cleaning up.

"I need a hawker," I say to the falconer that night, my fingers clamped over my phone in a deathgrip.

"You need to leave," he says. "Travel. Take the rail as far as you can."

"Leave? Dad and I made this house. Get your fucking bird over here now!"

He takes three audible breaths before answering. "If the crows are that angry, they may attack Yui."

"You're more worried about your bird than a person? Do you know how many stitches I've gotten, you fucker! You fucking— Hello?"

He hangs up on me.

It may be for the best I lost Dad's gun. After killing Barb I must've dropped it on the solar farm, left it to run. The last thing I remember is arriving home, breathless and empty handed.

"Please look for the gun," I said to the Gonzalez girl. Teen. "It was my father's, and I don't want any kid to find it and get hurt."

"Oh, I found it already while tending the goats."

"You did?" I asked. "Then where is it?"

"At the ranger's office, or maybe they shipped it away already I don't know. I turned it in straight away. It was by the open gate at plot seven. Thought that's what you would've wanted."

I gave it a long think and decided maybe I did.

Once I harvested light. Now I wait in the dark. Once I had a blue sky. Now I have an earthen prison. Once I lived with purpose. Now I only hope to escape.

A bus will pull as close to my house as the driver can, tomorrow morning. A social worker arranged it. I already have my seat reserved for the high-speed rail to New Tollan. Don't own any suitcases, but I've stuffed some clothes in a backpack. A family will move in to keep house while I'm gone.

Not sure if I'll ever be back. I don't know what Dad would do if he saw me leaving everything. I failed him and everyone. Feels like the end of the world, or at least my part in it.

Anyway, the next day, I get on the bus.

The crows stopped their stone throwing, if the Gonzalezes can be believed. The Gonzalezes are a big family, so I asked them to tend to the solar farms.

They sent me a video. Must've watched it hundreds of times already, and I expect to replay it a hundred more on the train. From the footage I recognize my solar panels. They're from plot twelve, by the creek and sycamore grove. I also know the Gonzalez kids by sight. The rest, by god, that I don't get. I see it, but I don't believe it.

Maybe the video is doctored, some hoax to rub poison oak over sore spots. It's a taunt, an insult, a cruelty. Unless it's real. The more I imagine it might be true, the more something loosens in my core, the more I can breathe deep, the more I begin to grin.

In the clip, a pair of children with frizzy hair run toward the arrays and throw. Peanuts and cashews fly from their hands. The nuts land on the solar cells, plinking like raindrops. Crows dive after the food with caws of delight.

* * *

A.E. Marling writes on pages, cards, and buildings. A member of SFWA, he has penned several speculative-fiction novels and written for *Magic: The Gathering*. The author also shines words in light on buildings as a projection activist (@AEMarling).

Moth City (Diversity)

Art by Yen Shu Liao
Text by Christoph Rupprecht

Solarpunk Creatures Project Entry #17 (Early Spring 87/2143)

Main Text

After several weeks here, things are slowly becoming clear. The diversity is key: no giant moths and earthworms, no city. At least as long as the toxins remain in the soil. The moth eggs are what keep people here healthy, and the moths certainly won't hand them over just like that. But folks here have turned the city into a huge garden, with plants producing compounds said to foster caterpillar development. Those giant moths value their sentience, no surprise there! So everyday life is full of bartering and haggling. The moths also insist on feeding the stuff to equally enormous earthworms. Hard to find conclusive proof (must return to Moth City in the future for further study), but the plausible hypothesis? The moths hope more earthworms means better soil and thus improved plant growth. Or, as rumor has it, sentient earthworms. In the past such talk led to trouble, but these days a Multispecies City Council makes sure there's space to deal with the frictions and differences required for peaceful coexistence of species. Their transport planning certainly works!

Side Text

It's unclear where exactly the giant moths came from (more to study for my colleagues trying to understand the Big Change era). Most fascinatingly, living together is influencing both human and moth cultures. What is still a mostly trade-based relationship seems to be evolving, though those artists co-housing with moths still raise both eyebrows AND antennae.

Moth City

Moth egg container made from broad leaf and sticky silk.

egg detail

Things are slowly becoming clear. Diversity is key: no giant moths and earthworms, no city. At least as long as the toxins remain in the soil. The moth eggs keep people healthy, and the moths know that. But folks turned the city into a nursery of plants that somehow foster caterpillar sentience. The haggle is real! The moths also feed the stuff to equally enormous earthworms. Hard to find conclusive evidence, but the plausible hypothesis? More worms means better soil and improved plant growth. Or, as rumor has it, sentient earthworms. Such talk might cause trouble, but these days a Multispecies City Council helps deal with the friction and differences required for peaceful coexistence of species. Their transport planning certainly works!

Where did the giant moths come from? (note: team up with historian to understand the Big Change era). Coexistence obviously influencing both human and moth cultures. Still a mostly trade-based relationship but evolving, though those artists co-housing with moths still raise both eyebrows AND antennae.

Moth caterpillar have their own lane in streets

Human urban forester trading with a Moth

Plant material collecting bags

Kombucha Atoll (Adaptation and Ingenuity)

Solarpunk Creatures Project Entry #21 (Summer 89/2145)

Main Text

Rich dude's technofix gone bad, salvaged by adventurous creatures: not the first time! The main ship, the Harvester, got hopelessly SCOBY-infested and was let go. After drifting for years, folks realized the reef ecology now all over the place provides clean drinking water, food in the form of reef fish and of course the edible fungi growing all over, chance to do meaningful restoration work, a community of like-minded people. First it was going with the currents, now they gently steer the Harvester to patches of floating garbage, feeding the mysterious plastic-devouring assemblage of species in the process. Now and then they veer close enough to the coast to trade and welcome new folks, but the restored old satellite link keeps them in touch when further out. Apparently they're working with scientists to see if the SCOBY can adapt to other parts of the ocean… adaptation and ingenuity: vital to clean up our ancestors' mess, little by little.

Side Text

SCOBY: symbiotic culture of bacteria and yeasts, hence the name Kombucha Atoll. Not convinced it helps the reputation of the place, but the boat villagers don't seem to mind. Must not forget to acquire a sample of their local fermented brew… for further study.

* * *

Yen Shu Liao was lucky to grow up with abundant, accessible, and unbridled nature. Their nurtured loved for nature expanded as they immigrated as well as lived long term from Continent to Continent, developing a global perspective. Balance, growth, sustainability, and innovation are values that led them to the solarpunk world. Visual art is their way to navigate this world.

Kombucha Atoll

Rich dude's technofix gone bad, salvaged by adventurous creatures not the first time! The main ship, the Harvester, got hopelessly SCOBY-infested and was let go. After drifting for years, folks realized the reef ecology now all over the place provides clean drinking water, food in the form of reef fish and of course the edible fungi growing all over. Chance to do meaningful restoration work, a community of like-minded people. First it was going with the currents, now they gently steer the Harvester to patches of floating garbage, feeding the mysterious plastic-devouring assemblage of species in the process. Now and then they veer close enough to the coast to trade and welcome new folks, but the restored old satellite link keeps them in touch when further out. Apparently they're working with scientists to see if the SCOBY can adapt to other parts of the ocean... adaptation and ingenuity vital to clean up our ancestors' mess, little by little

SCOBY: symbiotic culture of bacteria and yeasts, hence the name Kombucha Atoll. Not convinced it helps the reputation of the place, but the boat villagers don't seem to mind. Must not forget to acquire a sample of their local fermented brew ...... for further study.

Solarpunk Creatures project entry #21 (summer 88/2148)

THE WETLANDS VERSUS THE MAYOR

Jerri Jerreat

The Mayor was a friendly fellow, a mop of sandy hair, good teeth, mild eyes. He had a firm handshake when accepting petitions, promising to do his very best. Everyone liked him. He was also a fastidious dresser.

The Mayor religiously wore white shirts (light blue was *union worker*, pastels, *absurd*), but enjoyed choosing his daily tie. To meet children carrying a heartfelt petition, he wore a yellow tie with teddy bears or lightning bolts. To meet those fretting about affordable housing, he wore a navy striped tie. To meet eco-groups (*sigh*) asking for electric buses, community gardens, or to save a wetland or woodland, he wore a green tie, or one with tiny green trees on it. Ironic, *obviously*.

He had a set of phrases such as, "What hard work you've all put into this! I'm so impressed!", or "Was it difficult to get so many signatures?" or, "What a pleasure it is to meet citizens who care so deeply!" He liked to switch them up, like the ties.

The Wetlands, now, was a different sort. She embraced several major rivers and creeks spilling into a famous Lake. Irrepressibly optimistic, she danced salsas and chaînés around insectaries and symphonies of birds, amphibians, and fish. The city had a respectable history, if colonial (no massacres at least), and the Wetlands had generously forgiven past wrongs to her. Behind the Wetlands was her young neighbour, a friendly shoreline Forest, some trees two centuries old. Small streams journeyed through the Forest to reach the Wetlands. Together, they all broke the force of storms, cooled summer heat, and beckoned in hikers, squirrels, fungi, turtles, water striders and tiny worlds of moss. The Forest and Wetlands often whispered and chuckled together at life, enjoying a fine breeze or a loon's call.

Humans came from far away to take fossil-fueled boat rides past all this sweeping greenery, wearing sun screen, sipping martinis.

The Mayor had Plans. A city needs tax dollars to finance beautification intended to entice wealthier citizens—attractive flagstone walkways, lookouts and promenades, with flower gardens. Trees, dotted about, add to the charm. A Forest, though, is a *waste of money* and hides people housed in tents. A Wetland is a *swamp*, catches plastic bags, laundry detergent jugs and Styrofoam. It ruins a view. A Wetland hides ducks who drop their business on sidewalks, or worse, *geese*, who stroll about as if they paid taxes, *belonged* there. Some tourists are frightened of geese. Swans are all right, he reckoned, in the far distance, or in a painting. And if a Wetland becomes too large, there's nowhere to tuck your sailboat or yacht in. Or to let middle-class families wade, searching for those rounded rocks you've had trucked in from up north, or university students to play frisbee, drink and—*actually,* thought the Mayor, *university students are a pain.*

(The Wetlands laughed into fouettés.)

The Mayor slipped all Developments through with amiable promises. He insisted that concrete towers, ten or twenty-story buildings, would create a "walkable city." "Intensification," he argued, is the green way to go, and never mind that there were no forests or nature to offset all that heat-amassing concrete. People could walk to get their groceries! (As if.) To be honest, these towers were rather tall, dark and shadowy and meant a small park needed to be paved over for parking, but they would certainly bring in tax dollars. The Mayor adored them. "We must build for a Climate Crisis," he proclaimed blithely, and smiled for the camera, fingers crossed.

This time a "significant" Wetland with Protection Regulations beside a lovely scruffy Forest, was in the way of a proposed yacht club and two thousand riverside condos.

Just imagine the taxes.

The Mayor pressured the Planning Committee (some, old pals on the same side of the tennis court, if you get what I mean), into hurrying this Development along.

"We need Progress!" he argued to the councillors. "We can't be left behind by other cities! We need to move into the modern age! Attract high-tech and financial business!"

"What about our own people without homes?" countered a young councillor. "We have a waiting list here of nearly ten years for affordable housing?"

The Mayor turned his famous smile into devastating scorn. "You're new on Council. You haven't seen all the steps we've made to offer emergency shelters and to speed up affordable housing." He raised one eyebrow. "Also, these condos will have some bachelor units! Let's get on with it, shall we? We don't want to be left behind or the Developer will find a different city to invest in."

That councillor swallowed but dared again. "But—once we clearcut a forest and cover a wetlands, how do we handle extreme storms? And what about the world's loss of biodiversity?"

The Mayor laughed heartily and shook his head. "Biodiversity isn't a problem around here! I was stung by a bee last weekend just trying to have a quiet coffee outside!"

The older councillors laughed along with him.

The Mayor lowered his voice as though confiding to friends. "And this wetlands is just a stinky marsh. Have you smelled it lately?" He pinched his nose. "Disgusting! As is that forest! I wouldn't let my kids walk in there! It's just a hiding place for a lot of ruffians and their junk. There are stolen *shopping carts* in there, *tarps, cans with sharp metal edges*—it's just a garbage heap! And dangerous."

(The Wetlands paused mid-plié.)

He used words like Heritage, Tourism, Housing, Community, A New Tomorrow, Sustainable, and threw in two EV-charging stations, with full-colour mock-ups of a family standing on a pier. In the photo, the child points at a handsome yacht in the distance.

***

People strode and marched along the shoreline, waving large squares and shouting. This was becoming common, thought the Wetlands. Was it weekly? A flotilla of canoes and kayaks surrounded her frilly edges, banging their paddles. The humans seemed terribly upset.

The Wetlands sympathized; she blew sweet-smelling kisses over them. She wished she could help. She splashed her friend, Forest, good night, and rippled softly into a deep restorative nap. This would all smooth over like a bad storm from the east. Humans were often upset. It was difficult to fathom.

***

The Wetlands had bad dreams, vague nightmares. She woke up to a tornado of chain-saws, and giant mechanical monsters chewing and eating.

Over two thousand trees lay dead. Her friend—was gone.

The Wetlands, in shock, froze, and closed her eyes. There was no dancing, no thinking, no breathing. No movements. It was simply— too much.

A layer of clay slid over her, then another. Then a blanket of concrete.

Underneath it all, the Wetlands was still, quiescent, as though Sleeping Beauty's spell had been cast over her. Her mind seethed, but her feet did not even twitch. Her graceful hands were petrified into fists.

***

The first spring after the glorious condos had been built, a fleet of ducks and geese shat all over the Lexus and Cadillacs. Ring-necked or buffleheads, mergansers, wood ducks, mute swans and trumpeters. They trundled up and down the streets, honking, looking for familiar reeds and cosy nesting sites.

There were complaints to the Mayor, but he reassured everyone that this was just "a transition time."

Green-striped map turtles and red and yellow-striped painted ones searched for favourite logs in vain. They struggled to climb the steep walls, but were unsuccessful. They swam further on, further away. Most did not find nests.

Then that autumn, the first storms swept away all the lawn furniture, the Thai ironwork, the Greek statuary. A small sinkhole, mink-sized, appeared along the shore. A flagstone fell in.

***

The Wetlands smoldered and planned all that winter, lying in a fairy death under the concrete. Her legs quivered. Her toes began to point, then flex.

***

The next spring the Wetlands woke. She rose and rose and, nothing to embrace her, began flamenco dancing furiously across streets and cars and underground parkades, quite cheekily. There was a terrible loss of Mercedes.

After that, the Wetlands returned in guerilla forays, fierce tarantellas, and saucy foxtrots, kicking up longer and wider sinkholes. The earth beneath all that wet weight began to soften and crumble. It was carried away in rogue underground currents just as if a curled finger were beckoning.

Ransom, perhaps.

***

The Mayor gazed out from his limo window in the impermeable paved parking lot, listening to a report of the damage on his cell. His forehead was creased. His daughter had brought home a painting of a wetland filled with birds. Even his family was betraying him.

Meanwhile, he heard woodpeckers working merrily at reflections in shiny barbeques. It sounded just like gunshots.

This is war, he thought. But I can wait this out. I shall win.

A wave crashed, nearly twenty metres inland, startling him.

"Had enough, sir?" asked the driver, itching to get safely away. The parking lot was no longer safe.

"Yes. Fine. Let's go."

As the car left, another wave rose up, higher, stronger, searching for reeds and willows, old friends, meeting algorithms of sand and gravel, iron and coal.

Those will not stand forever.

***

A dozen years passed. This time the Mayor had not been re-elected. The youngest Councillor replaced him, the one who'd questioned the development. She was an artist, with science courses in Climate Change under her belt. She was also a terrible dresser, often a plaid shirt over black slacks, a thrift shop blazer. She listened, though, to delegations, to councillors, to science. She encouraged a vote to spend money on restoring wetlands and planting fifty small Miyawaki forests across the city. Also, half of all parking lots to be required to become permeable or treed. Owner's choice.

A new approach to development had begun.

***

The Wetlands had been fighting for a long time. One day she saw humans return again with loud machines. She was about to gather herself into a wild force when she saw—she heard—the humans were breaking down the concrete shore walls.

The machines cracked it in pieces, let it fall. More humans arrived. They created rocky shoals, anchored log tangles to it, above and below water. It took them weeks to remove the concrete and foreign clay, but they did their best.

The Wetlands was surprised. *Very* surprised. She shook her skirts out, looked backward over her shoulder at them. She didn't know how she felt about humans anymore.

The flotilla returned, small boats laden with soil, compost, and straw. People squinted against the sunlight on newly freed water as they handplanted shore grasses. They tested the water, the new soil, brought more plants and seeds from nearby. On the shore, humans were bent over, smiling, positioning willows and sumac in messy clumps.

The Wetlands had tiptoed backward, offstage, to observe this work. She tried to make sense of it. One day she realized that the giant square condos on shore were all crooked now, their footings wet, the land unstable. (She grinned, and did a little jazz hands.) The ugly buildings looked different now to the Wetlands, glaring at them out of habit. Smaller. The closest one had been removed.

The Wetlands could not help a tiny hip circle, a hair flick.

There was a burst of sound onshore, bubbling child laughter, and the humans all cheered. New water slithered out from the shore in one place, a familiar creek, chuckling in delight. The Wetlands splashed *Hello! How Are you? Where have you been?* She could not suppress a grin. She had been shimmying up that shore, wriggling and swaying in abandoned garages and cracks in the sidewalk for over a decade. She would not stop—though these new areas looked very interesting. (She eyed the shoals.) Her dancing had been relentless, her memory long.

***

Twenty years after the condo build, the Wetlands are back. Truly back, her fists have cracked open lingering cement and tar, thrown in seeds, forcing growth everywhere the bulldozers have overlooked. She's singing her family home with a grand-battement. The muskrats have heard, the water snakes, turtles, insects. Fish scales glint underwater, all colours and sizes. The teals, kingfishers and chickadees are arriving and a hundred different songs fill the air. Everyone is *reviennent,* water spiders, midges, dragonflies, even the fairy shrimp.

Humans are paddling along the shore, monitoring and planting more, smiling.

The Wetlands smiles back.

***

Thirty years after the destruction, a human family tiptoes along a deer path in the young Forest toward the famous Wetland. The mother works in Nature Restoration. Her father, the old Mayor, sits down quietly on a wooden bench under a willow near the shore. He is wearing no tie. He looks around, straining his neck like an owl to see as much as possible. The woods are noisy, rustling, alive.

After several minutes his grey head falls, deep in thought. He notices a flake of bark on the end of his bench, ragged edged, a sort of a pattern of browns, cinnamon near the small edge. He reaches out to brush the bark off and—it opens. Two glorious orange wings, red edged, Jackson Pollock splotches. ("A comma," his daughter will say, incomprehensively, later. "Or a question mark.") He inhales sharply, then studies it. Such rich colours! So hidden! He marvels at the tiny furry body between the twin paintings. It pulses. It breathes.

The family has slipped up to the shore; mother takes the youngest's hand. They hold themselves still to admire the coveys of ducks and geese, and a silent row of ruby-edged turtles on a log. Red-winged blackbirds are trilling in alto. Flycatchers, swallows and sandpipers, tail-dip, swoop or tiptoe. There is a humming in the air; pollinators are working. A velvety deep brown mourning cloak brushes past them like a tissue, close enough to see the yellow edging and light blue dots.

There, over there, is a grey heron, standing like a ghost among tall bullrushes. The child is pointing.

Around them all, arms flung out in joy, the Wetlands is jitterbugging.

* * *

Jerri Jerreat's writing, from Anishinaabe, Haudenosaunee territory, appears in *Grist/Fix: Imagine 2200 Climate Fiction for Future Ancestors; Flyway: Journal, Alluvian, Feminine Collective, Yale Review Online, The New Quarterly, Glass and Gardens Solarpunk Winters; Glass and Gardens: Solarpunk Summers,* & others. She has a growing pile of protest signs by the door & directs YouthImagine TheFuture.com. Find her at jerrijerreat.com/ or Instagram: @jerrjtree

LEAF WHISPERS, OCEAN SONG

Tashan Mehta

This is a love story.

Like all good love stories, it begins with the moment of meeting. They are five. Jen is hanging upside down from a branch, crisscrossing her eyes and pulling her mouth wide with her pointer fingers so that she can stick her tongue out. Lu is standing at the roots of the tree in silent judgement. This is the only person in the colony her age? The child she is meant to make friends with? She casts around for an adult who can save her. *Try it*, Jen urges, her hands now stretched to the ground as she gently swings her body. *No thanks*, Lu says and resents, immediately, the indignities that growing up will force upon her (such as "making friends").

Later, Lu will see this moment as prophetic, for growing up is indeed terrible. School is a collection of children she doesn't understand and cannot befriend; they follow one set of rules in front of adults but immediately switch to a new, unspoken set of rules when the adults disappear. When she finally gets home and falls into her book, she is relieved; she has survived one more day of the gauntlet. She is also a little scared, if she is being honest, although she doesn't know who to tell this to. She watches the children taunt Jen in the bus, throwing scrap paper at her and scratching their armpits while ¬¬making monkey sounds. Jen doesn't seem to mind, until she does, and then she's screaming-snarling-clawing-at-faces as kids hoot and scream-laugh louder. Lu is scared this will happen to her; bullying doesn't seem very discerning about picking targets.

Jen and she are not friends, even though they are the only children in the colony. Once, as they are climbing off the bus, Lu sees that Jen is crying and wants to touch her shoulder. But it is a bad idea; to be associated with the bullied is to be tainted, so she doesn't. In bed that night, she reminds herself that Jen is weird. Remember her hanging from that branch with her pink tongue coming out, like she was part lizard and part monkey? Childhood is hard enough without friends like this.

***

College is better. No one looks at reading books like a personality trait, and Lu finds a collection of friends she thinks are fun and then, about a month later, decides she will die for. Her college is old stone with staircases that crisscross above each other and provide a deep sense of atmosphere, which Lu appreciates. She is studying linguistics—that bachelor's degree with famously rich job prospects, her best friend Mae jokes—and she loves the rigor of it, the song of sound and meaning. She dates, but these are not as successful as her friendships; she is too occupied with grand questions like "What is Love?" and "How Do You Know When You Find It?" to truly invest in the person opposite her. Mae, who also studies linguistics, tells her she is overthinking dating but if you don't take the time to think about love, which supposedly all the writers and poets never shut up about, what precisely was worth thinking about?

Essay deadlines, Mae tells her wisely, *and sex. Good sex*, she amends.

Lu doesn't keep a partner for very long. She doesn't see the point.

Jen reenters her life during Lu's second job. It is at a start-up in the field of non-human languages; the research is new but revelatory, and Lu is once again galvanized by the potential of language. The company works out of an apartment in Colaba, the team leaning around big plants to talk to each other and smoking on a sea-facing terrace. Lu cannot remember being this happy.

So when Jen comes to the office, Lu imagines this is retribution; all good things, as Mae says, must end. Jen is a consultant, "foreign-returned" (Harvard, one of her colleagues tells her later) and already making waves in the field. She's unrecognizable: chic, easy, funny. Everyone loves her.

The first time they are introduced, Lu's palms are sweating. She expects this new, cool Jen to smile cruelly when her turn comes, and say, *Oh her! Of course I know Lu. She refused to be friends with me in school. Watched me get bullied for years. Cute story.* She is so convinced in this narrative, she decides to lead with an apology. But Jen doesn't recognize her. She holds out her hand and says *Pleased to meet you* with the same bright smile everyone gets.

Lu doesn't know if she's pleased or upset by this. She decides she is pleased.

Jen is brilliant. Even though she is Lu's age, she is light-years ahead, grasping the ins and outs of non-human communication with a dexterity that surprises everyone but Lu (she hasn't forgotten the girl hanging upside down from a branch, like she was part lizard, part monkey). They're working with the Great Collection, a global project that seeks to map existing knowledge on non-human languages. Apes, cats, and dogs form the majority of the data, but the information is slowly expanding to insects and marine life.

So far, the only sectors interested in the project are the tech space (*Love bird watching? Introducing an app that tells you the name of the bird AND what it's saying!*) and pet corporations (*Wondering what kibble your dog likes? Curious whether your cat really loves you? Now you can know!*). But the potential is startling. It's not only about communicating with different species—it's about learning from them. How do dogs smell cancer? Why do cats taste the air and what does it tell them? What principles do ants use to organize themselves? Non-human languages would mean people no longer had to guess; the creatures themselves could tell them. Lessons, wisdom, stories—every single thing human civilization unlocked with the emergence of language could now be enriched by new voices and forms of wisdom. When Lu thinks about it, she gets shivers.

It's clear now that non-human languages use their bodies more, and soon Lu's colleagues are ambling across the office or writhing on the floor as Jen corrects their posture. *The real gold mine,* she tells them over Bombay sandwiches, *is plants. Trees live for thousands of years! Imagine the wisdom, the stories.* This is what Jen spends most of her time on: plant language, her passion project.

One night, Lu returns to the office for a parcel and finds Jen working late. She's bent over her laptop, tongue poking out between her teeth. She looks so much like the 10-year-old Jen doing a craft project that Lu is destabilized for a moment. Then Jen looks up, sees her, exclaims, and begins to pack up so they can leave the office together.

At the banyan tree outside the building, Lu stops. *Do you remember the first time we met?*

Jen is blinking at her, her mind probably still on plant syntax. *It was in Hindu colony, by the triangular garden*, Lu says, possessed by some spirit of stubbornness. *You hung upside down on a tree.*

Er…

Smiling! Jen is smiling, one of those polite smiles you give people when you realize they need you to remember something but you clearly don't. Lu is horrified (why did she say anything?) and then suddenly adamant.

You must remember, she insists. *We were the only children in the colony our age.*

Jen shrugs. *I'm sorry, awful memory.* She glances at the banyan tree. *Upside down, you say? Impressive. What did I use, my ankles?*

No, you…

The next thing Lu knows, she's climbing, possessed by a madness to reawaken Jen's memories. God knows how she makes it to the branch—she's not the most athletic person—but she's here, clinging on. When she looks down (bad idea, never look down) she sees Jen, lit by streetlights, looking like a zookeeper prepped to talk an insane penguin off the ledge.

Lu, I'm not sure what this is but maybe you should come down…

Jen has a point. Lu isn't sure what this is either, but she's committed to the role now so she shimmies along the branch and then gingerly sits up, her feet dangling. How do you know if a branch is strong enough to hold your weight? Do tree climbers run calculations?

…Lu…

I'm going to die, Lu thinks and then, before she can overthink it, she squeezes her knees to hold the branch, and swings upside down.

When she opens her eyes, the world is still here. She did it! She did it and didn't die! *Like this*, she tells Jen proudly, swinging gently back and forth. For a moment, she just enjoys the feeling—hanging upside down is like occupying a non-human language for the first time, where the world upturns and everything old seems suddenly new. Then she pulls her mouth wide with her pointer fingers and sticks her tongue out.

Jen starts to laugh, a helpless lovely laugh that comes straight from her belly and tells Lu two things. Number one: she, ordinary and book-ish Lu, has managed to surprise the brilliant Jenifer. And number two: of course Jen remembers.

You, Lu says, still swinging, *are a truly terrible person.*

Jen is laughing so hard, she has to lean against the tree. *How else*, she says, wiping her eyes, *was I to get you to try it?*

Lu doesn't believe much in beginnings—any event of significance has multiple beginnings if you look at it closely enough. This love story, for example, began when they were five, then began again when Jen walked into the office, and tonight, here, is another beginning, of old and new forged together.

But this beginning has a different significance, for it is also the beginning for the world itself. Tonight, a fishing boat spots Opi in the ocean.

***

Opi takes seven months to reach the shore. Lu and Jen are huddled at Mae's house, watching it on the laptop. Those huge tentacles whooshing out of the sea. Waves, taller than any tree, slamming onto the beach. Fish, flapping on sand, stunned and dying.

There is no language to describe Opi. Pictures of it are so distorted no one can agree on what they're seeing. Sketch artists draw illustrations that are optical illusions, like the Penrose triangle. *It's like we're in Abbott's Flatland*, Mae whispers, *watching a three-dimensional creature from a two-dimensional perspective.* Indeed, marine biologist Margaret Blu would say something similar in her first televised interview on Opi: *In all our stories, we assume aliens would come from the sky. We should have been looking at the oceans.*

Opi has arrived in Goa, its body stretching from Chapora to Sinquerim beach. Dogs gather at the line between sand and jungle, barking hysterically. Fishermen set up barricades to guard it; they say Opi is a visiting god from the sea.

I'm going to Goa, Jen says, *and you should come. This is history.*
They won't let you anywhere near it.

But here Lu is wrong, for a week later, Jen gets a call. It's a sister of a conservationist friend that Jen worked closely with last year for mapping lichen in Goa. She's working on the core team established to understand Opi: marine biologists, conservationists, local fishermen. She tells Jen: *We think it's speaking.*

And so Jen is flown out as an expert non-human linguist with a "unique understanding of local culture" (she says this to Lu at the airport with a half-laugh). Lu goes with her. They rent two huts in a small beach shack hotel near Anjuna beach, and Jen spends her days in top-secret meetings. Lu wanders around the carnivals set up just outside the barricades: news channels and journalists but also locals and tourists, eating bhutta and roasted channa and staring at whatever bits of Opi they can see. Lu buys trinkets from the stalls (*a shell dislodged from the ocean by Opi itself, madam, very rare, usually 500 rupees but for you 400*) and wonders what she is doing here. After the awe wears off, she cannot understand why she won't book a ticket back. It's Jen who is wanted, not her. She's come under the guise of studying Opi—that's how her boss gave her leave—but she's not doing much studying, is she? She'll be more useful back at the office.

But each night when Jen comes back, kicks off her shoes, and they sink into the sofas at the café with a glass of urak, Lu forgets about leaving.

It's a marvel, Jen whispers. *They think it's from the Mariana Trench, but they're not sure. The fishermen won't let the scientists experiment on it, and I agree. Lu, I can't explain—being near it... it's like being in a different slice of reality. You feel different. Did you notice the dogs stopped barking today? They've been slipping under the ropes to lie next to it. Crabs are scuttling closer; even star fish seem to wash up near it. It's doing something, we just don't know what.*

And the speech? Lu asks eagerly.

Too vast. It's sound, scent, song, feeling, thought—just everything you can imagine. Sandeep said he saw a glimpse of a vision the other day; he thinks it was Opi speaking to him. I don't know. Nothing in our tiny world prepared us for this.

These nights, Lu feels like an explorer in the old world, wonder at every corner, history always in the making. Then morning comes, Jen leaves, and Lu goes back to worrying.

It's Jen who ends their stay at the shack. *They want me to come onto the team full time, properly*, she says, looking into her drink. *They have a house for me, so I'll move out tomorrow.*

What should she do with this confusion of joy and hurt? Jen is a friend, she reminds herself, and we are always happy for friends. But Jen in Goa is not the same as Jen in Mumbai, sharing Sunday morning bagels or browsing Trilogy library. It is astonishing to her that in the face of such sublimity, she can be selfish.

I'm happy for you. Lu reaches out her hands to her brilliant, beloved friend (friend?) and means it.

Jen won't take her hands. She looks directly at Lu and talks fast. *You'll come with me, of course. I've already spoken about you, I've been speaking about you for days, and they'd love to have someone with your expertise come on board. I was hoping to have the offer letter today, but these take so long. You must come. Lu, I won't let you say no. It's an incredible opportunity; forget understanding non-human languages, I think Opi is going to change how we communicate at an intrinsic level. Don't tell me you like your life in Mumbai too much or you're happy in your job; none of it matters, because this is so much bigger than us. You'll make a new life here, I promise, and it will be wild and exciting and so much more than we could have dreamed of. Don't say you don't want wild and exciting because you do, even though you like schedules and want to be in bed by 10pm. So you're coming, yes? Yes. Yes? I won't let you say no.*

All of this is said so smoothly, so quickly, that the logic of it knits around Lu. Of course Jen wants her here, she cares about her career, she's a good and non-selfish friend. It's only five months later, when lying in a garden and watching fireflies erupt from a leaf, that Lu considers that this was Jen's version of a love letter.

***

They kiss in the third month of moving to Goa. Mae finally convinces Lu to act on her feelings, unrequited or not, and Lu composes a speech that she reworks four times (after which Mae refuses to read more drafts). It includes phrases like "Our Friendship Means Everything to Me" and "I Absolutely Understand If You Don't Feel the Same Way" (Mae cuts this line in each draft, and Lu adds it back in). In the end, she doesn't use the speech, because Jen is explaining how complexity theory might help them interpret Opi's language, and Lu is so overcome, she kisses her. It's a terrible kiss—their teeth clash and Lu thinks she cut Jen's lip—but now Jen is kissing her back and things are decidedly wonderful. They both panic after that, have lunch to discuss their panic, and after lots of talking about "How the Friendship Means Everything" again, decide to be together.

God, Mae says on the phone, *you guys are exhausting,* but Lu can hear her smile from here.

Work on Opi is thrilling. Lu looks forward to the gentleness of the beach, the warm-wash of a different reality. The air smells of salt and cold currents, and the days blur into a haze of golden light, leaves, and bird call. Opi's arrival has meant a burst of funding for non-human languages, and the Great Collection is now a sprawling digital archive that births its own niche research fields. There are enough languages in the database for the team to cobble together theories about Opi's complex sound/smell/song/sight language, and draw slowly closer to understanding it. The key, Jen believes, lies in plants and fungi, maybe even stones—in organisms that can live as long as Opi.

Opi sits, waiting.

Jen and Lu move in together. They rent a decrepit bungalow in Assagao because Jen saw it on her morning run and fell in love. It used to be the house of a Catholic priest, and pale Jesuses are still nailed to the walls, red bulbs perched over them. It has this epic collection of thirty stairs to the main veranda, with the garden (all weeds now) arranged in matching layers. They both love it. Lu sets to work on the mold on the walls, and Jen throws herself into the garden. Lu can hear her practicing her plant speech on the lemongrass.

I got it wrong, Jen says. She's lying on her back in the garden, sun on her face. *I used to think if we can speak another's language, we can learn from them, hear their stories. But it's so much more than that. Language doesn't just tell you things, it lets you become them.* She turns her face to the side, stares at her lemongrass rustling in the wind. *It helps you belong.*

Lu doesn't fully understand what she means; she's never looked at a plant and imagined walking in their shoes, the same way she can with a human; she's cannot see them and think "family." But Jen can, and Lu lives the sunlight of that second-hand wonder.

Do you feel like that when you look at Opi? she asks, pulling a twig out of Jen's hair.

Jen shakes her head. *Opi is like... the universe. Do you know The Pale Blue Dot, that picture of Earth from space, where our whole planet is nothing but a spec? Opi is like that picture: startling, petrifying, alien. A reminder of how insignificant we are, of how life plays out in a magnitude we cannot imagine. Opi's language is too large to understand fully; it makes me feel… awestruck. Maybe terrified. It's like standing in front of a god.*

In the eighth month of their moving to Goa, Opi begins to speak.

What they thought was speech until then was only Opi pausing, a simple breath in for a creature that lives on a time scale they cannot comprehend. All those sounds and songs were Opi's exhalation, the stray fray-ends of communication meant for no one in particular.

When Opi speaks now, it is meant for them.

The only way to describe it in human language is song—song that drifts in your ear at all times of the day, like it lives in your head, song that wakes up people on the opposite side of the world, that calls the monkeys to gather on trees and the iguanas to pause. Lu is napping when it starts, and she wakes up because Jen is draped over her, holding Lu's face in her hands, crying—with both elation and sorrow it turns out, because they know just enough to know this is Opi and it is telling them a story that touches the very nerve of life, but they don't know enough to understand it.

***

Leaf Whispers, Ocean Song hits the shelves nine years later. Jen is so nervous, she curls herself up in a blanket like a snail, only her eyes poking out. Lu cuddles her and feeds her tea and biscuits, and keeps her favorite lemongrass plant close by. The first review of the book calls it a "a triumph in the field of non-human languages" and "a masterpiece in reimagining ourselves" and although the reviewer hasn't done a very good job grasping the nuances of Jen's work, Lu is happy to forgive him. More reviews follow the same theme, and Jen gently emerges from her blanket.

Opi still sings. Lu can hear it as she shops for groceries, as she dozes on her flight, as she roots out the colony of ants that have made a home in her flour. Most people tune it out with muting devices, but those who keep listening find that the language grows *in* them. They begin to dream of dark waters. Of strange, luminescent animal-plants, shape-shifting sand, and different ways of seeing. Lu sees an entire island once, buried under the ocean and populated with a strange civilization. Jen sees folktales made by different organisms, stories where humans aren't the center but only a part. *What a part we play, Lu. Small, hapless, giddy on the shortness of the time we live. We're a civilization of mayflies.*

It's not just the visions. Opi has turned them inside out; it sings in time scales they cannot grasp, whispers in dimensions they cannot comprehend, and suddenly, each person on Earth has a mirror to their own mortality, to the flimsiness of their human-centric ideologies and imaginations, to how fleeting they are in the gushing memory of other species, lands, and stars. Suddenly, it is as if the cosmos has turned its huge, unblinking eye upon the world, as if it is saying, *look*, inviting them to see themselves through the eyes of forever.

And once you look, you cannot look away.

On one of her short visits to Goa, Mae asks Lu if she is ever jealous of Jen—*you know,* she spins her finger in a wheel, *the book tours, the praise, the way the popular narrative has made her the center of Opi research, not the team.*

Lu says no. But she is not being entirely truthful.

A year after the book comes out, Lu leads Jen to their favorite cliff in Goa and there, with the wind bending the trees in half, she asks her to marry her. Jen says no.

***

Just as every story of worth has multiple beginning, perhaps they also have multiple ends, moments that push it to the brink and hold it there, at the cusp of shattering. What pushes it over? What brings it back?

Lu would do anything to know.

She packs a small duffel bag. Jen is sobbing; she is trying to hug Lu; she is begging. Lu keeps packing. Only when Jen kneels on the floor and says, *I evoke our friendship. Forget our relationship, forget being partners, forget it all—you once said to me, this friendship means everything to you. By that friendship, please,* does Lu stop. She sits on the edge of the bed, hands tucked between her thighs, waiting.

Jen doesn't say anything Lu doesn't know. How she doesn't believe in marriage, how the institution binds and holds in place, how they don't need it. *The world is so vast,* Jen is crouched by Lu's knees, clutching them, *forty years ago we didn't believe it was possible to talk to plants, and now look at us. Look at what Opi has done, what it's shown us. How can we go back to the old models of living, of shaping ourselves only around people and imagining two-person families, how can we not think of new ways to bond, relate, and live?*

Lu only half listens. Opi's song layers over Jen's words like a strange soundtrack. It's ridiculous that after her college years of "What Is Love?" she picks someone who doesn't know the answer. She thinks, I should call Mae and tell her I lied. Tell her she phrased the question wrong. Because Lu doesn't want book tours or academic awards—she wants Jen, but Jen is only half in the world of the human. So yes, she is jealous, because Jen has ears and eyes like no one else and it makes it difficult for her to stay. Five-year-old Lu saw it in the girl hanging with her tongue out. Five-year-old Lu was wise enough to steer clear.

Say something, Jen whispers.

Lu stands. *I heard you,* she says, then picks up her bag and leaves.

She stays in a small beach shack; she wants to be close to Opi. Leaving her partner and her home in the same night feels too much, and she clings to Opi for comfort.

The carnivals have packed up, but the dogs are still here, sleeping in a quiet sea. Lu picks her way across them, petting those that lift their heads. She slips under the barricade and walks towards the waves, near a tentacle. There is that shift again, a walk into a different piece of reality.

Opi is dying. The team has known this for a while, but they've been holding off telling the politicians because they can't decide what to do about it. Several on the team believe that Opi came here to die, that this song is its farewell. *In my culture*, Zenobia says, *upon our death, we give our bodies to the vultures as a last act of charity. Opi is doing the same; its song is its gift.* Not everyone agrees, especially in cultures where death is traditionally fought.

Now Lu touches the tentacle. The song in her head doesn't change, but her emotions do: they settle in her like sediment, leaving only air and lightness. She curls up next to the tentacle and goes to sleep.

The next morning she goes home. Jen is sleeping on the top step, cocooned in a blanket, only her eyes visible. The whole garden is bent towards her. She wakes when Lu walks up the steps, and the look on her face—hope and despair and *please*—cracks Lu's heart.

Yes, she says before Lu can speak. *If you will still have me, yes, I'll marry you.*

Lu shakes her head. They sit together quietly on the front step, watching the sun rise higher. Then Lu turns to Jen and takes her hands. *Promise me, here and now, that you will commit to this. That you commit to co-creating a reality and life with me, that you will see me as I am always and accept me, that you will work, Jenifer, work hard for us at every turn. I mean it.*

Of course! Of course I do—

You have to promise.

Jen touches her forehead to Lu's. *I promise*, she whispers.

Okay, Lu says. *I promise too. And I understand, and I take back my proposal. Love is just an endless series of beginnings anyway, of learning to commit every day. This one is today's.*

***

Twenty-five years later, Opi dies. It sings until two weeks before the end, and the sudden silence shakes the world. They have not understood much of what it said, but it has changed them. Exactly like the first men who travelled to the moon, they have left their planet and looked back on it; what they have glimpsed will forever alter how they think.

Jen does not witness the passing of the world's greatest visitor. She dies four months before Opi. She is at a conference, away from Lu. And so Lu is sitting in their home, drinking chai on their veranda when she gets the call. *Brain aneurysm*, they tell her, and the inexplicability of it maps perfectly onto the suddenness. As if the world just said, *Enough*, and took Jen away.

***

Two years after Jen's death, Lu returns to their house in Goa.

Mae thinks it will be good for her. *You lost your love and then gave up a home—it wasn't wise. People need their anchors.* But the house wasn't a home without Jen, although Lu doesn't tell Mae this. She goes back because she wants to see Opi and because, honestly, leaving has not made anything better: Jen is still dead and the world a little less.

Opi's skeleton sits in the same spot, its skull a white hill across the horizon, its tentacles pale rivers in the sand. Crabs and small creatures have made homes in the bones, an entire ecosystem. Wise, wonderful Opi. Even in death, it gives. At the boundary between beach and jungle, there are offerings: marigold flowers, cracked coconuts, little paper fish and swans. A battalion of dogs sleep near the body.

It is this that nearly makes Lu cry: these animals, standing guard over the object of their love. She envies them—at least they are near their beloved—and then is ashamed. Always self-centered in the face of the sublime.

She arrives at the house in the early morning, when the sky is changing color but the sun hasn't pulled itself over the horizon. The garden is overrun, shrubs and trees entwining to form a jungle. Lu cannot see the steps to the main house, and the house itself is barely visible, only the roof showing. She stands by the gate for a long time, unwilling to unlock it. What should she do with this pain? Here is a little piece of the world made with Jen, that is meant to have Jen in it, but is only empty.

She enters, finally, because her taxi is scheduled an hour from now, and she might as well sit on the steps instead of standing in the sun. The garden whispers as she enters; the plants scrutinize her, wondering who this stranger is. A bougainvillea catches on her shirt and it tears. She wants to weep. Wild cats slink in the undergrowth, their yellow eyes blinking. She sits on the top step and presses her face into her knees. Loss gets easier, they tell you. The bastards were lying.

When she looks up, the Old Cat is observing her, the one Jen believed was immortal. Lu calls to her, but the cat disappears into the foliage. Then two kittens are gamboling around Lu's feet, exclaiming at her pink toes and how big they are, asking each other how tall she is, and can they climb her, and is her hair soft, and her cheek looks so padded, should they try and scratch it, will it be satisfying? Lu scoops them up before they can cause too much harm, and goes into the house.

Spiders have run amok in the corridors, and giant cobwebs—the kind Jen would call masterpieces—clothe each corner. Lizards as large as her forearm perch on the walls, watching her. They don't run. This is their home now; Lu is the guest. All along the ceiling and the walls, moss sprouts in soft, furry green, filling the house with the smell of broken leaves and fresh air. Beetles scurry along the floor with weeds sprouting through its cracks; when they see Lu, they collapse onto their backs dramatically, playing dead (Lu can hear them say "dead, dead, dead" like earnest students practicing their lessons) and then trying vainly to get back to their feet once she passes. *Jen. Jen. Jen.* The house is saying her name, everywhere, all the time, all at once. How much more alive this would be to her, to her ears that could hear the most delicate of patterns and her eyes that could see the smallest of creatures.

It's the wonder of it, Jen says to her once. *How connected we are to everything else, how we're small and big, and fleeting and timeless. Lu, it's… it's a love story.*

Lu doesn't have the same ears or eyes. All she has is the love she held for Jen, and its pale echo of meaning.

Lu.

She thinks she imagined it, but there it is again: Lu. And now she can hear it everywhere, a steady chant under Jen's name.

Lu, the weeds between her toes are saying, *welcome back, look how much we've grown.*

Lu, the lizards say, *are you planning to sleep in the bedroom because the bed is broken and we made a nest among the wet wood; we'd like very much not to have to make one again, so let's talk.*

Lu, the moss says, *little one, small one, your pain is so vast and heavy. Set it down.*

And now she does cry, crumbling to the floor as the two kittens entangle themselves in her hair.

We remember, the jackfruit tree says, its leaves whispering against the window frame, *how she sat on the steps when eating fresh fruit, so she could spit the seeds into the earth.* Oh, it used to drive Lu insane: every monsoon, there would be a new crop of mismatched fruit trees sprouting from the soil, right near the house.

We remember, the stone floor says, *how she used to run down these corridors barefoot, pressing her toes into us for coolness and comfort. We have not forgotten her laughter.*

She used to pick us up, a beetle murmurs from behind a leaf, *and carry us outside. If we were stuck on our backs, she would always upturn us.*

We remember you weeping, the mint plant whispers; it was planted right near the breakfast table where Lu heard the news; it has now grown all across it. *We felt your pain. Don't cry, little Lu. Jen is here, nothing dies.*

Lu doesn't know how she finds the strength to stand, to stumble onto the veranda. She was right; the garden is scrutinizing her. She was wrong; it isn't calling her stranger but family. The bougainvillea that tore her shirt was only trying to hug her (Jen was very big on teaching them how to hug). The cats that slunk away were only furious she failed to feed them for so long. She smells the lemongrass before she hears it, finds it in the jungle between the cashew tree and a hibiscus plant. It's taller than her now. Jen's favorite, even though she pretended she didn't have favorites. *Lu*, it rustles, and it doesn't have to say more.

Because somehow, Jen has given Lu her eyes and ears. She's shown her their family.

***

It is the first day in their new house. Jen walks down the corridor, ignoring the cracked walls, with Lu right behind her, who tries not to look at broken beams. The house smells of age and decay; it is filled with light and green. Then Jen is calling her, and they crouch by a rock near the front step. It is covered with a thin pattern of ash-green.

Lichen live for centuries, Jen whispers, as if they are in a temple. *The oldest living one is eight thousand years old.*

You're making that up.

I swear, map lichen in the Artic, you can google it. Imagine, something so ancient in our house. It's like a god. It's like being blessed.

I love you, Lu thinks, although they have not said the words to each other yet. I love you, and your mind and heart. I will do anything to keep you.

***

In front of a ruined bungalow, a taxi pulls up at the appointed time. It waits for five minutes, then ten, then it calls the appointed number once, twice. In the shadows of an old garden, the driver doesn't see a woman crouched by a stone that is always open to the sun, a faint pattern on it. The woman's fingers are on the pattern—which is, in fact, a 100-year-old lichen—and she is listening as it tells her stories of the house, the land and two women who came to live there for 30 brief years. Impossible to think she believed Jen was dead—for here she is, breathing through the memories of the earth.

***

Tashan Mehta is the author of *Mad Sisters of Esi* and *The Liar's Weave*, which was shortlisted for the inaugural Prabha Khaitan Woman's Voice Award. Her short stories have featured in *Magical Women*, the *Gollancz Book of South Asian Science Fiction Volume 2* and *PodCastle*. She was fellow at the 2015 and 2021 Sangam House International Writers' Residency, India, and writer-in-residence at Anglia Ruskin University, UK. You can find her at tashanmehta.com

...before you travel onwards, might we ask for your help again?

This book is both a collection of stories and a small research project. Remember the survey we asked you to fill out before you started reading? To understand how stories might contribute to building better futures for humans and nature alike, please tell us what you think.

Simply visit the link below and fill out our second reader survey:

https://creatures-postsurvey.multispecies.city

Thank you again for your help!

Visit https://survey.multispecies.city to learn about the results (it may take a while before we can share any).

About the Anthologists

Christoph Rupprecht (he/him) is a geographer based in Japan. When he's not researching sustainability, food, agriculture, green space, degrowth, and solarpunk with a more-than-human lens, you might find him reading science fiction, hanging out with plants, trying to make cheese, or taking a nap. He believes the imagination holds the key for jointly building sustainable and just futures for all life.

Deborah Cleland (she/her) is an activist/ performance artist/ researcher, with all the compromise and circuitous life paths that those slashes imply. She dabbles in interactive theatre and games, site-specific place-making and creative non-fiction, hoping to bring social justice and other solarpunk ideals to life through writing and performance. She lives on Murramarang/Yuin country on the south east coast of Australia.

Melissa Ingaruca Moreno (she/her) finds her happy place in the intersection of multispecies thinking, design, and futurism. In her PhD she explores how to transform urban design to care for the wellbeing, sensorial worlds and agency of more-than-human species, and to enable multispecies cohabitation. These days you find her in a communal biolab in Berlin, at awe with bioluminescent mushrooms that are teaching her to reconnect with darkness at nights, and engaging people in reimagining multispecies futures of nightscapes. She feels at home in communities like Mycohackers (enthusiasts that design with fungi) and other global networks of foresight and nature-based urbanism.

Norie Tamura (she/her) is a social scientist in Japan, researching agriculture, forestry, and fisheries. After working as a consultant in those areas, she moved to academia. Growing up in the Western Japan metropolitan area, she repeatedly discovered alternative universes in rural areas, and came to realize that knowing and experiencing a different world is the key to envisioning a different future.

Rajat Chaudhuri (he/him) is a bilingual author and climate activist. His works include novels, short story collections, translations (from Bengali), and edited (or co-edited) anthologies of speculative and solarpunk stories. His previous novel, *The Butterfly Effect* was twice listed by Book Riot as a "Fifty must read eco-disasters in fiction" and among "Ten works of environmental literature from around the world". A Charles Wallace Creative Writing fellow, his fiction also appears in the climate futures video game *Survive the Century*. Chaudhuri's new climate novel *Spellcasters* has been just published. He lives and writes in Calcutta.

Sarena Ulibarri (she/her) lives, writes, and plants trees in the American Southwest. She is the author of two novellas: *Another Life*, about a solarpunk community in Death Valley, released from Stelliform Press in 2023, and *Steel Tree*, a science fiction retelling of The Nutcracker, released from Android Press in 2023. Her short fiction has appeared in *Lightspeed, DreamForge, Solarpunk Magazine*, and elsewhere. Her essay in *Strange Horizons*, "Hope and Horror in Climate Fiction" won the 2023 Utopia Award for Nonfiction. She is Editor-in-Chief of World Weaver Press.

World Weaver Press, LLC
Publishing fantasy, paranormal, and science fiction.
We believe in great storytelling.
WorldWeaverPress.com